11-13-03

5R

The Pursuit of Alice Thrift

**Center Point
Large Print**

**This Large Print Book carries the
Seal of Approval of N.A.V.H.**

ELINOR LIPMAN

The Pursuit of Alice Thrift

CENTER POINT PUBLISHING
THORNDIKE, MAINE

This Center Point Large Print edition
is published in the year 2003 by arrangement with
The Random House Publishing Group.

The text of this Large Print edition is unabridged. In other
aspects, this book may vary from the original edition. Printed in
Thailand. Set in 16-point Times New Roman type by
Bill Coskrey and Gary Socquet.

ISBN 1-58547-362-6

Library of Congress Cataloging-in-Publication Data

Lipman, Elinor.
    The pursuit of Alice Thrift / Elinor Lipman.--Center Point large print ed.
        p. cm.
    ISBN 1-58547-362-6 (lib. bdg. : alk. paper)
        1. Women physicians--Fiction. 2. Interns (Medicine)--Fiction. 3. Interpersonal
relations--Fiction. 4. Boston (Mass.)--Fiction. 5. Courtship--Fiction. 6. Large type books.
I. Title.

PS3562.I577P87 2003b
813'.54--dc21

                                                                                    2003053235

For Mameve Medwed,
dear and exemplary friend

YOU MAY HAVE seen us in "Vows" in *The New York Times*: me, alone, smoking a cigarette and contemplating my crossed ankles, and a larger blurry shot of us, postceremony, ducking and squinting through a hail of birdseed. We didn't have pretty faces or interesting demographics, but we had met and married in a manner that was right for SundayStyles: Ray Russo came to my department for a consultation. I said what I always said to a man seeking rhinoplasty: Your nose is noble, even majestic. It has character. It gives *you* character. Have you thought this through?

The *Times* had its facts right: We met as doctor and patient. I digitally enhanced him, capped his rugged, haunted face with a perfect nose and symmetrical, movie-star nostrils—and he didn't like what he saw on the screen. "Why did I come?" he wondered aloud, in a manner that suggested depth. "Did I expect this would make me *handsome?*"

"It's the way we've been socialized," I said.

"It's not like I have a deviated septum or anything. It's not like my insurance is going to pick up the tab."

Vanitas vanitatum: elective surgery, in other words.

He asked for my professional opinion. I said, "There's no turning back once we do this, so take some time and think it over. There's no rush. I don't like to play God. I'm only an intern doing a rotation here."

"But you must see a lot of noses in life, on the street,

and you must have an artistic opinion," said Ray.

"If it were I, I wouldn't," I said for reasons that had nothing to do with aesthetics and everything to do with the nauseating sound of bones cracking under mallets in the OR.

"Really? You think the one I have is okay?"

"May I ask why you want to do this now, Mr. Russo?" I asked, glancing at the chart that told me he'd turn forty in a month.

"Let's be honest: Women like handsome men," he said, voice wistful, eyes downcast.

What could I say except a polite "And you don't think you're handsome enough? Do you think women judge you by the dimensions of your nose?"

Next to me he smiled. The camera mounted above the monitor played it back. He had good teeth.

"I haven't been very lucky in love," he added. "I'm forty-five and I don't have a girlfriend."

"Is your date of birth wrong?" I asked, pointing to the clipboard.

"Oh, that," he said. "I knock five years off when I'm filling out a job application because of age discrimination, even at forty-five. Bad habit. I forgot you should always tell the truth on medical forms."

"And what is your field?"

"I'm in business, self-employed."

I asked what field.

"Concessions. Which puts me before the public. Wouldn't you think that if everything was okay in the looks department, I'd have met someone by now?"

I hated this part—the psychiatry, the talking. So

instead of asserting what is hard to practice and even harder to preach in my chosen field—that beauty's only skin deep and vastly overrated—I pecked at some keys and moved the mouse. We were back to Ray's original face, bones jutting, cartilage flaring, nose upstaging, a face that my less scrupulous attending physicians would have loved to pin to their drawing boards. If it sounds as if I saw something there, some goodness, some quality of mercy or masculinity that overrode the physical, I didn't. I was flattering him to serve my own principles, my own anti–plastic surgery animus. Ray Russo thought my silence meant I wouldn't change a hair.

"Vows" would reconstruct our consultation, with Ray remembering, "I heard something in her voice. Not that there was a single unprofessional moment between us, but I had an inkling she may have been saying 'No, don't fix it' in order to terminate our doctor-patient relationship and embark on a personal one."

Reading between the lines, and knowing the outcome, you'd think something was ignited in that consultation, a spark between us, but I wasn't one of those attractive doctors with a stethoscope draped around her shoulders and a red silk blouse under her lab coat. I was an unhappy intern, plain and no-nonsense at best, and hoping to perform only noble procedures once I'd finished my residency, my fellowship, my board certification—to reconstruct the soft tissue of poor people, to correct their birth defects, their cleft lips and palates, their cranial deformities, their burns, their mastectomies, to stitch up their torn flesh in emergency rooms so that no scar would force them to relive their horrible accidents. I'd hand off to my less idealistic and more affluent associates the nose jobs, the liposuctions, the face-lifts, the eye and tummy tucks, the breast augmentations, and all cosmetic procedures that make the marginally attractive beautiful.

Ray Russo should have consulted someone who would graduate from the program and set up a suite of sleek offices in a big city. I wished him well and sent him home with the four-color brochure that covers the gruesome steps of rhinoplasty.

Why did I take his phone call six months later? Because I didn't remember him. He dropped the name of my chairman, which made me think he was a friend of that august family—as if he'd sensed I was worried about my standing in the department and my ambivalence toward my then chosen field. Of course, I am summarizing for narrative convenience. Why go into detail about our history, our motivation, our sweet moments, if I'm going to break your heart soon enough? I could add that I have a mother who worries about me, a mother whose motto is "*Go* for a cup of coffee. It doesn't mean you have to marry him," but I'm not blaming her. This is about the weak link in my own character—wishful thinking—and a husband of short duration with a history of bad deeds.

If I sound bitter, I apologize. "Vows" should revisit their brides and grooms a year later, or five or ten. I'd enjoy that on a Sunday morning—scanning the wedding announcements stenciled with updates: NOT SPEAKING. DIVORCED. SEPARATED. ANNULLED. CHEATING ON HIM WITH THE POOL-MAINTENANCE GUY. GAVE BIRTH 5 MONTHS

LATER. IN COUNSELING. CAME OUT OF THE CLOSET—any number of interesting developments that reveal the truth about brides and grooms. Ray's and mine could have multiple stamps, like an expired passport. It could say DIDN'T LAST THE HONEYMOON or SHOULD HAVE KNOWN BETTER. Or, across his conniving forehead, above that hideous nose, succinctly and aptly, LIAR.

2
Later Classified as Our First Date

RAYMOND RUSSO'S SELF-IMPROVEMENT campaign began with a stroke of Las Vegas luck: He won a free teeth-bleaching, upper and lower arches, in a dentist's lottery. It explained his too-easy grin and his drinking coffee through a straw during what would later be classified as our first date. We were side by side, on stools at the Friendly's in the lobby of my hospital. Conversation was stalled on my medical degree, which evoked something close to reverence, expressed in boyish, gee-whiz fashion, as if he'd never encountered such a miraculous career trajectory. Was it not flattering? Was I not psychologically pummeled every day? Insulted by evaluations that described my performance as workmanlike and my people skills as hypothermic? Was I not ready for someone, anyone, to utter words of admiration?

"I can't be the only woman doctor you've ever met," I said. "You must have gone to college with women who went on to medical school."

"Believe it or not, I didn't."

"There are thousands of us," I said. "Maybe millions.

A third of my medical school class were women."

"Well, keep it coming," he said. "I know *I* was happy when you walked into the examining room. It helped me more than some guy saying, 'Your nose is fine the way it is.' I might have thought he wanted to keep me homely—you know—to reduce the competition."

I hoped he was joking, but humor comprehension was never my strong suit. I asked, "Did I take measurements that day, or a history?"

Still smiling, he said, "You don't remember me at all, do you?"

I said, "It's coming back to me. Definitely." Studying his nose in profile, I added, "I'm not a plastic surgeon. I just happened to be in the wrong place at the wrong time."

"Just the opposite! Thanks to you, I'm going to live with this nose of mine and see how it goes. I know a couple of guys who had nose jobs—I'm not saying they were done upstairs—but I think they look pretty fake."

I stated for the record—should anyone more senior be listening—"We have some true artists in the department. You could come up and look at the before-and-after photos. They're quite reassuring."

He waved away the whole notion. "I could die on the table, and then what? My obituary would say 'Died suddenly after no illness whatsoever'? 'In pursuit of a more handsome face'? How would my old man feel? It's his nose I inherited."

"General anesthesia always carries a risk," I said, "and of course there's always swelling and ecchymoses, but I doubt whether the hospital has ever lost a rhinoplasty patient."

He smiled again. He tapped the back of my hand and said, "You're a serious one, aren't you?"

I confirmed that I was and always would be: a serious infant, a serious child, a serious teenager, a serious student, a serious adult.

"Not the worst quality in a human being," Ray allowed.

I said, "It would help me in all the arenas of my life if I were a touch more gregarious."

"Highly overrated," said Ray Russo. "Any doofus, any deejay or salesman, or waitress, can be gregarious, but they can't do what you do."

It sounded almost logical. He asked if a cup of coffee was enough for dinner. Didn't I want to move to a booth and have a burger? Or to a place where we could share a carafe of wine?

I didn't.

"My car's in the hospital garage," he continued. "I slipped into a reserved space, figuring most docs must've left for the day." He took from his pocket a fat wad of bills, secured with a silver clip in the shape of a dollar sign. After much shuffling, he said he had nothing smaller than a fifty.

"I've got it," I said.

The $2.10 tab must have been viewed as a silent acceptance to dinner, because soon he was helping me on with my parka and leading me up a half-flight of stairs and through the door marked GARAGE. Parked under RESERVED FOR DR. HAMID, Ray's car was red and low-slung. Its steering wheel was wrapped in black leather.

"Seat belt secure?" he asked. "Enough leg room?" He patted the dash and said, "Just got my snow tires on today and my oil changed."

I said, "I never learned to drive."

He laughed as if I'd said something amusing, and turned to the parking attendant, who announced, "Three-fifty."

The attendant studied the fifty, handed it back, agitated it when Ray didn't take it. "C'mon," he snapped. "This isn't Atlantic City."

Ray said, "Can I pay you tomorrow? She's a surgeon here. I pick her up every night."

Snarling, the man waved us through.

When we'd pulled away, I said, "I don't like lying. I could have paid."

"He doesn't care," said Ray. "He gets paid by the hour regardless of how much is in the till when he cashes out."

After a few blocks in silence, he asked, "Do you have a roommate?"

"Why?"

He grinned. "I'm making conversation. A guy has to start somewhere. I could've asked about brothers and sisters. Teams you follow. Astrological sign."

"Do *you* have a roommate?" I asked.

"Me? I'm forty-five. A guy with a roommate at forty-five probably wouldn't be out on a date in the first place."

So I'd been right: *date*. His intentions were personal. I asked what made him call me up after all this time.

"It's what people do, Doc," he said. "Guys take a chance, because all of us have pals who met someone on a bus or a bar stool and asked for her phone number. So you think, Have a little courage. What's the worst she could do?"

"But why now? Why wait until I can't even remember who you are?"

"There were complications," he said.

I might have asked what they were, if only I had been curious, interested, or less exhausted.

By this time we were in front of the restaurant. Ray waved away the valet and said he'd take care of it himself—this *was* a parking lot for the patrons' use, wasn't it? Had he misunderstood the sign?

He didn't like the first table the hostess offered, so we waited until something with the right feeling opened up, the proper footage from the kitchen and the restrooms. It was an Italian fish and chop house with a Tiffany-shaded salad bar and beer served in frosted mugs. Without consulting me, he ordered the appetizer combo plate and a carafe of the house wine. He turned to me. Red or white?

I started to say that the sulfites in red wine gave me—

"Good," he said. He smiled the way you'd smile for an orthodontist's Polaroid, clinically, a gum-baring grimace. "Just had a bleach job," he said. "I'm supposed to avoid red wine, coffee, and tea."

The waitress pointed to the wine list, under the leather-bound menus, with the end of her pencil.

"I'll let her pick," he told the waitress. "She must have good taste. She's a doctor."

"What kind?" asked the waitress.

I said the Australian Chardonnay would be fine for me. One glass.

"I meant what kind of doctor."

"Surgeon," I said. "Still in training."

"Not your garden-variety surgeon," said Ray. "A plastic one."

The waitress did something then, squeezed her elbows to her waist so that her chest protruded a few degrees more than it had at rest. "I had plastic surgery," she said, "but I didn't go crazy. Would you have known if I didn't tell you?"

I said no.

Ray said, "Isn't it nice that you can speak about it so openly."

"She's a doctor," said the waitress. "I wouldn't have asked otherwise."

"I didn't know you before, but they look great," said Ray. "Did you feel that having larger breasts would improve your quality of life?"

"Yeah, I did," said the waitress.

"And have they?" asked Ray.

"I like 'em," said the woman. "I guess that's what counts."

Ray told the waitress that I had talked him out of a nose job and he'd done a complete one-eighty: He went in wanting one and came out a new man.

"Because she likes it the way it is?" asked the waitress. "Because when she looks at you she doesn't see the shape of your nose but the content of your character?"

"Nope," said Ray. "None of the above."

"I don't know him at all," I said.

"It was an office visit," said Ray. "I came for a consultation. And now I'm buying her dinner because she saved me ten thousand bucks."

The waitress looked thoughtfully at her pad and said, "I'll be right back with your drinks and your appetizer."

I told him, "Everybody has a procedure on their wish list or a scar they want to show me."

He asked if plastic surgery was more lucrative than the regular kind.

"It can be. Not if you volunteer your time and pay your own expenses to operate on the poor and the disfigured."

"You do that?"

"I hope to."

"I've seen those doctors who fly planes into jungles. The parents of these deformed kids walk, like, hundreds of miles to bring their Siamese twins to some American doc to separate, right?"

"Hardly that," I said. "That's major, major surgery, with teams of—"

"Maybe I'm mixing up my *60 Minutes* segments," he said. "But you know what I mean—the freaks of nature." Our waitress returned with the wine and said she'd be back with the appetizer combo platter. Ray raised his glass. "Here's to you, Doc, and to your future good deeds."

I said, " I don't understand why you wanted to have coffee with me, let alone a full-course dinner."

"You don't? You can't think of any reason a guy would want to see you outside the hospital?"

I said, "If this is leading up to a compliment, I'd

prefer you didn't. I wouldn't believe it anyway."

He reached over and turned a page of the menu so *"Pesce"* was before me. "Doctors—they watch what they eat and they know about good cholesterol. What about a piece of salmon?"

I said fine, that would be fine.

"And here we go," said Ray as the waitress made room on the table for our oval platter of deep-fried, lumpen morsels. "I'll have the usual," he said, "and the lady will have the salmon."

"Cooked through," I said.

Ray winked at me and said, "If she looks at it under the microscope, she doesn't want to see anything moving."

"Remind me what your usual is . . ."

"Vingole," he said. "Red."

The waitress asked if she could at some point talk to me in the ladies' room. It would only take a sec.

"Ask her here," said Ray.

"Can't," said the waitress. "She's gotta see it."

I said no, I couldn't. I was in training. I wasn't qualified. I'd only rotated through plastic surgery. No, sorry—shaking my head vigorously.

"Are you okay?" Ray asked her. "I mean, is there, like, an infection?"

I was immediately ashamed of my lack of even basic medical curiosity. Here a civilian was saying the right thing, exhibiting a bedside manner that years of schooling had not fine-tuned to any degree of working order in me. So I said, "Is something wrong, or did you just want to show me the results?"

She turned away from Ray and whispered, "One of the nipples. It looks different than before, a little off-kilter."

"Did you call your doctor?" I asked.

"I'm seeing him in a week. So I'll wait. It's probably nothing."

Ray broke off a piece of bread and dipped it into a saucer of olive oil. "How long could it take, Doc?" he asked.

THE NIPPLE WAS fine—merely stressed by an ill-fitting brassiere—but it gave Ray an early advantage, establishing him as a more compassionate listener than I. He was now drinking a glass of something that looked like a whiskey sour. Mathematically half of the appetizers were awaiting my return. "How is she?" he asked.

"Fine. But I'd like to explain why I resisted. It's not like the old days. The hospital's malpractice insurance doesn't cover diagnoses based on quick glances in the ladies' room."

He smiled and said, "She could sign a release that said, 'My patron at table eleven, Dr. Thrift, is held harmless as a result of dispensing medical advice to me in the ladies' room of Il Sambuco.' "

I said, "If I seemed a little cold-hearted—"

"Nah. You'd be doing this every time you left your house."

I might have expanded then on my life: That when I left the house, it wasn't with an escort at my elbow, introducing me left and right as Dr. Thrift, surgeon. I didn't socialize. I worked long hours and went home comatose. The hospital was teeming with people who wanted to talk, idly or professionally—it didn't matter. My day was filled with hard questions, half-answers, nervous patients, demanding relatives, didactic doctors. Why would I want to make conversation at night?

"Speaking of your house," he said, "you never answered my question about roommates."

"I have one," I said.

"Another doctor?"

"A nurse, actually."

"Are you friends?"

"We share the rent," I said. "But that's the extent of it. Occasionally we'll eat dinner or breakfast together, but rarely."

"How'd you pair up if you're not friends?"

"An index card on a bulletin board. I think it said, 'Five-minute walk to hospital. Safe neighborhood. No smokers.'"

"How many bedrooms?"

"Two. Small."

He launched into a discussion of the rental market—about places I could probably afford that had health clubs, swimming pools, Jacuzzis, off-street parking, central vacs, air-conditioning, refrigerators that manufactured ice . . .

I tried to stifle a yawn. "I'm usually in bed by this hour."

"Is she a good roommate?" he asked. "Considerate and all that?"

"It's a guy," I said. "Leo."

"Gay?" he asked.

I said, "Not that I pay attention, or not that he's flagrant in his dating habits, but when he does entertain guests, they're women."

This was what I deserved for agreeing to dine with a garrulous ex-patient. I asked if this was normal social intercourse for him—drilling virtual strangers about their home life and housemates.

"I'm getting to know you," he said. "You're welcome to ask me questions, too."

So I asked, "Do you live in an apartment?"

"A house." He bit his lip. "Alone. At least now."

"Now?" I repeated.

He drained his whiskey sour and blotted his mouth with his big maroon napkin. "I was married," he said. "And then I was widowed."

The waitress was back with our entrées just in time to hear his declaration. After leaving the plates, she stayed, as if waiting for the next cold blast from my arsenal of bad manners.

"I'm so sorry," I said to Ray. "How long ago?"

"A year and a day," he said.

I said to the waitress, "I think we're all set for now."

"More bread when you have a chance," said Ray.

I asked how his wife had died.

"Not from natural causes."

"Automobile?"

"Yes," he said. He raised his wineglass. "If you don't mind, I'd just as soon not go into the details. It's too upsetting."

"Of course," I said.

He scooped a littleneck from its shell and chewed it

with something like rapture.

I dug in, too. My salmon was dry, but I'd brought that on myself.

"Good?" asked Ray. "Because I was hoping you'd really like this place."

"Excellent," I said.

And this is exactly how a woman agrees to see a man a second time after finding him neither interesting, intelligent, nor compelling: He announces that he is a recent widower, vulnerable, like a man without an epidermis. That you are his first plunge into the treacherous waters of the Sea of Dates. Thus, when he finds the courage to ask if you'd like to do this again sometime—try another place, maybe Chinese or Ethiopian, maybe take in a movie—you say yes or you say no, and you understand that the look on your face and the speed of your answer will harm him, help him, or possibly save his life.

3
Leo Frawley, RN

IF YOU HAD seen my apartment, you would have guessed I was a clerk in a convenience store or a stitcher in a third-world sweatshop. I'm not bragging. I grew up in a three-story house with china and silver, a cleaning lady who came in every Thursday, and parents who sent me to college without financial aid. But four years later, I was sleeping in a bedroom that made me nostalgic for the claustrophobic shoe boxes I occupied in college. When I looked around my room and wondered why I said yes to the first place advertised on the housing board, I reminded myself of the extra twenty-five minutes of sleep I gained because of my proximity to the hospital, that I didn't need a coat to run the three blocks to work if it was above 40 degrees Fahrenheit, and that Leo Frawley was an exemplary roommate.

Leo would have said the same about me: I barely used any utilities. I didn't watch television, play CDs, or touch the thermostat; my presence, especially in the refrigerator, the medicine cabinet, and the kitchen cupboards, was negligible. I was never around or underfoot; when present, I slept deeply.

Signing a lease was an act of faith on my part. I knew nothing about Leo except for the superficial impressions I gleaned in our one cafeteria meeting. He was pleasant, well-spoken, and apparently popular. Coworkers greeted him, juggling trays across a single arm to hail him from all corners of the room.

"You have a lot of friends," I observed.

"You will too when you've been here as long as I have."

I said I would be quiet, considerate, and neat. I wasn't the liveliest wire he'd find in the city of Boston—quite the contrary, in fact—but I'd never disturb his sleep or monopolize the phone or be late with my rent.

"This could work," he said.

I asked if he could give me references, and he wrote a half dozen names and phone numbers on a napkin. The only local area code belonged to his mother, who he later told me had been prepped not to sound tight-lipped and disapproving if women called about the ad. Mrs. Frawley reported that Leo was the cleanest of her whole brood, and that was saying something because among her thirteen offspring she had one priest, one nun, one actuary, one pharmacist, two librarians, and a lab technician for the U.S. Food and Drug Administration. And while she didn't know why a girl would want to share an apartment and a toilet with a man, Leo would be the one of all her boys whom she'd recommend for the job. I thanked her and said she should be very proud of him. We were colleagues at the same hospital and he was clearly held in everyone's high esteem.

"He's named for a pope," she told me.

Not wanting to discuss anything too personal or too statutory with Mrs. Frawley, I asked Leo himself whether he walked around the apartment in states of undress or thought it was important to knock before entering a roommate's quarters.

"I might duck from the bathroom to my room with a towel wrapped around my middle. Is that what you meant?"

I said that was acceptable, certainly. I had lived in a co-ed dorm for one semester in college until I could be relocated.

"A guy who grew up with eight sisters knows how to knock," he said. "He also knows that a bathroom isn't available the minute he wants it."

I should have dropped it then, but I pressed on. Had any women—specifically former roommates or coworkers—ever complained, formally or informally, about his personal conduct?

Leo said, "Have I done or said anything so far that suggests that?"

I liked the way he answered, with dignity, and I liked the slight offense he'd taken. And in many ways, my initial rudeness has made me a better roommate. I knew as soon as I'd seen the look on his face that I had needlessly challenged a man who, after all, could bathe neonates and give breast-feeding lessons to their postpartum mothers.

Once I had moved in, I asked Leo why he needed to advertise on the community bulletin board, given the hordes of admiring fellow nurses and his geographically desirable apartment.

"I didn't want to live with another nurse," he said.

I asked why.

"You know," he said.

I said I didn't. I wasn't great at human-relations nuances. Was it because there would be too much shoptalk? Too much bringing the work home?

"Not so much the work," he said. "More like the extracurricular stuff. There's quite the grapevine. Let's say I had a visitor. And let's say someone from the NICU observed that guest coming out of my bedroom in the morning. Word would get around."

I thanked him for what I thought was a tribute to my discretion. I said, "Not only am I uninterested in your social life, but I wouldn't recognize a grapevine if I were harvesting grapes from it."

"Excellent," said Leo.

We followed the ground rules seamlessly: rent and utilities split down the middle; food separate, with both of us having the right to throw away leftovers growing mold spores. A chore wheel was posted on the refrigerator and rotated weekly. Suggested courtesy guidelines: seven minutes for showers; baths up to twenty minutes; no music after ten P.M. No dirty dishes left in the sink. Kitchen trash should be emptied and not allowed to overflow or smell. And after six months, he'd let me know if he thought our arrangement was amenable.

WHEN WE INTERSECTED at the hospital, Leo introduced me cheerfully. It was especially nice if he was with a smart little girl patient—just the three of us on an elevator—and then he'd say, "I'd like you to meet my friend Alice. She's a doctor. In fact, she's a surgeon. Isn't that a great thing to be?"

If only I could have smiled like a good role model and said something inspiring. If only I could have looked approachable enough to prompt one dad in my department to ask me to join him and his sixth-grader for lunch on Take Your Daughter to Work Day.

And did I mention that every female nurse in the hospital knew Leo? He was a friend to all—registered, practical, aide, candy striper—regardless of what floor or service or shift they worked on. If I were dispensing advice to men on how to meet women, how to be popular without having to be a matinee idol or ever leaving your workplace, I'd advise them to follow in Leo's footsteps: Get a job in a teaching hospital. Allude often to your training in the medical corps of the U.S. Army. Wear scrubs. Smile often and easily. Attach a miniature stuffed koala bear to your stethoscope.

I myself was short of friends when I moved here for my residency. Apparently, if I believed my own reputation, I was not "fun." Sometimes on Monday mornings in medical school I'd hear references to weekend parties, kegs, harbor cruises, but I didn't experience them first-hand. When I decided to go into surgery, my lab part-ners—so-called people persons and future family practi-tioners—said, "How perfect."

I graduated second in my class, which I thought was a good prognostic of how I'd perform as a resident, but apparently it was not. I had some trouble bridging the gap between the patient's surgical site—that disem-bodied, exposed rectangle of skin awaiting a scalpel—and the patient's mind, soul, and figurative heart. I thought it was helpful to disassociate the two, to forget I was cutting into a live human being; to pretend it was dead, formaldehyded Violet or Buster, my two cadavers from Gross Anatomy.

How had I gotten so appallingly ineffective with actual people? I thought I had a nice way about me—I was particularly adept at delivering good-news bulletins to relatives in the waiting room, but even that drew crit-icism. Once in a while, a next of kin complained that the frown on my face as I walked into the lounge scared him or her to death. But wasn't it mere concentration? It was never enough—my excellent knowledge of anatomy, my openings and my closings, my long hours. What people want, I swear, is a doctor with the disposition of a Montessori teacher.

None of it is easy. Male patients are not thrilled to see you, especially in urology and vascular. Athletes want their bad knees, shoulders, ankles, and elbows fixed by doctors who look like them—Nordic, buff, handsome, confident, certainly not female. Everyone experienced in trauma works around and over you in the ER—faster, surer, nimbler, louder. I began to think that high marks in medical school were an indicator of nothing, and that a few parties along the way might have honed my social-ization skills more than long nights at Countway Library.

I was the medical equivalent of the kid picked last for the kickball team: Honor roll doesn't matter; sex, race, or national origin doesn't matter. The only thing that mattered was if you could kick a ball over the head of the second baseperson and get someone else home.

AT THE SIX-MONTH juncture, during one of our rare syn-chronized breakfasts, it was I who asked Leo if he'd like to find a more compatible roommate.

"In what sense?"

"More fun. More charismatic."

"Hey," he said. "What's wrong?"

I said, "I think you're too polite to tell me that it's not working out. Everything is fine on the surface, but maybe you could find someone more suitable. You know—maybe we're like those married couples who never raise their voices, but all the same aren't happy."

"I'm happy," said Leo. "I think this is working out fine." Then he asked if it was me—was I the discon-tented one looking for an out?

"Just the opposite," I said. And then I tried to define my position, that I was proud to be his roommate because of the high esteem if not popularity he enjoyed at the hospital; proud to have my name on his answering machine's outgoing message.

Instead of looking pleased he said, "But you have to be content inside your own skin."

I said that wasn't possible at this juncture. Work was all-consuming, especially while I was so bad at it.

"You'll get better. Interns, by definition, are here to learn."

"I may have made a terrible mistake," I told him.

His expression grew alarmed: One of his neonates? One of his preemies? "When?" he asked.

"I don't mean a specific terrible mistake. I meant, it was a mistake to think that good grades were transferable to the actual practice of medicine. I don't have the aptitude in any of the areas they evaluate us in."

Leo thought for a minute, then said, "You work hard. You haven't ever taken a sick day, as far as I know. And you haven't had any major goof-ups, correct?"

"No one would leave me alone long enough in the OR to take out the wrong organ or amputate the wrong limb," I said.

"Do you want me to talk to someone?" he asked.

"Like who?"

"I know people," he said. "I could feel them out for how you're doing and where you stand. Maybe you're worried about nothing."

I said I knew how I was doing, and besides, I needed the truth more than I needed the anesthetic tact they would administer out of friendship to him.

Leo said he hadn't always been this comfortable on the ward. I should have seen him on his first medevac flight. Boy, was that a scary couple of hours. And not much hand-holding for trainees.

I said I recognized that in a million years, or even if I spent a million dollars on therapy, I'd never have his personality, his good humor, his unflappability, or that way he could walk into a patient's room and say just the right breezy thing to make his or her pain or nausea or approaching syringe recede.

"You notice all that?" he asked.

"I hear about it. It's common knowledge. I think some of the pediatric residents steal your lines. And your patients, let's face it, worship you. Babies, toddlers, girls, boys. Not to mention their mothers."

Have I mentioned that Leo is handsome? Perhaps not when you break it down, feature by feature, and factor in some patches of facial seborrhea. But altogether it's a successful package, with its curly blond hair, well-defined mouth, and pale blue eyes that look like they've just finished having a good laugh. He was probably a gawky teenager, and I do see vestiges of acne scars on his red face, but overall he bears that winning combination of an elfin face on a tall, broad-shouldered man.

He said then that his late father thought he was wasting those very talents I was referring to, the gift of gab, the ability to walk into a room and—pardon the bragging—win friends and influence people. "So you know what that means, right? To a Boston-Irish father?"

I shook my head.

"State senator or state rep with an eye to an eventual run for the governor's office."

"Is that what you'd like?"

"Absolutely not," said Leo. "He didn't like telling people that his son was a nurse. He used to say 'orderly'

30

because he thought it sounded manlier, but I put a stop to that. He changed it to, 'Leo trained in the army medical corps and works at a Harvard hospital. No, not married, but he dates a different nurse every night.'"

I said, "It's not so much your gift of gab. It's bigger than that. It's a quality of mercy combined with your ability to make a joke."

Leo smiled and said that was a nice compliment. Very nice. Thanks. *Quality of mercy*—wow.

"Maybe some of it will rub off on me," I added.

He said—another tribute to his diplomacy—"You have other strengths, Alice."

"Name one."

"Brains, for starters. I mean, let's say there was an entire hospital staffed by smiling volunteers, happy LPNs, and class clowns like me. It would certainly lose its state certification in a hurry."

I said that was a ridiculous argument, but thank you.

"What exactly are you worried about?" he asked. "Your private life or your professional life?"

"Professional," I said. "I don't know if I'll be invited back for a second year. And then what? I'll have to start over again. And what would that be? Who's going to want a resident that was asked to leave?"

"Does that happen?"

"All the time. It's a pyramid system. They start with seven, and prune every year."

He sighed. Even Leo couldn't put a positive spin on my prospects.

I walked over to the counter and came back with the coffeepot. "Let's just say my answer to that question had been 'personal' instead of 'professional.' Would you have some insights? Have you noticed me doing anything egregious during social exchanges?"

Leo upended the sugar dispenser and let several teaspoonfuls pour into his cup.

"Be honest," I said.

He squirmed in his chair, closed one eye. "If you put a gun to my head, I'd probably say that at times you remind me of my sister-in-law Sheila."

Leo had twelve siblings, so there was always a family member he could cite as a role model or bad apple. "I hasten to add that Sheila is probably the smartest of any of my brothers' wives."

"But?"

"But she's not the person I'd marry if I had my eye on the governor's mansion."

I said, "Massachusetts doesn't have a governor's mansion."

Leo closed his eyes, exhaled as if exasperated.

"Is your brother running for something?" I asked.

Leo shook his head.

I said, "I ran for office once, in high school, but I lost. I would have been perfect for the position of class secretary because I'd taken shorthand one summer and would have been able to take the best notes of anyone else, but apparently that mattered very little."

"Everything in high school is a popularity contest—which can't be a startling revelation to you."

I tried to remember back to the three straight years I ran, and for the three straight years I was trounced by girls who weren't even members of the National

Honor Society.

"Don't take this wrong," said Leo, "and don't answer if you don't want to, but did you date in high school?"

He didn't let me answer. He patted my hand and said, "No matter. What a stupid and shallow question, right? As if you'd even remember. *My* high school social life is certainly a blur."

He poured himself a second bowl of cereal and filled it to the rim with milk. "The guy who calls here? Is he a friend?"

"I had dinner with him once."

"And?"

"And he'd like to do it again."

"Have you called him back?"

I said no.

"No, permanently, or no, not yet?" he asked.

"He's not my type," I said.

Leo offered no rebuttal, but I knew what he was thinking: How could Alice Thrift, workaholic wall-flower, have collected any data or constructed a model on something as theoretical as her type?

4
We Entertain

THIS IS WHAT we imagined: Nurses and surgical residents conversing in civilian garb. RNs impressing MDs with their previously underappreciated level of science and scholarship. Exhausted doctors sipping beer while sympathetic nurses circulated with pinwheel sandwiches. Doctors asking nurses if they could compare schedules and find free Saturday nights in common.

When every nurse accepted our invitation and every resident declined, Leo and I had to scramble to provide something close to even numbers. I volunteered to call my medical school classmates who were interning in Boston—there were two at Children's, some half dozen at MGH, a couple more at Tufts, at BU . . .

"Friends?" he asked.

"Classmates," I repeated.

I know what was on his mind: my unpopularity. That the words *party* and *Alice Thrift* were oxymoronic, and now Leo was experiencing it firsthand. I said, "Let's face it: I have no marquee value. My name on the invitation doesn't get one single warm body here, especially of the Y-chromosome variety."

"We're going to work on that," said Leo.

"On the other hand, since I'm not known as a party thrower, my invitees will expect a very low level of merriment."

Leo said, "Cut that out. It's not your fault. We're aiming too high. Interns are exhausted. If they have a night off, they want to sleep."

I said, "That's not true of the average man, from what I've read."

"And what is that?" Leo asked.

"I've heard that men will go forth into groups of women, even strangers, if they think there's a potential for sexual payoff."

"What planet are you living on?" Leo asked. "Why do you sound like an anthropologist when we're just bullshitting about how to balance our guest list?"

We were having this conversation in the cafeteria, Leo seated, me standing, since I usually grabbed a sandwich to go. He didn't think I ate properly, so after he'd rattled a chair a few times, I sat down on it.

"If I called my single brothers, not counting Peter," he said, "and they each brought two friends, that would be six more guys."

"Is Peter the priest?"

"No, Joseph's the priest. Peter doesn't like women."

"Okay. Six is a start."

I unwrapped my cheese sandwich, and squeezed open the spout on my milk carton. "I know someone," I finally said.

"Eligible?"

I nodded. *So* eligible, I thought, that he was pursuing Alice Thrift. "Not young, though. Forty-five. And widowed."

"Call him. Forty-five's not bad. Maybe he could bring some friends."

I said, "Actually, he's the one leaving those messages."

"He's been crooning Sinatra on the latest ones," said Leo. "What's that about?"

"Trying to get my attention." I took a bite of my sandwich.

Leo said, "No lettuce, no ham, no tomato?"

I pointed out that I never knew how long lunch would languish in my pocket before consumption, so this was the safest thing to take away.

Leo paused to consult our list of women. Finally he said, "I see a few of my colleagues who would be very happy with a forty-five-year-old guy. And even more who would pounce on the widower part. How long ago did he lose his wife?"

"A year and a day." I looked at my watch's date. "As of now, a year and two weeks."

"Call him. Tell him you and your roommate are putting together a soiree of hardworking primary-care nurses, who—studies have shown—sometimes go out on the town looking for a sexual payoff just like the males of the species."

I said, "I wasn't born yesterday. I know people have sexual relations on a casual basis."

Leo studied me for a few seconds, as if there was a social/epidemiological question he wanted to ask.

I said, "I've had relations, if that's what your retreat into deep thought is about."

"I see," said Leo.

"In college. Actually, the summer between my junior and senior years. I was a camp counselor and the boys' camp was across the lake."

"And was he a counselor, too?"

"An astronomy major at MIT, or so I believed. He knew all the constellations."

"Sounds romantic," said Leo.

I said, "Actually not. I had wondered what all the fuss was about, so I decided to experience it for myself."

"And?"

I swallowed a sip of milk and blotted my mouth. "Not worth the discomfort or the embarrassment or the trip into town for the prophylactics. And to make it worse, he expected follow-up."

"Meaning?"

"That we'd do it again."

"What a cad," said Leo.

"I found out later he wasn't an astronomy major at all, but studying aerospace engineering. And in a fraternity."

"Did you ever see him again?

I said no, never.

"So that would be . . . like five years ago?"

I shrugged. After a pause, I wrapped the remains of my sandwich in plastic and put it in my jacket pocket.

"Not that it's any of my business," said Leo.

I said I had to run. Would catch him later—I had the night off so I'd do some vacuuming.

"Alice?" he called when I was a few paces from him. I returned to the table.

"I want to say, just for the record, as a fellow clinician, that the fuss you've heard about? With respect to relations? The stuff that, according to movies and books, supposedly makes the earth move and the world go round? Well—and I say this as your friend—it does."

I didn't have an answer; wasn't sure whether his statement was confessional or prescriptive.

"What I'm getting at," he continued, "is that you might want to give it another shot someday."

RAY BROUGHT HIS cousins George and Jerome, two men in leather jackets over sweaters knit in multicolored zigzags. "Missoni," said Ray when he saw me studying them. He repeated in his introductions to everyone, "Cousins? Absolutely. But like brothers. No, better than brothers—best friends." Or—whichever suited the race or ethnicity of the nurse he was addressing: *"Paisans."* *"Confrères."* "Homies."

Not to say he was ignoring me. Quite the opposite. He helped in the manner of a boyfriend of the hostess. He stomped on trash, refilled glasses, wiped up spills, chatted with the friendless, who would have been me but for the refuge offered by a kitchen and hors d'oeuvres–related tasks. Ray may have watched too many situation comedies in which suburban husbands steal time from their guests to peck the cheek of their aproned hostess/wife. I had to say repeatedly, "Why are you doing that?" disengaging him in the exact manner that my mother swatted away my father. It hardly discouraged him; if anything he was inspired to discuss what he perceived as my discomfort with/suspicion of intimacy.

I said, "I know men have very strong drives, and I know you've been lonely, but I think you're being overly familiar."

Happily, guests were interrupting us. Leo poked his head in every so often to remind me that there was a party going on in the other rooms and that I should leave the dishes for the morning.

"Let's go see how our guests are faring," Ray said cheerfully.

Leo had indeed dipped into his supply of brothers for the occasion, which was of great genetic interest to all observers. One had black hair and the fairest, pinkest skin you'd ever see on a male old enough to have facial hair; another had Leo's build and Leo's ruddy complexion, but an angular face and brown eyes that seemed to come from another gene pool. The Frawleys were mixing warily with the Ray Russo contingent. One red-haired brother asked a cousin, "So, how do you know Leo?"

"My cousin's going out with his roommate," he answered. I corrected the misapprehension. Ray and I were acquaintances, I said.

The cousin grinned. "If you say so."

I explained to the brother that Ray had lost his wife a year ago and only now was getting out socially.

Cousin George said, "He was really faithful to her memory. He didn't do a thing until she was legally pronounced dead."

I told him what Ray had told me: the accident, the head trauma, the coma, the life support, the horrible decision. I asked if any of her organs were donated and George said, "Um. You'd have to ask Ray."

I asked if she'd been wearing a seat belt.

George said, "I doubt it."

Leo was now doing what he had threatened to do during our planning phase if things didn't coalesce on their own—dance. He was taking turns with a flock of nursing students, all undergraduates from the same baccalaureate nursing program, and all friends. They looked alike, too: Their hairdos were the ballerina knots, streaked with blond, that were popular with pretty teenagers. I didn't think we should invite anyone under twenty-one because we were serving beer and wine, but Leo had prevailed. Now they were taking turns being twirled, and each one's raised hand revealed a few inches of bare midriff and a pierced navel.

"Wanna dance, Doc?" Ray asked.

I shook my head resolutely.

"Would it make a difference if it was a slow dance? You must have learned a few steps of ballroom dancing for those teas at that fancy college."

I didn't remember telling him where I'd gone to college, but I must have mentioned it over dinner. I said, "Okay, a slow dance."

"I'll talk to the deejay," said Ray. He turned to his cousin. "Georgie—put something on that the doc might enjoy dancing to."

"Will do," said George.

A little human warmth generated from a clean-shaven jaw can go a long way. I may have exaggerated my ineptitude on the dance floor; any able-bodied person can follow another's lead when his technique constitutes nothing more than swaying in place. It helped that he didn't talk or sing, and that his cologne had a citric and astringent quality that I found pleasing.

If Ray said anything at all, it was an occasional entreaty to relax. "You're not so bad, Doc," he said when the first song ended. "In fact I think you might like another whirl."

He hadn't let go of my hand. I looked around the room to see if we had an audience. Leo was consolidating trays of hors d'oeuvres, but watching. He arched his eyebrows, which I interpreted to mean, Need to be rescued?

I shrugged.

A nurse with closely cropped hair dyed at least two primary colors took Leo's hand and led him out to the patch of hardwood that was serving as the dance floor.

"Having a good time?" Leo asked me.

"You better believe it," Ray answered, flashing a thumbs-up with my hand in his.

A PHONE CALL woke me. Was I in my own bed or in the on-call cot? It took a few seconds to orient myself in the dark before remembering: I had the weekend off. Good. This would be the hospital calling the wrong resident.

But it wasn't. It was my mother, her voice choked.

"Is it Daddy?" I whispered.

"It's Nana," she managed, discharging the two syllables between sobs.

"What about Nana?"

"Gone! One minute she was alive and the next minute, gone! Pneumonia! As if that wasn't curable!"

My grandmother was ninety-four and had been in congestive heart failure for three months and on dialysis for nine. I said, "The elderly don't do well with pneumonia."

I looked at my bedside clock: 3:52 A.M.

"My heart stopped when the phone rang because I knew without even answering," my mother continued. "Here it was, the phone call I've been dreading my whole life."

"Is Daddy there?" I asked.

My father came on and said, "I told her not to wake you. What were you going to do at four in the morning except lose a night's sleep?"

"Ninety-four years old," I said quietly. "Maybe in the morning she'll realize that it's a blessing."

"I tried that," he said. "Believe me."

"Tried what?" my mother asked.

"To point out to you, Joyce, that your mother lived to a ripe old age, was healthy for the first ninety-three of them, and any daughter who has a mother by her side at her sixtieth birthday party is a pretty lucky woman."

"It's not the time to count my blessings," I heard. "I'm crying because she's gone, okay? Do I have to defend myself?"

"Be nice to her," I said.

"I am," he said. Then to my mother, "I know, honey. I know. No one's mother can live long enough to suit her children. It's always too early."

My mother raised her voice so I could hear distinctly, "Some daughters hate their mothers. Some mothers hear from their daughters once a week if they're lucky. I talked to mine every day. Twice a day. She was my best friend."

"When's the funeral?" I asked.

"We haven't gotten that far yet," said my father. "She still has to call her sisters."

"I called you first!" I heard from the far side of their bed.

"Sorry to wake you," my father said. "I couldn't stop her. You're on her auto dial."

"I have to get up in two hours anyway," I said.

I BRING UP this relatively untraumatic and foreseen death because Ray counted my grandmother's funeral as our third date. He was a genius at being there for me when I didn't want or need him. He called the Monday after the party and got Leo. "Her grandmother died, so I don't know when she'll get back to you," he said.

Ray paged me at the hospital, and without announcing himself said, "I'm driving you wherever you need to go."

I said that was unnecessary. I had relatives in Boston who were going to the funeral, and my father had worked out the arrangements.

"Absolutely not. What are the chances that they'll want to leave when you can leave and return when you have to return? Zero."

I said, "But, Ray: I don't know you well enough to bring you to a funeral."

"I'll wait in the car," he said.

"It's not an hour or two. There's the service, then the burial, then I'm sure there will be a lunch for the out-of-town guests back at my house."

He said quietly, "I know all too well the number of hours that a funeral can consume."

I said I couldn't talk. Someone's ears needed tubes. To end the conversation, I yielded. I said he could pick me up at six A.M. And just in case he didn't spend the whole time waiting in the car, he should wear a dark suit.

I also said, "Ray? I don't want you to construe this as anything but what it is—transportation. I'm being completely forthright here. If you want to drive me all the way to Princeton as a friend, I'd appreciate it, but otherwise I'll make arrangements with my cousins."

"I get it," he said. "I think I was a little too pushy at the party, coming on too strong in the kitchen. But I know that. That's why I called your apartment—to apologize. Besides, I have my own guilt to deal with."

"Guilt? Because you went to a party?"

"More like, if I ever told my parents that I had feelings for a woman so soon after Mary died, they'd be furious."

I asked, "*Your* parents? Or are you talking about your parents-in-law?"

Ray said, "Let's not talk about parents, especially with your mother just having passed."

"Not my mother, my grandmother."

I heard a low chuckle in my ear. "You did sound kind of blasé for a gal whose mother just died."

"She was ninety-four and comatose," I said.

"God bless her."

I was at the nurses' station on Fletcher-4. I caught one nurse rolling her eyes at another. They'd been listening.

I hung up the phone and stated for the record, "My grandmother died last night, unexpectedly."

"We heard," said one, not even looking up from her fashion magazine. "Unexpectedly, despite being ninety-four."

"No one's sympathetic when they hear ninety-something," I said. "They think that makes it easy, as if it's overdue and you should have been prepared."

They exchanged looks again. I wanted to say, What am I doing wrong? Did I sound brusque or unfeeling? Have we met before? Instead I said, "I'm Dr. Thrift. This is my first night in ENT. You probably know my housemate, Leo, from pediatrics. Leo Frawley?"

The younger one sat up straighter and hooked stray blond tendrils behind her ears. "I know Leo," she said.

"And you are?"

"Roxanne."

"I'm Mary Beth," volunteered her deskmate. "I used to work in peds."

"We're sorry for your loss," said Roxanne. "I'd be, like, devastated if my grandmother died—no matter how old she was."

I took a tissue from their box, touched it to each eye, and said with uncharacteristic aplomb, "I'll be sure to tell Leo how kind you were."

5
A.k.a. the Transportation

HAD I REALLY thought that Joyce Thrift's social reflexes and nuptial dreams would fail her on that January day, just because she was laying her mother to rest?

Ray whistled appreciatively when we pulled up to my parents' house, a sprawling Dutch Colonial, previously white, now yellow with pine-green shutters—a new color scheme they'd forgotten to tell me about.

"How many square feet in this baby?" Ray asked, squinting through his tinted windshield.

I said I had no idea. One doesn't think of one's childhood home in mathematical terms.

"How many bedrooms?"

"Five."

"Five! For how many kids?"

"Two. But one is a guest room, and another's my mother's studio."

"For what?"

"Fiber art," I confessed.

Ray looked engaged, which was his psychological specialty: filing away facts that would later make him seem uniquely attentive. "You mean like weaving?" he asked.

"Weaving's part of it. She incorporates different elements—wool, feathers, newsprint, photographs, bones."

"Human or animal?"

I said he could ask her himself. She'd be thrilled to discuss it since her relatives and friends had grown tired of her shaggy wall hangings, both as a topic of conversation and as an art form.

"Maybe on a future visit, but I certainly wouldn't bring it up today," said the master of funereal etiquette. He pointed to the silver van in the driveway and read approvingly, "Fêtes by Frederick."

"The caterer. People will be coming back after the cemetery."

"Buffet, you think?"

"Something low-key. When my grandfather died, we had finger sandwiches and petits fours."

"So what's the plan? I meet you back here?"

I looked at my watch and calculated aloud, "Funeral at eleven, then to the cemetery, then back here for an hour. How does one-thirty sound? I'll come out to the car."

"Doc," said Ray. "That's terrible. You're not going to run in and run out like you've been beeped. This is your grandmother who died, not some second cousin twice removed."

"Two-thirty, then?"

"I wouldn't mind going to the church," said Ray. "I

46

find that even if I don't know the deceased, I get a lot out of it."

What could I do but include him after the gas and mileage he'd invested in the trip and his curiosity about fiber art? I said, "I think I'll be riding with the next of kin in the limousine. But if you want to go to the church, I'm sure that's fine." I reached for the door handle. "I should probably have this time alone with my mother, though."

"Absolutely," said Ray. "I don't want to be underfoot while she's getting dressed."

I wasn't worried about my mother, who could be gracious in any tragedy. But I needed to take her aside and explain that the rough-hewn man in the red car was a mere acquaintance and—not that she'd ever entertain such thoughts on a day like today—wholly unsuited to any other role. And the Swarthmore sticker on the back windshield? Not applicable; a relic from the previous owner.

"Mind if I run in and use the toilet?" Ray asked.

I said okay. There was a powder room just inside the front door.

"Thirty seconds, and that includes the hand-washing," he promised.

He took his gray pin-striped jacket from its hanger, put it on, tugged at his cuffs, smoothed his silver tie against his sternum. "Not bad, huh?" he asked.

Already on my way up the stone walk, I didn't look back. I opened the front door and called, "Anyone home?"

Ray was right behind me. "Wow. Nice place."

There was a party-sized coatrack in the foyer, bearing

so many wooden hangers that I stopped to ponder the scope of the after-funeral fête. I pointed to the half-bath and Ray darted toward it.

My father appeared at the top of the stairs in a black velour bathrobe and hospital-blue terry-cloth slippers. When he reached the bottom step I gave him a hug that was slightly longer than our semiannual perfunctory squeeze.

"You okay?" he asked.

I said I was, of course, sad, but still, when one saw as much untimely and sudden death as I did, then it's hard to view ninety-four as—

"We were able to get Frederick on practically no notice at all," announced my father. "I mean, we only wanted tea sandwiches and a few salads, but he was Johnny-on-the-spot."

Ray emerged from the bathroom in the promised thirty seconds, his right hand outstretched. "Ray Russo," he said, "a.k.a. the transportation."

"We left at six," I said.

"Luckily I make my own hours," said Ray.

My father smiled uncertainly.

"First-Prize Fudge," said Ray.

"Fudge?" I said.

"Mostly to seasonal concessionaires. I have a box for Mrs. Thrift in my car, if you think that's not a frivolous gift at a time like this."

My father turned toward the stairway and yelled, "Joyce! Alice is here! And a young man."

Within seconds my six-foot mother was descending, buttoning a black dress with chiffon kimono sleeves. She forgot, in her role switch from grieving daughter to hostess, to kiss me. We weren't much for public or private displays of affection anyway, but I patted her back and checked her fastenings. "You missed a few buttons," I whispered.

I could tell from the way her vertebrae were aligned that she was greeting Ray bravely, ambitiously. "I'm Joyce Thrift," she said. "And you are . . . ?"

"Ray Russo," Ray and I pronounced in unison.

"Are you a colleague of Alice's?" Her glance dropped to his feet and to shoes that were too pointy for a man in medicine.

"He drove me," I said.

Ray bowed his head and took two obsequious steps backward. "I think it's best if I wait in the car so as to give you your privacy," he said.

"Absolutely *not!* Alice? Take Mr. Russo into the kitchen and see what goodies Frederick is willing to part with."

I said, "Mom—Mr. Russo actually drove me as a favor. He wouldn't even let me pay for the gas."

When she looked to each of us for clarification, my father added, "She means this gentleman is not a car service. Mr. . . ."

"Russo," I supplied.

"Mr. Russo is in sales," said my father.

"Which reminds me," said Ray. He made it to the door in three long strides and was back in twenty seconds—time that passed in silence among the Thrifts—holding a gift-wrapped box that could have housed a VCR.

"Milk chocolate marshmallow, Black Forest, and penuche," said Ray. "No nuts, just in case anyone's allergic."

"Fudge," said my mother. "I'll be taking great comfort in this over the next few weeks."

"Or maybe," Ray said with a nudge to her elbow, "once you taste it, over the next few *days*."

My mother handed me the box. "Tell Frederick . . . I don't know: the blue Wedgwood platter?"

"This size comes with its own serving tray," said Ray.

My mother looked down and blinked at her stockinged feet. "I should finish dressing," she murmured.

My father turned her toward the steps. "She's barely slept since we got the news," he said.

"Maybe Alice could write me a prescription for something."

I understood that this was my mother putting an MD at the end of my name. "You know I can't write prescriptions yet," I said. "Let alone in New Jersey."

"She doesn't need any sedatives," said my father. "She's exhausted. She just needs this day to be over."

"Warm milk works for me," said Ray. He winked. "Especially with a shot of brandy in it."

"Let me give this to Frederick," I said. "It weighs a ton."

"There's five pounds in there," said Ray. "Which means more than a quarter pound of Grade A sweet creamery butter and at least a quart of evaporated milk. We list the ingredients on our Web site."

"Perhaps I *will* lie down," my mother said.

"You have a beautiful home," said Ray, crossing the foyer to inspect a bronze death mask, reputed to be of Pocahontas.

"Of course you'll come to the funeral, Ray," my mother said.

He said, his back to us in connoisseurship, that he didn't want to intrude.

It was then that I saw a glance pass between my parents, and I realized that the invitation was not hospitality but fear that a purveyor of carnival fudge might, if left alone, pillage the mourners' residence. "We insist," she said.

"Whatever feels right to you," said Ray, now studying one of my mother's canvases. "I can stay here or I can slip into a pew that's a good distance from the immediate family. That way, no one is going to ask, 'Who's the guy?'"

My mother said, "I think anyone who drives seven hours—"

"It took us under six," I said.

"Anyone who drives five-plus hours to a stranger's funeral should absolutely attend the service," she continued. "And if anyone jumps to conclusions . . . that's the last thing I'm concerning myself with today."

"I'd be honored," said Ray. As he turned back toward us, his voice and face slumped. "You'd think I'd have an aversion to funerals after my personal misfortune, but it's quite the opposite."

"Misfortune?" echoed my mother.

"Ray was recently widowed," I explained.

"No!"

"Automobile accident," he said.

"When?" asked my father.

"A year ago Inauguration Day—ice, snow, sleet, you name it," said Ray. "The car had four-wheel drive and traction control. I thought it was foolproof."

"Air bags?" my mother asked.

Ray said, "I can't even discuss that aspect of it because it makes me shake all over with rage. Suffice it to say, they didn't deploy."

"You poor man," said my mother, flexing the fingers of one hand in the direction of the powder room to mean, Someone get me a tissue.

"I insist you lie down," said my father. "There's a long day ahead, and lots of people wanting to discuss their own mothers' deaths, and it's going to take a lot out of you, sweetie."

"That's exactly why I didn't bring up my own tragedy," said Ray. "And if someone starts talking about theirs? You give me a sign and I'll come over and I'll be your ears so you don't have to listen to their story, okay? Would you let me do that much?"

"Yes, I will," said my mother. "I only wish you'd been here to answer some of the phone calls."

"We had to let the machine pick up," said my father.

Ray shook his head. "People. Why is it so hard for them to use their brains?"

"Exactly," said my mother. "This has been like taking a graduate course in psychology. People you barely know send you fruit the minute they see the obituary, while some of your best friends don't even call."

"They don't want to bother you," I said. "Or maybe

they hung up when they got the machine."

My mother began her climb to her bedroom, both hands on the banister.

FREDERICK WAS ALONE in the kitchen, wearing chef's full regalia plus striped pantaloons and red plastic clogs. When I announced the fudge delivery, his lip curled; he pointed to a remote pantry counter.

"My mother wants it put out," I said.

"I have truffles," he snapped.

Perhaps it was then that I felt a twinge of something for Ray—call it sympathy, loyalty, charity—born of a caterer's condescension. "A guest brought it," I said. "A guest who got up at five A.M. this morning so I wouldn't have to take a bus."

With the edge of a linen towel, Frederick wiped a drip of red goop from a platter. "And you are?"

"Alice."

Frederick said, "The problem is, Alice, that this isn't a pot-luck dinner. Everything is planned, down to the color of the sugar cubes. Serving fudge with truffles is like serving steak with roast beef."

"It's the guest's livelihood," I said. "And no one but you will notice if there's a surfeit of chocolate."

Just outside the kitchen door my father was giving Ray loud directions. "Cool," Ray repeated after each prescribed left or right turn.

There was a pause on our side. Finally Frederick asked, "You're the older daughter?"

I said that was correct. We'd met at my mother's sixtieth—

"The doctor?"

I said yes.

He smiled benignly, then asked, "And where does a doctor cross paths with a fudge salesman?"

I couldn't muster an answer; couldn't even choreograph my own exit as I pondered what it was about me that invited caterers to condescend.

"Must be serious, judging by the color of your cheeks," Frederick continued.

I said, "Any color on my face is utter astonishment and, and, dismay, and frankly—"

The door swung open and Ray was at my side. At first I thought the object of his survey was the grandness of the built-in appliances and the curve of the granite countertops, but he was looking for his gift.

"In the pantry," said Frederick.

Ray popped a pastry triangle in his mouth. "Spinach," he said.

"*Spanokopita,*" said Frederick. "Though not fully defrosted."

"Not bad," said Ray. "Not what I expected. I thought it was going to be sweet—a miniature turnover, like with fig inside." Ray chewed, swallowed, popped another triangle in his mouth. "You Greek?" he mumbled through the phyllo.

Frederick shook his head in the smallest possible arc, and turned back to the sink.

Ray looked at me: You see that? You gonna let the kitchen help diss your guests?

I said, "Frederick? My mother wanted you to make up a nice plate for Mr. Russo."

Frederick crossed to the refrigerator, returned with a plastic bag of some curly purple vegetal matter. "She didn't mention this to me," he said.

"We've been on the road since six A.M.," I said.

Ray helped himself to a deviled egg, then another. "Don't bother. I'm gonna head out so I can get a good seat."

"I don't think you have to worry about a crowd," said Frederick. "She outlived every one of her friends."

"I lost my wife at a young age," said Ray, slipping an arm around my waist. "So good genes mean everything to me."

I moved a discreet step away and said, "My other grandmother died at sixty-two of non-Hodgkin's lymphoma."

"I did the brunch," said Frederick.

I said I might lie down for a short rest myself before the limo arrived, if they'd excuse me.

Ray grinned. "These doctors! They can catnap on a dime. I swear—ten minutes of shut-eye, and she's up for a triple bypass."

Frederick smiled knowingly.

Ray's eyes narrowed. "I'm not saying that I'm well versed in this lady's personal habits—if I read that smirk correctly."

Unfazed, Frederick blinked and turned to me.

"I've never done a triple bypass," I said. "I've never even watched."

Alice Makes Up Her Own Mind

COVERING FOR OUR vacationing pastor was a woman with a crewelwork stole, who ruined the funeral by eulogizing my grandmother as "Barbara."

At the fourth or fifth misstatement, my mother barked from behind her handkerchief, "Betty!"

The minister looked up; smiled indulgently at the grieving heckler.

"Her name wasn't Barbara," clarified a male voice in the back.

Everyone knew it was the homely pin-striped stranger who'd arrived ahead of everyone else and whose signature was first in the guest book: Raymond Russo, Boston, Mass.

"Betty," repeated the minister. "How careless of me." She smiled again. "My own mother was Barbara. I think that must say something, don't you?"

My mother was having none of it: Her stored grief found a new cause, a new enemy, in the rainbow-embroidered figure of the overly serene Reverend Dr. Nancy Jones-Fuchs, who was told in the recessional, in frigid terms, that her services would not be needed graveside.

Ray was the only one who had thought to slip the Book of Common Prayer beneath his overcoat. My aunt Patricia suggested we honor my grandmother Quaker-style, which was to say, in silence. After several minutes, Ray opened the prayer book. We looked over. He offered it to my mother first. "I couldn't," she said. Nor could Aunt Patricia, which left my father, who looked to me.

"I could read a psalm," Ray offered. "Or just say a few words. Whatever you think she'd like."

"Read," I said.

"The Twenty-third Psalm is on page eighty-two," whispered the funeral director.

Ray's recitation was from memory, eyes closed, and more heartfelt than I expected. When he finished he said, "I didn't know Betty, but I wish I did." His voice turned breezy; he tapped the coffin genially with the corner of the prayer book. "Sorry you have to have a virtual stranger here, Betty, reading the last prayer you'll ever hear, but I guess I know you at least as well as that lame minister did. Boy, was that annoying. And I think you and I would've been great pals if we'd crossed paths earlier." He looked to my mother, who nodded her permission to continue. "I should be an old hand at this, but I didn't have the composure to say anything at my wife's grave. She passed away around this time last year. So maybe this is God's way of giving me another shot at it. Which reminds me—if you run across Mary up there, maybe you can buy her lunch and tell her it's from Ray." He raised an imaginary glass. "So here's to you, Betty: Ninety-four rocks. You had, what? Like, twenty presidents? Four or five wars? I hope you kept a journal or you talked into a tape, 'cause I'd love to hear the high points."

"She did," said my mother.

"Which?" asked Ray.

"Videotaped. On her ninetieth birthday."

57

"God bless her," said Ray.

"Amen," said the funeral director.

"Amen," we echoed.

"Now what?" asked my mother.

EACH LUNCHEON ATTENDEE was called upon to share her indignation: What an insult. What a besmirching of Betty's memory. *Imagine* living for ninety-four years and getting eulogized under another name. And who the hell was *Barbara?*

When the crowd thinned and the cousins drove away, Ray and my mother moved on from ministerial misdeeds to fiber art. I had to remind him that we had a long drive ahead, and that I had to be back at work at six A.M.

"You're not staying over?" my mother cried.

"We've discussed this," I said.

"One day off for the death of a grandparent?" my father said. "What kind of hospital is that?"

"A five-hundred-bed teaching hospital," I said.

"The show must go on," said Ray.

"Call her department. Let them page the goddamn head of surgery," my mother said. "Tell him it's an outrage. I need my daughter here."

I darted between my father and the kitchen door. "Dad," I said. "Please don't. It's not like a regular job. We don't take sick days. No one asks for a day off unless it's life or death."

"Which this is," my mother said.

Ray took her hand. "Mrs. Thrift? What if we stayed for another coupla hours?"

"Alice makes up her own mind," she said.

Ray guided her to a dining room wall where they stood in front of "Flotsam and Jet Set." "Of the ones on the first floor, this is my favorite," said Ray.

In docent fashion, my mother asked if he could explain why.

"The seaweed. The lobster claw. It reminds me of home."

"Can you tell that the wood is charred? I think it must have been kindling for a clambake." She pointed to a crumpled piece of paper. "This was a contrivance on my part, but I'm not apologizing for it."

Ray moved closer, cocked his head, and read, "Nokia Issues a Profit Warning."

"From *The Wall Street Journal*, obviously. Which I found in the trash and not, strictly speaking, on the beach."

"Do all your canvases tell a story?" he asked.

My mother said they did, but not *her* story. The beholder's. Each composition was a Rorschach test. If someone saw, for example, capitalism or disorder or impotence—whatever one would call it—that justified her flexing her artistic muscles to add, for example, a piece of newsprint that wasn't necessarily organic to the site.

"I'm all for flexing artistic muscles," said Ray.

"The majority of my pieces are pure fiber. This one's atypical, and for some reason I felt it belonged here, around food."

Ray said he'd entered this room solely for the art-work, but as long as he was here, he'd have a few shrimps for the road. What a spread. What generosity.

What a wonderful family we were.

I FOUND FREDERICK and my father at the stove, drinking scotch and eating Frederick's signature spiced nuts directly from the sauté pan.

"Way too much food," said my father in greeting.

"I *told* Joyce that people don't eat after a funeral, but she's always afraid of running short," said Frederick.

"How's this: Next time you'll pretend to follow her orders, but you'll only make what you think is the right amount," said my father.

"Just what Frederick needs," I said.

"What's that?" asked my father.

"More authority."

"Your daughter's employing irony," said Frederick. "She thinks I wasn't as obsequious as I should have been with her boyfriend."

"Ray is not my boyfriend," I said.

"I just can't see it," he explained. "Someone as serious as Alice—not just academically but also in the *joie de vivre* sense—who takes up with a traveling salesman. Your parents didn't send you to MIT and Harvard so you could practice medicine from a trailer," said Frederick.

I told my father I had to speak to him in private. He led the way to the pantry and I followed. "You know what he's basing all of these insults on? Fudge! Isn't that ironic? Someone makes a living cooking little pastry triangles and decorating platters with dots of liquefied fruit pulp, and that makes him a judge and jury."

"Can someone earn a living in fudge?" asked my father.

I said I had no idea. None. In fact, we had never discussed the fudge business before this trip.

"I'm not siding with Frederick," my father said. "What if people judged me on my wife's product?"

"Don't be rude, you two," called my mother from the doorway. "People are leaving. They want to say goodbye." And to Frederick, "Alice and her father always had this bond . . ."

"I think we both know she's the son he never had," said Frederick.

How could he say that? He must have known that my younger sister, Julie, was too short-haired and pierced for my mother's taste, and that I was, by default, increasingly her hope for a wedding and grandchildren.

My father and I ventured back.

"I'm coming up to visit you soon," my mother said.

"Me?"

"In Boston. Do you realize I haven't taken one day off since Nana went into the hospital? It took me this long to realize that with a mother's death, the umbilical cord is finally cut. Not that I resented it. I loved that umbilical cord. I used to brag about it: that ours—mine and Nana's—was made of some space-age material. Indestructible and indomitable. Now I have to form new alliances and visit some museums."

I said, "You have Julie, too. She's a good candidate for a new alliance. I think she's got an easier schedule than I, so it might be more satisfying for you."

"Julie," said my mother, "thinks that I don't like her friends."

"You don't," said my father.

"All I know," said my mother, "is that Julie had boyfriends all through high school, that she was even a little boy crazy, and now I'm supposed to forget that and embrace her . . . so-called lovers."

"It could be a phase," said my father.

"It's biochemical," said Frederick. "It's not a choice."

"Please," said my mother. "It's all about sisterhood and politics."

The kitchen door swung open to reveal the politely inquisitive face of Ray. "Someone must have taken the wrong coat," he said. "There's one left on the coatrack and it doesn't belong to . . ." He looked toward the foyer, then pronounced, "Mrs. Gordon."

"Gorman. I'll handle this," said Frederick.

We waited. The dispossessed Mrs. Gorman raised her voice and cried, "In January? I'll catch pneumonia with nothing more than a coat thrown over my shoulders."

"Why me?" moaned my mother. "What kind of idiot goes home in the wrong coat?"

"Frederick's taking care of it," said my father.

"Maybe we'll leave now," I said.

"Unless we can help with the coat mix-up," said Ray.

"You'd be doing us a favor if you took some food back to Boston," said my father.

"No problem," said Ray.

Frederick came back through the swinging door and went straight to the phone. He punched some numbers, tapped his foot, fixed his eyes on the ceiling, and whispered to us, "She knew *exactly* what the problem was: two black Max Maras, same fur trim, different sizes."

"Polly's?" asked my mother.

"Polly's," Frederick confirmed.

My mother said, "Let them work it out on their own turf." She opened the door and said, "Marietta? Polly's not home yet. Can you just swing by her house tomorrow and swap the coats? I'm exhausted."

"Hers is enormous," said Marietta.

"*Maybe* a size ten," Frederick whispered. "More likely a twelve."

"Can't you just roll up the sleeves?" asked my mother. "Or borrow something for the ride home?"

"I can't believe she could even get into mine," Marietta whined.

I left the kitchen and said to Marietta—the bridge partner famous for wearing a size zero and having quadruple-A feet—"I know it wasn't your fault, but you might consider name tags or a laundry marker."

Marietta burst into tears, prompting my mother to do the same.

"You two aren't crying over the coats, are you?" I asked.

My father joined us and demanded to know what I'd said to my mother to provoke this outburst.

I said, "She's crying because Marietta's crying."

"Take your mother upstairs," he said. "I'll drive Marietta home."

"You didn't bring your car?" I asked her.

My father said, enunciating carefully, "Alice? I don't think you understand that Marietta lost her own mother last fall, and sometimes when someone's crying about a lost coat, it's not about a lost coat at all."

How was I supposed to know that Marietta's mother had died? All I'd ever heard about Marietta was that her life was an endless, frustrating search for clothes and shoes that didn't fall off her body. I said, "I'm very sorry for your loss. I hope it wasn't painful or prolonged."

Marietta sank a little, so my father propped her up by her bony shoulders.

He shook his head and mouthed a string of indistinct words that turned out to be *amyotrophic lateral sclerosis*.

"Which was hell for her and hell for me," Marietta shouted. "So I haven't had much time to sew *name tags* in my clothes."

"Alice didn't know," said my father.

Ray joined us by the coatrack. "Hey!" he said. "I could hear you from the back porch! What are you yelling at Alice for?"

I told him that Marietta's mother had succumbed to a long, drawn-out, and debilitating disease, which no one had told me about until now.

"Then take a page from my book," he told her. "My wife died recently but I know how to conduct myself at someone else's funeral."

My father was trying to console Marietta at the same time that he was signaling Ray to refrain from uttering one further syllable.

Now barefoot and seated on the stairs, my mother murmured, "It never fails."

"What never fails?" I asked.

"Your social graces," she said. "Or lack thereof."

"Maybe Alice is too busy devoting her brain to medical science to bother with some of the niceties that other people have time for," said Ray.

"I have friends who are doctors who could be anchorpeople," sniffed Marietta. "Or social directors on cruise ships."

"Are they surgeons?" I asked.

My mother sighed. My father looked to Ray.

"Maybe I'll take Alice home now," he said.

WE STOPPED TWICE for coffee. I didn't say much—even less than usual—because I was working up to something like an expression of gratitude. Between sips I said, "I don't go home a lot because I usually manage to say something tactless, and everyone stays mad for a couple of weeks."

"Until?"

"Until my mother calls and complains about my sister. No one apologizes. It just goes away."

"I've heard of worse things," said Ray. "In some families, people stay mad. No one calls and pretends everything's okay because they all hate each other's guts."

I told him this trip was different. I always left like this—earlier than planned. But no one ever walked through the door with me. No one ever came to my defense or pointed out that the Mariettas of the world were the ones deficient in social graces.

"And?"

"I guess that was me saying thank you."

"You're welcome."

A few miles later he asked, "Who did this to you?"

I asked what he meant.

"Your parents? Is that who? Did they ever build you up? Tell you you were smart and pretty—their precious daughter, their pride and joy?"

"Pride and joy, sure," I said. "But because of what I did and not the way I looked."

I could see that he was studying my profile, searching for a diplomatic counterpoint. "What a pity," he finally said. "To think that all these years—how many? Twenty-five?"

"I'll be twenty-seven in two months."

"To think that in all these years you've been carrying around this image of yourself as—how would you define it? Unattractive?"

"Yes," I said.

"I don't want to hear that anymore," he said.

I didn't flinch when his hand moved to my knee, an act that seemed more brotherly than sexual. Or so I thought. He left it there until he had to downshift, a good fifteen miles later. When it found its way back, higher on my leg and decidedly less fraternal, I let that pass, too. I was only human. No one else was driving me out of state or banishing derogatory adjectives from my vocabulary. No one else's pupils dilated as I described my two weeks in a remote village in British Honduras with the Reconstructive Surgeons Volunteer Program, aiding the shunned. In a few years I'd be thirty. My sister was a lesbian. I was a heterosexual with the potential to be the favorite child. And here in the adjacent bucket seat, stroking my unloved leg, was a man.

"WHAT I MEANT by 'stay,'" said Ray, "is pretty much universally understood to mean *not go home*. As in *sleep over*."

I explained, just inside the front door of my building, that overnight parking was prohibited on Brookline Avenue, and, furthermore, overnight guests were not allowed under Leo's and my covenant.

Ray said, "I've never heard of such a thing! Whatever happened to consenting adults? Is this a halfway house or something, with rules about sex, drugs, and firearms? C'mon. Who are you kidding? You're making this up, aren't you? Why not just tell the truth? Why not say, 'Ray? I'm scared to have a man in my bed.'"

"I'm not," I said. "I just think this is premature and unwarranted."

"'Premature and unwarranted,'" he parroted. He moved closer and took my hand. "But I'm a red-blooded guy who's pretty good at translating body language and I seem to recall you didn't mind having my hand on your knee earlier this evening between Sturbridge and Natick on the Mass. Pike."

I said maybe, but that was depression authorizing what appeared to be intimacy. Physical contact didn't have to be sexual, did it?

"Pretty much," said Ray.

I confessed that I wasn't a red-blooded gal. I didn't know the signs and didn't seem to be endowed with the hormonal cues that the rest of the population possessed. "Frankly," I said, "I'm baffled as to why you want to see or drive or sleep with someone who gives nothing back."

It was then he declared, "It's so obvious, Alice: I want to spend time with you and make love to you and wake up next to you because I'm crazy about you. And I have been ever since I walked into that examining room and found that the doctor was a woman, no wedding ring on her finger, and with a pretty uncluttered field once I asked around."

"Whom did you ask?"

"The secretary! She said you weren't married."

I said I doubted that very much. Yolanda would never entertain personal questions about me or any other house staff. Even if she wanted to she couldn't because we'd never discussed anything remotely extra-departmental.

Ray grinned. "I wheedled it out of her. It wasn't so hard."

"Was fudge involved?" I asked.

Ray didn't answer.

"She has a notorious sweet tooth. Everyone teases her about it and bribes her with Godiva truffles." Everyone but me, that is. Yolanda was overweight, sedentary, and had a family history of Type 2 diabetes.

"So how about a kiss?" he asked.

I waited, shrugged, switched my pocketbook to the opposite shoulder, announcing finally that a kiss would be acceptable. I closed my eyes.

Nothing happened. I heard him step away, and when I opened my eyes he was three respectful paces back, tightening the knot in his tie. "You know what?" he said.

"I'm not going to force you. Your expression is like a kid biting into a fish stick when he was expecting a French fry. I have more pride than that."

I asked, as any good clinician would, "Was it what I said, or the way I said it?"

"What does it matter? I wanted to kiss you, and now I don't."

It was excellent psychology: In an instant he was the hurt party and I was the villain.

"Not sixty seconds ago I said I was falling in love with you," he continued, "and all I get in return is a blank look and the third degree about which secretary said what."

"Not blank," I said. "Surprised, or maybe just exhausted. And you're the one who brought up Yolanda."

"Either way, it's not very flattering," said Ray, "although I don't expect much from this life anymore. Me, Ray Russo, average ordinary widower without a bachelor's degree, let alone an MD or a CPA after my name, thinking he can turn the head of Boston's most eligible doctor."

I mumbled something to the effect that anything was possible. I'd seen in my own circles a famously obnoxious second-year resident chafe daily against her equally disagreeable chief resident, yet at the Christmas party they announced their engagement.

"Are you saying there's hope, or are you saying, 'Let's be friends, Ray. You and I are from different worlds, and even though this is America, where everyone is allegedly equal, and even though you dress well and drive a cool car and own your own business, I'm looking for a guy who I could take to a doctors' dinner party and wouldn't embarrass me or get drunk or talk back to the host.'"

Of course I had to counter with something democratic and egalitarian. I said, "I took you home, didn't I? And, by the way, I really appreciated your talking back to my father today, which I think demonstrates your high self-esteem as well as your ability to think on your feet."

"My street smarts, you mean?"

"That, too. Definitely. And your pluck."

"Gee, thanks. That's what I want people to think: That guy has pluck."

"Are you mad?"

"Nope. Not mad. Discouraged, maybe. And still lonely, but don't you worry. That's my cross to bear." He walked to the door and said, barely mounting a wave, "See ya."

"See ya," I said.

He opened the door, but hesitated on the threshold. "Good luck with everything, Doc. I hope you have a great life and you get to fix, like, every harelip along the Amazon."

"I appreciate that," I said.

LEO'S BEDROOM DOOR was closed. His voice and that of an unidentified female's could be heard in what sounded like playful conversation. As a courtesy, I knocked on his door and said, "I'm home," to save all of us the embarrassment of louder noises or their spilling into the hallway in any state of undress.

I should have been thinking of my deceased grandmother as I fell asleep, or agitating over my most recent evaluation, but instead I was puzzling over how I'd thrown cold water on Ray's torch. Was there a book I could read on the subject: *How to Restore a Man You've Rejected to His Previous Station as Platonic Friend? On Your Own Terms, Without Leading Him On?*

Did I owe Ray an apology? Should I be thinking, Fruit? A gift certificate? A presidential biography on tape?

Leo would know. I'd ask him in the morning.

HE KNOCKED ON my door at 5:45 A.M. "Aren't you supposed to be across the street in fifteen minutes?" he yelled.

I groaned. I had hit the snooze button twice and fallen back into a deep REM sleep, stuck in a dream filled with cousins and stained glass. "Coffee's on," said Leo. "I think if you take three minutes for a shower, two minutes to get dressed, five minutes to eat your cereal, you'll have another five minutes to cross the street and get up to the floor. *If* you get your ass in gear this second."

None of this—reveille or raisin bran—was typical of our arrangement. Immediately I grasped what was happening: He was playing the solicitous and thoughtful roommate because he had an adoring audience.

"Is your guest still here?" I asked. When he didn't answer I said, "I thought I heard a woman's voice coming from your room last night."

I was sitting on the edge of my mattress now, staring dully at my feet. There were specks of mauve polish left on a few toenails, remnants of a summer spruce-up. I probably had some nail-polish remover somewhere. "I'm up," I called. Then louder, "Leo? You still there?"

"In the kitchen."

"Alone?"

"She didn't stay over, if that's what you mean."

I put my robe on, a souvenir in thin yellow cotton from a VA rotation, over surgical scrubs and took a seat at the kitchen table. I said, "I think I'll have that coffee before my shower." I shook a cupful of flakes into a bowl. "Was it someone nice?" I asked. "Someone new and exciting?"

He shook his head. "Just someone to watch a movie with."

"Was it a funny movie?"

"In places," said Leo.

"Because I heard laughter."

He was at my elbow, holding our phone and dialing a number. He handed me the receiver and said, "Here. It's ringing. Tell them you came back by train this morning and you'll get there as fast as you can. Mention the word *funeral* so they'll remember it wasn't a vacation day."

Yolanda answered. I told her I was doing my best to get there for rounds but would undoubtedly be late.

"Funeral," Leo whispered.

I nodded. "I think you probably remember that I was at my grandmother's *funeral* all day yesterday."

Yolanda said without any indulgence in her voice, "So when should I tell them you'll get here?"

"Maybe fifteen minutes, if I run."

Leo held up his hands and flicked both sets of

fingers three times.

"More likely thirty. I just got in. And my roommate is in the shower so I have to wait my turn."

Leo flashed a thumbs-up.

"The most I can do is pass on your message," said Yolanda.

I looked up and mouthed, Not happy. Leo reclaimed the receiver and said, "Yolanda? It's Leo Frawley, soaking wet. Look, she's in no shape to make rounds. Can you finesse this? I mean, like a half hour? It's not like she was out partying last night and couldn't get out of bed this morning—you know what I'm saying?"

She must have said something like, "Dr. Thrift? Partying? That's a good one," because Leo answered, "Yeah, well, there's a lot to be said for keeping your nose to the grindstone when you're expected to work eighteen-hour days."

I stood up, tapped my watch, and pointed across the hall to the bathroom.

He hung up quickly and asked, "How was yesterday? Awful?"

"Very sad. And the minister was a complete stranger, so that didn't help."

"I guess I meant, how did Ray work out as an escort?"

"Good and bad."

He pointed to the chair I'd just vacated and I sat back down. "Good as transportation. Good at taking my side in a family fracas. Bad at being grammatical and appropriate."

"I could have predicted that," said Leo. "There's something slimy about him. And he tries too hard. He's

73

clearly waging a campaign to win your hand."

"My hand?" I repeated. "You mean, as in marriage?"

"Of course. He's not a kid. He's a widower. Don't you read magazines? Men who were once married get hooked up again as soon as they can because they know single men die younger than married men. Ask any actuary."

I said, "Don't be ridiculous."

"Then you're blind. He's looking for his next wife and he thinks her name is Alice."

I took a long gulp of coffee. "Okay. Maybe he is. But it's only human nature to look for someone who can return his feelings, and when he realized I couldn't, he finally gave up."

Leo said, "I don't want to make you any later than you already are, but I think I have more to say on the subject of Ray—namely that he kept coming back without any encouragement, so why would he bow out now?"

I said, "Maybe you and I can grab a sandwich in the cafeteria."

"If my five minutes overlaps with yours, you mean."

"Or tonight."

"Can't tonight," said Leo.

"Same woman?"

"Dinner with my mother," he said. *Mutha* was how he said the word: *Dinna with my mutha.*

I waited, thinking he might sweep me up into the party, in that way of large families with boardinghouse tables and bottomless stews.

"You didn't want to come home and have dinner at

74

my house, did you?" asked Leo. "Is that what I'm reading in your face? 'Leo, invite me to your house because I haven't had a really stringy piece of meat in months, and I'm dying to be interrogated about my life, my sleeping arrangements, and my grandmother's last days on earth.' "

I said, "Actually, I'd welcome the opportunity to observe you in a family context."

Leo said, "Is that Thrift-speak for 'Excellent! I've been dying to meet your mother, Leo'?"

I didn't see the difference, but I said yes, it was.

8
Leo's House

WE TOOK THE Riverside Line to Kenmore Square, then switched to a Boston College car, outbound. When stymied by a turnstile, I had to confess that I hardly ever took public transportation.

"Why not?" Leo asked.

"Too busy working to go anywhere."

"You know what?" said Leo. "I'm sick of hearing that. *I* work hard, and I know a lot of residents who do, too, but they get out. They wear beepers. Yet you seem proud of the fact that you have no life."

Was he right? Was I going to be like Dr. Perzigian, chief of thoracic surgery, famous for making rounds at five A.M.; for getting married in scrubs in the hospital chapel; for missing the birth of his son while repairing a knife wound close to the aorta of a philandering city councilman?

"Because," Leo continued, "it's getting a little monotonous."

I said, "Then I'll have to be monotonous because all I care about is getting invited back next year and eventually becoming chief resident and after that getting into a plastic surgery program."

Wouldn't you think a speech like that would provoke a statement of support? Instead, to my shock and to the fascination of the two teenage girls sitting in front of us on the trolley car, Leo said, "I chose that word deliberately because I'm in charge of the social development of Alice Thrift."

I harrumphed. The high-schoolers turned around in frank fashion to assess me. I stared back schoolmarmishly so they would mind their own business. Leo tapped one of them on the shoulder and asked in his friendliest pediatric bedside fashion, "Don't you think my friend here should spend a little more time worrying about life outside of work and less about preserving her reputation as Alice the overworked?"

The two girls, both of whose hair was streaked maroon, looked at each other and smirked.

"No, really. Don't give me attitude," said Leo. "I grew up with a houseful of sisters, so I'm not deterred by a couple of funny looks."

The one next to the window asked smartly, "Haven't you ever heard of, 'Don't talk to strangers'?"

"I'm a nurse and she's a doctor," said Leo, "so that doesn't apply, especially in the middle of a trolley car, surrounded by potential Good Samaritans."

"They're probably fourteen years old," I muttered.

"Fifteen," said the one in the aisle seat.

"A good demographic," said Leo. "I have a couple of nieces around that age and I can always depend on them for an honest appraisal of my shirt, my tie, my hair, my shoes, my date, my taste in music, you name it."

One mumbled, "Music?"

Leo named people or groups or albums—I'd heard of none of these entities—which broke whatever final layer of ice needed melting with these two strangers in front of us, their eyebrows pierced and their fingertips stained orange from some triangular chiplike snack they were sharing.

Do you see what Leo represented in our arrangement? Charm of the easy, fluent, unaffected variety— meant to be instructive, but a constant reminder of my own unease.

LEO HAD WARNED me, but still I was shocked by the quantity of Jesus iconography on his mother's walls and horizontal surfaces. She lived in Brighton, in the same house in which he'd grown up, still containing some of the thirteen children she'd raised there: Marie, the divorced special-ed teacher, a foot shorter than her brother and 50 percent more freckled, had his round, elfin face; Rosemary, the travel agent, from the dark-haired side of the family, wearing a fashionable and no doubt expensive suit with a double strand of pearls; and Michael, the baby, age twenty-six, wearing a T-shirt bearing the name of a gym.

Mrs. Frawley had ginger-colored ends on her gray hair and bobby pins serving as barrettes. She introduced herself as Mrs. Morrisey. When she excused herself to check the oven, Leo explained that her friends and her priest had convinced her that marrying Mr. Morrisey a few years back—also widowed, also lonely, the owner of a red-brick duplex in Oak Square—was a good idea. The new Mrs. Morrisey had decided rather quickly that her friends were wrong; that being a wife to Mr. Morrisey involved duties beyond housekeeping and companionship that she'd been led *not* to expect.

The less said the better, Rosemary confided once we'd taken our seats in the dining room. "He calls once in a while but Ma won't come to the phone."

"And you don't ask her for an explanation?"

Marie said, "She moved into his house after the wedding, and was back here in less than a month."

"She implied that he raised his hand to her," Michael whispered, "but we think it had to do with the bedroom."

"Wouldn't she tell you outright?" I asked. "Or file charges if he really did hit her?"

The four Frawley children twisted their mouths in various directions, all telegraphing the same thing: Enough said.

Leo added, "We think part of the deal up front was separate bedrooms, which Ma took to mean no wifely duties and no honeymoon."

Marie put her finger to her lips and everyone but me nodded in complicitous agreement.

Raising her voice so it would carry to the kitchen, Rosemary said, "Leo tells us that you're a surgeon."

I said yes, I was. But just starting out, and it was a long road ahead, much competition, much narrowing down of the field.

"She worries about everything," said Leo.

Mrs. Morrisey came back through the door with a roasted chicken on a cutting board. "The plastic thing popped up like it was supposed to, but I left the bird in because the baked potatoes weren't ready. It might be a little dry," she announced. "And, Rosey, get the vegetables out of the microwave, please. Use the Fiestaware."

"Need another set of hands?" Leo called after his sister.

"You stay here with our guest," said his mother. "Marie will get the drinks."

"The chicken looks delicious," I said.

"I hope there's enough," said Mrs. Frawley. "Leo didn't tell me until this morning that he was bringing a guest."

"The choices seem to be milk or water," Marie said from the doorway.

"Milk," I said. "And don't worry about having enough to go around. I don't eat much; in fact a baked potato would be fine."

"You're not a vegetarian, are you?" Marie asked.

Leo turned to me with a grin. "*Are* you? I don't even think I'd know the answer to that."

I said no, I wasn't. I liked everything.

"Why wouldn't you know that?" Michael asked his brother.

"Because she works all the time, and when she's home, that's the night I'm out. Which is why we're perfect roommates."

"Out working," asked his mother, "or out carousing?"

79

He grinned. "Carousing." He got to his feet and approached the roast chicken on its ancient cutting board, cracked and wooden, the very kind that health officials ask consumers to replace with hygienic plastic.

"Who wants white meat who isn't a Frawley?"

"Maybe a small slice," I said.

Leo said, "You're our guest. You're going to get several slices because I can scramble myself a couple of eggs or make myself a bologna sandwich if need be."

Marie said, "I would've picked up another chicken on my way home if Ma had called me."

"Wouldn't we all," murmured Leo.

Mrs. Morrisey said, "I have an apple pie and a half-gallon of harlequin ice cream."

"Pass the plates, please," said Leo.

We said grace, and thankfully we didn't have to clasp hands around the table. Mrs. Morrisey looked at me for a long few seconds before picking up her knife and fork.

"Go ahead, Ma, ask," said Leo. Then to me, "She's dying to know if you're Catholic."

"I'm sorry," I said. "I'm not."

Leo said, "*And* . . . ? That's only half an answer. She wants to know what brand of church you belong to."

"I was raised Unitarian."

"She's heard worse," said Leo.

"How'd you and Leo get together?" asked one of the sisters.

I explained that Leo had posted an ad on a hospital bulletin board and I answered it.

"She called Ma for a reference," Leo said, and laughed.

"What did you say?" Michael asked his mother.

Mrs. Morrisey, unamused, said, "That I didn't see why a girl would want to share an apartment with an unrelated man, but if that was her only option, then Leo was polite and clean."

"Thanks, Ma."

"And named after a pope," I said.

It was not the right thing to say. Mrs. Morrisey concentrated very hard on sliding her peas off her fork between tight lips.

"Which is a historical fact I found very interesting," I added.

"All my children are named after saints or popes," she said.

"I'm named after an aunt who was a WAC in World War Two," I volunteered.

"Did she make it back alive?" asked Michael.

"Definitely. And lived to ninety and died in a veterans' hospital."

Mrs. Morrisey asked, "Was it the VA in Jamaica Plain?"

"No," I said. "The VA in Loma Linda, California."

"The children's father died at the VA in Jamaica Plain, which turned out to be a blessing because Cardinal Law happened to be visiting the day he slipped into a coma, and it was the cardinal who performed his extreme unction." Mrs. Morrisey held her napkin under the tip of her nose.

"We were there," said Marie. "We all met him."

"I heard about your grandmother," said Mrs. Morrisey. "I'm very sorry for your loss. Was it very sudden?"

"It was and it wasn't. I mean, all death is sudden from the medical standpoint that one second a person's alive and the next second he or she is dead."

"I never thought of it that way," said Mrs. Morrisey.

"She had a lot of things going on medically, but the official cause of death was pneumonia."

"Old man's friend," said Leo.

We all looked up for an explanation.

"Old man's friend," he repeated. "That's what pneumonia's called. Because it ends the suffering."

"I never heard of such a thing," his mother sniffed. She squeezed her baked potato so its insides erupted. Without being asked, Rosemary passed the margarine.

Nor had I heard of such a thing. I asked Leo if that was a common expression on the wards.

"Probably not," said Leo. "It's just one of those things doctors mumble when the shoe fits."

I put my fork down. "Do you mean because the patient's old and feeble and on life support, and his family's trying to decide whether to remove the feeding tube or take him off the respirator? That pneumonia settles the question for them?"

Leo said, "Maybe we can discuss the fine points later."

"Are you saying nobody would even *start* IV antibiotics?"

His eyes darted to his mother and back to me. "We do everything that's humanly possible. Then it's in God's hands," said Leo. "If you catch my drift."

His mother grumbled, "Don't think I don't know what goes on in these big-city hospitals with their Jewish doctors and their Congregational chaplains. Which is why I want to die at Saint Elizabeth's."

"I know, Ma," Leo answered. "We all know that. Can you pass the oleo back this way?"

"You're giving Alice the idea that you don't like Jewish people," said Rosemary.

"What *I* don't like is this talk of pulling plugs at my table."

"Mom's internist is Jewish and she loves him. Don't you, Ma?" said Marie. "He's on the staff at Saint E's."

"Dr. Goldberg," said Mrs. Morrisey.

"Goldstone, actually," said Leo.

I said, "I shouldn't have quizzed Leo about the pneumonia protocol at the table. I get anxious when I hear something I think I should have learned in my medical ethics elective—such as, Would you begin a comatose geriatric on a course of antibiotics?—because I want to find my own medical lacunae and fill them in."

"What Alice is trying to say is that this is her first year, so there's lots of gaps in her knowledge. And when she hears something she doesn't know, she loses all sense of time and place and what's appropriate dinner conversation in order to launch a tutorial," said Leo.

"I do?"

"I'm teasing you," said Leo. "Sort of."

"I think it's the truth," I said. "I do panic when I hear something I think I should have retained."

"Don't they give you tests?" asked his mother.

"Every day's a test," I said.

"Not literally," said Leo. "She means that she always has to be on her toes."

"Why would you put yourself through something like that?" asked Marie. "Is it worth it? All these long hours and blood and people dying?"

"Surgeons make a lot of money," said Michael. "Maybe you work straight out for a couple of years, but then it's someone else's turn to burn the midnight oil, which is when you start seeing some real money."

"Alice isn't in it for the money," said Leo.

"What do you see yourself doing when you're graduated or certified or whatever it's called?" asked Michael.

"Reconstructive plastic surgery in the Third World."

"And who foots the bill for that?" he asked.

I explained that one might have to perform cosmetic surgery on the well-to-do for, say, six months of the year, and their money would support the philanthropic endeavors.

"What if you had a family?" asked Marie. "Would you take them with you to the Third World or would you leave them at home with your husband?"

I said, "I can't think in terms of a conventional nuclear family."

"Maybe her husband could be a missionary and they could do their work together," suggested Mrs. Morrisey.

"What a good idea," said Leo. "Do you know any eligible missionaries you could introduce Alice to?"

"Don't be fresh with me," said his mother.

"Actually, Alice has an admirer," said Leo.

Everyone turned to me. I said, "Leo is exaggerating."

"Leo thinks he's a creep," said Leo.

"What does Alice think?" asked Rosemary.

I sighed. "This man's wife died a year ago and his

pursuit, I think, is largely sexually motivated."

Mrs. Morrisey huffed and muttered something to herself.

"I didn't mean that it was reciprocal or that I encouraged him. I was just trying to explain his attentions."

"All men want the same thing," said Mrs. Morrisey, "and that particular thing is not dinner-table conversation either."

"You had thirteen children," said Michael.

Mrs. Morrisey slapped her fork onto her place mat. "Leave the table!" she barked.

Leo laughed.

"You, too!"

"Ma! He's twenty-six years old. You can't ask a grown man to leave the table because he alludes to your having had carnal knowledge."

"We have company," murmured Rosemary, "and I'm sure it's very awkward for her to be in the middle of a family squabble."

"My family fights every time I go home, and it's usually provoked by something I say. So don't worry about me." I tried to affect the smile of a good guest. For added amenability, I said, "I don't think this chicken is dry at all."

"This one was fresh. You lose a lot of the juices when you defrost a frozen bird."

"My mother doesn't cook much," I said. "Especially now that it's just the two of them at home."

"How many sisters and brothers do you have?" asked Michael.

"One sister. Who lives in Seattle."

"Is she married?" asked Mrs. Morrisey.

"Not yet," I said.

"Can we get back to whatever it was we were talking about before Michael had his mouth washed out with soap?" asked Leo.

Marie—clearly the family mediator and diplomat—turned to me. "I think we were talking about the demands on you at work, and I was asking, *Is* it worth it? Is all the hard work and sleepless nights and—you said it yourself—the *panic* worth it for some kind of professional dream that might be unattainable?"

The most unexpected thing happened at that point: I felt like crying. I disguised the quaking of my lips by taking two long swallows of milk from my glass, then by blinking rapidly as if the problem were ophthalmologic.

"Are you okay?" Leo asked.

"I didn't mean—" began Marie.

"I must have been thinking about my grandmother," I said.

"Of course you were," said their mother. "But she's in Jesus' house now and free of pain, God rest her soul."

Still, I was hoping to prove myself the kind of pleasant conversationalist who gets invited back. "Where does purgatory come in?" I asked. "I mean, under your afterlife guidelines, wouldn't she still be there?"

All the Frawleys were taking sips from their respective milk glasses or searching inside their potato skins for neglected morsels.

"Alice needs a weekend off," said Leo.

I KNOW THAT some people are equipped to analyze their failings and to pose leading questions such as "Did I do something wrong?" or "Are you upset?" to the silent person in the seat next to them, but I had neither the vocabulary nor the inclination. As the trolley car negotiated the twists and turns of Commonwealth Avenue, Leo kept his eyes shut until I heard him say, "Just to play devil's advocate for a minute . . ."

"About?"

"About your job. Whether you really have no aptitude for surgery, or whether it's your former A-pluses talking."

I asked what that meant, and how did he know what my grades were?

"I'm guessing you're one of those people who moaned and groaned about how badly they did on their organic chemistry exam until it came back with a big red hundred and five on the top of the page because you got everything right including the extra-credit question."

Calmly I said, "I'm the worst resident they've had since the legendary one in the eighties who was asked to leave even though he was engaged to the niece of the head of the hospital."

Leo said, "You don't have to be asked to leave. You could decide for yourself."

I said I didn't understand.

Leo coughed into his mittened hand. "Have you ever

thought of dropping out of the program?"

Only ten times an hour and with every withering look and every truthful evaluation, I thought. "Not really," I said. "I can't imagine giving up my goals for something as trivial as professional humiliation. When I start thinking about my shortcomings, I say, 'You graduated second in your class in medical school. How can you be so bad? If you study harder you'll get better.'"

"What about the fact that you feel like a failure every minute of the day?"

"I can improve," I said. "It's still early in the year. It could all click into place tomorrow."

"Doctors switch fields," he said. "Surgeons go into anesthesiology. Internists become allergists. You earned your degree. No one would take that away from you."

"No," I said. "I'm no quitter."

"I'm only being hypothetical," Leo said. "I'm only thinking of you and what could make you a happier person."

"In the short run," I snapped.

"No," said Leo. "In the long run."

"I'm no quitter," I repeated.

RAY WAS WAITING on the stoop when we returned, smoking a cigarette that he snuffed out as soon as I appeared. He was wearing a shiny black quilted parka and a black watch cap that did nothing but suggest *burglar* and call attention to his nose. He stood up and said, "I paged you, but you didn't answer."

"I wasn't at the hospital."

"You remember me, I'm sure," said Leo.

"The nurse," said Ray. "Of course. How ya doin'?"

I pointed to the streak of ash on the granite step behind him and asked if he'd been smoking.

"First time in a decade," he said, "which I blame on some very disturbing news I received one hour ago." He stared at Leo for several long seconds before adding, "It's kind of personal. I was hoping to talk to Alice in private."

I said, "Leo's very easy to talk to. Much better than I am."

"I hope no one died," said Leo.

"Nothing like that," said Ray. "It's closer to an emotional crisis—some facts that have come to light. And I didn't have any supper, so I was hoping Alice might keep me company while I grab some *nachos grande* and a beer."

Leo checked with me. I nodded once reassuringly, and he trudged inside.

THERE WERE THRONGS of well-dressed people at the bar, businessmen and -women, many drinking from martini glasses; many laughing in that brittle, automatic way that substitutes for meaningful discussion. "Straight ahead," said Ray, steering me from behind, his hands on my shoulders, his body swaying as if I had agreed to lead a conga line. "The dining room's in the back," he instructed.

When we were seated at a small, far-off table, and the dour hostess had left, Ray said, "No people skills. None. Would it have killed her to smile? And why Siberia? There's a dozen better tables."

I said, "Don't make a fuss. It's quiet back here and we can talk. Let's just order."

Ray was suddenly distracted and grinning at some new piece of sociology. He cocked his head toward a smart-looking twosome, smiling tentatively at each other over their menus. "I'd put money on the fact that they just met out front, he bought her a drink, they decided they had a little thing going on, and one of them said, 'Wanna grab a bite?' "

"You know that from merely looking at them?" I asked.

"Doesn't take that much," said Ray. "No offense."

"How do you know they're not married, or siblings, or coworkers having a tax-deductible dinner?"

He leaned over and asked, "Doc? Have you ever been to a bar before?"

I said, "Of course."

"Has anyone ever approached you and asked if you'd like a drink?"

"Other than a waiter?"

Ray patted my hand. "I mean, has anyone ever flirted with you? Asked you to dance? Asked if you'd like to go someplace quiet and talk?"

I knew where this interview was leading: from not terribly personal queries to the carnal questionnaire—*if ever, when, with whom, how did I like it,* and, worst of all, *how did I feel?*

By way of answering, I opened my menu. Finally, when I looked up and saw he'd held the same stare of cross-examination, I tried, "Your bad news? Can we discuss that instead?"

He took a sip from his water glass, swallowed, bit his bottom lip. "Stop me at any point if this gets too uncomfortable for you. But my wife, Mary? She had a boyfriend."

"When?"

"When we were married! For the whole time, in fact. Some guy she worked with."

I said, "I never asked you what she did."

"She was assistant manager of the Kinko's near Northeastern. But you're missing my point, which is that I'm devastated."

I asked how he'd found out and he said, "From my former sister-in-law."

"That doesn't sound right. Why would anyone besmirch the memory of her dead sister, especially after the fact?"

"Because it was eating away at her all these years— that Mary was cheating on me and thinking she was getting away with it."

"But why now?"

"Because she has a big mouth and I was talking to her on the phone and I told her I'd met someone—actually I might've said I was in *love* with someone—and out came the whole ugly truth, which I think was her way of encouraging me to move on."

I said, "Even if it is the truth, what does that change in the here and now?"

"Everything! I visit her grave and I go to church like clockwork. Do I continue in that vein—Mary the saint— or do I get to the bottom of what Bernadette told me?"

"This Bernadette's no friend of yours," I said. "Why

would you take anything she said at face value?"

Ray leaned toward me, his voice even. "Because it has the ring of truth."

"Well, just forget about it," I advised. "Order some food and a glass of beer and we'll change the subject."

"I don't think you get it: This isn't some little piece of gossip that has no bearing on anything. This is a huge piece of news. Throughout my marriage, for the entire three years we were together—"

Now it was my turn to look up from my menu and stare. "Did you say three years?"

"We *knew* each other for three years. We were actually married for sixteen months, which I'd always looked back on as one long extended honeymoon."

I said, "I guess I assumed—"

"Because of how shaken up I was? And how saddened I was for a whole year since her demise?"

I pointed out that sixteen months was hardly a lifetime, so if Mary *had* been cheating over the course of the entire marriage, it was a relatively short period of infidelity.

Ray took a paper napkin from the dispenser and blew his nose. "I took my marriage vows very seriously and I'm a little surprised that you're taking Mary's side."

I said I most certainly was *not* taking Mary's side. I was just trying to examine all facets of the situation. "Maybe she had no choice," I offered. "Maybe it was sexual harassment."

"Baloney! Sexual harassment. Mary was as tough as nails. No one messed with Mary if they didn't want a boot in the groin."

Another mental adjustment was needed, this time from docile wife and mother of Ray's future children to extremely tough cookie. I asked how old Mary was when she passed away.

"Twenty-eight," said Ray. "She liked older men. This guy, Patrick, from work? Would you believe fifty-two? She had a father thing, but I didn't care. If I had fifteen years on her and that's what she liked—hey, why not?"

A waitress was finally at our side. "I'm going to have the burger with Muenster and caramelized onions, no lettuce, no tomato," said Ray. "And whatever you have on draft."

A dozen breweries and seasonal batches were described before he heard the right name.

I said I'd have nothing now; maybe a piece of pie later.

"Nothing to drink?" asked the waitress.

"She's a doctor," said Ray. "No drinking when she's on call."

"We get a lot of doctors here," said the waitress, and cocked her head in the direction of my hospital.

When she'd gone, I said, "I'm not on call. You don't have to make up excuses."

"You know why I do that? I'm just so friggin' proud that you're a doctor. I guess I look for any occasion to announce it."

If it weren't for his previously announced emotional distress, I might have said that I took exception to his use of the adjective *proud*—that it was a word for parents, for teachers, for mentors; for one's own self to admit in the privacy of one's head. "We've discussed this before,"

I said, "but maybe I need to say it again: I'd prefer that you didn't lie."

"Lie?" he repeated. "Because I tell the waitress you're on call? Isn't that true? Don't you work around the clock? Didn't you work all day today and aren't you going back there at dawn?"

"Pretty much," I said.

"Okay. That's settled: no lie." He smiled as the waitress delivered his frosted mug. "After the day I've had, you wouldn't believe how good this looks," he said to her.

She said, "Okay, I'll bite. What kind of day did you have?"

"You tell her," Ray prompted me.

"It's a personal matter—" I began.

"Concerning my former wife, who was unfaithful the entire time we were married. With a guy she worked with. Who we even double-dated with."

"You didn't tell me that," I said.

"He and his wife had us over for dinner once. The happy couple—him with his arm around her shoulders, nuzzling her hair and making jokes in bad taste about their empty nest, implying that they had sex whenever they felt like it, in every room."

"Late wife or ex-wife?" asked the waitress.

"Late," he said. "Car crash. Which until today I never even considered to be any kind of divine retribution."

"Why would you," I asked, "if you just found out tonight?"

"Maybe I had my suspicions," said Ray.

The waitress took a step toward the kitchen. "I need

to put your order in. Sorry."

I was sorry I hadn't pleaded fatigue and said good night at my door. I sat there, conversationally dry, ill-equipped to offer therapy of any kind. I tried to recall what my more psychologically astute fellow residents murmured at the bedsides of overwrought patients. "Is there anything I can do?" I heard myself ask.

"You mean it?"

I hadn't meant it. I had no idea what was on a menu of helpful things I could be recruited for. I said that as a doctor and someone who saw a lot of suffering and heard deathbed regrets—not true—I believed that the surviving spouse should forgive and forget.

"Except, Doc," he said, "we're not talking about one mistake, one slip-up. We're talking about a wife screwing around every chance she got."

I took a sip of water, then asked, "Were you ever unfaithful to her?"

"Never! Not once. And why would I? A middle-aged guy like me, nothing special to look at and not exactly a world-beater, who lucked into this relationship with a young and very hot lady."

I asked him to explain that—"lucked into." How had they met?

"At work," he said.

"Yours or hers?"

"Mine. At the Topsfield Fair. I was at my booth, and along comes this *really* good-looking girl in leather pants. I mean, like, exceptionally good-looking—long dark hair, big brown eyes, suede boots that came up past her knees—and she asked me for napkins because there's horse dung and cow manure all over the place, and then she had to wash her hands and I let her use my hose, and then, out of gratitude, she bought a pound of chocolate walnut."

"And how did that lead to your getting married?" I asked.

Ray said, "Give it a try, Doc. Take a stab at it."

I said, "Did you ask her out on a date?"

"Eventually. But how did that come about?"

"Over a telephone?"

"Correct," said Ray. "But who called who?"

"She called the phone number on the fudge box?"

He pantomimed something that seemed to mean switch it, flip it, turn that on its head.

"You're close: I asked her to write her phone number on her check when she paid for the fudge."

"So you called her up and asked her for a date and she said yes?"

"Nope. That would have been way too obvious. What I *planned* to do was offer her a tour of the plant."

I said I didn't know he had a plant. Where was it and how many workers did he employ?

"It's not my plant per se. But let me finish. When I introduced myself as the guy at the fudge booth who helped her wipe the shit off her boots, she asked if the check had bounced, and even though I hadn't thought of that angle, I said yes, unfortunately it had. And where I usually charged a twenty-five-dollar fee for a returned check, I'd waive that if she'd have dinner with me some night."

I asked why he lied and why he'd let someone think

her check had bounced.

"I hadn't cashed it yet when I called her, but, believe me, knowing Mary as I do now, it would've bounced without any help from me."

The waitress, with a ketchup bottle squeezed between her bicep and her rib cage, was approaching with Ray's meal. His oval platter overflowed with French fries, the version I liked, long and thin and still wearing their skins. I took one without asking permission, prompting him to say, "I hope you realize that tasting food from the plate of a member of the opposite sex without asking is an act of intimacy. Here," he said, tilting half of the fries onto my place mat, "have as many as you want."

I said, "I don't see how taking a French fry is an act of intimacy."

"Yes, you do! You wouldn't help yourself to a French fry on a stranger's plate."

"Maybe an act of familiarity," I said. "Or hunger."

"Whatever." He held the ketchup bottle at a perfect 90-degree angle over his hamburger and waited patiently for something to flow. "Where was I with Mary and me?" he asked.

"Dinner in exchange for a fictional returned-check penalty."

"Right. So she agrees to have a drink with me the next night, a weekday. I negotiate for the weekend. We settle on Friday and a place in Central Square because she lives on the Red Line." He replaced the top half of the bun with a twist and checked the sides for oozing. "But wait. The rest is definitely *not* history: She didn't show. However"—and he grinned broadly—"I not only had her phone number on the check, but her address. So I get in my car and I drive over to Davis Square. No one's home. I wait outside. She pulls up around eleven, eleven-fifteen. Someone else is driving. But I don't get too upset because he just drops her off and she doesn't give him a backward glance. First thing she sees is my Porsche—two cars ago—and I'm waiting on the sidewalk, leaning against it, nice and friendly. I say, 'Miss Ciccarelli. I think you forgot our appointment.'"

He paused to take a gleeful bite from his burger, as if expecting me to pronounce his mating behavior clever and audacious.

"I would have called the police," I said.

"Except, Doc, you don't understand the world the way I do. Mary knew that a guy who dresses like me and owns the kind of cars I do is not a stalker. He's a guy on a romantic mission, like in a movie when the hero's waiting for the girl when she gets home from work, exhausted and a little down in the dumps. Did I mention I was holding a single red long-stemmed American Beauty rose?"

"No, you didn't."

"I was pissed, but I figured, what the hell? What do I have to lose? She stands me up, so I'll give it one last try. So what do you think happens next?"

I asked if this narrative really required audience participation. I didn't say that his Socratic method reminded me of rounds, of interns being called upon to recite, to provide answers and differential diagnoses, and of constant failure on my feet.

Instead of answering, I poised the ketchup bottle over

my own fries, inducing a few drips. He asked if I was sure I didn't want anything else. I said yes. I didn't want him to call the waitress back, delaying his consumption of his hamburger, prolonging the night.

"Okay! I love this part: Mary sees me on the sidewalk. Well, sees *someone*. It's dark, so how could she recognize me when she's only laid eyes on me once, and plus it's too dark to see the rose. But this is one tough broad. She doesn't flinch, doesn't make eye contact. I say, 'Mary, it's Ray Russo. We had a date to meet in Central Square.' She said, 'Oh, shit. Didn't the bartender tell you that I had to work and couldn't make it?' I say, 'Gee, Mary. No. And you must think I'm a fucking moron to believe that one.' You know what she said? I'll never forget it. I even told this at our wedding reception in a little speech I gave: She goes, 'Well, you don't have a choice, asshole, because if you don't get the fuck off my property, my next phone call is to nine-one-one.'"

I blinked. I tried to remember how this man and I had ever intersected and what possible turn of events had led me to this table and this conversation.

Ray said, "Excuse my language. I wanted to quote her accurately so you'd get the full flavor. So anyway, I laughed, which was exactly the right thing to do. It cut the tension and showed her I had a sense of humor. Before you know it, we're sitting on her front porch having a pretty good conversation. About forty-five minutes later, maybe an hour, we were . . . how should I say this? Getting to know each other even better."

I waited for some exposition. When none was offered, I asked if he meant they had sexual intercourse.

Ray blotted his bulging mouth with his napkin, nodding emphatically. "Like you wouldn't believe."

"Safe sex?" I asked.

"Sure," he said. "I'm always prepared. And so was Mary, as it turned out. She bought condoms at Costco, like a dozen gross at a time."

I answered as best as I was equipped to on this topic. "There must have been some extremely strong chemistry if you had sex after a forty-five-minute conversation."

"You could say that. You could also say that Mary was a highly physical individual." He picked up the salt and pepper shakers and made them face each other. "Like you and I have a conversation? To communicate and maybe pass the time? Not Mary"—and here the salt and pepper shakers went horizontal—"she might have been a sex addict if I hadn't come along."

"Wasn't anyone home?" I asked.

"She didn't care! She had a couple of roommates, but everybody minded their own business when it came to entertaining guests." He picked up his mug, nodded firmly, and swallowed a few gulps.

I said, "I'm fairly speechless."

"Over what aspect?"

"Mary. I have to reconfigure my mental picture of her."

"From what to what?"

"From . . . I don't know. I used to picture you were grieving over someone very sweet and wifely. But now she reminds me of the fast girls in junior high I was afraid of, the ones who smoked and drank and had boyfriends and beat people up behind the tennis court."

He looked puzzled. "I never talked about Mary before?"

It was my turn to signal to the waitress for a beer. I said carefully, "I don't understand why her sleeping around would come as a shock. I mean, if she had sex with you the first time she ever spoke to you—"

"Second time."

"Okay, second time. Doesn't that say she had, at the very least, an extremely erratic moral compass?"

"I didn't try to change her," said Ray. "In fact, I kind of liked it as it applied to me."

Our waitress brought me Ray's choice—Valentine's Day Pale Ale—and asked if I wanted my pie now. I said no thanks, just the bill. Ray added, "She's playing shrink, asking me the tough questions. Which is just what I need right now—tough love. Face the facts. Who's to say I wasn't in denial from the first time I laid eyes on her?"

"Who?" asked the waitress.

"Mary!"

"His late wife," I said.

"Oh, right. Sorry. The one who died."

"Don't be sorry," said Ray. "She was a slut."

The waitress dragged her astonished gaze from Ray to me.

Ray gestured, an introduction. "Which is why I'm here with Alice—this is Alice, by the way—and why my values and my morals have changed, like three hundred and sixty degrees." He reached across my grease-spotted place mat to squeeze my hand.

Did this constitute an emergency? I thought so. As soon as his eye contact wavered, I withdrew my hand, found my beeper, and induced several insistent and non-negotiable chirps. "Damn it," I said, getting to my feet, grabbing my jacket by the scruff of its neck. "Gotta run. You stay."

"I thought you weren't on call," he said.

"Disaster drill," I answered.

"I told you," Ray said. "She's a slave to her profession."

I surprised myself when I hesitated beside the table. "I'm thinking of quitting. It's not making me happy. In fact, it's making me miserable."

"You do look pretty catatonic," said the waitress.

"What about your dreams of helping people?" asked Ray. "What about all those deformed children in the jungle who need operations? Are you gonna bail on them because you're a little miserable?"

"Can't talk now," I said, taking a manly swig of ale. "Duty calls."

"Need a taxi?" the waitress asked.

I said no. It was faster to walk—ten minutes tops; seven if I jogged. Thanks.

"Don't jaywalk, and watch the ice," Ray called after me. "And, *número uno,* no more nonsense about quitting, agreed?"

I stopped at the threshold between restaurant and bar to wrap my scarf around my neck. The crowd had not thinned. The patrons looked up, but only long enough to see that it was the woman in Gore-Tex and Thinsulate, leaving alone. Once again, my hand went to my pager,

which announced that I was needed, desperately, somewhere else.

10
I (Nearly) Kill Someone

LET ME BEGIN by saying that it was my thirtieth hour of
duty, every one of them on my feet. The sun had risen,
set, then risen again when I was summoned to the OR for
the lowly job of holding a retractor during a gallbladder
operation. Defensible or not, I dozed off—I swear, for
one second—and lost my grip. My rebounding retractor
hit the surgeon's hand, causing damage I don't particularly want to discuss. Blood spurted everywhere. The
surgeon screamed. He swore. He threw something sharp
across the operating field, missing me, everyone
claimed, on purpose. The patient didn't exsanguinate or
die. But it was bad. I wanted to flee, but the surgeon
ordered me to stay so that he could narrate, in the most
sarcastic and derisive tone imaginable, every remedial
step; how he was obliged to insert, painstakingly, a T-
tube into the previously unnicked and profoundly important common bile duct, *Dr. Thrift*.

Perhaps, if I had been a star, his pet, he wouldn't have
carried on so. Now wide awake and gripping the
retractor with two hands, I felt the surgeon's antipathy in
every inhale and exhale, every glare above his mask.
Thank you, Dr. Thrift. Thank you for the damage control
ahead. Thank you for sabotaging me; thank you for
making me look like a goddamn incompetent and liar—
I who predicted that Mrs. Romanowski would have clear

sailing and a complete recovery will now spend hours I can't spare justifying her lifelong complications.

Did I mention that this ogre was president-elect of the American College of Surgeons? That I'd failed to impress him in the past, on rounds, in situations that now seemed utterly benign and inconsequential? Even in the best of circumstances—delivering good news from pathology to a post-op patient—Dr. Charles Greenleaf Hastings could render me nervous and blank.

He was right: I'd been assigned a minor, practically janitorial job, yet had started a chain reaction with results far out of proportion to my lowly responsibility. If I clung to the bottom line—live patient versus dead one— I suppose I could consider myself lucky. And perhaps someone else, someone cocky and capable—someone who just two days before *hadn't* inserted a central IV into an accident victim's artery instead of his vein— would shake this off as sleep deprivation or God's will. But I took these traumas for the signs that they were, that the near-murder of two people in the same week should spare future patients from my lethal ministrations.

I didn't call home, or consult my fellow interns, nor did I run into the arms of the sole surgeon on staff who had a heart and a daughter my age. I went to the gift shop in the lobby, still blood-splattered, ignoring alarmed glances, and borrowed a box of ecru stationery, promising to pay later. The saleswoman grasped that it was a matter of great urgency. "Take it," she said, retreating behind the cash register. "Just take what you need and go."

I washed my hands, found a desk, found a pen. I

wrote in a shaky script befitting a woman in shock,

> *I hereby resign from the program, effective imme-*
> *diately.*
>
> > *Very truly yours,*
> > *Alice Jane Thrift, MD*

11
Now What Do I Do?

I STAGGERED HOME, ran a bath, fell asleep in the tub, and was startled awake in tepid water by a pounding on the bathroom door. As usual, it took me a few seconds to get to the border of consciousness and remember where I was. "Leo?" I moaned.

"Are you okay?"

I pulled the plug and stood up, shivering and now crying.

"Are you ill?" he yelled. "Can you open the door?"

I said, "I'm not sick. Don't come in. I'm getting out of the tub. I fell asleep. I quit the program."

After a long pause he asked if I had said "quit."

I put on my ancient bathrobe—quilted, dingy white polyester patterned with sprigs of blue forget-me-nots—wiped my face on its sleeve, and finally opened the bathroom door. He opened his arms, whereupon the shriveled, failed, limp, damp, medically hazardous me walked into them. "I had no choice," I told him. "I made a horrible mistake today, on top of a pretty bad mistake on Monday that I didn't even tell you about because a senior resident caught it and fixed it—"

I saw him glance at the water, then turn over my left wrist.

"Don't be ridiculous," I said.

He guided me down the hall and sat down next to me on the couch. "Now tell me what happened," he said.

I provided the plainest and most self-recriminating account of having fallen asleep holding a retractor.

Leo didn't gasp, didn't look horrified, hardly reacted. *"And?"*

"First let me say that the patient was obese, so the surgical field was down there pretty deep. I couldn't see anything, so it was unbelievably boring. And I hadn't slept for days. Next thing I knew—chaos."

Leo blinked and asked calmly, "Did the patient die?"

"No, but—"

"What was the surgery?"

"Cholecystectomy. But wait—"

"I know what you're going to say: The surgeon nicked something."

"Common bile duct and the hepatic artery. Lacerated."

"Which surgeon?"

I coughed out, "Hastings. Charles."

"Ay," said Leo and flopped back against the sofa.

"First he yelled, 'Out, out, get out of here. And don't ever show your stupid face in my OR again, missy.' But then he said, 'No. You stay and you listen to me, because you're never going to make this mistake again.'"

"Like that? In that tone?"

I said yes, but worse—louder, meaner. I went deaf and blind. I hung on to the retractor for dear life, frozen to it for what seemed like hours. And as soon as he stalked out of the OR, and I was free to go, I went. For good.

I expected to be anointed with everything Leo was famous for—empathy, compassion, commiseration—with extra credit for having amputated the rotting and putrid limb that was my surgical career. He said, strangling the words, " 'Missy'? He called you 'missy'? In the OR?"

"That was the least of it. He lectured as if he were talking to a kindergartner: 'This is what we call a Penrose drain, Dr. Thrift. This is a surgeon's knot. This is the anesthesiologist, who will now extubate the patient—who, by the way, will soon need the name of your lawyer.' "

"What a fucking nerve," said Leo, now on his feet and pacing around the living room. "What a son of a bitch."

"Why did it have to be him?" I wailed. "Why couldn't it have happened on someone else's watch?"

"He'll be sorry," said Leo. "Mark my words."

"No, he won't! This was war. He's probably proud of himself. He's probably hoping this lives on as a Hastings legend, passed down through generations of surgical interns."

"He had no right to treat you like that! I don't care how many arteries got nicked. You didn't do anything worse than let a retractor slip, which could have happened to anyone."

I swallowed whatever tearful *mea culpa* was on its way and asked, "Really?"

"I'm sure it happens every day," he said. "I mean, not necessarily here but somewhere, in some OR . . . definitely."

"But he said there would be months of chronic problems now because of scar tissue, and he had to put in a T-tube—"

"Okay," he said. "Okay. So that happens. Accidents happen. No one died. Did you do it on purpose? Did you volunteer to assist and then screw up, or did you get dragged into the OR, exhausted, and given a sleeping pill by the name of 'hold the retractor for a few hours'?"

"This isn't the reaction I expected," I said.

Leo pointed toward the front door. "First thing tomorrow morning I want you to march back to the hospital and tell them that you are *not* leaving. You'll explain that you dashed off a letter of resignation in the heat of the moment, but after speaking with your lawyer—"

I clamped our one throw pillow to my face and said from behind its matted fringe, "No way."

He sat down again. "Not only do I want you to march over there, but you're going to demand that Hastings apologize to you and to every person who witnessed his tirade."

I lowered the pillow. "Are you crazy?"

"He bullied you! He not only insulted and humiliated you but he discriminated against you. Luckily, we have an OR full of witnesses." He considered that for a few seconds, then asked enthusiastically, "Any nurses get an earful of this?"

I said if he thought he could assemble a team of

people willing to side with me against the all-powerful Dr. Hastings, well, lotsa luck. Besides, wasn't it his considered opinion that I should quit and end the misemployment misery? Wasn't that the subject of a recent Green Line career-counseling session?

"Not like this," said Leo. "I wanted you to walk out the door with your head held high."

"That's impossible," I said. "And I guarantee that whoever opened my letter of resignation tonight took his wife out to dinner to celebrate."

Again Leo stood up. "This could take some intervention on my part."

"What would that be? A picket line of nurses? Leo's Ladies for the Ethical Treatment of Interns?"

He said with great dignity, "Not at all. I was thinking of blackmail."

My head-shaking stalled mid-objection. "Blackmail?" I repeated.

"Creative blackmail. I've got the goods on Hastings."

Something—a prick of hope? a cc of revenge?—made me ask, "What *about* Hastings?"

"An indiscretion. Caught red-handed. By me. In the film library."

"When?"

"A year ago, maybe more. But I'm a patient man. I knew it would come in handy."

"I find it a little suspicious that you're only telling me this now."

Leo said, "Alice. Be serious. I didn't know you a year ago. And besides, do we have the kind of relationship where I'd come home and tell you a juicy story, let alone use *blow job* in a conversation with you?"

I said, "I'm not naïve. I know about hospital affairs. I wouldn't have been shocked."

"Ha," said Leo. He went into the kitchen, came back with two tall cans of Budweiser, and handed me one.

Enunciating as if I were a novice lip-reader, Leo said, "We want to embarrass Hastings."

I asked what the actions of two presumably consenting adults had to do with my sorry state.

"He created that sorry state," said Leo.

"With my help," I said.

"Stop seeing everything so objectively! Do you think there's a hospital rule that if you make a mistake, you have to leave?"

"No?"

"I've made plenty of mistakes," said Leo. "Everyone has. If you're lucky, you don't kill or maim anyone and your supervisor says, in effect, 'Go and sin no more.'"

I asked if Hastings was a married man.

"Absolutely married. With kids."

"Who was he fooling around with in the film library?"

Leo said, "Does that matter?"

"A film librarian? A radiologist?"

"No one you know," said Leo.

"Doctor or nurse?"

"It doesn't matter," he repeated. "What matters here is that Hastings was violating our sexual harassment policy and his marriage vows." Leo took a swig of beer, crossed his arms defiantly. Finally he said, "Okay. I have two words for you, which will put this transgression into perspective. And those two words are *cleaning woman. Que solamente habla español.* So I think we can say with reasonable assurance that he used a little sign language or high school Spanish, or force, or, most likely, his wallet to achieve his desired goal."

I asked Leo if he'd reported what he'd seen.

He said, "I was afraid it might backfire and end up punishing the woman. Neither one saw me. I opened the door and backed right out again. I stood guard outside so no one else would burst in on them."

"That's a little odd," I said.

"She'd have died of embarrassment. I figured one day I'd have my moment alone with him—maybe side by side at a urinal—and I'd lean over and say, 'Doc? I saw you in the film library, with your fly open and your eyes closed, and if you ever ask anyone else in this hospital for sexual favors who doesn't ask you first, I'll beat the shit out of you.'"

I said, "Leo! I'm shocked. I can't believe you'd threaten someone with physical violence."

"How do you think we handled things at Saint Columbkille's High School? By filing grievances or beating kids up?"

"Did you ever get your moment alone with him?"

"I did. In an elevator. I said, 'Morning,' when he got on. No answer. So after a few floors I said, 'Saw you in the film library a couple of weeks ago.'"

"No!"

"More or less. His head jerked around. I said very cordially, 'Leo Frawley, RN. I don't think we've formally met.'"

"Did he answer?"

"His whole body froze, then he said, 'I have no idea what you're talking about, and if I were you, I'd be a lot more careful about how you speak to your superiors.' I said, 'Are you saying I have the wrong guy? Or I'm lying? Because I'll raise my right hand and swear to it at the hearing.'"

It must have been the effect of the alcohol entering my bloodstream because I heard myself saying, "If a pollster calls me tonight and asks me to name my most admired American, I'm going to say, *'Leo Frawley.'*"

"Now, that," said Leo, "is an extraordinarily winning and gracious statement."

"For me, you mean?"

"For anyone."

I would have liked to generate another winning and gracious statement, but nothing suggested itself. I fished an old tissue out of my pocket and blew my nose.

He asked if I was hungry, and I nodded. He went into the kitchen. I heard the refrigerator door open, some shuffling of our lamentable provisions, then, "How about eggs?"

I said that sounded perfect. Could he do soft-boiled?

"Walk me through it," he said.

I joined him in the kitchen and narrated: Boil the water, add the egg with a metal spoon so the egg wouldn't receive the full assault of the boiling water, time it—I'd had success with four and a half minutes— then remove.

He nodded. "You sit. Toast?"

"If we have any."

He supplied a shot glass for an egg cup. Everything—eggs, butter, grape jelly, toast—was from his larder. As I ate, I caught him smiling at something. "What?" I asked.

He said it was the incision I'd made, slicing the top half-inch off the egg with my knife. "What's that all about?" he asked. "I've seen people do that on TV, but never in real life."

"Habit," I said.

"But why? Doesn't it waste part of the egg, which is a pretty skimpy meal to begin with?"

I said, "It's a way in, that's all. Instead of peeling the top and having a jagged border, you get a nice clean edge. You don't burn your fingers. Plus it's faster."

"Now I know," said Leo. "Thank you for that."

I sprinkled salt on the exposed yolk and dipped in. "Perfect," I said.

"Eggs for supper are always therapeutic," said Leo. "Especially when consumed in a comfy bathrobe."

I looked down at said garment. The stitching that formed every rhomboid was unraveling, and two of its transparent plastic buttons were missing. A powder-blue ribbon, once a bow at the neck, was in shreds. "It used to be pretty," I offered.

"First," said Leo, "I see ratty bathrobes with peep-holes all the time, so you don't have to apologize for missing buttons to a professional such as myself."

"And what's second?"

"Nothing's wrong with you that a good night's sleep and a pep talk and maybe, somewhere along the way, a little fun wouldn't have fixed."

Not that again, not from Leo. I said, "I've heard it all.

Lighten up, Alice. Smell the roses, Alice. Carpe diem, Alice. As if that's what's wrong with me: not enough fun. As if I can change that by—what's your prescription? Take tango lessons? Go on a picnic?"

Leo said, "You're right. I apologize. I guess I was suggesting that you could find ways to enjoy life more, not that the essential Alice Thrift would have to change. Just her outlook."

I spread jelly on my toast and swilled some more beer to show that I wasn't all business. "How in the world, if I follow your advice and go back to work, would I find more opportunities to enjoy life?"

"You could socialize with people in the same boat, such as your fellow interns, for example."

"I've tried that. No one wants to socialize with someone who's bad at work and bad at play. No one except Ray Russo."

Leo stood up, found another beer in the refrigerator. "What's up with that relationship?"

I said, "That's an upgrade—*relationship*."

"What would you call it?"

I shrugged. I explained that each time I left Ray after a . . . get-together? a quasi-date? I thought I was saying Good-bye, No more, The end. But then he'd turn up again.

"It must be a *little* flattering when a guy won't take no for an answer."

"He likes the doctor part. When I mentioned I was thinking of quitting, he said, 'Don't you dare.' "

Leo smiled, an ironic twist of his mouth. "Don't tell me that Ray and I are on the same side of an issue?"

I said, "If I ever told him how Hastings insulted me in front of everyone in the OR? I think he'd find out where he lives and wait for him on the sidewalk after dark. With a tire iron."

Leo straightened up. "Has he ever shown any signs of violence with you?"

I said no, of course not.

"Then why would you say that?"

I checked my bathrobe and regripped the gaps. "Just a sense I get of how he solves problems . . . his notion of how the world works."

"Do you ever get a sense of his good qualities?"

I could enumerate several impulses Ray possessed— love of travel, loyalty, availability—that were not criminal proclivities, but otherwise I was stumped. "Isn't this meeting about my professional life?" I asked.

"Meeting?" He smiled. "Is this a meeting? Or is this supper with your roommate?"

I said, "I know you want to help, and I am taking your various recommendations under advisement, and this definitely qualifies as supper . . ."

"But?"

"I'm not you. Maybe Leo Frawley can confront people and sue them, but I can't."

He patted my arm, looked stumped, looked up at the microwave clock. He coughed, then raised a finger as if asking for one more indulgence. "Did you hand your letter of resignation to your chairman, or did you leave it with his secretary?"

"Neither. I left it on his desk."

"What time?"

I said I thought it was around six.

He rapped the table with his knuckles. "Excellent. Let's go get it."

I said, "But I just told you—"

"No, different plan. This doesn't stop you from quitting again tomorrow. This just gives you an extension."

I shook my head. "Bad plan. His office will be locked. Alarms will go off. Security will arrest us."

"Wrong. We'll find someone with a passkey. We'll enlist the cleaning staff. We'll say . . ." He closed his eyes for a few seconds, then opened them, wide and inspired. "How about this: We'll tell the truth! We say, 'Alice had a horrible day, the worst, and she wrote a letter of resignation which she left on Dr. Kennick's desk, but now she's changed her mind. Can you let her in? She'll show you the letter, and if we're misrepresenting anything, you can detain us, or frisk us, or call our mothers.'"

I looked at Leo. It was so simple. He had such faith in himself and the truth and the goodwill of every custodian, hospital-wide. "Do I have to accompany you on this caper?" I asked.

"Absolutely. No one is going to rescue your letter on my say-so alone. C'mon."

I said, "We'll have beer on our breaths. Won't that undermine our mission?"

Leo smiled. "Mission," he repeated. "That's my girl."

LEO WAVED AT several passing janitors before hailing
Ruben, whose premature twins, he told me, had been
born with respiratory distress syndrome at thirty-one
weeks.

"How're my boys?" Leo asked, grinning broadly.

Ruben wrapped an arm around Leo's shoulders and
squeezed. "Beautiful! Healthy. Eat good. Sleep good. No
problem."

Leo introduced me as his roommate, which caused
Ruben to peer first at my ID and then at my bustline.

"We need your help," said Leo.

"Anything for Dr. Leo," Ruben said.

Leo elbowed me, which I understood to mean, Correct him at a more propitious time.

"It's no small favor," Leo continued, "so promise me
you'll refuse if you feel the slightest bit compromised."

Ruben wouldn't hear of it. Big, small, upstairs, downstairs, today, tomorrow—no problem.

Leo lowered his voice. "Dr. Thrift needs to get into
Dr. Kennick's office to pick up a letter she left there by
mistake—"

"Which, originally, I meant for him to read, but I've
changed my mind."

Ruben winked at Leo.

"What?" I asked.

"Nada," said Leo.

"I distinctly saw him wink."

Leo shielded one corner of his mouth as if relaying a secret. "He thinks you're talking about a love letter."

Ruben winked again with greater conviction.

"I most certainly am not," I said. "I'm referring to a letter of resignation provoked by a very unfortunate slip-up in the OR, which, in the heat of the moment—"

"Made her quit," said Leo.

"No good," Ruben said.

"No kidding," said Leo. "And our thinking is that Kennick hasn't seen this I-quit letter yet, so no one will be the wiser if she can deep-six it."

"What's it look like?" asked Ruben, his right hand now fishing deep into a trouser pocket, from which appeared several dozen keys.

"A rectangle," I said. "Cream-colored. I think the manufacturer is Crane, so it should have a watermark. There's no address or stamp, just *Dr. Kennick* hand-written on the front, in script. I should have brought a sample envelope with me from the box."

Again Leo signaled: *Relax.*

Ruben unplugged his vacuum cleaner. "No big deal," he said. And we were off.

IT WAS NOT in plain sight on any horizontal surface in Kennick's office. "*You* look," Ruben said, beckoning from the doorway. "I'm not touching nothing."

We changed places: Ruben as lookout and me holding his feather duster for the appearance of house-keeping. I groped along the wall, found the light switches, experimented; dimmed the crime scene back to near-darkness. Kennick must have had the day off because his credenza held an avalanche of mail. I approached the stack gingerly, upsetting nothing, lifting only corners of the fat shrink-wrapped journals and flyers hawking surgical symposia on tropical isles. And finally at the bottom—ignored, insulted, entombed—was my handwritten surrender. With my nimble surgeon's fingers in a pincer grip, I liberated my letter and ran.

LEO TURNED ON the front burner of our narrow gas stove, and beckoned to me for the sacrificial offering.

"Don't burn yourself," I said.

"Fat chance," he said. "*You're* burning this sucker, and then we'll think of something symbolic to do with the ashes."

He turned a knob and produced a circle of blue flame. "*Low* is fine," I advised.

One corner caught immediately. I dropped the envelope and stomped on it. What remained was singed but highly readable. "Do I have to finish the job?" I asked.

"No," said Leo. "It was plenty symbolic—your attacking the letter as if it were a poisonous copperhead."

"And this was an exercise in what?"

"Too early to tell," said Leo, "but something along the lines of a new day dawning."

"I think it burned the floor."

"Just a smudge," said Leo. I followed him to the sink, where he tore a paper towel from our freestanding roll and wet it.

"Let me," I said.

He waved me away and set to work, sprinkling Bon

119

Ami on the smudge, frowning as he moved to old, unrelated stains.

I silently tested an unfamiliar phrase, then said aloud, "I have a sudden craving for pizza."

Leo looked up. "Pizza?"

I said, "Sure."

"I was thinking *pizza* myself, not thirty seconds ago." He pointed to our junk drawer. "Look in there. Mimo's take-out menu. Order whatever you like."

The drawer yielded graduation programs, expired coupons, wax-paper lunch bags, unopened bank statements, a flurry of Chinese menus, and, finally, Mimo's.

"What do you like?" he asked.

Prompted by the alphabetical list of toppings, I threw out, "Anchovy?"

Leo leaned back on his haunches and said reverently, "Wow. I had no idea."

I said that plain would be fine if he preferred. Was that the same as a cheese pizza? The menu said a small pie was six slices, which should be plenty.

Leo's expression changed to something mildly self-conscious. He said we'd probably need a large. Okay if he called in a large? His treat.

"Leftover pizza's good," I said. "I had a roommate once who ate cold pizza for breakfast."

"Actually, someone's coming over later. When her shift ends."

"Who?"

"Meredith," said Leo. "From labor and delivery? She gets off at eleven."

I said I hadn't rotated through labor and delivery.

Was she a nurse?

"Nurse-midwife, actually."

"Is she a new friend?"

He shrugged.

"A girlfriend?"

His reply sounded unnaturally hearty: "Whoa. When does that designation kick in—*girlfriend?* Yikes. Hard to say."

"Is this her first visit?"

He shook his head, but barely.

I said it was good to get an extracurricular report, belated or not. Might I ask how long they'd been a two-some?

He offered some unintelligible body language, mostly shoulders.

"You don't know?"

More ducking and shrugging. "Guys aren't good at those kinds of questions," he finally replied.

I said I didn't mean to make him uncomfortable. But I was asking no more than what he had asked about Ray.

He thought that over, pulled out a kitchen chair, sat down, and folded his hands. "Fine. What do you want to know?"

"Is she intelligent?"

"Yes, definitely. Always at the top of any guy's list of desired attributes."

"Does she have a college degree?"

Leo smiled and said, "Yes. Would you like me to have her SAT scores sent?"

I said no, of course not.

"She delivered my latest niece," he said. "My brother

Christopher's first baby, if you were wondering how we met."

I hated the next question but I asked it anyway. "Is she attractive?"

"Most people would consider her attractive."

I offered a compliment of my own—that Meredith was obviously quiet and considerate.

Leo asked how I'd come up with that.

"I meant that she must be quiet and considerate because I've never heard her arrive and have no idea what time she leaves."

Leo turned a little red in the face. He mumbled something about her being just the opposite. Quite lively. And personable. Patients adored her.

The opposite of me, he meant.

He took the menu from me and walked to the phone. I heard him order; I noted how he sounded and looked engaged, no doubt charming even the pizza maître d'.

"Thirty minutes," he reported. "You'll eat yours as soon as it gets here. No need to wait up for Meredith."

I said, "Three's a crowd. Even I know that."

He walked back to the table and sat down again. "I feel as if I've sprung something on you and you're upset. I can hear it in your voice."

I said, "Not at all. I understand. Didn't you choose me as a roommate over the nurse candidates in order to protect your privacy? Don't worry about me. If I seem surprised, it's my own fault for not paying attention and for wearing earplugs to bed."

"Literally?"

"Literally."

The next minute he was standing behind me, kneading my shoulders in a professional manner and staring off into space. "Maybe I've been playing it close to the vest . . ." he began. "No one at work has caught on. I'm not one to make any big announcement, especially before I know if it's going to last more than a few dates."

"Has it? Is it serious?"

Leo said, "I'll have to go look up *serious* in the dictionary before I answer that."

When I glanced over at our bookshelf, Leo gave my shoulders a reproving squeeze. "That was a joke, Alice. Guys don't like to label things. It's . . . nice. So far, no problems. Neither one of us talks about the future." His tone changed from philosophical to charitable. "Although I know she's definitely looking forward to meeting you."

"Is she?" I asked, my voice chillier than I'd intended.

"You *are* pissed," said Leo.

I bumped my chair a few inches to slip out of his grip. "I've been meetable for a long time, haven't I? Sleeping one room away, probably using the same bathroom glass and bar of soap. And we've no doubt passed each other in the hospital corridors a dozen times." I lifted my ID and jabbed my own picture for emphasis. "Alice Thrift, MD. Friend and roommate of Leo."

"Don't blame Meredith," he said. "She almost introduced herself to you a couple of times at the hospital, but then chickened out."

"Hard to introduce yourself to someone who's invisible," I muttered.

"Don't say that! You're not invisible. I hate when you talk like that."

When I didn't answer, when I sat there with my arms folded and my cognitive functions trying to grasp what had been revealed and why I'd been perturbed by it, Leo actually smiled. "Can I boil you a therapeutic egg?" he teased. "Four and a half minutes, no waiting?"

I said no, thank you. The pizza would be here soon.

"How about some black coffee so you can stay up past eleven?"

"To meet her?"

"*Yes,* to meet Meredith! No excuses; no more slipping in and slipping out like people with a secret. Whaddya say?"

I answered with an aplomb I credit to my socially appropriate parents but rarely invoke. I said that I was looking forward to meeting Meredith, too. Not tonight— I was dead—but soon. Maybe we could all go to a bar together or to the planetarium some night, the four of us. Isn't that how two roommates and their respective friends of the opposite sex fraternized? By consulting their schedules and organizing a double date?

13
Ms. Bravado

DR. KENNICK PUT me on probation. I could continue my surgical pursuits if—as he so crudely phrased it—I pulled no more Alice Thrifts.

He had me beeped at home. Leo heard the summons, slipped out of bed, carefully closing the door behind him, and intercepted me in the kitchen for a pep talk: Falling asleep on the job was yesterday's news; today the headline was HASTINGS ON THE HOT SEAT, right? I was to throw around the words *intimidation, discrimination, harassment,* and *debilitated by exhaustion.* Got it?

I outlined my worst fears: Kennick must have seen the letter of resignation despite our caper. He must have gotten a late-night phone call and an earful from Hastings. We must have triggered a silent alarm, prompting security to study its surveillance tape.

Sitting opposite Kennick in a tweed armchair, I soon learned that there *had* been a late-night rant of a phone call, and it had been, indeed, an earful. Probation won by a hair's breadth over separation because he, Dr. Kennick—red-faced as he alluded to "a colleague's attack that erupted into something unbridled and, frankly, uncalled for"—was still quarterbacking this department.

I asked if this was tantamount to giving me two months' notice.

"It's up to you: If there are no more serious mistakes, we'll most likely lift the probation. If we see measurable improvement, you'll earn more responsibility. If we see no improvement, we'll be forced to sit down and assess the danger you pose to the patients."

I said I was bound to improve. If only he could have a little confidence, I might get some, too. Didn't that make sense? Trial by fire wasn't my best working milieu.

"You knew what you were getting into," he snapped. "We all did it, and now you have to do it. This is what separates surgeons from the rest of doctordom. Exhaustion never excuses a mistake." Sports analogies flowed: one more strike and I was out; fumble again and I'd be sidelined; let anyone down, be he playmaker or water boy, and I was off the team.

Leo would be crushed. He had pictured me walking away with an apology from Kennick and the promise of one from a humbled and chastened Charles G. Hastings. Instead, I accepted what now sounded eminently fair: two months to shape up; two months to show my stuff; two months to make the starting lineup.

I remembered to state for the record that I'd been bullied, harassed, humiliated, discriminated against, screamed at. In front of witnesses.

"Which I don't dispute—"

"—by a loudmouth asshole," I heard myself say.

"That loudmouth asshole is the next president of the American College of Surgeons," Kennick stated, adding a notation to my file.

Ms. Bravado kept her head erect for the walk out of his office, past Yolanda, who was trying to look as if she wasn't enjoying every slippery inch of my career descent, down the hallway to the ladies' room, to the farthest toilet, into which I vomited. I didn't mean to linger, didn't have time for dramatics like these, but some combustion of adrenaline and fatigue had rendered me lightheaded. I sat on the floor and invented a conversation, whereby a sympathetic soul would inquire from the row of sinks, "Are you all right in there, miss?"

"Just nerves," I'd answer. "I'm on probation—a first for my department. No one's ever been this bad."

Next the phantom stranger would ask, "Is your nausea, by any chance, morning sickness?"

"Yes," the other, chatty me would offer. "I just found out. I haven't told anyone yet."

Where was this tableau and conversation coming from? No one had impregnated me. No one had even tried. No pair of legs was visible outside my stall. I fluttered my hand in front of the optic sensor to induce another flush, then checked my pulse. I was alive. I recognized my surroundings: gray tile, white grout, white porcelain. These were my Keds, my white jacket, my plaid skirt, my brown tights, my ID. How odd—using my imagination, writing a playlet starring an alter ego of mine, an Alice who had a life and missed a period. I wiped my mouth with toilet paper, then went out to the sinks. I didn't want to look in the mirror but I did: My eyes were red and my skin was pale; my hair, in what remained of yesterday's single braid, was unkempt. An expression of my father's came to mind: *Sad Sack.* I was sick of that face; sick of myself. I needed to do something immoderate, big, drastic. But what? The possibilities were hardly endless: I could walk away and never come back. I could switch to a specialty that wouldn't kill me. I could sue Dr. Hastings. Murder Dr. Hastings. Cut off my braid. Take vitamins. Take amphetamines. Call Ray and tell him to leave me alone. Call Ray and tell him I'd like to have sex.

Sex. I rinsed my mouth with cold water and dried my hands. Intercourse in my own bed, I reasoned, would take less time and energy than dinner or a movie. And I could be asleep within minutes following the act. Ray would be pleasantly surprised. "You mean it?" he would ask, his eyes grateful, his voice cracking with repressed emotion and pent-up testosterone.

Maybe it would put color in my cheeks. Maybe I would like it.

Your place or mine? I could say. I looked into the mirror, blotted my upper lip with a brown paper towel, and whispered as libidinously as I could, "Your place or mine?"

I CARVED ONE minute out of my duties to call the housing office. My timing, pronounced the young man on the other end, was awesome. A tenant had most unfortunately lost his life and had *just,* like, this morning, been discovered! The police would be finished with their investigation by the end of the week, tops. It was a studio apartment with a small terrace and a Murphy bed, available as soon as the carpet was industrially cleaned and fumigated.

I asked if I could wait until the police report was in and whether the tenant had died of anthrax, Legionnaires' disease, or foul play that might implicate a neighbor.

The young man lowered his voice. "Off the record?"

I said yes, please.

"Sleeping pills. Not to worry."

"Was he a surgical resident?"

"Anesthesiology. But it was personal—a bad breakup. He left a note."

I said I was sorry. I'd take it. I gave him my name, my beeper number, and my solemn promise that I'd have a check on his desk by five o'clock.

I WENT LOOKING for Leo in the cafeteria during the half hour he favored for lunch. There was a woman eating with him—wearing the professionally serene expression and natural fibers of a midwife. Around her neck, under her long brown hair, were both a stethoscope and a strand of beads that looked like shellacked seeds. Older, I thought. Thirty-five, forty. That would be fine with Leo the open-minded, the lover of all humanity.

"How's it going?" he asked enthusiastically. "I can't believe I didn't get debriefed. You talked to Kennick, right? Everything okay?"

"Well, I'm still here." I offered my hand to Meredith. "I'm Alice. The roommate."

She said, "Leo told me about your trials and tribulations. I hope you don't mind his sharing that with me."

I said, "*Trial* is right. I'm on probation. Two months during which I'll be under the microscope." I held up my hand to ward off Leo's reply, sure to be another call to action. "I do have good news," I announced.

Ever the optimist, Leo grinned. "Hastings's busted?"

"No, nothing about that—"

"Thankfully, Hastings does no OB or GYN procedures, so we never overlap," Meredith informed me.

I nodded once and turned back to Leo. "You knew I was on the waiting list for hospital housing?"

He said huh, no, he didn't know that.

"Well, amazingly enough, a studio opened up today, which is practically required now that I'm on probation. I'll be a tunnel away from the hospital."

"But you're only across the street now," he said.

Standing behind Meredith, I could easily convey with a minimal thrust of my chin: Now you'll have your privacy.

"Is it definite?" he asked. "Have you signed anything?"

I said I had.

"Which building?" asked Meredith. "North or south?"

"North," I guessed.

"I've heard they're nice," she said.

Leo said, "No, they're not! They're overrun with married couples and babies and plagued by fire drills."

"You love babies, hon," Meredith murmured.

I said I was supposed to be getting labs for my chief resident, stat.

"This seems kind of sudden," said Leo.

"That's the nature of a waiting list," I said. "An apartment comes up, you make an instant decision, or you kiss it good-bye."

"You'll still see each other here," said Meredith. "Probably as often as you did when you were roommates."

"Not so fast with the past tense," said Leo. "We're still roommates."

Meredith smiled, got to her feet, touched Leo's shoulder in a farewell love tap. "I'm a champion mover," she said to me. "I'm famous for helping friends pack and relocate and unpack. Just say the word."

"I only have my clothes and books and a toaster oven," I said. "But thanks just the same."

She put out her hand. "Really nice meeting you. I know I've been something of a ghost roommate, but now we don't have to be strangers. I'd love to have lunch another day when you have more time."

"I'm the ghost," I said. "And as far as lunch is concerned, I never have more time."

Meredith's bright smile faltered. Leo said, "No time and no manners."

As soon as she walked away I said, "You won't miss me. I was never there. I just took up a bedroom and wrote a check, but I wasn't a real roommate."

Leo said, "I tried to help. I tried to be your friend. I didn't know I wasn't allowed to have a girlfriend."

"That's what you think? I'm moving out because of her? She's irrelevant. Today's headline is, MY NUMBER CAME UP FOR HOSPITAL HOUSING."

"If you say so," said Leo, wadding his sandwich wrapper and denting his soda can.

I stood by the table before finally asking how long he was going to stay mad at me—he, Leo, the eternal optimist; he whose glass was not only half-full but vitamin-enriched.

He made a sour face, which turned slightly indulgent after a few stubborn seconds.

I said, "I'll continue to pay my share of the rent. I mean, what else do I spend money on? I can swing both for a while. The new place is subsidized."

He said, "I might be okay rent-wise. We've talked about it as a possibility."

"We?"

"Her commute is ridiculous," he answered. "Would

you believe Winchester? For a midwife?"

I said I had to run. I couldn't let the team down. The team was waiting to hear if Mrs. Jacobs was acidotic.

"What about the other parts of your life?" he asked. "Are you going to make friends in the new building? In the laundry room? Because I felt we were making some progress in that arena."

"Which arena?"

"Human relations. Good times. Fun."

I said, "I'll socialize. I'll definitely meet new people. And I think you're forgetting Ray. I haven't given him much of a chance. Maybe, when I have my own place, I'll get to know him better."

"Ray?" he repeated, now on his feet. *"Ray?* Are you saying this to get my goat? I mean, is *boyfriend* such a textbook concept that you'd let a slimeball fit the bill just because he won't take no for an answer? I find that so goddamn depressing that I don't know what else to say."

People were watching. Leo Frawley rarely frowned and never glowered; never raised his voice except to hail a friend or cheer a patient.

I said I appreciated everything, every kind act, every morsel of food from his side of the refrigerator, but I hadn't known he was such a snob. And what nerve to insinuate that I was asocial and eremitic. I'd learned at his knee—the most popular guy in the world—hadn't I? Wasn't it logical that I'd take a turn for the sociable under his tutelage?

"Overnight?"

I said his timing was appalling. It had been a very rough twenty-four hours, if he recalled. With my voice

132

choked, I added, "I felt nauseated and diaphoretic after talking to Kennick. And I've just pulled myself together to carry out my first lowly gofer errand. So I'd appreciate no more so-called advice about Ray Russo or anyone else."

"I can't believe we're arguing," said Leo. "I don't know how we came to this. I can't believe you'd get so weird over a woman staying over—"

"I'm on call tonight," I said coldly, backing away. "And tomorrow night I may or may not be home after work."

"Alice—" he tried. He reached for my wrist, but I yanked it free and strode away.

14

I'm a Normal Person

WITH PROFESSIONAL AND residential upheavals looming, I didn't undertake anything socially drastic. I purchased a greeting card, a black-and-white photograph of the Leaning Tower of Pisa, and wrote inside, *Hi! I'm moving to my own place on Feb. 1, an exceptionally clean studio in hospital housing. Will call when I get a phone. Or you can page me. Sincerely, Doc.* I mailed it to First-Prize Fudge and wrote *Personal* on the envelope. I hadn't heard from Ray since I'd beeped my getaway from the bar near Fenway Park, but even I knew, in my uninsightful way, that between the lines of my cheerful tidings lay a bold invitation.

He didn't answer. I tried to remember what I'd written; I also tried to remember what traits he possessed, other than his willingness to abide my company, that made me want to resuscitate the friendship. He wasn't intelligent or attractive. He wasn't interesting, except perhaps as someone I might have interviewed—after venturing into a bad neighborhood with a tape recorder and a whistle—for an undergraduate sociology course. In his plus column I could write *entertaining* and *outgoing* and *shares food*. If I were prone to oversimplification and romance, I might say, *Opposites attract,* but that very notion seemed so unscientific, so puerile, that I dismissed it out of hand.

AS MY MOTHER folded each of my undergarments into thirds and arranged them in my suitcase, she asked nonchalantly, "Have you ever heard, in your medical travels, of Asperger's Syndrome?"

"It's neurological. A form of autism, I think."

"Nicknamed the Little Professor Syndrome." She frowned at the compromised elastic in a dingy pair of cotton underpants and lobbed them into my wastebasket. "Sufferers have very high IQs—sky-high—but their social skills are nonexistent," she continued. "Your father read the piece, too, and we can't stop talking about it. He's been doing some research on-line and found a study at Yale." She walked to the closet door and asked me to face her. She put her hands on my shoulders, signaling, Pay attention. Head up. Make eye contact. "How are you today, Alice?" she enunciated in Beginning Conversational English.

I shrugged. "Tired. Depressed."

"Good," she said. "That makes me feel better." She

went to her shaggy woven book bag and took out an underexposed Xerox, its pages stapled and highlighted in pink. "It was the cover story in last Sunday's magazine section . . . and now I'm quoting directly: 'When you ask them at first, "How do you do?" they will say something like, "Why do you want to know?" They simply don't understand social games.'"

I said, "Are you talking about me? You think I'm autistic?"

She held up an index finger. "Wait, I underlined it. . . . Here it is: 'Asperger's kids cannot decipher basic visual social signals. This leads people to see them as emotionally disturbed. Or brilliant.'"

I took the pages from her and skimmed the opening paragraphs.

"Ring any bells?" she asked at my elbow.

I read silently until I came to ". . . a neurological disorder that disproportionately affects males," pointed that out as if it settled the matter, then asked, "Don't you think that if I were autistic, someone would have diagnosed it by now?"

"Not this kind! It was only made an official syndrome in 1994."

"And do you think a lot of autistic kids graduate from college *summa* and go to Harvard Medical School?"

She frowned. "I wondered about that, too. But you could have something less than a full-blown case. You could be compensating because Daddy and I are such extroverts that you learned coping strategies."

Had I learned to cope and compensate? I walked over to my bed, which was stripped to the mattress ticking, and lay down on my side, facing the wall.

"There are a lot worse neurological problems a person could have," my mother coaxed. "You could have been born with cerebral palsy or epilepsy or Tourette's. Asperger's is a walk in the park compared to—"

"I don't have Asperger's! And you're not qualified to diagnose anyone, either. First of all, mostly boys get it. Second of all, I'm a normal person who might be challenged in the personality department, but that's all. And how do you think it makes me feel to hear that my mother thinks I'm autistic?"

"*Feel?* Feelings are exactly what I'm looking for," she said. "There aren't enough in this family since Nana died. I want you and me to have what Nana and I enjoyed for sixty-two years, which is to say an exquisite friendship."

She picked up the pages again and flipped to another highlighted passage. "'Consider Glenn Gould,'" she read. "'The eccentric Canadian pianist, who died in 1982 and who retired from the concert circuit at thirty-one, was notorious for his bizarre behavior: He had a phobia about shaking hands, ate nothing but scrambled eggs and Arrowroot biscuits, and rocked incessantly at the keyboard.'" She tossed the pages onto my night table. "I'm finding this very reassuring, because I know you don't have a phobia about touching people. You not only have to touch them but you have to cut into them and probe their organs and glands. Correct?"

"Correct."

"But let me ask you this—is the reverse true?"

"The reverse of what?"

"The reverse of a hand-shaking phobia. In other words, do you like to be touched?"

Did I? While I tried to remember, she jumped in. "Stop me if I'm getting too personal, but I've had a lot of free time lately to imagine what goes on inside the head of Alice Thrift. I mean, is physicality something you think about? Yearn for? Jump into with both feet when the opportunity presents itself?"

I said, "That's three different questions."

"And look how long it's taken me to ask you even one! Nana knew more about what was going on inside my head than I did. Even when I'd moved away from home, she knew where I was going, with whom, when I was menstruating, and what I was making for dinner. I could tell her anything, and she never recoiled, never shrank from any personal details. Her EQ was off the charts."

With her daughter maybe, inside their two-person cocoon. I didn't point out that Nana's so-called EQ dwindled in the company of her grandchildren. Julie and I were dropped off at her apartment when my parents couldn't find a baby-sitter, and it was understood that we would bring our own food, and then get tutored in contract bridge by displaying our hands solitaire-style on her card table.

I said, "I don't think a mother and a daughter should talk about personal concerns, because sooner or later the daughter is going to have to hear something she'd rather not know."

She smiled coyly and sat down on the edge of the bed.

"When your father and I first met—"

I put my hands over my ears. She pried them away and snapped, "Don't act so autistic."

I said, "If you insist, I'll listen. But remember that I'm not Nana."

"I don't insist," she said, then plunged ahead: "Your father and I despised each other at first sight. I thought he was brash, rude, egocentric. He was getting his MBA, while I always fell for the boys who wrote for the literary magazine." She smiled a private smile. "Poets, of course. When along comes this guy—micro, macro, macho. All business, and I mean that literally."

"I've heard this story," I said.

"No. You've heard the sanitized version. What might be instructive is the truth: that I slept with him not too long after we met, just for the fun of it. Just to get it over with, just to be with someone who wasn't sensitive and artistic—without the slightest intention of falling in love. But that's where it happened: in bed. Well, there weren't any etiquette books that tell you where to go from there. You jump into bed because you want to be like those girls who hung around the Village, who had sex without looking back, and what happens? You wake up, happily twisted in the bedclothes, wanting to be Mrs. Bertram Thrift."

I blinked. "And your point is?"

"My point is that I could confide every word of this to my mother. My girlfriends were too conventional— go steady, get pinned, get engaged, buy your trousseau, get married, lose your virginity on your wedding night in the Plaza. I knew that I could tell my mother everything, and she wouldn't call me a slut or, worse, dissolve into tears."

"How did you know she wouldn't?"

"Because of how she raised me. She wasn't ashamed of her body or her bodily functions, and that kind of thing sets a tone in a house. If one takes a bath and voids with the door open and if one's daughters can perch on the edge of the tub and have a conversation with their naked mother, some threshold is set." She lowered her voice to confide, "Once, right after her divorce, we spent a week at a nudists' colony in upstate New York, one that accepted children. Her friends didn't know. She wasn't a committed nudist, but she was curious. We didn't go back because she didn't particularly like the people, and I think, between you and me, she was looking for some male companionship at that stage. Ironically, it proved to be an unbelievably dull vacation. Everyone talked politics, everyone was married, nobody flirted, and everyone sagged." She smoothed her dark hair back toward its French twist. "I tried very consciously to continue that tradition and hold court in the bathtub, but you and Julie and God knows your father would close the bathroom door when you walked by. Maybe I should have tried harder."

"Why?"

"Because! I might have broken down some resistance. I might have made you more open, more physical, more . . . unconstrained. And Julie! I should have tied her down and made her bathe with me in order to demystify the female body so she wouldn't grow up to see it as a sexual object!"

I said, "I don't think it works that way."

"The point being—one of several points I wanted to make—that it's not too late. I'm here for you now. God closed the door that was Nana and opened the one marked 'Alice.'" She nudged me with her hips until I moved closer to the wall, then lay down next to me.

"Doesn't this feel good?" she asked. "Doesn't it make you want to talk late into the night?"

I said, "Not really."

"Go ahead," she said. "Tell me something. Anything. Big, small, as long as it comes from here." She rapped her fist against her left breast.

"Like what?"

She waved her arms above both of us. "The sky's the limit. Your dreams and aspirations. Your fantasies. A handsome internist you spotted across a crowded room."

I could conjure only round-shouldered, myopic internal-medicine residents, married nonetheless. I said, "Well, you know it's always been my dream to do reconstructive surgery on patients in the Third World."

"I know," she said. "But why?"

"Why? Because in many cultures the disfigured are shunned. Imagine having the power to return someone to society and to rescue him or her from loneliness, if not total isolation or even death—"

"And this is important to you—rescuing primitive people from loneliness? Are you sure you'd be good at that?"

"I'd learn. I have ten more years of training before I'd be eligible to even—"

"I didn't mean surgically. I mean psychiatrically. Do

you think that you have the interpersonal skills to be a humanitarian?"

I said, "You asked me about my dreams and I told you. Is that so hard to understand—someone who's born with a cleft lip makes her way to my clinic and leaves with a perfectly aligned vermilion border?"

"You're right, absolutely." She smiled. "What else do you want to confide in me? Anything more immediate? More Alice-centered?"

I closed my eyes and said, "No, thank you."

"I'm sorry. I apologize. I know that if it can be learned in a textbook, you'll study till you get it right, so what am I worried about?"

I said, "Well, here's something you can worry about: I almost killed a patient during a gallbladder operation this week. How's that for a good juicy secret?" I abridged the rest: the exhaustion, the retractor, the nicked hepatic artery, the hostilities, the sentence.

"Terrible," she murmured. "You must have been scared to death. But thank goodness no one died . . . and now, how humiliating to be watched like a hawk." She waited a beat, tapped my forearm to signal a new topic. "What about your love life? That's more along the lines of what I was trying to elicit."

I said, "You know I'm working a hundred and twenty hours a week—"

"What *I* know is that it takes a special man to understand and to accept that. Probably another doctor, don't you think? Which is why I like the ring of *hospital housing*."

I said, "I work with doctors day and night. I don't

have to go to a dance in the common room to meet any."

"Dances? Really? They hold dances in your new building?"

"No. And if they did, do you think I'd go?"

Her right arm crossed over her face and covered her eyes.

After a minute I tried, "Mom? . . . Joyce?"

She answered with a sniffle and plucked a tissue from my bedside box. After another interval I nudged her and said, "Okay. Here's an inside scoop: Once I'm settled in, I'm going to invite Ray over for what I'm labeling a housewarming."

"Ray?"

"Ray Russo. The man who drove me to Nana's funeral?"

"Not the candy vendor?"

I said as a matter of fact, yes.

"Have you been seeing him?"

I said no, hardly, but hc'd taken the day off from work to attend a total stranger's funeral, and this was my way of saying thank you.

She rolled onto her side, propped herself on her elbow, and peered at me. "You're beet-red. What kind of thank-you did you have in mind?"

I could have said, "Beans and franks and a video." I could have said, "No comment," or, "None of your business." But she was stretched out beside me, still sniffling, still wearing black, and building monuments to sixty-two years of mother-daughter candor. So I said, "I'll probably make sandwiches and buy a bottle of wine, and then, if all goes well, I'll lower the

Murphy bed."

"For what?"

"For what normal, sexually active people do on a bed."

She sat up. "Please tell me you're joking, Alice."

I said no, of course not. When did I ever joke? And why did the suggestion of me having sex render her flabbergasted?

She inhaled and exhaled as if exercising great forbearance. "Believe me, I'm not objecting to the sex. Far from it. I'd put myself up against the most broad-minded parents in this entire country. What I'm reacting to is 'First we have dinner and then we have intercourse.' It just sounds so passionless. So . . . autistic."

I said I wished she'd stop throwing medical terms around. As for passion, hadn't she just spent the last half hour bragging about her active dislike for my father, precoitally?

"Your *father* was a graduate student at Wharton! Your intended partner sells granular fudge out of the trunk of his car. I just don't see it. Is it convenience? Or desperation? Or—you won't like this one bit—pity?"

I climbed over her and returned to the closet. After much pointless clanging of hangers I called out, "You may think you're as broad-minded as anyone in America, but you won't acknowledge Julie's girlfriends, and you think I can't date someone unless he has diplomas framed in his office."

"Does he *have* an office?"

"Probably."

"Did he go to college?"

"It hasn't come up."

After another silence she asked, "Are you attracted to this Ray?"

The only acceptable answer was yes, so I said it: Yes, I was attracted to Ray. Pity had no role here, at least not on my side. He'd been very attentive and gentlemanly. There had been no pressure. Well, maybe he'd asked for a kiss after the round-trip to New Jersey, but that was hardly worth reporting since most people kiss as casually as I might order a pizza. But I'd been thinking things over. Ray was a normal man with healthy needs. Now it was my turn to signal that I was a mature adult, and ahead of me was the hurdle that mature adults have to jump.

She crossed to the closet and wrapped her arms around me. "Nana and I went round and round on this for years. 'Has she or hasn't she? Will she or won't she?' She was sure that somewhere along the line, at some frat party or junior year abroad, you lost your virginity. But not me. I always maintained that, if it had happened, I'd know. And now you've told me, in advance. On one hand, I'm depressed over your choice of partners. On the other hand, I'm thrilled that you're confiding in me now."

I said, "Actually, Nana was right. I had sex once in college; at summer camp, actually."

"With a man?"

I said yes, a counselor at Tattaho.

"Voluntarily?"

"Of course voluntarily. He paddled across the lake in a canoe, and we sat on the dock for a while and reviewed our sexual options, and then we found a spot behind the infirmary and we did it."

"And then what?"

"We discarded the used condom in the dining hall Dumpster, and I went back to my bunk."

"I meant, were you in love? Was this a romance? Was it everything you hoped it would be? Did you keep in touch after camp?"

I said no, none of the above. I hadn't enjoyed it, so I hadn't seen any reason to repeat the experience.

"Till now?"

I stopped what I was doing—stuffing the overflow of dirty clothes into my bulging laundry bag—to wonder aloud, "Have you ever thought about how in every country, no matter how remote, in every culture, every religion, and every climate, people copulate? Since time immemorial, men and women—without classes or manuals, without anatomical diagrams or scented candles—have sought out partners for sex. I find it quite fascinating, and I think if it's so natural to every species, then I shouldn't have dismissed it out of hand."

"I see," said my mother. "So this upcoming date of yours is more or less an anthropology experiment?"

"Is that so terrible? I mean, isn't everything?"

She looked away, plucked another tissue from my bedside box.

"I thought you'd be happy that I was thinking about something that could be categorized as interpersonal," I said.

She didn't answer. Her shoulders sagged; her glance wandered back to the highlighted pages.

I tried to think of a topic that would cheer her up. "My new building has a laundry room," I tried. "And a health club with a juice bar."

"Which means what?" she snapped. "More venues for your research?"

Would I ever do anything right? Intercourse was wrong. Virginity was wrong. Socializing with a man below my station was wrong. I couldn't please my mother; surely couldn't measure up to a dead nonagenarian as confidante and bosom buddy.

I said, "I'm very tired. Maybe we should call it quits for the day."

She raised her head and shook off the burden of my company. "I'm not giving up. Who knows when we'll talk again. I mean *really* talk, like this, meaningfully. I don't have to like every choice you make—Nana certainly didn't when it came to me. Now we'll finish packing like the excellent team that we are, and we'll drive these boxes across the street and toast a new beginning. I brought a bottle of champagne." She smiled brightly. "We'll do a few loads of laundry, and you'll share with me your anxieties about next Saturday night."

I said, "Saturday night?"

"Your date! Your housewarming *à deux!*"

I said, "I'd have to consider that date provisional because I haven't heard from him in several weeks."

She held up her hand in protest. "I refuse to be discouraged. You didn't invite Ray for dinner and sex because he's *Ray*. You invited him because he represents manhood, a physical tool. So if it's simply a matter of joining hands with a partner and jumping over a hurdle—there's plenty of fish in that sea."

I nodded and tried to look amenable. But I noticed that in the face of her eagerness to banish Ray and to substitute another token, I felt a tug of loyalty. Hadn't I promised to contact him when I got my phone? How clear it seemed now: Rapprochement was *my* responsibility, *my* move. I had interpreted his silence as lack of interest. But maybe he was sick and didn't have health insurance; maybe his office never forwarded my card. He could be sitting by the telephone or his wife's headstone, gift-wrapped penuche at the ready, waiting for my call.

Was my mother right? Was I ill-equipped to rescue primitive people from loneliness?

The time had come to find out.

15
Advanced Social Outreach

MY MOTHER HAD brought a tape measure, scissors, and shelf paper, insisting that she'd raised me to line drawers and refresh them with sachets. Since she was willing to do the fitting and cutting, I left her to the task while I swiped surfaces of the already immaculate kitchen. Feathering my nest made her cheerful, as if it symbolized a fresh start and social potential. Soon she moved from lining drawers to inspecting kitchen cabinets, marveling aloud at the remarkable cleanliness of the former tenant. I refrained from mentioning that Dr. Richard A. Gale, whose name was still on my buzzer, whose next of kin had left me his pot holders, refrigerator magnets, spices, and U. of Michigan shower curtain, had died on the premises from a broken heart.

I approached the Murphy bed, probably Exhibit A in the coroner's inquest, fearing that the fumigators had overlooked its hidden planes and squalid sheets. Holding my breath, I pulled the mattress down to horizontal. "How wonderful!" my mother exclaimed at the sight of the brand-new plastic-encased mattress, pale aqua and silver, labeled "extra firm."

"See? I'm all set. A bed, two chairs, two tray tables."

She countered with, "Bookcase, bureau, coffee table, nightstand, vanity, television, stereo . . . I hardly know where to begin."

I led her to the closet and showed her the white wire baskets that slid in and out on tracks. Similarly, built-in bookshelves, designed by a thoughtful architect who knew studious doctors would be the sole tenants. Wouldn't these built-ins do? And I could stick the journals in the linen closet, where my modest supply of sheets and towels left plenty of space.

"If it's the money, I'll buy you what you need. And when I get home I'm going through Nana's apartment and seeing what pieces would fit in here. My God! You don't even have a couch! Or a desk!"

"Can we change the subject?" I asked.

"What was the big impetus to move, especially if it's only across the street? You got along fine with your roommate, didn't you?"

I said yes, I did. Leo had been an excellent roommate, but I wanted my privacy and—even though he was too polite to have asked me to leave—I sensed the timing was right.

"Because of the probation?"

I said yes. The probation. Precisely.

It was a trick question, maternal lie detection. She pounced. "Explain to me why you'd invite more upheaval at the time you were being put under the microscope at work. I'd think you'd need a shoulder to cry on and a set of strong arms to take out the garbage."

She'd met Leo only once, but of course she would have memorized his musculature. I said, "Leo has a new girlfriend."

"So?"

"She was staying over every night."

After a few long seconds of reflection she came up with, "Were they very loud?"

I said, "Loud? Not at all. She slipped in after eleven and I never heard a thing."

Upon further meditation she asked, "Was she paying her share of the rent?"

I said no, of course not. We weren't operating a guest house. Girlfriends and boyfriends stayed free.

"I wonder if I'm hearing the truth," she mused. "I wish there was an electronic readout of your thoughts like the headlines in Times Square."

I might have indulged her by asking, What do you think I'm not telling you? But I couldn't bear another evocation of Nana and her emotional talents. I looked at my watch. It was only three-fifteen. She had promised to spend the day getting me settled, buying dishes, buying bath mats and pillow shams and cute imported baskets, all to get my new home shipshape in a Martha Stewart vision of what a bachelorette's studio could be. I said, "Mom? Do you need to stay any longer? I mean, I'm unpacked. I don't think there's anything left to do."

She answered with a squeal of exasperation. "Why do I bother? Why did I think we'd reward ourselves with a delicious dinner after the work was done? Why do I persist in thinking I'll reach you?"

I said weakly, "You've reached me. Definitely. I think we've covered a lot of ground today and I'm definitely beginning to feel my feet slipping into Nana's shoes."

"Is spending time with me so unpleasant that you couldn't bear another—what time is it anyway?—five or six hours of my company? I pictured we'd shop, stop for a break, have a cappuccino, then come back here, shower, dress for dinner, call a cab, have a wonderful meal and a delicious bottle of wine. Most children would be grateful. Even if they were faking it they'd go along with the plan as a way of thanking said mother for her time and effort. Especially if she'd already made the reservations."

I knew she was right but I couldn't travel the distance between what she was asking and what I could bear. I asked, "If we went out for dinner, would we have to talk about feelings and men and sex?"

"I think it's good for you, the desensitizing, so those subjects won't seem alien and uncomfortable. So soon enough I can ask, 'What's new?' and you'll know what I'm *really* getting at."

I said, "You want me to be more responsive, or nicer, but if you listened to me you'd know I'm too scientific for that. Every minute of the day I'm dealing with life-

and-death matters. My career is on the line. I don't have time for trivial things like which member of the opposite sex has crossed my field of vision or who has slept in my bed."

"I suppose that's true," she murmured. "I suppose we could talk about life and death and war and peace." With visible effort, she reset her features, signaling that another one of life's lessons was bubbling to the surface. "Alice," she began, "when one is engaged in conversation with people, one can't be blunt unless that person specifically asks for bluntness. You have to be diplomatic. If your mother is visiting and you've had enough, you could say that you felt as if you were coming down with something. Or that you had made other plans—as much as you'd love nothing more than dinner out—so could you take a rain check."

I said, "I don't lie."

"I'm not asking you to lie. I'm teaching you about *white* lies. Which is what you say when you don't want people's feelings to be hurt."

I told her I understood what she was saying: Do unto others, et cetera. But I wasn't proficient at censoring the blunt sentences that my brain transmitted to my mouth.

"Is there anyone besides me you can practice with?" she asked. "Because I'm not letting myself get aggravated. I'm giving you your space. I'm going to find a hotel room and spend the night and walk the Freedom Trail in the morning without letting this exchange ruin my Boston holiday. I'm also going to forget that you asked me to leave the way you'd hang up on a telemarketer."

I said, "You don't have to worry. I practice diplomacy all the time with patients. A doctor can't just walk into the hospital room and say, 'Looks bad. Couldn't be worse. Do you have your affairs in order?' The one time I did that, the family asked that I be taken off the case."

"That's a relief," said my mother. "That shows you have a feedback mechanism. But I'm worried about this"—she swept the room with an outstretched arm—"your living alone. Not even a roommate with whom you can practice your social skills."

I said I was well on my way to improving my skills. Leo, who was renowned for his empathy, had provided a very good foundation.

"Was?" she repeated. "Past tense? Can't you still be friends?"

I said, "Yes, certainly. Leo and I intend to meet for lunch in the cafeteria just as we always did, and he'll help me improve my personality."

It felt dishonest and artificial to let the suggestion stand that Leo and I would carry on as friends, or even that interns got a lunch hour, but wasn't that the whole point of a white lie? To make the listener comfortable at the expense of truth?

IT SEEMED ODD to be entering the cafeteria in blue jeans and a pullover without a white coat and without a figurative stopwatch ticking in my head. Sunday nights were brightly lit and bustling here; fewer house staff but more visitors. The salad bar was at its weekend best, which meant Parker House rolls instead of commercial sliced white, and mint jelly in paper

152

thimbles at no extra charge.

In an act of extreme social outreach I placed my clam chowder and American chop suey at the opposite end of a long table where a person, a male doctor of near-retirement age, was already seated. I knew this was a collegial thing to do; doctors slid their trays onto tables without being invited and introduced themselves with ease. Perhaps at some point in my professional future this tablemate might nod pleasantly when his subspecialty intersected with mine. He was holding a paper napkin to his tie as he ate the other featured soup, Scotch broth. "How are you this evening?" he asked.

"Not great," I answered.

His smile froze. "Is someone sick? A family member?"

I said, "No, sorry. I'm not a visitor. I work here."

"House staff?" he asked.

"Intern, surgery."

"My condolences," he said. He nodded at the chair next to him. "Why don't you slide down here so I don't have to shout."

As I approached, he rose, offered his right hand for me to shake, murmured a few syllables that must have been his name, then said, "Would you care to tell me why you're not great?"

"I did something apparently unforgivable in the OR, and now I'm on probation for two months."

He returned to his soup, spreading a new paper napkin against his tie. "You must be the intern who fell asleep holding the retractor," he said calmly. "I *did* hear about that."

"From Dr. Hastings?"

He said, "I don't remember from whom."

"I'm a scandal," I said, "but of the most boring and occupational kind."

He picked up his spoon, hesitated over the soup, put the utensil down again. "Would you mind a little advice from a veteran of many medical skirmishes, not to mention blunders?"

I said, "Quit? Switch to something more humane? Do research? Join the army? Do physicals for an insurance company?"

"No, it's only this: Put this mistake behind you. If you dwell on it and rage against Dr. Hastings, it's only going to keep it alive and gnawing at your insides."

I said, "This was war. He started it, and it's not up to me to call a truce. If it were criminal to harass and degrade another human being, he'd be in jail."

He said quietly, "I like an outspoken dinner companion, but one should be careful talking about a colleague in a public space."

"Are you his friend?" I asked.

"We all know Charlie Hastings. *Friend?* I wouldn't go that far."

"I have nothing to lose. He hates me. He tried to get me fired. He didn't, but I'm on probation and will probably make a horrible mistake tomorrow, and that'll be the end of me."

He smiled. "Would you care to tell me your name?"

I asked why.

"Not for any nefarious purpose. Just good manners."

Sprinkling oyster crackers onto my chowder, I said,

"I'm the hopeless Alice Thrift."

"Pleased to meet you, Dr. Thrift."

I asked what kind of a doctor he was. "I started out in surgery," he said.

"And what are you now?"

"Still, after all these years, after all the headlines about our shrinking numbers and our malpractice muddles—OB."

I said, "I've always found it a little peculiar when men choose OB. Of course I was delivered by a male obstetrician, but now, today, it seems odd that a man would devote himself to anatomical parts he didn't possess without any hope of ever experiencing any of the sensations associated with them."

He didn't answer right away. After a few resolute bites of his chef's salad, he said, "I chose OB because, for the most part, it's a joyous field. Ninety-seven percent of the time the outcome is a healthy baby and a happy family. Women come to me to deliver their babies because I'm good at it, because I know my stuff even if I don't possess a uterus or a cervix, and I stick around no matter how long it takes their babies to be born. I should note that in some fields—mine, for instance—being there, i.e., compassion, is just as important as skill."

I said, "Well, I seem to have neither."

He said, "I can't speak to your surgical skills, but I'd probably agree that your small talk could use some . . . thawing."

I said, "Believe me, I know that all too well. My mother thinks I have Asperger's Syndrome. Maybe I should switch to pathology, where the cadavers don't care about small talk."

He said, "I know you meant that as a joke, but pathology is a very rewarding field. Path reports are the backbone of what I do."

I asked if he knew Meredith—what was her last name?—the midwife? He smiled what I took to be a faint, ironic smile and said, "Of course. Everyone knows Meredith. A force to be reckoned with."

"She's my former roommate's girlfriend," I told him. "Do you know Leo Frawley? He was my roommate until today."

He stirred his soup slowly, in circles around the rim. "And what happened today?"

"I moved."

"Suddenly?"

"An apartment came up"—I gestured in the direction of the towers—"so I grabbed it."

"Lucky. Most of my residents recount tales of the legendary waiting list."

"It's only a studio," I said. "Most people want at least a one-bedroom. Besides—this one is stigmatized. Its former tenant died there and wasn't found for a while."

"Who?" he asked sharply.

I said his name was Richard Gale, but that's all I knew.

"Not one of mine, thank God. But still, horrible news . . . tragic . . . such a waste."

I asked him to repeat his name.

"Henry Shaw. Please call me Henry."

"Really?"

"There was a time when I could convince residents to

call me by my first name, but I've practically given up trying." He patted his bald head. "Apparently I'm too distinguished to be called anything but 'Doctor.'"

I said, "I'd like to call you Henry." I picked up my fork and started on my American chop suey, which was actually baked and crispy and unusually delicious. "Moving must have given me an appetite," I said.

"And you couldn't plan your move on a day off?"

I said, "It *is* my day off."

When Dr. Shaw didn't say anything, I pushed on. "The easiest thing was to run over here for a bite, no coat, no boots. Convenience won over the institutional food and that smell"—I sniffed the air—"instant mashed potatoes and giblet gravy." I forced a smile. "And look what pleasant company I found on a Sunday night. . . . Are you attending a birth?"

He smiled. "All done."

"A girl or a boy?"

"Boy."

"Long labor?"

"Not too bad." He shrugged modestly; very long, in other words.

I asked why he was still here.

"Just want to make sure everything's okay. There was a little excitement with the umbilical cord, but he's fine. More trauma for the dad than anyone else, watching it through the camcorder. I'm just going to swing by the nursery for a look-see." He frowned at his beeper readout. "And another on the way. Early. Thirty-five weeks."

I said, "You seem so . . . unfrazzled at the prospect of

another delivery and being up all night."

"Sometimes I get frazzled," he said, "but I keep it to myself. I've seen too many doctors snap at everyone around them, conduct I find most unbecoming. If you can't control your temper and you explode under pressure, then you should find another line of work."

I didn't want his dinner break to be over. Maybe I should switch to OB so I could sit at the knee of Dr. Henry Shaw and let my frazzlement melt away, dissolved by the tears of ecstatic and grateful patients. I asked how often he did C-sections, and did he like surgery?

He said, "I actually do like surgery. Not the emergencies, not when we're racing against the clock. But for the most part, there's the pot of gold at the end of my particular surgical arc."

I must have looked blank because he added, "The baby!"

I said, "Sorry. I was having a little reverie of me holding a retractor while you were dissecting down to the uterus, and my staying awake because a baby is more exciting than a gallbladder."

"You had your difficulties during a cholecystectomy?"

I said, "The retractor hit the surgeon's hand—"

"St. Louis, Missouri, Barnes Hospital, 1964, the first month of my first year. I fell asleep for a second during a hysterectomy and, *bang,* retractor hit scalpel."

"And what happened?"

"Luckily, nothing. No veins or nerves were damaged—only my pride."

"Did the attending cause a huge scene?"

"I don't remember one. He asked rather quietly if I'd like to let someone else take over. I slunk away and got drunk, which doesn't help my recall."

I whispered, "Dr. Hastings threw his scalpel at me. I don't think he was actually aiming at my head, but I didn't know that when he launched it. He could have blinded me or nicked my external jugular."

"Prima donna behavior," he grumbled. "Ego on parade."

I said, "I'm not saying it wasn't a major goof-up on my part, but it wasn't ignorance or incompetence. I mean, I fell asleep. I couldn't help it."

"The hours are insane," said Dr. Shaw, "but no one listens to me. The fraternity of surgeons likes to perpetuate its hazing rituals."

I liked that very much—"hazing rituals." Leo hadn't thought of that particular characterization when arming me with my closing arguments.

Dr. Shaw looked at his watch. "As much as I'd like to get one of those whoopee pies I resisted in line, and continue our conversation, I have to check on my moms."

I said, "Hope all goes well tonight."

He touched my wrist. "Tell me your name again."

"Alice Thrift."

"Good luck to you, Dr. Thrift. Don't let the bastards get you down." He picked up his orange tray, walked a few yards away, then returned. "If I may, one more little piece of unsolicited advice: The night is young, so don't go straight home to bed. That's the temptation—believe me, I remember—but you can sleep when you're old like me. Dig out that winter coat. Find some fresh air beyond the tunnel and the hospital."

"You mean, get some exercise?"

"That, sure. But I guess I meant, go find some young people, especially ones who don't work here. Go talk about what's happening in the wider world and try not to think about this one."

Was such a stable and paternal fellow directing me to a bar or a club or a sports arena? I asked for suggestions.

"Call a friend," he said. "Or jump on the subway. Take it over to Harvard Square. Walk around. Follow the music into a coffeehouse—do they still have coffeehouses? Check the listings in the *Globe*. There's always a lecture you can slip into or a party you can crash."

How could I tell him that crashing a party was as appealing to me as parasailing or bungee jumping. He meant well, which I couldn't say about many of my self-appointed guidance counselors. And it was so nice to see concern rather than impatience or distaste on an adviser's face.

I said, "I'll try. I could take a nap first, then go out. I have a friend I've been meaning to call. I'll do that right now. Thanks."

"I want a report," said Henry. "And don't let me hear that you hit the snooze button and slept straight through till six A.M."

He wanted to hear from me; my new friend Henry wanted a report. I said, "I promise it'll have substance and content. I promise I'll call my friend."

"Good. Go out. Have fun. Have lots of fun. Something tells me it's overdue."

I smiled and said, "I may have to sugarcoat this report. I mean, the night is young. Who knows what kind of mischief I could make?"

Henry said, "That's very considerate of you, Alice. I have three daughters who never educated me. I can only tolerate the whitewashed version. So, yes, thank you. You're very kind."

We both knew he was humoring me—that a man who brought forth babies had a high threshold for the facts of life. I considered running after him to enfold him in a hug, but I wasn't sure about the professional ethics of such an act. Instead I waved fondly. I bought a whoopee pie and headed home.

16
Slow-Normal

BECAUSE I'D PROMISED at least two members of the Alice Thrift Improvement Committee that I would reinvent myself, I felt obliged to find a telephone. The Boston directory listed no Ray or Raymond or R. Russo in Brighton, nor did any actual human telephone operator leap to my aid. After straining to remember the names of his cousins from my party, I came up with George, who was both listed and at home.

"He's got a private number," George said, dropping his voice to a whisper.

I assured him that I wouldn't disseminate it to any unauthorized persons.

"Can't. Once I gave it out and Ray got really pissed, so let me call his cell and either him or me will get back to you."

I told him I was calling from a pay phone in the lobby of my building because I'd neglected to order one of my own—in fact, I didn't realize that was the custom when one relocated.

"Number?" he repeated.

I dictated the ten digits from the dial and told him I'd wait for—what was his estimate of a realistic response time? Five minutes? Ten?

"Stay put," said George. "I think Ray will want to talk to you even if he can't get out tonight."

I didn't question that. Everyone I knew had obligations and occupations that restricted their social ventures.

"Give me the address, just in case."

By now I wished I hadn't involved a third party. Ray's not responding to my note was an eloquent answer. George would feel obliged to pass on a humiliating "Can't you take a hint?"

I said, "This is getting complicated. Just tell Ray that if he wants to talk to me, call now, and if he doesn't want to talk to me, I'll understand."

George had nothing encouraging to say and apparently no freedom in which to say it. "Stay in the booth and pretend you're fishin' around for quarters so nobody else cuts in," he advised. "We don't want Ray getting no busy signal."

Booth? There were no booths in this day and age. Or persons in need of a public phone. I sat down on the craggy carpet and waited.

A UNIFORMED GUARD was shaking my right shoulder and asking me to vacate the premises. I explained that I was the new tenant in 11G and was merely resting while waiting for a call.

"One second you're on the phone, next second, you're in a heap. Like, I wasn't sure if I had a situation on my hands." This guard looked as if he were still in high school and as if he'd borrowed both his shirt and his cap from an older brother. "All you docs are alike," he said. "Some go up in the elevator and it comes back down. I find them sleeping standing up. Pretty creepy. I wake them up and we try again."

"Did I miss any calls?" I asked.

He said not that he knew of, but he'd been over there, at the desk. Which he'd better get back to now that I wasn't comatose or homeless. Could he help me to the elevator?

I didn't have to answer because at that moment Ray Russo walked through the front door holding a big plastic bag declaring NOBODY BEATS THE WIZ.

"Sir?" said the guard, hurrying back to his post.

"I'm here to see Dr. Thrift," said Ray, and, with a wink, cocked his index finger at me.

"Right behind you—the lady on the floor."

Ray raised the bag to eye level. "Hey, Doc. A house-warming present! Two-point-four gigahertz. Caller ID, call-waiting ID. I can return it if you don't like the color."

How was such a thing possible? That George reached

Ray, that Ray found a store open on a Sunday night, bought me a phone, and drove to an address I'd never supplied?

He scrawled a celebrity squiggle on the sign-in clipboard, breezed past the desk, pulled me to my feet, then kissed the hand I'd extended.

"Aren't stores closed on Sunday nights?" I asked.

"The phone, you mean? I've been driving around with it for a coupla days—since I got your card—and out of the blue George calls and announces, 'Doc called from the lobby of her new building.' And you know where I was? Crossing the BU bridge. I swear to God. On a Sunday night, I'm here in eight minutes." He turned back to the guard. "I parked out front—"

"Sorry. For deliveries only. Gotta move it. You want the hospital garage: a left and another left."

I sensed that some wink or signal or body English must have passed between them because the guard announced, "In that case, as long as you're gone by midnight."

"Well?" said Ray, grinning broadly, wrapping an arm around my shoulder. "Shall we?"

I led him toward the elevator, conscious that my navy-blue cotton sweater had assumed the shape and color of a faded sweatshirt. My sneakers were ancient red Keds, purchased for freshman phys ed, and my jeans had been fished out of my laundry bag. I had expected some time to prepare myself for a male visitor, and had no idea how one disappears and performs discreet ablutions in a studio apartment with company present. In the elevator, Ray peered into my face, then rubbed his knuckles diagnostically against one cheekbone.

I asked what he was doing.

"Your skin has a pattern on it, like you were sleeping on a burlap bag."

After exploring the indentations myself, I explained that I'd fallen asleep on the carpet waiting for George to call back.

"Good detective work. Good memory, too. And lucky that Georgie's a cousin on my father's side."

I asked why it was necessary for him to have an unlisted number.

"Customers," he said. "I learned this pretty quick, that when you're dealing with chocolate and all that entails—gift emergencies, cravings, blue laws—people call whenever the mood strikes like it's their God-given right to order fudge at two A.M. It's not enough to leave a message on my voice mail. They have to call my home number. Like they're desperate. Like it was life or death." He smiled. "No more going through Georgie for you! You're getting my cell-phone number." He opened the bag so I could peer into it. Inside was an unwrapped box depicting an animated woman speaking into a crimson phone. Not only would I be able to talk to friends for four-point-five hours without recharging but I could store fifty of their names.

THE TOUR TOOK thirty seconds and inspired no compliments.

"Now what?" Ray asked.

I produced my two folding chairs from the closet as well as the champagne my mother had left in my narrow refrigerator.

"I didn't think I was ever going to hear from you again," he said after swirling and examining the contents of his paper cup.

I devoted myself to stuffing frayed threads back into a hole in the toe of my left sneaker.

Ray tapped my knee. "Could I have a little eye contact here?" He moved his chair so that we were facing each other. "Words," he ordered. "Say anything. Start with 'I' and add—whaddyacallit—an action word."

"A verb?"

"Yeah. A verb and then maybe another whole set. Something that explains what's up."

"You mean . . . ?"

"Not calling, then writing, then moving, then calling."

"I decided I'd like some company," I managed.

"Really? Was I at the top of this company list? Second, third, bottom?"

"First."

"In other words, the move was a mistake. You had a roommate and now you don't, and you felt lonely so you went through your address book and came up with old Ray."

I said, "It's not very scientific to declare something a failure on the basis of one day, is it?"

"I don't operate on the basis of scientific. Here's what I know about a new place: You open the door and you think, Ahhh, the moment I was waiting for. Space. Freedom. Privacy. Or you walk in and say, Shit. Now what do I do?"

The truth was that his presence, this invitation, could be traced directly to my mother and to my foolhardy confession involving a contemplated dip into carnal waters. But now that Ray was here, seated in a manner that a family counselor might have employed for a truth-telling exercise, I was conversationally impotent. Any leanings and sensations I'd experienced when alone now seemed impossible to summon.

"Well," I began, "one impetus was a nice fatherly man, an obstetrician I had dinner with in the cafeteria, who advised me to get out of the house."

Ray's eyes narrowed. "Was he asking you out?"

"Absolutely not. He was trying to diagnose my social failings, and was taking me under his wing."

Ray smiled. "Like me. I took you under my wing, didn't I? I guess you like that."

I told him this Dr. Shaw had recommended an outing to Harvard Square—

"First, forget finding a parking space, and second, what do you think you're going to see on a Sunday night in February besides Harvard students lined up at an ATM?"

"I was thinking music or a lecture, or going to a coffeehouse."

"There are closer places than Harvard Square to get coffee," said Ray.

"It's not the beverage. It's the getting out and the not falling asleep after supper."

"Nothing wrong with sleep if you need it."

"Except," I pointed out, "the paradox of sleep: You wait and hope for it all day long, look forward to it, crave

167

it, and then that time actually arrives, and your head hits the pillow. It's sheer bliss, and you close your eyes and then, *snap,* it's morning and you have to face the exact thing you were trying to escape from."

"Not me," he said. "I make my own hours."

That reminded me to inquire about what he did in the off-season—such as now.

"There's still orders to fill—people who buy fudge at the fairs who come back for more—and I call on small grocers and specialty shops."

"What about warm climates? There must be fairs somewhere in the country all year round."

"Think about that. Can I travel in warm climates with a couple hundred boxes of fudge in my car? No way. I'd need a refrigerated van at the very least."

"Is that out of the question?"

He grinned. "Trying to get rid of me?"

I said, "I called you. In fact, I went to the trouble of tracking you down through a third party, which is hardly an act of avoidance."

With one eye closed as if it were a matter of great delicacy, Ray asked, "Do you know other people besides me who you'd classify as friends?"

I began my inventory—Claire, who was my college roommate sophomore year; Laura, one of my lab partners in Gross Anatomy; and of course my sister, Julie, who would have to have an asterisk next to her name because she lived in Seattle—

Ray was shaking his head, vetoing every name. He took me by the hand in crossing-guard fashion. "C'mon," he said. "We're fixing this."

I tried to resist; tried to get some traction on my carpet but my soles were worn smooth. Then he was opening the door, and I was following, indulging an element of something—intellectual curiosity or childish hope—as if Ray knew something I didn't know; as if there were a cure for me at the end of the hall or behind a curtain: a friend from my past or a new job or the winning ticket—life repair as practiced on television talk shows.

But he'd led me only one door away, and he was ringing its bell. A man appeared, holding a copy of *The New England Journal of Medicine*, wearing a look I knew—sullen and superior.

"Is the lady of the house in?" Ray asked.

"There is no lady of the house," said the man, and closed the door—not a slam, but all the incivility I needed to lose my microscopic spirit of adventure.

"C'mon," said Ray. "Don't be discouraged. There's bound to be a friendly face on this floor."

I said, "Is that what you're doing? Canvassing door to door until you find me a friend?"

"I'm not gonna put it that way, believe me."

With me making myself small in my own doorway, he knocked on the door directly across the hall. A woman's voice called out, "Who is it?" and Ray answered, "Your new neighbor."

"Which new neighbor?"

"Across the hall."

The voice said, "Sorry! My new neighbor is a woman. Nice try, bud. I'm calling security."

Ray pointed at me, then at the door, calmly, almost wearily, as if he were a veteran of talking women out of summoning the police.

I stepped closer and addressed the painted aluminum. "Um. Hello? I'm your new neighbor in eleven-G. That was my friend, who thinks he's doing me a favor by dragging me around to apartments in order to meet people. Sorry."

"What's your name?"

"Alice Thrift."

There was a thunk of a dead bolt, and the door opened. My new neighbor was smiling cynically. Her hair was spiky, the ends the color of Cheddar cheese and the roots dark in a fashion I knew was deliberate. Many small hoops decorated both earlobes. She extended her right hand for a hearty shake. "Sylvie Schwartz," she said. "Excuse the paranoia."

Ray waved. "I'm the go-between, Ray Russo. Nice to meet you, Sylvie. You live alone?"

"I should hope so," said Sylvie. "I mean, six hundred square feet?"

"Same as hers? Studio with kitchenette?"

"That's the rumor. I can't say I've ever been inside the infamous eleven-G."

I asked if she had known Dr. Gale, my predecessor.

"I know his wife." She pointed down the hall. "She took up with the guy in eleven-C and moved in with him. No one, including the wife, had a clue he was so devastated."

"Am I missing something here?" asked Ray.

"The previous occupant committed suicide," I said.

"It was all so amazingly civilized until it became apparent that something horrible had happened in there," said Sylvie. We nodded, a private and somber signal between medical professionals verifying *decomposition*.

"Those civilized guys are the ones you have to watch out for," said Ray. "They're bombs waiting to detonate."

Sylvie said she'd invite us in for a drink but her place was a mess and she was going to hit the hay in about ten seconds.

"You, too, huh?" said Ray, grinning. "Same line of work?"

"More or less. We're all house staff in this building. I'm in medicine," said Sylvie. "Third year."

"Intern," I said. "Surgery."

"Hideous," said Sylvie. "How'd you happen to get five minutes off tonight?"

"It's not all that bad," I said. "I mean, it works out to about—"

"Do you have a boyfriend?" Ray asked Sylvie.

"No, I do not," Sylvie said. "But I think whatever the subtext of your question is, Ray, I'll be a very nice neighbor who can lend Alice a cup of sugar with the best of them."

"Hey, no offense," said Ray.

"Knock on my door anytime you're ordering take-out," she said to me. "I'm always happy to share a couple of dishes rather than eat one Kung Pao chicken by myself."

"Me, too," I said.

"Okay, then: Welcome to the biosphere. Thanks for making the overture."

The grouchy man opened his door, a new journal in

hand, and barked, "Would you folks mind taking your conversation inside?"

"We're winding this up," said Sylvie, "so we won't be disturbing you any longer, Anthony. Sir."

"Who does he think he is?" I muttered when the stranger had retreated.

"Chief resident, clinical pathology," Sylvie whispered. "And chief wet blanket on eleven-north, if not the entire hospital campus."

I uttered a silent prayer to the gods of personality: Please don't let me usurp Anthony's title.

"WE NEED ANOTHER scouting trip," Ray said when my door was closed behind us.

"For what?"

"Finding you a friend." He cocked his head toward the hallway. "This one's too aggressive. If she took you under her wing, she'd break a couple of ribs in the process."

"But I liked her. Not only does she get what my life is like, but she lives alone and likes Chinese food."

"I'm not saying you have to drop her like a hot potato. I'm just saying our work isn't done."

I said, "Please, no more door-to-door solicitations."

"Do you mean tonight, or not ever?"

I said, for the sake of diplomacy, "Tonight. Next time I talk to you, I'll give you a head count of how many new girlfriends I've acquired."

"Next time?" Ray repeated. "Are you calling it a night? Because according to my body clock, this is when the fun begins. We can go to Harvard Square if that's

172

what you want to do. I know a couple of bars over there frequented by professor types."

I knew I was breaking my promise to Dr. Shaw vis-à-vis sleeping versus living, but didn't I have an obligation to my patients and my career to stave off sleep deprivation and its resultant catastrophes? I informed Ray that a fatigued brain functions the same as an inebriated one. "Do you mind very much?" I asked in what I hoped was a benevolent manner.

"Actually, I do. I've got a parking space until midnight, so I'll stick around. You can get into bed if you want to. I can watch TV."

"I don't have a TV."

"Then I'll find something to occupy me. Anything need fixing around here?"

I said the management had been too self-conscious about the previous tenant to leave one single thing unfixed.

"Do you have a bathtub?" Ray asked.

I said I did. Why?

"Because one of my vices is long soaks in a steamy bathtub. I only have a fiberglass shower at my place, so I try to sneak baths in whenever I see porcelain."

"No," I said. "Sorry."

"Doc, let's just say that you had a washer and dryer and I didn't. Would you consider it inappropriate if I brought over a load of laundry?"

I said, "I think you know the difference."

"I know what you're getting at but you're taking a big leap. This is me soaking in your tub, as advertised, period. This is not me using a bath as an excuse to undress inside your apartment and then oh-so-casually appearing with a hand towel covering my privates and my butt hanging out the back."

I said, "I'm not squeamish about that. I see naked men every minute of the day. It's a question of routine. I take my shower at bedtime, and I'm not used to having company while I bathe."

He looked around. "I could make up the bed for you while you're in the shower. You can go directly from bath to bed. Fall into it. Ahhh, picture that: no fuss, no heavy lifting. Like a chambermaid had slipped in."

"Maybe some other time."

"You had a guy for a roommate, like, twenty-four hours ago. How was that different? Is it that I strike you as the kind of lowlife who'd spy on you through the key-hole?"

I said, "Not only is there no keyhole, but that kind of behavior wouldn't have occurred to me in a million years."

"Me, neither," said Ray.

To apologize for impugning his motives, I relented. I told him I was trusting him to be a perfect gentleman and not let history repeat itself.

"And what history would you be referring to?"

I said, "I'm sorry to bring up your late wife, but I can't help remembering that the first night you showed up at her door, you ended up having intercourse."

"That was Mary," he said. "You're you. We're talking about a different species of human animal here."

I said, "But really. How well do I know you? Am I let-ting a sex offender take a bath in my new apartment?"

Ray said, "No, you are not. And thanks for reminding me." He took the phone from its box, plugged a wire into the base and another into the wall. He picked up the receiver, listened, frowned.

I confessed that I hadn't called the phone company yet, but would do so ASAP.

"No matter. You've got two neighbors as eyewitnesses. They could finger me so fast that I'd be picked up before I crossed Park Drive."

"That's reassuring," I said.

He smiled. "Sheets and blankets anywhere I might find them?"

I pointed to the linen closet.

Armed with a towel and my one intact pair of pajamas—a gift from my sister, who judged puppies and dog biscuits to be a proper motif for flannel—I slipped into the bathroom and locked its door. Soap? Leo had always attended to the purchase of soap. A search under the sink rendered five bars of sandalwood soap and an unopened four-pack of toilet paper. Poor Dr. Gale, buying in bulk in happier times.

I showered quickly; wet my hair, washed it with soap due to an absence of shampoo. Five minutes later, my teeth were brushed and my pajamas were covering every inch of my skin from larynx to ankle.

Ray was slipping my pillow into a pillowcase in expert fashion. "Snazzy pj's," he said after a glance over his shoulder.

"They were a gift."

"A joke gift?"

I said I didn't think so. They were from my sister, a

sincere dog lover.

He plumped my pillow and centered it mathematically against the headboard.

I said, "No shampoo but there's soap. Did you find a towel?"

"I found *the* towel."

He took a few steps toward the bathroom but came back. "Doc? Do you think you'd manage your life any better if you didn't work a hundred hours a week? I mean, if you were a schoolteacher or a secretary, do you think you'd have towels and shampoo and more than one set of sheets?"

I said, "I honestly don't know."

"What about before this? Like in medical school? Did you live without furniture and food and small appliances?"

I said I did, but those things just seemed to appear without me.

"You must've had a pretty good-natured roommate. You probably used her stuff and she didn't mind because you were paying for half of it anyway."

I said I thought that was correct. I'd had two medical-school roommates, so the shelf in the shower held multiple bottles of hair products. Leo and I had had that arrangement, too.

"What about when you're done? I mean, finished being a resident. Do you think you'll be able to function?"

"I function. I may not have every single personal-grooming product I might need, but who does on the first day in a new apartment?"

"You're right," said Ray. "It's just that your place feels kind of bare-bones, which would be pretty god-damn depressing if I thought it was going to be permanent."

I said, "I'm going to buy a magnet to hold a shopping list. Leo had one on our refrigerator." I pointed to the bathroom. "Water's running and I don't want any floods. I'm going to sleep."

Ray leaned toward me. It wasn't what I expected from someone raised on the mean streets, who'd been married explosively to a brazen woman half his age. The kiss, when it landed, was soft, careful, and brief.

DESPITE MY INITIAL wariness and the astringent new-mattress smell, I fell asleep immediately. It might have been minutes or an hour when a sound woke me—my name combined with a moan. "Doc?" I heard, with a follow-up, louder, "Alice?"

I had to orient myself: Home? Hospital? Pager? Person? *Ray,* I remembered. Bathtub. I turned on my bedside sconce and followed the noise to the bathroom. "Ray?" I said. "Are you all right?"

"Doc," he said. "I think I fainted. I think something's wrong."

"What happened?"

"I don't know. I soaked for a good long time, then I sat on the toilet and I got dizzy."

I had no choice. I said, "I'll get my sphygmomanometer. Maybe you have low blood pressure and the combination of that and the heat—"

"You don't think I had a stroke or anything?"

I said, "No, I don't. Hold on. I'll get my bag."

"The door's open," he said in a voice weak enough to frighten me.

I returned in seconds and opened the door. He was standing up and he was naked. He had a hairy body, mottled, overheated skin, a tattoo, a penis. "I never fainted in my life," he said, "and I'm talking, like, a thousand baths that were at least this hot."

I threw his towel in the general direction of his pelvis, and took his wrist.

"You can do that without a watch?" he asked.

I shushed him, and after fifteen seconds pronounced his pulse slow-normal.

"What do I do now?" Ray asked.

"You'll sit down somewhere and I'll take your blood pressure."

He took my arm and walked slowly. I said, "You could have concussed falling out of the tub, or worse. Bathroom accidents are the number-one cause of home injuries."

"I must have crumpled into a nice neat pile or else I'd have split my head open."

I opened my deluxe black alligator bag, my parents' graduation present, unreturnable because of the monogram. I wrapped the cuff around his bicep and its tattoo—a crown that was either a religious icon or a beer logo. After two careful readings I announced, "Ninety over sixty. Fainting can happen even when the systolic is at seventy."

"I don't care what they say at that hospital of yours," said Ray. "You're *good*."

"How hot was the water?"

"As hot as I can stand it. Not a good idea, huh?"

"There's another possibility," I said. "Unrelated to the bath."

"What's that?"

I hesitated before saying, "Straining at stool."

"Guilty as charged," he said happily. His towel had slipped into loincloth position. "Want to take it one more time, Doc? Make sure it's not going to happen again?"

I agreed because it was putting me in my most professional light at the same moment that—despite a possible vasovagal and my head-to-toe flannel pajamas—his penis was asserting itself against the terry cloth. Still, I have to give Ray credit for propriety. He seemed genuinely embarrassed. He gestured downward in case I hadn't noticed. "Sorry, Doc."

Apparently my silent shrug looked like ignorance, prompting clarification.

"My boner? I assumed you noticed. Sorry. I promised I wouldn't disturb you, and then this stupid thing has to happen."

"As long as you didn't hurt yourself when you fell off the toilet—that's all I'm concerned about." And because I didn't want him to think I was an inobservant clinician, I added, "I did notice your erection, but I wasn't fazed. The human body has a mind of its own, so there's no need to apologize. And it's nice to have confirmation that a vasovagal faint can be followed by a compensatory rise in the systolic pressure."

"You think so?"

I thought no such thing. I was only employing words

that distanced me from the ongoing situation in Ray's nearby lap.

"Doc? I'm not getting fresh, but I think you should give yourself a little credit here. Honest. Sometimes when this happens . . . it has a personal meaning."

I looked down, at him, at my own properties. I wondered if my bare feet or the smell of perfumed soap had betrayed me. I murmured something medical, something about the male sexual response, about contextual misinterpretation.

"He's the judge of that," said Ray. "Maybe he's saying that you here, in your pajamas, on your bed . . . well, we have ourselves a context."

I look back and see that moment as a crossroads. I can imagine freezing the scene, wherein I might have pronounced him cured and dischargeable. "You're fine," I might have said briskly. "Your pulse and blood pressure are normal. Everyone faints once in a lifetime and this is nothing to worry about. Good night and good luck."

Have I mentioned that I've seen a lot of genitalia in my professional life, belonging to men of all ages in hospital beds with nothing between me and them but the occasional threadbare johnny? And, empirically speaking, not all penises are created equal?

So at this juncture at which I might have stopped, considered the consequences and complications of responding in kind, I didn't show Ray the door. I, Alice Thrift, allowed one and eventually both of Ray's hands to roam unchecked over my pajama top. Further, I accepted those caresses and participated—willingly if not obligingly—in the fits and starts and flannel-free gratifications that inevitably ensued.

17
Venues Not Available to Me

I'D READ ABOUT orgasms, of course, but had been skeptical about whether their notoriety was deserved, and whether I'd ever be among the subscribers. Manifestation, in my case, was a surprise: One second I was noting pleasant physical sensations, and the next I was not myself. In other words, on my first night in the north tower, I emitted sounds that may have alarmed or annoyed my new neighbors.

"Was that what I think it was?" Ray asked after my symptoms had decrescendoed and his own had subsided.

I nodded and said only "My goodness" until I caught my breath.

"Look at you," he said. "All red and sweaty and grinning from ear to ear."

I said, "I doubt whether that's completely accurate."

"Well, I'll say it: Wow. One minute I'm in a heap on your bathroom floor, and the next thing I know . . ." He gesticulated—arms waving, legs seizing, hands flapping.

"What?" I asked. "Next thing you know, *what?*"

He turned serious, exceedingly so, and touched my face with his knuckles. "What happened here. You, me, us. My cock, your snatch, the bombs bursting in air. . . . Do I have to spell it out?"

I said no. I'd been to countless lectures on human sexual response. I reached for the blood pressure cuff and stethoscope and motioned for his upper arm. After the proper interval I announced, "One-ten over seventy. Perfect. You should have no fears about operating a motor vehicle."

"Who's operating a motor vehicle?"

I reminded him about the midnight parking deadline and my own personal sleep requirements, already breached.

"I know this by heart," said Ray. "You're exhausted. You tell me this every time I see you. But we're past that now. Something really important happened here tonight. Maybe I'm a little old-fashioned, but I don't take sex lightly."

Which reminded me of Mary Ciccarelli and sex at its most casual, less than an hour into her acquaintance with Ray. I said, "There's no need to inflate this and attach sentiments to it, because I'm perfectly comfortable with recreational relations."

"I bet," said Ray.

I tucked the frayed quilt up to my armpits and secured it before I asked, "Ray? I want to ask you a question and I want you to be honest: Did you actually faint, or was that a ruse?"

"Ruse? Like I was faking it? I swear to God, Doc. I sat on the toilet and next thing I know I'm on my ass on the floor. I didn't know where I was at first, and then I remembered, so I called your name. Maybe it was God's way of putting us on the same page."

I asked what that meant—"putting us on the same page."

"Getting us together. Getting you to see me as something other than a guy who tries too hard and keeps turning up like a bad penny. What I'm saying is, maybe God maneuvered me into a medical emergency without any clothes on in order to get me on your radar screen."

I asked if he really thought God concerned himself with the social lives of people like us, given the billions of diseased and dying in his purview.

"Good point," said Ray. "I guess it was just a figure of speech. I come from a religious family where God was thanked for every good thing that happened, no matter how dinky."

I said politely, "I understand that perspective," and I truly did, thanks to Leo, who had explained after dinner at his house that my scientific, irreligious, textbook views of life and death sounded like heresy to his mother, whose belief system could be summarized as "He's got the whole world in His hands."

"Do you believe in God?" Ray asked.

I said, "I believe in science. So one could advance the argument that belief in science is tantamount to a belief in order, and there could be a larger force in the universe that is the architect of that order."

"I like calling it fate," said Ray. "I like thinking about how I won a teeth-bleaching, which got me looking in the mirror, which made me walk into plastic surgery and there you were. Then a couple of months go by and I faint and who comes running when I call for help?" He grinned and gestured as if I were waiting in the wings for my cue. "The very same Dr. T.!"

"Dr. T. is exhausted," I said. "And fate is decreeing that you depart the premises to prevent her killing any innocent patients tomorrow."

"Hey!" he snapped. "That's stinkin' thinkin'! You're not going to kill anyone—tomorrow or ever. You just need some confidence and some practice. One of these days, it's all gonna click—like learning how to drive a stick, or hitting a golf ball. Practice makes perfect, but you can't get the yips every time you pick up a club or get behind the wheel."

I dismissed his advice as the cheerleading of an outsider who meant well but didn't understand the difference between swinging a golf club and resecting a colon. I told him I appreciated the pep talk, but he was proving my case. If he stayed, we'd talk. I had to sleep. Thank you and good night.

"I was kinda hoping to spend the night," he said.

I shook my head. "I have to get up at five-thirty. I only have one pillow. Your car is illegally parked. Maybe another time."

He sat down on the edge of my bed. "Is there time in your busy schedule for a good-night kiss? I'll make it quick." When he leaned in for the actual compression of lips, my arms went up and circled his neck, causing a lingering farewell and inducing a near-reluctance to part that was unanticipated.

DR. SHAW'S SECRETARY could have been hired for her soothing voice and maternal susurrations alone. She explained that Dr. Shaw wasn't taking on any new patients, but that partners Goh and Garfinkle—excellent doctors both—were. Should she get their books?

I said, "It's really just to follow up on a conversation

184

Dr. Shaw and I began last night in the cafeteria. I'm a surgical intern—"

"Does this involve one of his patients?"

I said no; it involved me, and the subject was social rather than gynecological.

This appeared to stump her momentarily, but she recovered in time to ask if it was a pressing matter, or could he return the call at the end of the day.

"Any chance I could run up and talk to him between patients?"

"You're house staff?"

I said yes. Alice Thrift, MD. I didn't want to leave things up to the vicissitudes of our schedules, but I supposed I could simply wait until I bumped into him again in the cafeteria.

She lowered her voice. "Can you run over at noon? The office closes for lunch until one. He usually takes a snooze on his office couch, but doesn't mind being interrupted."

I said, "I'm on a very short leash, so if I don't turn up today, I'll try to make it tomorrow. Or the day after."

I could hear another line ringing and an intercom buzzing. "Got a pencil?" she asked.

"Why?"

"I'm giving you his private line."

"That's awfully nice of you—"

"And his home phone number, just in case."

I winced. "Should you do that?"

"It's my home number, too," she said.

I HAD BEEN unable to answer the first three questions

posed during morning rounds—about the patient's symptoms, about her history, and about her pending tests. My fellow residents answered smartly on all sides, with no sidelong apologetic glances for their role in pounding the dunce cap into the vertex of my skull. The sole sympathy emanated from the patient—herself in pain—a college student who would turn out to have appendicitis, the diagnosis of which was obscured by her mobile cecum. Whereas a week earlier I might have observed the emergency appendectomy, might have snipped off the offending organ or stitched her up, I was not even invited to scrub.

Truly, it was a test of my gumption: How high could I keep my chin up and for how long in the face of a campaign to rid the surgical world of Alice Thrift? Here is where the true champ digs deep and discovers reservoirs of fortitude, brains, and ambition. Here is where she shakes her fist and—as her pager beeps and the chief resident barks—vows to be better and to prove all her detractors and tormentors wrong.

Not me. I'd lost my character somewhere in this hospital, ground under the heels of a few attendings and carried off in the squalls of their tantrums. All I needed was one person to come along and say, "It's not skill. It's not native talent, or brains, or hands, or a gift from God. It only takes practice and a little more confidence. Next time you'll get it right; and if it's not the next procedure or the next suture, it'll be the one after that. Hasn't anyone pointed that out to you?—'See one. Do one. Teach one.' Medicine's motto? Surgery's subtitle?"

Looking back, I wonder how I missed that aphorism.

Perhaps it was something that generations of senior residents have passed down to junior residents after work, over pizza and beer, in venues not available to me. When Ray Russo advised, in effect, "Practice makes perfect. Give it a chance," I ignored it as the sunny outlook of someone whose ups and downs involved fudge sales and box scores—not continual worries about life and death.

EVEN THOUGH I called at a very decent eight-thirty P.M., I woke up Dr. Shaw. I apologized for disturbing him, and for being in possession of his phone number.

"Jackie gave you the number with the full expectation that you'd use it," he said. "Now tell me how you are and how your Monday—is today Monday?—went."

Suddenly I felt ridiculous and tongue-tied. The presumptuousness of waking up a nearly retired obstetrician, who also happened to be a near-stranger, to confide anything at all made me question my state of mind.

"I'm listening," he prompted.

"It seems so silly—to bother you at home about trivial matters. Your answering service is probably trying to reach you right now."

"I'm not on call," he said. "Tell me what's going on."

I said, "Well, as promised, I called up the man I've been seeing—marginally seeing—but for the most part ignoring, and he came over within minutes."

"Obviously glad to hear from you," Henry said, unable to stifle a yawn.

"Well, here's the part I needed to discuss with someone: I did a very foolish thing."

"You probably didn't."

"I gave him a tour of my new apartment, which is quite devoid of interest, but for some reason he was rapturous over my bathtub."

"Go on," said Henry.

"He made a very good argument for indulging himself before he left."

"Indulging himself?"

"Taking a bath in my tub. He only has a stall shower."

"And this foolish thing? Would that have been unprotected relations?"

"Absolutely not!"

"Good. I had to ask. What's your question?"

I said, "I guess it would be in the area of where I go from here."

There was a pause, during which I detected the amplified sound of a palm sliding over a mouthpiece and a muffled conversation behind it.

A woman's voice said, "Alice? It's Henry's roommate, Jackie. From the office? Can I be of any help?"

"Roommate?"

"Longtime companion? Girlfriend? But trust me, this is no scoop. We've lived together since our respective divorces, a hundred years ago, way before bosses couldn't take up with their secretaries."

I said, "I'm so embarrassed, calling your number as if it were a relationship hotline."

Jackie laughed. "You're not the first miserable intern to call after hours and pour her heart out to Henry. That's where I come in. He hands the phone to me when it gets personal. You must have touched on sex, which has been known to give him the heebie-jeebies."

"Me, too."

"Tell me what you're worried about," she said firmly.

I didn't know exactly, so I came up with a slight over-statement. "I'm worried," I told Jackie, "that the man I had sex with last night will think we're engaged."

"Trust me," said Jackie. "No man in America thinks that having sex is tantamount to proposing marriage. Not in the last two centuries, at least."

"He's a widower," I said. "He's been celibate for a year out of respect for his wife, so this was a momentous occasion. He said as much. But I'm confused by the fact that we had, to the best of my knowledge, in the vernacular, great sex."

"And this is a problem?"

I said, "Not on the face of it. But there isn't much else to recommend him."

"In twenty-five words or less . . . ?"

I summarized: traveling salesman, bad grammar, rough-hewn, had an unlisted number, a swagger; was transparently impressed with my being a doctor while not even using anatomically correct names for body parts.

"Being rough-hewn and a traveling salesman aren't fatal flaws."

I said, "I know that."

"Because I hear something in your voice that sounds as if you're asking permission to fall in love with someone who might be less than your parents' ideal son-in-law."

I objected. I said that successful sexual congress was one thing, but falling in love was not applicable, especially with Ray Russo.

"If Henry weren't listening," Jackie confided, "I'd tell you about a few crushes I had in my youth on boys who had to pick me up at the corner because they weren't allowed within a hundred yards of my house."

"Ray is lonely," I said. "Various friends of mine have pointed out that men who were once married know the actuarial tables and want to remarry as soon as possible."

"But I'm guessing that he wouldn't want to marry someone he didn't love, life expectancy or no life expectancy," said Jackie.

"If you met him, you'd understand what my reservations are."

"Bad grammar isn't fatal. And as for swaggering, I refer you back to my high school crushes. Maybe you're having a delayed adolescent rebellion, dating bad boys with no college prospects."

I said, "You must think I'm hopeless and friendless and devoid of common sense and insight."

"Don't be silly. I'm enjoying myself immensely. When do I ever get the chance to give solicited advice? So here it is: Let nature take its course. Don't talk yourself out of anything. Give him a chance. Keep him under wraps if you think your friends won't approve. If the doubts continue—and I mean real doubts, not ones borrowed from your friends—you can always break it off."

I heard a muffled conversation taking place between them, then Henry's voice back on the line. "Jackie wants to meet you. And I don't think she means with a sliding-glass panel between you. I think she's hoping you'll come for dinner some night when neither of us is on call."

I said, "Really? You'd invite a total stranger to dinner?"

He said, "I raised three daughters and she raised two sons. We don't think it's a big social undertaking to feed an extra mouth or two. And neither of us would categorize you as a stranger after this particular conversation."

The "extra mouth or two" worried me and rendered me silent. How many strangers would I have to converse with over dinner?

"Bring your friend," he continued. "We want to meet him. Jackie and I are good judges of character. And a little nosy. Our kids weren't quick to bring their paramours home—still aren't—so we've got some repressed parenting bottled up. Just let us know if either of you is vegetarian or kosher or lactose intolerant."

I said, "I know you won't like him."

Henry said, "Now, wait a minute. As long as you asked for my advice, I want you to consider this: Almost every day of my working life I meet patients—pregnant women with whom I share a common goal and almost always an eventual happy ending. And round about their sixth month, they bring their husbands in, or partners, or whatever the fashionable term is this decade. I'm almost always surprised. Most of these men are nervous; the ones who aren't nervous seem either stupid or overconfident or too blasé about what the fetus represents, which is responsibility or adulthood or the end of freedom. What it's made me is nonjudgmental, because if I let my first, second, and third impressions prevail, I'd spend a lot of time worrying about my mothers' postpartum lives. Eventually I see everyone in labor and delivery, and of course some still give me pause, but for the most part, if they've come this far and they're having a child, I get a glimpse into the core of them, and it leaves me feeling pretty damn good."

I thought of Ray leading me across the hall in search of a friend; I thought of his voice, muffled and confused, calling for help from the bathroom floor. And further, there was that little matter of how much I liked his hot cheek against mine, and his lips working their way down my spinous processes.

"There must be something to recommend him," Henry prompted.

I said, "Well, I don't have to be charming or interesting around him. He seems happy to keep the conversation rolling. And he notices what I need—a telephone, an answering machine, a computer, health and beauty aids, friends."

"So you're saying he's thoughtful."

I said I wasn't sure. But yes, Ray seemed to care about me and even worry about me and my life skills.

"Now we're getting somewhere," he said.

In the background I heard, matter-of-factly if not clinically, "Ask her what she's using for birth control."

He must have declined with a strenuous shake of his head, because Jackie came back on the line and said, "Henry's fading fast. I think he wants me to wind this up."

I said I was getting beeped myself. Dinner would be lovely. Thanks.

Why had I said that? Dinner would *not* be lovely. I

dreaded this dinner. Ray would interpret the invitation as our coming out as a couple. Jackie, the common-law, support-staff girlfriend, would be so tolerant and egalitarian that I'd leave thinking Ray's good qualities superseded his bad. And at the head of the table would be Dr. Shaw, the patron saint of odd couples, the national spokesman for Doctors Without Sleep Who Have a Life.

I quickly added, "But, unfortunately, I'm going to have to decline due to my awful schedule."

"Nonsense," said Jackie. "Saturday night, seven sharp. Bring the boyfriend."

"He's not my boyfriend," I said, but she'd already hung up.

18
The Life of the Party

RAY SEEMED SUSPICIOUS that I'd invited him to a dinner party in a doctor's private home on what he deemed a swanky street in Brookline.

"How come?" he asked. "Why me?"

"As my date."

"Was I invited specifically, or is it one of those 'Alice Thrift and Guest' deals?"

"Specifically."

"Because . . . ?"

"Because that's how normal social intercourse proceeds: You meet new people, they get to know you, they invite you to dinner."

"Is he your doctor?"

I said no; Dr. Shaw—Henry—was my friend. As an

obstetrician, he was outside my orbit professionally, but at least I could claim him and his life partner, Jackie, as . . . work pals.

"Who else is going to be there?" Ray asked.

"Just us."

"When?" asked Ray.

I said, "This Saturday," hoping to hear that he had long-standing plans with cousins, or that business was taking him out of town to a confectionery convention at the Javits Center.

"I accept. Do you know if they're allergic to nuts?"

I said I didn't know. I had to run. I was in the ER today, and ambulances were arriving every thirty seconds.

"Can I see you tonight?" Ray asked.

I said—because it was easier than expounding on exhaustion and laundry and romantic uncertainty—yes. But did we have to go out? Would he mind if we did nothing?

"Stay in?" He chuckled. "No problem. Why would I want to go out when all I've been thinking about is you in your pink pj's; no, correction: you with your pink pajamas in a ball at the foot of your bed."

I was supposed to be calling an underage patient's next of kin—concussion and abrasions from skateboarding, not life-threatening—but was struck immobile by Ray's depiction of me as an object of sexual desire.

"You there?" he asked.

Nurses and residents were milling around the desk, eyeing the phone. I whispered, "I can't talk."

"But you've been thinking of me, too, right? My

clothes in a heap. No pj's, no nothing?"

"Affirmative," I said.

"I'll bring dinner. What are you in the mood for?"

"Anything."

"Love ya," I could swear I heard as the receiver left my ear.

He arrived with three large subs in the Italian genre, cut into quarters so we could mix and match. He also arrived with a gift-wrapped pillow. "Top of the line," he said proudly. "Goose down, but not the scratchy kind with the quills poking through."

I said, "Let me pay you for it."

Ray said no, absolutely not. And hadn't my parents taught me that you don't offer to pay someone when they bring a gift?

I said, "It doesn't seem right that you have to spend your money, especially in the off-season, on basics for my barren apartment."

"You don't have time to shop," he argued. "I do." He put the subs down on my kitchen counter along with the bottle of Chianti he'd brought, and put his arms around me. He kissed me, then backed away to ask what I was thinking and why I looked as if I were trying to solve a math problem.

"Don't be silly," I said. "I wasn't thinking about anything."

"Don't you like the way I kiss?" he tried again.

I said, "I do like the way you kiss. In fact, that's exactly what I'm trying to assess—what happens when we kiss and why."

"Doc," said Ray. "Are you for real? Do you seriously have to look at everything under a microscope? I'm not saying that for my benefit. I'm saying it for yours. Have you ever just sat back and enjoyed something? I mean, anything? A movie? A funny joke? A lobster dinner?"

I said, "I'm sure I have."

"I'm not complaining. But I don't want to be a social worker, either. I'd like to think this is a two-way street."

I said, "I'm trying."

"Maybe the answer is, Don't feel the need to tell me what you're thinking when it's a dose of cold water."

"I know that," I said. "But a person who is afflicted with my personality can't just will herself to be a good conversationalist."

He asked if I ever watched television.

I said I had on occasion. Why?

"Because. It shows how normal conversation flows back and forth and how people act when they're in love or maybe just have the hots for each other. Or how they tell a patient he's terminal, or how they shoot the shit during a coffee break at the hospital."

"What program is this?"

"Any daytime drama. There's a lot of raw emotion and passion. But at the same time, you would know that the person who's delivering the lines doesn't really mean it, either. They're acting. They're faking it. Life is like that: You have to put the song across even when you don't feel like it." He winked. "Even when you're the most exhausted person who ever lived."

He walked over to the counter and narrated as he unwrapped the subs. "Eggplant parm, meatball, and sausages and peppers. They make their own. A little soggy, but that goes with the territory. Ever gotten anything from Manero's on Hanover Street?"

I said no, I hadn't, but added—with conspicuous feeling and verve—that they looked scrumptious and that I was starved.

He found two plates, divided the sandwiches artfully, and asked, "Where to?"

"I have tray tables," I said.

"Not my style. We'll lower the bed and eat on that."

I said okay, but let me strip it and put down place mats.

"Ever eat in the nude?" he asked.

I said no, not since infancy.

"This way we can go for broke—let the sauce dribble down our necks and then we can take a bath together."

I said all right. Nude dining and tandem bathing—sounded like it would be both liberating and romantic. Had he brought more condoms?

Ray smiled. He said, "Yes, doctor. I most certainly did. You think Ray Russo would ever dream of having anything but safe sex with you?"

I said I appreciated his taking that particular responsibility since I'd feel self-conscious buying contraceptives at the hospital pharmacy. Had he also brought a corkscrew? Would we need napkins under these circumstances? Should I disrobe now?

THERE WAS A knock at the door during dinner, shocking me into imagining the scene through the eyes of a potential visitor: two adults feeding each other chunks of messy food, detritus of which was staining their faces and points below. At the moment the knock came, Ray was on his knees, tracing my areola with a piece of sausage.

Calmly, he put his finger to his lips and shook his head.

I opened my eyes wide, a question: I shouldn't answer?

He mouthed, They'll go away.

Reflexively, nervously, I sang out, "Who is it?"

"Sylvie Schwartz!"

Ray shrugged: Damage done. It's all yours.

I called back, "Sylvie? I can't come to the door right now. I'm . . . indisposed."

"Did I wake you?"

I said, "Um, no. I mean, I'm in bed, but I can't come to the door."

"Whoops. No problem. Just thought I'd ask if you wanted to get sushi or some Thai food."

I said, "Thanks so much for asking. Any other time would be great."

"Don't worry," said Sylvie. "I get the picture. Sorry to interrupt."

Ray made a face that seemed to be saying, See what happens when you don't play dead? You're busted.

"I'm glad you came by," I called out.

Ray rolled his eyes.

"Have fun," she answered.

After she'd retreated and her door had closed, I said, "That was really nice of her to follow up on her promise, don't you think? She said she was going to invite me to dinner, and now I know she's sincere."

Ray said, "You're getting more popular by the minute. Pretty soon I'm going to have to take a number."

I said I understood that reference—*take a number*—like patients in the fast-track clinic of the ER.

"I was thinking *deli counter*," said Ray, "but sure—same thing."

"I couldn't just ignore a knock on the door. I mean, it could have been someone in distress. And even though tonight wasn't convenient, there's bound to be other times when I'll really welcome her company."

"I'm surprised you didn't invite her in and offer her the leftovers."

I pointed out that that would involve opening the door and, even if I had a robe on, she'd see the stains on my face and neck. And him in my bed.

"You wouldn't be ashamed of that fact, would you?"

"Do you mean ashamed of you? Or did you mean embarrassed to be caught incorporating food into my foreplay?"

"Me," he said. "Raymond J. Russo."

"That would be hypocritical, wouldn't it? Inviting you over but hiding you from my neighbors? I wouldn't do that."

Ray sighed. "Just say something unscientific that'll make me feel good. That's all I'm asking for here. That I'm a guy to you, and not a lab partner."

I said, "You are definitely a guy. Don't forget I meet men every day, and this has never happened before. Also, you might recall that I was the one who called you on Sunday night—"

"The night you'll never forget? The night the earth moved and all the animals in the forest stood up on their hind legs and listened to the sound, far away, of Alice Thrift thrashing around on her Murphy bed?"

He was being metaphorical, so I didn't contradict the ludicrous laws of nature he advanced. He was also being amorous, trying something new along my neck, nibbles interspersed with flicks of his tongue. "There's eggplant and meatball left," he murmured. "And one juicy piece of hot sausage that's getting bigger by the moment."

Another colorful figure of speech. Ray was chock-full of them.

A SURVEY OF my closet on Friday night was discouraging. There was my graduation dress, black, but sleeveless, purchased in anticipation of a hot June day under a polyester robe. I put it on and went across the hall.

"What's this?" Sylvie asked.

"I'm going out tomorrow night."

"What's the occasion?"

"A dinner party at Dr. Shaw's. OB? Lives with his office manager, Jackie?"

"Good for you," she said, and—because I was pinching the material at my hip and looking dubious— "What's your question?"

"Can I wear a sleeveless dress in February?"

Sylvie opened her door wider and I walked in. It was my apartment's twin, but a polar-opposite fraternal one. There were plants by her windows, artwork on her walls, apples and pears in a bowl on a real table, copper pots and pans hanging from hooks above her stove. "Wow,"

I said. "This looks like a real home."

"Yours will, too," said Sylvie. "You just need the time."

"And some taste," I said.

"First," said Sylvie, "the dress. Very basic. You can't go wrong. But one suggestion, if you don't mind. Accessorize."

"Such as?"

"Hold on."

She went toward her closet, and returned with a garment that reminded me that clothes didn't have to look like school uniforms. It was a black sweater—soft, even a little fluffy; it had black beads sewn here and there, not enough to embarrass me, but just enough to dress me up.

"Here. Like this." She guided me into it, then pushed the sleeves halfway up my forearms. "Room to show off a big bold bracelet. And the bolero length is excellent. It accentuates your waist."

I said, "Really? I can borrow this?"

"Definitely. What about earrings?"

I touched my earlobes. "No holes."

"Not a problem," said Sylvie.

She disappeared again. I heard drawers opening and closing. She returned with a basket holding what she said was her past—a Girl Scout lanyard, a needlepoint choker, Mardi Gras beads, pop beads, clip-on earrings, and frayed friendship bracelets. She dumped the contents onto the kitchen counter, and spread it into a single layer. I vetoed a daisy cluster of jet and rhinestone earrings and declined papier-mâché parrots the size of laboratory mice. I started to say that I could probably find screw-back pearls in my own junk basket. Sylvie looked up from her sorting to study my lobes. "Ever consider getting your ears pierced?" she asked.

I backed away a step and said no, never.

"One hole per lobe," she said. "Not Swiss cheese like mine. A nice hoop would look very nice when your hair's pulled back. Nothing gaudy. Just that added little *je ne sais quoi*."

"Maybe," I said. "At some point when I've finished my training."

She laughed. "In case one fell off into the surgical field?"

I said, "The surgeons I answer to don't wear earrings."

"Speaking for myself, I never leave the house without them," said Sylvie. "In fact, I'd be happy to do the honors right now."

"What honors?"

"Hul-lo. Pierce your ears. Me. Now. I've done all seven of mine."

"But I'm going out tomorrow night," I said. "I don't want my ears to be bleeding."

"Nonsense," she said.

I didn't want to say aloud that she was an internist in training, not a surgeon, and that I wasn't sure about the hygiene of a kitchen operation.

"Sit," she said. "I'll get my instruments."

Obediently I backed down onto a kitchen chair. Sylvie bustled around, inordinately happy it seemed, and came back with a terry-cloth hand towel, several alcohol prep pads, and a sewing needle. Another trip brought a bottle of pHisoHex and a pair of gold earrings, little balls with a diamond chip in each center. Finally, ice cubes in a cereal bowl. "First, we always use earrings with at least fourteen-carat-gold posts. Second, we choose something that I don't wear anymore." She was at the sink now, scrubbing—hands, fingers, nails, sides of fingers, repeatedly, even working her way to the elbows. From the cabinet below the sink she removed surgical gloves—contaminating herself, I noticed—then set them aside on a paper towel. "I know, I know—not exactly OR standards," she said, "but I think I'm aseptic enough for the task ahead."

I didn't argue. See one, do one, teach one.

"*Regardez:* Not only do I use a new needle that's never pierced a living organism, but I sterilize it like so"—she struck a match from a box on the stove and touched its flame to the sharp end—"and now I cool it down with alcohol."

"Your hands," I prompted.

"No problem," she said. The gloves went on. An ice cube and a needle came toward me.

"Do you think I need a swab of Betadine?"

"Overkill. Not to mention ugly," she said. "Close your eyes. I've never lost an ear."

"Tell me what you're doing as you do it," I said.

"I certainly will not," said Sylvie.

I felt the ice, front and back. Then the puncture—manageable pain—then the journey of the needle. I asked if there was much bleeding. Sylvie said, "One drop . . . nice placement. Your lobes were made for this. Okay. Now the earring . . . sometimes hard to get it through to the other side. Sorry . . . almost . . . okay, got it! Earring back is now secure. We're halfway home. Want to see it, or should we finish the job?"

"Finish."

"More ice. Numb enough?"

I said it wasn't too bad. I thought about me looking for veins; about me trying to thread a line into a patient's superior vena cava. This was nothing; this wasn't even a junior membership in the academy of sufferers.

When both earrings were in place and I'd received my instructions for nightly turns and disinfecting, she brought out a bottle of wine.

I said I'd return the earrings as soon as I could buy a replacement.

"Or not," said Sylvie. "I'd like to think of them as your fashion starter kit."

Fashion starter kit. I asked Sylvie if this was a makeover—first a bolero sweater studded with shiny beads, and now earlobes studded with diamonds.

"No!" she protested, too fast to be believed. She cocked her head slightly; she looked at my naked wrists, at her costume jewelry, at my feet. "What size shoe do you wear?" she asked.

RAY PICKED ME up, dressed in his funeral suit and tie, looking more than presentable. My outfit was hidden beneath my parka, but I'd heightened the color of my lips with a tinted lip balm purchased at the hospital pharmacy, and had coiled my ponytail into a knot at the back of my neck.

"Doesn't she look great?" he asked the teenage guard

at the security desk.

The guard looked up and blinked.

I kept walking, and at the door quietly asked Ray not to put people on the spot. And what would a confirmation from a security guard, hoping for nice tips next Christmas, mean anyway?

"So sue me," said Ray. "It just flew out of my mouth. And as long as we're being honest, let me suggest that you don't have to knee a guy in the groin when he pays you a compliment."

"Did I do that?"

"Not literally. But you do like to swat it away, same as if it was an insult. And I don't say this to make you feel bad. I say it because we're going out in public now, and you look nice, and someone else might pay you a compliment tonight."

I said thank you for that advice. He looked very nice, too.

When we were in the car, driving west on Beacon Street per the directions, Ray asked if I wanted him to play it cool.

"In what sense?"

"Like, if we're standing around having drinks and I get the urge to put my arm around you. Or if we're sitting next to each other at dinner and I put my hand on your thigh. Is that something that's going to get you all goosey?"

I said, "Well, Jackie and Henry know that we've had sexual relations, so I suppose a gesture of affection wouldn't upset anyone."

He kept his eyes on the road but repeated slowly, each

word distinct: "They *know* we've had sexual relations? Is that what you people talk about in the doctors' dining room?"

I said, "There *is* no doctors' dining room."

"Then wherever it is you make sexual confessions."

"You sound mad," I said.

"I'm surprised. I thought you were the last person in the world who'd brag about her love life, especially if the guy you were doing it with was me."

Had I bragged about my love life? I didn't think so. "Love life" sounded active and fluid, whereas I'd only experienced what might be termed love episodes . . . love accidents. Confidences offered solely to illustrate my doubts about Ray as a boyfriend. I said, "I think your TV doctors confide such things in each other all the time. Isn't that what keeps the plots moving? Sexual disclosures in the workplace?"

"But that's not real life," said Ray. "Those people are hinting at juicy things that will make the audience tune in tomorrow."

I said, "I'm sorry. In the future I'll be more discreet. And to answer your original question: If you put your arm around me over wine and canapés, I won't get goosey."

"Thank you," said Ray.

THEIR HOUSE WAS stucco, crisscrossed with dark timber, chaletlike. A Christmas wreath was still on the door, and their mailbox was painted to look like the head of a cow. Jackie answered the chime as if she'd been waiting breathlessly with her hand on the doorknob. She was younger than Henry—by ten years? fifteen?—petite and energetic, with short blond hair brushed forward to frame her face. Pretty and fit, she reminded me of hospital coworkers who organized their fellow nurses into lunchtime jogging parties. She greeted me with a kiss, and accepted Ray's gift-wrapped fudge with such courtesy that no one would have suspected that we'd discussed his product as a liability.

"Everyone's here," sang Henry from a few yards behind her.

He took our coats and we followed him past the stairway, down the hallway of wood stained dark against bright white stucco walls. I stopped, causing Ray to bump against me. "More people?" I asked Henry.

"No surgeons," he said. "In fact, no doctors." And then we were at the threshold of what appeared to be a library. "Everyone knows everyone else," he boomed.

It made perfect sense: Someone of Jackie's social talents would have regarded her large dining room table, her blended-family supply of flatware, and thought, Cooking for six is no harder than cooking for four! Who would work as another couple? Henry must have connected the dots, reaching back to our cafeteria conversation, the nuances forgotten but names retained: Midwife Meredith and Nurse Leo, young folks whom Alice knows and will feel comfortable with.

"Did I get this right?" asked Henry. "Schoolmates? Roommates? Some such?"

"Roommates," said Leo, who was wearing a maroon V-necked sweater over a shirt and tie.

"I'm Ray," Ray said, extending his hand to Meredith,

who seemed as composed as another human being could be in the face of such a social collision. Her dress was loose and hemplike; her shawl was ochre. Her earrings looked like IUDs.

"Drinks?" said Henry. He pointed to a library table swathed in white linen. "I have a pitcher of martinis. I have beer. I have wine. Dr. Thrift?"

"Martini," I said. "Very dry. A double."

"Olive or a twist?"

"Both," I said.

Ray pointed to the brown bottle Leo was holding and said, "One of those would be super."

"Boys love their beers," said Meredith, who was sipping what looked like club soda.

Jackie, right behind us, looked from one face to the next. "Henry knew there was some connection. But I guess this was a surprise."

"Our paths haven't crossed lately," said Leo.

I said I'd been in the ER. Lots of kids, but no neonates.

"How's the new apartment?" he asked.

"Great. Very convenient. Immaculate."

"She needs stuff," said Ray. "The only furniture she has is built in. She didn't even know you had to bring a phone."

"You've seen it?" Leo asked.

Ray said quietly, "I got a tour."

Jackie said, "I don't know when she'd have time to buy furniture with the hours she keeps."

"All of us work around the clock," said Meredith.

"Not me," said Ray.

"I meant at the hospital."

"Are you a nurse, too?" Ray asked her.

"Nurse-midwife. Certified."

"No kidding? One of those people who delivers babies at home?"

Meredith looked toward Dr. Shaw and said quietly, "On occasion. In an emergency."

"Don't get me started," said Henry. "We've agreed to disagree."

"What do you think?" I asked Leo.

His glance went around the room, from Meredith to Henry and back to me. "We've also agreed to disagree."

"Am I missing something?" asked Ray. "What are we discussing here?"

"Home births," said Jackie.

Ray asked Leo, "So what's your beef with it?"

Leo said, "My beef is this: A home birth is about the mother, not the baby. It's about low lights and pot-luck casseroles and herbal tea and wanting to have a beautiful experience."

Henry said quietly, "Hear hear."

Meredith said to me, "Notice who's taking this position: the men."

"Not me," said Ray. "Anyone I know who's had their baby at home, it wasn't on purpose."

I said, "I haven't done much OB, except my clerkship in med school, so I don't know the statistics."

"There isn't a surgeon alive who's a proponent of home births," Meredith said. "So I doubt whether you'll be the first."

"Hey," said Ray. "She just said she hasn't done much

OB. You can't lump her in with other surgeons. She *hates* surgeons."

"In that case," Leo offered with a friendly smile, "maybe someday Alice will look around and say, 'What am I doing in a subspecialty that amounts to indentured servitude, answering to people who are aggressive assholes?'"

"Or maybe I'm doing much better," I said.

"Really?" asked Jackie. She had her hand on my back, waiting for a polite moment to announce, "There's smoked bluefish pâté and gravlax, if anyone feels like a nibble."

"How long does your probation last?" Meredith asked me.

"Two months."

"What an ordeal," she said. "Two months of people watching you, waiting for you to shoot yourself in the foot."

"I've heard worse," said Henry. "When I started out in surgery, I was given two *weeks* to shape up."

I detected charity and smiled. It couldn't have been true; if the word *probation* had ever appeared on his transcript, he'd have trumpeted it to me over our soup course in the cafeteria.

Ray asked Meredith what kind of paces she had to go through to become a midwife. Did she have to work for three days straight with maybe, if she was lucky, one catnap every twelve hours?

I said, "I don't have to work three days straight, Ray."

Leo was the only one who'd migrated over to the appetizers. He was leaning against a wall, several yards away from our circle.

Ray said to Meredith, "I'm guessing you have pretty regular hours—I mean, I know you deliver babies in the middle of the night, but I'm guessing you have a shift. You work a set number of hours and then another nurse takes over when it's quitting time? Is that right?"

"What's your point?" she asked.

"I have no point. I guess I heard something in your voice that gave me the idea that you thought Alice was on probation because she wasn't smart enough or good enough." He smiled. "So I guess it got my back up."

Meredith smiled, too, an icy smile of pure diplomacy. "I'm sorry you feel that way," she said. "I think no such thing. I have the utmost respect for doctors."

From the corner of the room, Leo laughed and lifted his bottle to his mouth.

Henry laughed, too. I did as well, although I wasn't sure where the humor lay. Ray's expression shifted slowly from malignant to benign. They were laughing at Meredith or her lie, or her skills as a debater. But definitely not at Ray Russo or the drip who brought him.

SEATING PLAN: THE hosts at the head and the foot of the table. Ray and Meredith on one side of the table, Leo and I next to each other opposite our dates. A caterer had furnished two roast ducks, crispy and sauced, and vegetables tied together in little bundles. "I used to cook," said Jackie, "but I finally got over my belief that my self-worth is tied to the number of hours I put into a dinner party."

"Me, too," said Leo. "One of the happiest days of my

life was when they invented take-out rotisserie chickens."

"This is duck," said Meredith.

"I like duck," said Leo. "I used to feed the ones at the BC reservoir, if I could wrestle some stale heels of bread away from my mother."

"Leo's one of a dozen children," I said.

"Thirteen, actually."

"All named after popes and saints," I said.

"How do you know that?" Meredith asked.

"From his mother."

"Alice came to dinner," said Leo. "Unfortunately, my mother's self-worth is not tied up in her cooking either, but that doesn't stop her."

"It was a very nice meal," I said.

Ray said, "Alice isn't fussy. She eats cafeteria food every day." He winked at me. "And the occasional submarine sandwich."

Henry said, "Jackie cooks plenty. She's being modest."

Jackie said, "Henry's wife took cooking lessons. I mean, serious cooking lessons from that woman in Newton Centre who trains women to cater their husbands' law firms' cocktail parties."

"Now now," chided Henry.

"What happened to her?" Ray asked.

"We divorced," said Henry.

Ray wagged his index finger back and forth, between the head and the foot of the table.

"He's asking if I was the home-wrecker," said Jackie.

"No," said Henry, and nothing more.

"Sorry," said Ray. "I only asked because I'm a widower and I like to know what happened to other people's wives."

Meredith asked Ray when he lost his wife.

"A year ago."

"A year and a few months," I said.

"Cancer?" Meredith asked.

"Car accident."

Everyone murmured his or her condolences. Meredith asked if the marriage had produced any children.

"Luckily, no," said Ray.

"Why 'luckily'?" asked Leo.

"Because they'd have lost their mother! They'd be motherless, with me on the road most of the time. Who needs that?"

"Ray's wife was quite young," I said. "They weren't married for very long."

"*How* young?" asked Meredith.

"Twenty-eight when she died." He swiveled his palm from side to side. "Maybe twenty-nine."

"Statistically," said Henry, "not that anyone heeds this anymore, but the ideal childbearing age is twenty-four—strictly in terms of what's safest for the mother and safest for the baby."

"My mother was nineteen when she had me," said Ray. "And I was her second."

"My mother was sixty when she had me," said Leo, and we all laughed.

In other words, it was fun. I enjoyed the fact that

Meredith was serious and aloof, so for once I didn't take home the trophy for the wettest blanket. We drank red wine with our duck, except for Meredith, who kept covering her wineglass with the palm of her hand as Henry offered refills.

"Sorry," said our host. "I keep forgetting."

"On call?" I asked.

"Or just a teetotaler?" asked Ray.

"Temporarily," said Meredith.

Jackie did a swivel in her seat. "So, Ray. How did you and Alice meet? It can't be like the rest of us—at work, by the vending machines, in the cafeteria."

"As a matter of fact, we did meet in the hospital," said Ray. He tapped one flange of his nose. "About this honker. I was thinking of getting a nose job, and she was the one in charge that day."

"Hardly," I murmured.

"You were the one I spoke to." He reached for the whipped cream and added another dollop to his remaining bite of dessert—a hybrid of chocolate cake and pudding. "And she talked me out of it. In like two minutes. I left thinking, Maybe I'm not so hideous after all."

He looked around for confirmation. Jackie said, "That shows good values, on both sides of the desk. Handsome is as handsome does."

"My old man used to say that," said Ray. "Which of course served his own purposes, because his nose made mine look dainty."

Suddenly Meredith said, "I'm not trying to obfuscate, and I'm certainly not trying to be coy."

"Huh?" said Ray.

"About the wine." She smiled modestly. "About not drinking."

Leo said, "Meredith—"

"Some of you know, and the rest of you probably figured out"—broad, contented smile—"I'm pregnant."

"Whoa. Not me," said Ray. "I figured out no such thing."

"Me, neither," I said.

"I can't plead ignorance," said Henry.

"Was it planned?" asked Ray.

"Not that you know me well enough to ask that," said Meredith, "but I'll answer: It wasn't planned, but we're delighted nonetheless."

"Goes to show ya," said Ray. "If you, a nurse, who knows this stuff cold, can have a slip-up—"

"I believe you mean *two* nurses," I said.

Leo said quietly, "People can take all the proper precautions and still have accidents."

"I thought we agreed not to use the word *accident,*" said Meredith, her hand caressing her abdomen.

"How old are you?" Ray asked.

Meredith hesitated, then said, "I'll be thirty-seven next month."

"High time," said Ray. "Because if twenty-four is ideal—"

"Have you told your families?" I asked.

"What do you think?" Leo answered.

"We'll tell everyone when I've made it into my second trimester," said Meredith.

I asked how far along she was.

"Ten weeks."

"You know that exactly?" asked Ray.

Meredith smiled.

"If you know when you're ovulating," I told him, "you can figure out when you conceive."

"Cool," said Ray.

"Is it too soon to make a toast?" asked Henry.

"Absolutely not," said Meredith.

Henry stood and raised his glass. "To a new life. To Meredith's baby—"

"And don't forget her daddy," said Meredith.

"Her?" I repeated. "You already know it's a girl?"

"No, we do not," said Leo.

"A hunch," said Meredith.

"Ha," said Henry.

"He, she, whatever," said Ray. Now he stood. "Good luck to the mother. And to the father. And to her doctor, and to our delightful hostess."

"Hear hear," said Henry.

"Are you getting married?" I asked.

Leo banged his fist against his chest, expelling a fake cough. "One monumental life decision at a time, please," he said.

"Why do you ask?" said Meredith.

"Alice is drunk," said Ray. "I think this was her first martini. I mean, ever. Then wine on top of that."

Leo, to my right, said, "Alice got her ears pierced."

"That's true," I said. "At home. With no licensed physician present."

There was silence for a few long seconds.

"Alice made a joke," said Ray.

SOMEONE OF MY scientific temperament, unlettered in social convention, would be prone to do what I did next: make an appointment to speak with Leo in private. I chose not to leave a message, which Meredith might parse on his answering machine. Instead I sent him a note saying, *I'd like to discuss something with you. Please advise by beeper as to convenient dates, times, and sites. Yours truly, Alice.* There was no line for *personal and confidential* on the string-tied, multiuse in-house envelope, so I just wrote, *Leo Frawley, RN, NICU,* and hoped that the famously challenged mail-room staff would find my addressee.

The morning after the dinner, I updated Sylvie. Even though she didn't know the principals, she was captivated by Leo's paternity plight. I had provided the facts as I knew them on what she announced was going to be a weekly bad-weather constitutional between our residence and the hospital along the city-block–length tunnel.

"Duped," said Sylvie. "Put to use like a withdrawal from a sperm bank. A turkey baster could have done the job without the messy human interchange."

"You don't know that," I said. "I think there's some love involved between the parties."

"She's how old? Forty?"

"Thirty-six going on thirty-seven."

"Tick-tock, tick-tock," Sylvie chanted.

"According to Leo it was an accident."

"With a midwife? Please. They're all *Über*-moms, even the ones without kids. They design a whole career around not just childbirth but childbirth as the crowning achievement of a woman's life. Who do you think invented cutting your own umbilical cord and under-water births and planting fruit trees where you've buried the placenta? Midwives!"

I said I was sure that Native American cultures had been burying placentas ritualistically, or ingesting them, long before midwives—

"You know what I'm getting at: a baby at any price. This Meredith was, first and foremost, in the market for a father."

I said, "When Leo told me about Meredith, he sounded quite enamored."

"Bullshit! Leo's furious! One day he's getting it reg-ularly, and all of a sudden he has to start going to Lamaze classes. Believe me, she pulled a fast one."

This was why I enjoyed Sylvie's company, especially in her cynical mode: She was always happy to accuse and indict perfect strangers until they were proven inno-cent. It made me thirst for Sylvies in other spheres of my life. I'd long given up hoping that the sole other female intern, the glamorous Stephanie from Manhattan via Penn and Duke, would recognize that we shared a berth in surgical steerage. Sometimes, when I was splashing cold water on my face at five-thirty A.M., I tried to imagine what products and extra time it required to make eyelashes dark and distinct, and lids a canvas of silvery pastels. Even our names separated us: Alice and

Stephanie—nomenclature as destiny. Sometimes I would look at her, at the golden streaks in her excess of hair, and imagine that if an alien landed in our hospital, he'd never guess that Dr. Stephanie Crawford and Dr. Alice Thrift belonged to the same species.

And now came Sylvie, who after only a few days' acquaintance sought out my company, lent me clothes, pierced my ears; who yelled out greetings from the far side of the cafeteria and introduced me to any fellow elevator passengers of her acquaintance. I realized that other relationships with roommates in college and medical school were anemic and impersonal compared to the intimacy Sylvie induced on our inaugural hike.

"How long did you and Leo live together?" she asked.

"Six months, exactly."

"Just friends?"

This was how girlfriends talked as they power-walked. Every few lengths of the tunnel, residents waved in collegial fashion. I was beginning to see that she had a high profile inside an institution where most of us blended together into one white-coated blur. Sylvie, with her two-tone hair and her conversation-piece ear-lobes, stood out. Unlike the rest of us, she didn't appear downtrodden; didn't feel the need to announce how exhausted she felt. I'd been lucky to have landed across the hall from someone who was not only neighborly but immune to my social disorders. I worried aloud on this first Sunday morning, "I hope I'm not too dull a walking partner."

"You're not a kibitzer," Sylvie said. "You speak when

spoken to or when you have something to say. You're shy. Shy is fine."

I said I'd hardly ever heard my condition described as fine. Quite the opposite; usually only as a curse.

"I used to be shy," said Sylvie. "As a kid. But then I made a conscious decision to get over it."

"How?"

"I'm embarrassed to tell you. It's too lame."

"Please," I said. "If anyone needs to hear this, it's me."

"Okay. The nasty truth is: I took baton lessons. And I was astonishingly good at it. I could do twirls and catch it behind my back—you've seen this stuff. I joined the squad and in one year I was the lead baton twirler—superseding Kimberly Perreault, who never forgave me—to become the one who wore silver boots and tassels and led the parade. I'm not kidding. And this wasn't Texas or Alabama. This was Pittsburgh, Pennsylvania." She smiled. "If you ever tell a living soul, I'll deny it."

I asked how an external, athletic feat helped her to overcome her shyness. Wasn't it excruciating to get dressed up in a costume, presumably something scanty, and lead a parade through the streets of Pittsburgh?

"Well, this is even more embarrassing because it shows what a shallow little girly-girl I was. When baton twirling got me out of the house and invited to parties generally populated by cheerleaders and jocks, I came out of my shell. Isn't that loathsome? Popularity cured me." She shook her head. "My mother was torn: Was it better to have a daughter who was a wallflower or a daughter who sashayed across football fields in a short skirt and her midriff showing and who dated Catholics? I had to go to medical school to atone for my shallowness."

I had known baton twirlers and cheerleaders from afar in high school; none of them, I was fairly certain, had become doctors. I said, "I guess I pigeonhole people. Scratch any doctor and you get someone who was unpopular in high school, except to the extent that he or she ran for offices of clubs that would look good on their college applications."

"You do *not* pigeonhole people—not if you're dating what's his name, lover boy."

We had reached the hospital entrance, and did our about-face. Sylvie was right: The brisk walk had made me feel less bedraggled. I said, "I admire the way you can ask personal questions in a lighthearted way without sounding as if you're taking someone's history."

"Thank you," said Sylvie. "Now I'll definitely ask if your date slept over."

I said, "He visited for a while after we got back from dinner, but then he left."

"I get it," said Sylvie.

"We've just recently inaugurated that aspect," I said.

When she didn't ask a follow-up question, I amplified: "I meant the sex . . . it's only started since I moved here. The first time it happened by accident."

Sylvie laughed.

I said, "No, seriously. It was practically a platonic friendship, but he fainted in my bathroom and one thing led to another."

"I think it's all for the good and your work will benefit if you have a sexual outlet."

I shushed her. The tunnel's acoustics made it a less-than-ideal place for confidentiality. "What about you?" I ventured. "Any special friend I should know about?"

She stopped, kneeled down, retied a shoelace that looked perfectly secure.

"Did I ask the wrong question?"

She checked in both directions before saying, "I'm not sure you'll want to know about my 'special friend,' as you so quaintly put it. Due to aspects that might shock you and other aspects that make it less than kosher."

I said, "I'm not unenlightened. You'd be my friend no matter what you told me; no matter what category or gender of person your friend is. And I may have mentioned—because I'm so used to it and never give it a second thought—that my sister is a lesbian."

Sylvie laughed and got back to her feet. "I knew you were leading up to that. I thought I'd let you torture that sentence for a while before I said, 'Sorry. It's a man.'" She resumed her brisk pace, but I caught up with her in two strides.

"Is this guy another doc?" I asked.

Sylvie said, "Oh, yeah."

"An attending?"

"Why did you ask that?"

"Because of what you said about it not being kosher. I mean, if he were one of your attendings—"

"He's married."

I said, "I don't have any experience in that arena, but from what I've heard, affairs with married men result in unfavorable outcomes."

"Don't I know it," said Sylvie. Her elbows were pumping; it was getting harder for me to keep up with her. Suddenly she stopped and said a little wistfully, "Okay, here it is—another sappy piece of autobiography. It began with a very sweet kiss. Remember those? From our youth?"

I said sure I did. Yes.

"And unexpected. That can be nice. So picture this: It's late at night. You're in the film library and suddenly an attractive man is whisking you into an empty fluoroscopy suite."

"Film library" echoed off an ominous shape I couldn't name. My martinied brain and my residual fatigue were not helping my retrieval. I said, "You're the last person I would have expected to have turned to mush because someone lands a kiss on you."

She shook her head, pumped her elbows, didn't slow down. "Then I've misrepresented the situation. Said kiss was administered after several months of what I'd characterize as surreptitious meaningful glances."

I'd heard rumors of affairs. I'd even looked up from stitching or stapling or taking notes to intercept a meaningful glance between a surgeon and a resident, an anesthesiologist and a scrub nurse. But this was firsthand; this was a principal confiding in me. I asked if there had been any follow-up.

"Not much. He's busy, he's married, he's always in a crowd of residents or nurses."

"Can't he page you?"

Sylvie laughed. We walked a whole length of the tunnel, Sylvie wearing the expression of a woman with a tantalizing secret and me, evidently, looking stumped. "Don't try to guess," she said, "because even if you hit the nail on the head I'm not going to name names."

"How long ago was this kiss?" I asked.

"December thirtieth. Which you shouldn't perceive as me remembering it like some maudlin first-kiss anniversary. I only remember it because the conversation opened with him asking me if I had a date for New Year's Eve—"

"Out of the blue?"

Sylvie smiled as if thinking, Poor Alice. She's such a naïf in the ways of impulsive and adulterous displays of affection.

"Was he asking you out?"

"No. Just making conversation. I said I had no date and he said, kind of wistfully and anti-wifely, 'You're lucky.'"

"And *then* he kissed you?"

"Among other things," said Sylvie with a grin.

"In the fluoro suite?"

"Honey child: My bed is, as we all know, approximately a hundred and twenty paces from the hospital through this very passageway."

"And you weren't afraid that someone would see him entering your apartment?"

"Please. You know our floor. You have to be dead for several days before anyone notices your comings and goings."

And then I remembered where I'd heard "film library" in a sexual context, and why it was resonating in such nauseating fashion: a cleaning lady first, Sylvie second, or—more likely—fifteenth or fiftieth.

"What's the matter?" Sylvie asked.

"Nothing. Just something Leo mentioned once."

"Such as?"

I had to decide: Blow the whistle at the risk of bruising Sylvie, or protect a man who was smearing the good offices of the X-ray department. I said, wincing, "About witnessing an act of fellatio in the film library."

Sylvie laughed. "It certainly wasn't us. We moved to fluoro."

I wanted to ask, Is this special friend of yours named Hastings? But how would I proceed if her answer was yes? Was I up to the task of delivering a dire romantic prognosis?

"Is it the married-man part," she asked, "or the unabashed-sex part that's making you green around the gills?"

"Do you know this man well?" I asked. "Because I sense that this relationship is a combination of surreptitious glances and episodic sex."

She was saved from answering because at that moment, as we approached the double doors to the hospital, I spotted my nemesis, Dr. Charles G. Hastings, waiting for the elevator and checking his watch with his usual glowering impatience. Sunday morning had to mean an emergency, one that had been passed up the ladder from residents to—as he often reminded us—a full professor who should never be bothered at home. My arm went up to stop Sylvie's forward motion at the same moment that hers reached across to stop me in my tracks.

"Quick," I said. "Turn around."

We were halfway back through the tunnel before I said, "Sorry. I just didn't want to run into him. He's the one who was wielding the scalpel when I let go of the retractor."

Sylvie murmured something noncommittal.

Without having had much practice in saying oblique or coy things in my life, I tried a few now: "You probably wanted me to confront him, though, right? March right up in my sneakers and say, 'Hello, Dr. Hastings. Harassing any interns lately?' Which would be exactly what Leo wanted me to do the morning after my near-firing."

"Hmm?"

"Dr. Hastings? The one who wanted to throw me out of the program? I told you about that—the cholecystectomy?"

"Right," she said.

I said, "One of these days I'm going to have to work under him. And I have this fantasy where I'll say, 'You owe me an apology, Dr. Hastings. What you said and did was inexcusable. I spoke to a lawyer, and she agrees. One more harassment and we're going to sock you with a lawsuit—you and all of your kind.'"

Sylvie said, "What's gotten into you? *Lawsuits.* 'All of your kind.' Did you really consult a lawyer?"

"No. It was all Leo. He used to be the grievance chairman of the nurses' union, so we role-played until I got it right."

"Good man," she said, but wanly.

"Another lap?" I asked.

She said no, sorry. Couldn't. Had to read up on, well, stuff. Crohn's disease. For a talk. A stack of articles she'd clipped and never read. Besides, she was beat. Would probably have to nap before settling down with the journals.

I said okay. Exercise and confession now concluded. Back to medicine; back to *The Annals of Surgery*. And, likewise, back to sleep.

THE NEXT MORNING I not only diagnosed a pneumothorax but also got the chest tube into the pleural cavity on the first try. No one applauded, but the senior resident said, after hearing lung sounds, "Very slick."

Next day, still assigned to the ER: lacerated thumb belonging to fifty-two-year-old male, injury inflicted by lid of a tuna fish can. Same senior resident of the pneumothorax stepped aside; said, "Dr. Thrift is going to take over. As we all know, women are much better at sewing. And she's not just any old ER doc. She's a surgeon." Eight respectable stitches were the easy part, but I also told a joke—"Next time you might want to consider peanut butter and jelly"—evincing bedside bonhomie and inducing a grumpy laugh from the patient as I wound gauze around my very good work.

Friday: A sixteen-year-old girl presented, complaining of severe abdominal pain, accompanied by a jittery teenage boy whose jeans hung below the elastic waist of his boxer shorts. Patient moaning; reported having taken Ex-Lax to dispel the pain with no relief. Instantaneous and surefooted diagnosis by me: pregnant, in labor, possibly in transition; certainly in denial.

Early morning hours of the next day: Forty-eight-year-old man in cardiac arrest arrived by ambulance. Flat line. Much hyperactivity all around me. I was asked by a third-year resident to take over for him after five minutes of CPR. I did. I continued for my five minutes until he signaled, Okay, I'm back. We alternated for close to thirty minutes as others tried drugs, defib, everything at our disposal. Despite heroic efforts, he was never resuscitated. I did feel sad—this young man, his wife and children waiting to be told—but above all I felt part of a team that had done its medical best, seamlessly, loss of life notwithstanding, and proud that I never missed a compression or a count.

I am not saying that I deserve a Nobel Prize in medicine for what were, essentially, feats of first aid. Not at all. I wouldn't even present them as evidence of professional advancement. All I'm saying is that in the span of five days, no one had a tantrum at the sight of me. No one looked up from a gunshot wound or a blunt head trauma or a seizing accident victim and barked, "Not Thrift. Not her. Get me someone else."

MY SIXTEEN-YEAR-OLD PRIMIPARA, Amber Quinlan, had the far bed in a double with a woman whose side of the room was a florist's bonanza. I asked the teenager if she remembered me from the emergency room.

"It was a girl," she said.

"I know. I read your chart before I came in. Congratulations."

"Yeah, right. Just what I needed."

I asked how she was feeling.

She asked if I was a doctor; brightened when I said I was, and asked if I could write her a prescription for OxyContin.

My ER antennae vibrated: A patient was asking for a controlled substance cited in a recent memo as being a fashionable street drug. I said, "What do you need Oxy-Contin for?"

"Pain," she said. "Wicked bad."

I went back to the nurses' station, checked Amber's file, saw she'd been given Tylenol with codeine. I returned to her bedside and said, "Do you remember getting a pill about fifteen minutes ago?"

"No."

I told her she'd feel better soon, and said good night. As I made my turn, I was jerked back by Amber's hand clutching the hem of my white jacket. "My baby?" she asked. "Is she okay? They said she had to go into the special nursery."

"That's just a precaution. Because of your age and because you didn't have prenatal care."

"I took vitamins," she said. "I knew that I was supposed to do that much. And I drank chocolate milk, like, a lot."

I borrowed a chair from the roommate's side of the double, and closed the curtains around us. "What about your parents?" I asked.

"What about them."

"Did anyone notify them?"

"Someone had to call my mother about insurance and also 'cause I'm under eighteen. She left work and came here."

"How was that?"

"Freakin' out. Hysterical. Like, 'How could you do this to me?' And 'I'm not raising no baby so don't get any ideas about bringing her home.'"

"Is that what you'd planned? To bring the baby home?"

Amber said, "No way."

"Then you've decided to give her up for adoption?"

Amber said, "I've heard you can get money for it."

I said she'd have to talk to the social worker, but I doubted that very much.

"I knew a girl," said Amber, "and the family who was getting her baby sent her these big thick steaks in the mail so she'd eat right. And after the adoption was legal? She got a car."

I said, "Promise me you won't leave until you speak to a social worker."

Amber took a swig from a bedside can of Coke. "Is she going to tell me to keep it?"

A head appeared through the curtains. "Excuse me," she said. "I'm in the next bed so couldn't help over-hearing. But do you mind if I ask if the baby's father is Caucasian?"

Amber said, "What?"

Before I could define *Caucasian* or compose a sentence suggesting that the woman mind her own business, the roommate continued. "I know people who are trying desperately to adopt. I could put the two of you in touch."

I said, "This is a matter for social workers and adoption agencies and . . . and . . . responsible adults."

"Not true," said the roommate. "Private adoptions can be arranged through a lawyer."

"Enough," I said to her. "Please. She's sixteen years old."

"He's white," Amber said. "So's his mother. I never met his father."

"What does his father do?" asked the roommate.

"Please don't confuse her," I said.

When the roommate had receded back through the curtains, Amber said, "I was thinking maybe one of those open adoptions where the parents send you a letter and a picture once a year. And if I ever get my own place, she could come during school vacation."

I said, "I'm sure they'll find a wonderful couple who will take all of that under advisement."

"Go see her," said Amber. "They'll let you in. You're a doctor, right? You can go right up to her."

"You can go in, too," I said. "Day or night. You're the mother."

She shook her head.

"You want me to go for you and give you a report?"

Amber said, "Her face was kinda swollen. I want to know if there's anything wrong or if it's just from getting born."

"Are you sure you don't want to come with me? They like to get you up on your feet."

"I'll do it tomorrow. I have bad cramps, almost as bad as when I was having her."

I said, "That's normal. The medication should be kicking in about now."

"Come back after," said Amber.

ON DUTY, TALKING nonsense to Baby Girl Quinlan in her unflattering lavender cap, one big finger massaging her back, was Nurse Leo Frawley.

"How is she?" I asked.

"Fine. Just passing through on her way to the big-girl nursery," he said.

"Everything normal?"

"Yup. Breathing on her own, eating by mouth, pooping nicely. She's shipping out in twenty-four hours."

I told him I was in the ER when her mother came in complaining of abdominal pain, and had recognized it as labor.

"Good call," said Leo.

"It wasn't as obvious as it sounds. I mean, she could have been a regular fat girl with appendicitis."

Leo said, "And how clueless do parents have to be, or how absent or how wasted, not to notice their daughter's pregnant?"

I said, "That doesn't sound like the Leo I know."

"I've seen too much," he said. "The milk of human kindness dries up when you've taken care of as many crack babies as I have."

I said, "She may have been hiding the pregnancy, but she told me she drank milk and took vitamin pills."

"Over the counter One A Day—with iron if we're lucky—and no prenatal care," he said. "Big fucking deal." He smiled, though, as soon as he turned back to the baby. "She must have done something right. This one's lookin' good. Even her weight was decent."

I bent down so that I was eye level with the baby. "Kind of ugly, though, isn't she?"

Leo shushed me.

"You're not suggesting that she distinguishes between flattering and unflattering adjectives?"

"I never take that chance," said Leo. He turned back to the baby and crooned, "Right, sweetie-pie? All my babies are beautiful. Even the ones who are as homely as sin."

Now I tried it, a kitchy-cooing of my own design. I said, "Little girl? Nurse Frawley didn't say 'homely as sin.' What Nurse Frawley actually said was, 'Isn't she going *home* soon?'"

"She's not," said Leo. "At least not with Miss Foul-mouth Quinlan."

"You know that?"

"I know everything," said Leo. "It affects a bunch of stuff. Like none of us goes to the mother's room and gives the old breast-milk-is-best pep talk. Also, I was at the birth, or shortly thereafter. Let's just say a cursory evaluation of Amber's motherhood potential leads me to say, 'Good riddance to bad rubbish.'"

"On the other hand, she *did* ask me to check on the baby and report back to her."

"Sweet," said Leo.

"So can I tell her that everything's fine? Because she was worried about the baby's face looking swollen."

"She was a little beat up coming out, but that's normal. She'll be totally adorable in a week or two."

He moved to an incubator, which bore a child's

drawing by what I deduced was an older sibling, and a second fanciful poster-paint sign proclaiming MY NAME IS TYLER ANDREW.

I stayed by Amber's baby, who was tightly swaddled and propped on her side. Her face was red; a hematoma was blossoming under one closed eye. Usually I would introduce myself to a patient, but here I just whispered, "I'm sure you're going to have a great life, and that your adoptive parents will give you music lessons and ortho-donture if you need it, and send you to college and even graduate school. Okay?" I looked over my shoulder to make sure Leo wasn't close enough to hear. "And in her own way your birth mother really loved you, because no teenager takes vitamin pills and drinks milk unless she has a pronounced altruistic streak." I touched the worn flannel blanket that swaddled her tightly, then crossed to where Leo was rocking Tyler, still attached by tubes to various monitors.

I asked if that was part of the protocol—rocking the babies in rocking chairs.

Leo smiled. "Why, yes, Dr. Thrift. I think this might be considered a protocol—as well as calming a fussy baby. Not to mention soothing the nurse on call, espe-cially when he's tired and his other customers are asleep."

"I like that," I said. "I mean, do I ever get to sit down in a rocking chair when I'm stressed? Maybe *I* should consider neonatology."

"It's a gas. I mean, I see bad stuff, but now even babies weighing a pound and a half go home in a car seat wearing real baby clothes instead of doll outfits. Even when I'm in peds, I sneak back in to see my babies."

His babies. How could I not bring up the biological one in utero? I said, "You must be looking forward to sitting in a rocking chair with your own son or daughter."

Leo looked down at Tyler and said after a moment, "I'm sure I will."

"And Meredith must love babies, too, or she wouldn't be a midwife."

"Meredith—" Leo stopped. "Well, no one can say she doesn't live in a world that revolves around childbirth." He turned back to Tyler and said, "Okay, pal. How about a delicious snack?" And back to me. "He just started taking breast milk. You missed the party at lunch."

He went to the refrigerator and I followed as he explained that it was an unusually quiet night here in special care. During the day, it was Grand Central. Some parents camped out here, which was actively encouraged. Good for the mothers, good for the babies.

"Am I supposed to talk Amber into keeping hers?" I asked.

"No! She's what? Fifteen?"

"Sixteen."

"Why would you think it's a good idea for a sixteen-year-old single mother to raise her unwanted baby as opposed to some desperate couple who will worship her?"

"No sound reason. Just thinking of Amber down the road. She has this elaborate plan for open adoption and summer vacations when the baby's older."

"Anything's possible. A healthy white infant? Let her negotiate."

An inappropriate hypothesis passed through my brain: Might unwed Meredith give her out-of-wedlock baby to an infertile married couple? To mask the traitorous thought, I pushed it over the border into prepartum enthusiasm. "You'll be a wonderful father. Anyone who can appreciate these scaly, wizened preemies will certainly be a fabulous dad."

"You'd think so," Leo murmured.

"Are you saying you *won't* be a fabulous dad?"

"I'm saying . . . only that I would have liked to have been consulted first."

I recognized that this was a moment, unlike any ever seized by the Dr. Stephanie Crawfords of the world, to express solidarity and sisterhood. "Is that logical?" I asked. "How do you consult someone before a birth-control accident?"

Leo unscrewed the nipple of a tiny bottle labeled with Tyler's name, then headed toward the microwave. "Not to embarrass you with technical contraceptive details, but let's just say she was a firm believer in a method that is touted as being as effective as pharmaceuticals."

"Such as?"

"Don't make me say it. Let's just say that the character of one's vaginal secretions rules the day."

"Not that mucus method?"

"Bingo," said Leo. "Do you believe I put my faith in that earth-mother crap?"

I asked if there had ever been a study done.

"Yeah, right. A study where no one knows whether she was testing her mucus or inserting a diaphragm."

Leo rarely employed sarcasm. I said, "Sorry. I didn't

know I was asking such a stupid question."

"Didn't mean to snap," he said. Then: "I got your note. What's up?"

I said, "I don't know exactly."

He asked when I was free.

I said, "Sunday, Tuesday, or Thursday nights. After seven."

"Let's do Sunday. Your place? Because there's an occupancy issue at mine."

I said 11G, north tower. Right through the tunnel. If he could get away.

"Seven-thirty on Sunday. Do I eat before I come?"

I said no. We'd have dinner. I didn't own a table yet, but we could improvise.

"Let's go out," he said. "Ever been to Pho Saigon?"

I said no. But I'd like to.

"Good. Unless you hear otherwise, I'll pick you up at seven-thirty."

A baby emitted a near-soundless mewl and another joined in. An alarm sounded. Leo headed for it, reassuring me that it was all in a night's work—that these little ones forgot to breathe sometimes, but a firm prod was all it took.

20
Saturday Night

I HAD NO plans. Ray had left a message on my answering machine saying that he had to go to a wake. Kind of sudden. Long story. Would call later.

So at approximately eight-thirty P.M. I was alone,

enjoying the newly discovered phenomenon of restaurant delivery beyond the pizza genre (Greek salad and moussaka), when I heard cries from across the hall— male groans and expletives, followed by what sounded like a woman's shushing.

I turned off my radio. I couldn't make out what was being said, but the man seemed enraged. The woman was pleading. Or was she crying? Was it Sylvie?

I walked across the hall and rapped on the door. When no one answered I said, "Sylvie? Is everything okay in there?"

"Go away," said the male voice. "She's fine. Mind your own business."

Any good 911 operator knows that the voice one obeys is not that of the man claiming that his victim is fine.

Call security, I wondered? Enlist Anthony the pathologist in 11F? Adrenaline and fear and perhaps too many newspaper accounts of passersby ignoring the stabbed and the mugged propelled me to turn the knob of 11H. And though a chain barred my entrance, an obstructed and narrow slice of the scene revealed Dr. Charles Hastings, naked and writhing in apparent agony on Sylvie's sateen sheets.

"Sylvie? Are you all right?" I called.

"Oh, fuck," said Hastings.

Sylvie, whose leopard-print bra matched her leopard-print bikini underpants, came into view. "He thinks he ruptured a disk," she said through the crack in the door.

"Hi, Dr. Hastings," I called in his direction.

"Go away," he moaned.

"Maybe this is a good thing," Sylvie told him. "Now the two of us can get you into a wheelchair."

"I can't sit down," he yelled. "What the hell good is a wheelchair going to do?"

Sylvie unfastened the chain. Once inside, I asked her guest if he could walk at all.

"We tried that," said Sylvie. "His right leg is numb."

"You need an MRI," I said.

"Oh, really?" Hastings said. "You think I needed you to tell me that?"

"Shut up, Chuck," said Sylvie. "She's trying to help."

"I thought someone was raping you," I said.

Sylvie pulled the sheet up to Dr. Hastings's waist. "It was only histrionics," she said. "Only the howls of the man with the world's lowest pain threshold."

"I . . . am . . . in . . . agony!" he roared. "I need something for the pain!"

Sylvie said, "You can't walk. You can't sit. We have two choices here: We call an ambulance or we get a gurney."

"No ambulance! I want to go directly to X ray. And I don't want any goddamn first-year resident reading my MRI. I want Klein or Coughlin, period. I don't care who else is on call." He looked at me directly, sourly. "Don't I know you?" he asked.

Imagine: After all his flayings in public, all the injuries to my career and my soul, Charles Hastings didn't have the courtesy to put my name with my face.

I said, "I'm Alice Thrift. You tried to throw me out of the program."

"I. Am. In. Agony!" was his reply. "You idiots don't

seem to understand that."

Sylvie gave the frame of the Murphy bed a shake, as if reminding him of its potential to right itself and wreak worse lumbar damage. "And where do you think you're going without us two idiots? Home? In your imported leather low-slung driver's seat?" She pantomimed the shifting of gears with a whiplash-worthy thrust.

She turned to me. "I think we should let the punishment fit the crime. Idiot Schwartz will get dressed and find a gurney, while Idiot Thrift will stay here and keep Chuck company."

I said, "Let me—"

"No. It's my problem. If anyone's going to hijack a gurney, it's going to be me." Sylvie wriggled into jeans, found shoes under the bed, grabbed the first sweater that her bureau drawer rendered, and left.

Hastings glared and I said nothing. After another minute I offered, "She probably has an anti-inflammatory in her medicine cabinet."

"I can't take aspirin or ibuprofen. I have reflux."

I sat down on the farthest corner of the bed. After another silence I asked, "Did this come on suddenly?"

He curled his lip and turned his face away.

"How did it happen?" I tried again.

"Fucking your friend!" he yelled. "Is that what you're angling for? Some salacious details that you can incorporate into your fantasy life?"

I asked, with much dignity, "Do you think that was called for?"

"Do you understand what this pain is like? Have you ever had a ruptured disk? Have you ever even taken *care* of someone who ruptured a disk?"

I said, "For the record, I haven't rotated through orthopedics yet."

"Get my clothes," he barked. "You can do that much, can't you?"

I rose slowly and took my time collecting his boxer shorts, his socks, and his undershirt, which I then dropped on his chest.

"Now dress me," he said.

"I'm sorry," I said, "but that's out of the question."

"You're going to get me dressed, or I write this up."

"For what?"

"For refusing to help me."

I said, "I wasn't born yesterday. There is nothing reportable in feeling squeamish about putting underwear on your attending."

"Squeamish? Over what? A man's body? That's pathetic."

I said, "I didn't mean *squeamish* in the personal sense. I meant, you yell and scream at me when you're feeling fine, so I'd be very stupid to go near you with a suspected herniated nucleus pulposus."

With much grimacing and sighing, he lifted his arms and scraped his undershirt over his face, down to his neck.

"Please," he whimpered.

Just in case he was right; just in case I was violating some footnote to my Hippocratic oath, I took the boxer shorts from his chest and walked to the foot of the bed.

There was no way to oblige without lowering the blanket, so I did—past Dr. Hastings's proud genitalia, his thighs, his bony knees, his hairy legs, all the way to his ugly feet.

"Easy. Easy. Easy," he sniped as I shimmied his boxers up his legs. I looked away for the final journey up and over his pelvic region. I looked back at his face when it was over, and tried to see past the bluster and fury. I thought, Maybe I could summon the skills I'd read about under "The Doctor-Patient Relationship." He's injured and in pain, possibly frightened. I could summon a phrase or two that expressed goodness and mercy. Maybe, when he gets back to work, he'll mention my humanity to Dr. Kennick.

Just then, just when I might have pronounced one therapeutic sentence that recognized the absurdity of our situation and his extracurricular mortification, his fingers clasped my wrist. "I remember now! The botched cholecystectomy. Well, don't think there's any capital in this for you. Because if you ever tell a living soul about this, I'll have your ass in a sling, missy. This night never happened, understand?"

"Let go of me," I said.

"I don't even like the fact that you're friends with Sally, and I'm not afraid to make that abundantly clear to her."

I answered forcefully and eloquently. Unfortunately, the speech never left my head. *Surely you recognize that you are in no position to put anyone's ass in a sling. Surely you realize that you are a man who herniated his disk having relations with a woman half his age in violation of his marriage vows and of the hospital's sexual harassment policy. Does that arrogant brain of yours*

understand that if Sylvie—her name is Sylvie—knew
what you'd said about not approving of our friendship,
she'd laugh in your face? Tell me that you recognize that
you're at our mercy. That everyone within the sound of
your voice, in case you were thinking of yelling for help,
is another resident who will be witness to your trans-
gressions. Chuck.

"Get me my cell phone," he ordered.

I pointed to his jacket. "There?"

"Look in the pockets, for God's sake. Is that so hard?"

His camel-hair jacket hung over the back of a kitchen chair. The first bulge I found was his wallet.

"What are you doing in there?" he called.

I walked a few steps closer, wallet wide open. "Is this your wife?" I asked.

"Give me that!"

"What's her name?"

He tapped his cranium, above his right ear. "I'm taking notes. Up here. Every impertinent word you've uttered since you burst in here."

I turned the wallet face out. "Is it my imagination, or does she look a little sad?"

"Shut up! Either you make yourself useful or shut the fuck up. And where the hell is your friend? I want my phone. I asked for my phone a half hour ago!"

I found his wafer-thin phone, which I tossed in the direction of his lap. He caught it with a yowl of pain, and snarled into its mouthpiece, "Hospital operator."

I took a gulp from an abandoned wineglass that I hoped was Sylvie's, then remembered my moussaka fondly.

"Who are you trying to reach?" I asked.

"I'm trying to page Schwartz. Goddamn it. I'm in call-park. Now what do I do?" He looked up, saw me at the door, and asked forlornly, "Where are you going?"

"Be right back," I said. I slipped out, grabbed my take-out containers, and returned. I added more wine to a glass and sat down, purposely out of view. Sylvie's kitchen had a window that mine lacked, an accompanying bird feeder, and a view of an inner courtyard with a lamppost illuminating a wooden bench.

"Where the hell is she?" he asked again. "And where the hell are you?"

"Right here. I'm finishing my dinner. I'd offer you some but I don't think you should eat supine."

"Fuck you," he said.

"It's delicious. Greek food. Sylvie recommended this place: Mykonos. I think I taste mint in the dressing."

"I'm thirsty," he answered. "And I'm cold. Where's the thermostat?"

I heard the ping of the elevator down the hall. A few seconds later the door opened and Sylvie announced, as if she'd rehearsed on her way up, "Look. The gurney didn't fit, which makes perfect sense when you think about it because these are residential elevators—"

"Did you get a gurney or not?"

Sylvie called over her shoulder, into the hall, "Aaron?"

An enormous man with a shaved head, wearing the green scrubs of an orderly and with the biceps of a serious gym regular, stepped inside the apartment. "Hi, doc," he said. "How's it goin'?"

"The gurney's downstairs," Sylvie explained. "We just have to get you to the lobby. He bench-presses . . . what did you tell me? Five hundred pounds?"

Aaron laughed. "Close enough: around two-fifty on a good day."

"In any event, it'll be a cinch for him to lift you," said Sylvie.

"When I can't sit up? Are you crazy?"

"What's your choice, doc?" said Aaron. "Sliding down the banister?"

Sylvie turned to me and said, "We have a plan. How's *your* lower back?"

I didn't want to miss the spectacle of the hospital's biggest bully queuing up for what would be seen on a busy Saturday night as nonlife-threatening, i.e., take a number, Dr. Full Professor Hastings. I said fine, count me in.

Sylvie crossed to the broom closet. After stabilizing an avalanche of grocery bags, she returned dragging an ironing board.

"Have you lost your mind?" asked Hastings.

"What we got here is a creative emergency solution," said Aaron. "What's the big deal? You lie on an ironing board for two minutes? Ever been in combat? You think the wounded make a fuss over what kind of slab carries them to a helicopter?" He grinned. "Well, maybe they would if the slab was covered with orange Teflon daisies."

"I won't fit. It's too narrow and too short."

"We'll tie you on," said Sylvie.

"Got any rope?" Aaron asked.

"Rope *belts,*" said Sylvie.

"Like terrorists being subdued on a plane," I said.

"Get me a couple," said Aaron.

Sylvie produced three belts—one with replicas of ancient coins decorating it, one a leather braid of autumn colors, one black suede with silver-tipped fringe.

"Got any bungee cords?" Aaron asked.

"Not a one," said Sylvie.

"Neckties?"

"Just his," she said.

Aaron said, "That's nice, doc—you arriving all dressed up for your date."

I could see Hastings straining not to dislodge another expletive.

"I myself like a nice jacket and tie when I take a lady out—"

"Does anyone understand what I'm going through?" asked Hastings.

"Do we need rope?" Aaron mused.

"I have some that the previous tenant left behind," I said.

"Nah," said Aaron. "We'll wrap him good with an extra sheet, like a mummy. We can keep him immobile for the ride down. Right, ladies?"

"This is Dr. Thrift," said Sylvie. "Maybe you've seen her around."

From the opposite side of the bed, I offered my hand to the enormous Aaron. "Please call me Alice," I said.

AFTER INSULTING THE fourth- and third-year residents and insisting they bypass the attending on call for the chairman of the department, Hastings was admitted to a private room. Sylvie and I didn't stay.

I stood outside a phone booth while Sylvie called Mrs. Hastings. "Is this going to be a confession?" I asked her.

"Absolutely not," said Sylvie. "This is all business. This is 'Hello, Mrs. Hastings. Dr. Schwartz here. Your husband has been admitted to the orthopedic service with severe lower-back pain . . .'"

I shook my head. "It's not your job. Let him call his own wife."

"He refuses. He says she's not even expecting him."

"Because . . . ?"

"Because he's got her trained to think that he works around the clock."

"Every night?"

"Enough. Whenever he feels like it. Plus their house is in Marblehead, so he can use that as an excuse—too far to drive home once he's called in for a fake emergency."

After many rings, and after formal opening remarks addressed to what must have been the answering machine, Mrs. Hastings picked up. Sylvie started over—name, rank, and careful introduction of the phrase "Your husband's in the hospital."

"He didn't want us to make a fuss," she explained, "so he'll be furious with me for calling." There was a short pause, after which Sylvie restated, "Schwartz. Sylvie Schwartz. . . . No, internal medicine . . . different service. . . . No, probably just bed rest, but time will tell." Mrs. Hastings must have alleged that her husband was actually a pussycat, or that his bark was worse than his bite, because Sylvie then murmured, "That's a side of him we residents seldom see."

We walked back through the tunnel together. I asked if she'd like a cup of tea, but she said no. Quite the hideous night, and now she was going to change the sheets and try to forget her own lapses in sexual judgment.

I said, "Maybe the MRI will show he has a brain tumor, which is causing rash behavioral changes and making him worse than usual."

"Wouldn't that be nice," said Sylvie. "Unfortunately, the test was limited to the lumbosacral spine."

I asked if she thought he was going to find a way to punish us for this.

"For what? Getting him help? Escorting his dead weight down eleven floors and into the hands of an MRI maven?"

"Not that. For talking back. For shining a light into the film library. For reminding him he has a wife. For tossing his cell phone onto his testicles."

Sylvie threw her arm around my shoulders. "We're untouchable," she said. "We are a walking class-action suit. So stop worrying about punishment. He's the one who should be nervous. If he looks at you cross-eyed, he's dead meat."

Dead meat. I liked that expression. I filed it away.

LEO WAS LATE, but not egregiously: ten minutes and counting, which I'd learned from Ray to view as a grace period in the manner of a restaurant hostess. When the knock came at eleven minutes past the half hour, I opened the door, smiling hospitably as if he'd been on the dot—to find Meredith in a voluminous black coat and black felt sombrero, fanning her flushed face with red leather gloves.

"Ready?" she asked, collecting me with the professional smile of a tour leader.

I asked where Leo was, and she answered, "Double-parked downstairs."

I said, "I didn't know Leo had a car."

"It's mine. Sorry we're late. We were talking and lost track of time."

I asked if I was supposed to come with her, or was she canceling the plans I'd made with Leo?

Meredith frowned. "Did we get the time or day wrong? Sunday at seven-thirty, correct?"

"Correct," I said.

"Are you bringing your friend? Ray, is it?"

I said no. Because, frankly, I hadn't anticipated . . . an odd number. My understanding was that she'd be working.

"Leo told you I was working?"

I said, "I must have misunderstood."

She opened her coat to display her beeper on her

thickening waist. "I have two mothers past their due dates, so he was probably expecting another interrupted night." She smiled. "Poor Leo. It's awfully hard to get my undivided attention. I'm glad he feels comfortable enough to make plans with his women friends when I'm working."

Later Sylvie would tell me that she hadn't meant to eavesdrop, but that the patronizing tone wafting across the hall got her attention. At that juncture—as Meredith expressed gratitude for the charity of Leo's friends—Sylvie threw on something presentable, and invented a reason to open her front door.

"Hey," she said. "Anyone seen my Sunday paper? I never should have left it outside my door all day. People think you're working and won't miss it."

I introduced them, then waited for Sylvie's objective to announce itself.

Meredith mumured, "Leo is going to wonder what happened to us."

Sylvie turned to me and winked. "So, Alice," she said heartily, despite the coat over my arm and the keys in my hand, "want to order a double order of moo shu something?"

I said, "I'm sorry, but I'm going out for dinner."

"You and Meredith?"

"And Leo," I said.

"So that's three, right?"

I said yes, so it seemed.

"How about a foursome?" Sylvie asked.

"It's fine with me," I said.

"Do you know Leo?" Meredith asked.

"Why, no, I don't," said Sylvie, "but I like the sound of him."

"We really have to run," said Meredith.

"Get your coat, Syl," I said.

FROM THE BACKSEAT, Sylvie regaled her new acquaintances with the tale of Dr. Hastings's unfortunate night. I marveled at her ability to paint him as the villain and herself as the villainess and—a mere twenty-four hours later—extract its anecdotal value.

"But it must have been painful for you to see him for what he was," said Meredith. "I'm having a hard time believing that you're taking this so well."

"I have such bad taste in men," Sylvie explained, "that the only way to look back on these unfortunate liaisons without hating myself is to hate the former object of my affection."

"Sounds healthy," said Leo.

"How old are you?" Meredith asked.

"Twenty-nine in June," said Sylvie. "Doesn't that sound like I'm on the verge of something precarious?"

"Were you ever married?"

"Actually not," said Sylvie. She nudged me with her elbow. "But I've had a lot of honeymoons."

"Isn't Dr. Hastings in his fifties?" asked Meredith. "And married?"

"He told me he was separated," said Sylvie. "Isn't that odious?"

"And he pursued her for many months," I added.

"Meredith pursued me for months until I caved," said Leo.

"He's kidding," said Meredith. "Because if anyone did the pursuing in this relationship, it was he."

"We got that," said Sylvie. "Even from back here we sensed his gently mocking tone."

"Leo doesn't like to be serious. He thinks everyone, including me, is too earnest. He'd like it if we all made jokes twenty-four hours a day."

"What an insensitive fellow you are, Mr. Frawley," said Sylvie.

If the appellation "Mr. Frawley" sounded a note of intimacy in my tin ear, I could only assume that Meredith heard it, too. She took off her big black sombrero and placed it in her lap.

Leo said, "Alice? You're quiet back there."

I said, "I let Sylvie do the talking when we're together."

"She's an excellent audience," said Sylvie. "And you should have seen her going *mano a mano* with Hastings."

"No!"

"Absolutely. Tell Leo what you said to him."

"When?"

"When I was out looking for the gurney. You know . . ." She mouthed, The wallet.

"I opened his wallet and there was a picture of his wife—"

"Tell him what you said."

"I said that his wife looked a little sad."

Sylvie slapped the back of the driver's seat. "Isn't that great? I couldn't have done that because it would have been seen as sarcastic and belligerent, but Alice can say those things with an absolutely straight face and sound heartfelt."

I said, "I was heartfelt. I mean, I wanted to shame him, but at the same time I did think she looked a little sad."

"Was it a formal photograph or a candid one?" Meredith asked.

Leo snickered.

"Was that a humorous question?" Meredith asked.

"Probably not an intentionally humorous one," said Leo.

"Case in point," said Meredith. "Everything has to be a joke."

I said, "She was wearing what appeared to be a wedding dress."

"Which is kind of sweet when you think about it," said Leo.

"Why?" I asked.

"Because if they're both in their fifties, he's been carrying it in his wallet for twenty or twenty-five years, transferring it each time he bought a new wallet."

"Those are the guys to watch out for," said Sylvie. "The guys with the gallery of family photos on their office étagère."

"Do they have children?" asked Meredith.

Sylvie said, "He never mentioned any."

"Because I would think that the minute you had a child, that's the face you'd want to see when you open your wallet."

"I find that an illuminating statement," said Leo.

Sylvie said, "They probably had children, and the

state took them away."

Leo laughed and gave the steering wheel a thump. Meredith asked why she would say that.

"Another embittered joke," said Sylvie. "And a commentary on his cruel and unusual treatment of young people under his tutelage."

"She means me," I said.

"How about his sexual harassment of *me?*" said Sylvie. "Because even if you factor in the consenting-adult stuff, he started it."

"You're twenty-nine," said Meredith, evenly, pleasantly. "He's an attending in surgery, not medicine. So I'm not sure I see where the sexual harassment comes in."

"You are one-hundred-percent correct," said Sylvie. "You are so correct that I'm hanging my head in shame back here, and mentally composing a letter of reference to his next girlfriend."

"I didn't mean to sound critical," said Meredith.

I jumped in to add, "He's older, he's married, he's a full professor, he's powerful, so whether or not Sylvie thinks she's having run-of-the-mill consensual relations—"

"Meredith is saying it takes two to tango," said Sylvie. "One of us needed the strength of character to say a firm 'No, thank you.'"

Leo made a great show of hitting buttons on the silent radio. "Where is this stuff coming from? Am I tuned to the women's talk channel? I can't seem to shut it off."

"Leo doesn't like to discuss anything too earnestly, especially if it involves feelings," Meredith explained.

"He's a guy!" said Sylvie.

Meredith said, "I *really* dislike generalizing about men and women. I bend over backward, especially in my profession, to avoid thinking in terms of what are male and female behaviors."

Sylvie said, "Delivering babies? I would think that would be the bottom line, genderwise—I mean, in a good way—"

"Biologically and anatomically," I added.

"I mean, there are divisions, period. Unalterable ones. Ones that require a uterus and Fallopian tubes," Sylvie added.

I was seated directly behind Meredith, who straightened her shoulders but didn't answer. Her posture seemed to be saying, Don't patronize me, doctor.

Leo said, "If I put a pink cap on a boy baby the father usually goes a little ape-shit."

"Do you do that to make a point?" asked Sylvie.

"I never do anything to make a point," said Leo.

I corrected him—he who had rehearsed me to deliver stinging ultimata to Dr. Kennick; he who made me revoke my letter of resignation. He who'd been grievance chairman of the nurses' union for two terms—

"Really?" asked Sylvie. "You were grievance chair?"

"Someone's got to do it," he said.

"I was cochair of professional development in the union," said Meredith.

"Cool," said Sylvie. "Is that how you met?"

"No," said Leo. "Our tenures never overlapped."

"I was his sister-in-law's midwife," said Meredith.

"And Uncle Leo was working that night, so of

course I popped in."

"Every twenty minutes," said Meredith.

"I was nervous," he said. "It was Christopher's first."

I could see Meredith didn't like that—invoking the father's name instead of the mother's—but she turned her face toward the window, aborting another debate. I hadn't seen this side of Leo, his rising to the occasion for the sake of an audience, his willfully striving to get someone's goat.

AND NOW THE four of us were seated at Pho Saigon, the team of Meredith and Leo opposite the team of Sylvie and me. Finally, Meredith excused herself with a pregnant woman's shrug—uterus impinging on bladder, it reminded us; indulge me. As soon as she was ten feet away, Leo leaned forward and said, "I couldn't help it. She just assumed she was invited, so I couldn't tell her to stay home."

"It's fine," I said.

"So let me jump in and ask while she's out of earshot," said Sylvie. "Are you in love with this woman?"

Leo looked up toward the passage that led to the ladies' room, then down at the menu. "I'd have to say no."

"But now she's pregnant, and you're a reliable and responsible kind of guy?"

Leo said, "I seem to have this conversation every time I sit around a table."

I asked if he'd had this conversation around his mother's table yet.

"You don't seem to realize what that involves," he said, "or how it would upset my mother and several of her female children."

"In this day and age?" asked Sylvie.

"She's a devout Catholic," said Leo, "so her take on it would be personal anguish over the fact that I won't be with her for all eternity because of my sins."

"And you believe that?" asked Sylvie.

"It doesn't matter what I believe. It's my mother's belief that's going to drive her to her bed."

I said, "I've met his mother. She doesn't strike me as the type that falls apart too easily."

Leo looked up as there was movement in the restroom alcove: Meredith rejoining us.

"Everyone's looking very solemn," she said.

"We were discussing my mother," said Leo.

"I see," said Meredith. She opened her menu and appeared to read every classification conscientiously.

Leo turned to me. "So, Alice? How's the boyfriend?"

I answered, borrowing a phrase from modern life as overheard in the cafeteria, "Oh . . . Ray and I are having fun together. I take it one day at a time."

Meredith looked up. "Is he good company? Which is to say . . . do you find a lot of common ground?"

"She means," said Leo, smiling as if he were about to say something obliging, "that he seems not too bright."

Sylvie laughed. Meredith said, "Leo!"

I said, "Maybe you don't know him as well as you think you do. Or maybe a person can be good company for reasons that have nothing to do with IQ."

"I think Alice is in love," said Meredith.

"Let me answer that," said Sylvie. "Alice is finding something in Ray that isn't obvious to the outside observer—me included."

I said, "People have noticed improvements in me."

"Such as?" asked Meredith.

"I'm getting by on lcss sleep. I'm observedly less apprehensive at work. I sometimes say what's on my mind. I'm getting a television."

"You're dressing up," said Leo, and flicked one of his own earlobes to acknowledge my new ornamentation.

"So—" Sylvie added cheerfully, "it looks like I'm the only one who needs a boyfriend."

Leo blinked comically, as if picking up the strains of something faint. "That radio call-in show?" he said. "I keep hearing female voices asking for romantic advice." His head-swiveling attracted the attention of a waiter, who called from two tables over, "Be right there."

"Three Vietnamese beers?" Leo asked us.

"Sure," said Sylvie and I.

"Do you have milk?" Meredith called across to the waiter. "I don't see it on the menu, and I'm pregnant."

The waiter said, "Yes. One minute."

"I'll have a glass if it's skim," she said. "Other-wise—"

"Just do it," said Leo.

SHE WAS PAGED just as she was dipping into her soup, noodles expertly wrapped around her chopsticks.

"Don't tell me," said Sylvie.

Meredith actually smiled as if dispensing a lesson in self-possession to those of us who lived by being occupationally frazzled, then excused herself in search of quiet.

"Will she have to go in?" Sylvie asked Leo.

"Most likely."

No one said anything until she returned with a waiter in tow holding a take-out container. "I'm sorry, but I'll need the car," said Meredith.

"How many centimeters dilated?" asked Sylvie.

Meredith said, "Doctors rely on that much more heavily than we do in timing their arrival. We try to be with the mother from start to finish."

"Of course," said Sylvie.

"Good luck," I said. "Hope it's a quick one."

"I assume everyone's all right with taking the T home?" she asked, flinging her coat around her shoulders.

"Yes, no problem, fine," we answered with varying degrees of enthusiasm.

"Want me to walk you to the car?" asked Leo.

She was leaning down for a good-bye kiss, but stopped halfway and said, "Yes, I do."

HE WAS GONE long enough for Sylvie to comment, "Mark my word: trouble in paradise."

"Why don't we like her?" I asked.

She checked the door before answering. "We don't like her because we're picking up on the tension between the two of them, and we know there's a little rent in the fabric of this affair and maybe we can work a fingernail in there and do some further damage—"

"But why?"

"Why? Because Leo is so clearly unhappy and is being held hostage to Meredith's desire for a nuclear family. No, correction: desire for a baby, period. She doesn't need him! I can just picture the birth—a cadre of midwives tending to one of their own. Leo will be in the corner, dispensing the ice chips."

I asked—bravely, I thought—"Don't you think Leo can fight his own battles? I mean, you've known him for less than an hour, and you've become chairman of his grievance committee."

Sylvie smiled radiantly—not for me, but for Leo, who was striding toward us rather ambitiously.

WE WENT TO a bar—me feeling like the fun-hating, non-dancing, one-beer, suddenly exhausted third wheel. I tried to remember if I'd ever said anything proprietary about Leo, anything that would make this bald campaign for his attentions qualify as disloyal. When he left our little nightclub pedestal table for the men's room, I sipped my coffee in silence.

"What's the matter?" she asked. "C'mon. Something's wrong."

"I'm wondering if you want me to leave you two alone."

"Don't be ridiculous," said Sylvie. "What kind of friend would invite herself to dinner, then dismiss the very person who brokered the deal?"

"What deal?" I asked.

"Nothing. Bad choice of words. I meant, we're a *package* deal—you and me." She smiled. "The bells and whistles may be pure projection on my part."

"I hope so. He's practically engaged to Meredith." Sylvie rolled her eyes.

"She's pregnant. And what about you? You just had a romantic trauma twenty-four hours ago. You have to recover from that."

"I'm just having fun—meaningless, frivolous fun. So stop worrying. A little flirtation never hurt anyone. Think of it as social work: poor Leo getting some much-needed lighthearted companionship. "

"Are you trying to have sex with him?" I asked.

Sylvie laughed.

"Is that a *no?*"

"That was me expressing amusement at your phrasing, and the censure in your voice. *Shhh.* Here he comes. I'll try to tone down my scandalous behaviors."

"Let's not stay too late—"

"But I'm not tired," said Sylvie.

LEO DUTIFULLY ASKED me to dance after each round with Sylvie, but I was fixed stonily in my chair. "I don't know how to dance to this kind of music," I said.

"What kind of music *do* you dance to?" he asked.

"The kind of music they played at ballroom-dancing lessons in the eighties," I said.

"Good luck," said Sylvie.

"You two go ahead," I said.

Leo sat down, tapped my hand, asked if I was okay.

A month ago I would have answered with the "I'm exhausted" of old. Instead I said, "Clearly I'm in the way. You and Sylvie don't need a chaperone."

I felt glances being exchanged above my head. They

would be charitable, even affectionate, ones, though, because I'd brought these good-time Charlies together— such close friends of mine, the internist/baton twirler and the most popular heterosexual nurse in the world.

"Oh, stay," said Sylvie.

"Don't go," said Leo. "I mean, what would you be doing at home?"

Sylvie pointed to a chalkboard on the wall. "Look: They have pear Napoleon and Indian pudding."

"And mud pie," said Leo.

"We could share," said Sylvie.

I said, "No, thanks. I'm full. Maybe another time."

They shrugged and managed to disguise their delight. Leo insisted on accompanying me outside to hail a taxi with the ease of the lifelong city boy that he was. When a brown-and-white taxi stopped, I said good night. In response, he squeezed my shoulders and grazed my brow with his lips.

But this wasn't tenderness talking, or even regret. It was Leo saying, Thanks, Alice, old pal. I knew you'd understand.

22
I Move On

SYLVIE HAD ADOPTED me, and now Sylvie had sent me back to foster care.

I took it hard. I could have walked across the hall and said, "Let's talk," or, "I miss you." Instead I moped and cried over the rare thing I'd lost, the unexpected knocks on my door and the pleasure of her boisterous company.

Like a girl with a grudge in junior high, I barely nodded when I passed her in the halls.

Rapprochement was up to her, I reasoned. If she wanted to preserve our friendship, she should knock on my door. She should explain that it was an unfortunate misunderstanding, that she and Leo had danced and flirted and shared mud pie. Nothing more. *Whatever you're mad about, Alice, you should know this about Sylvie Schwartz: that in her book, girlfriends trump boyfriends, and comradeship trumps romance, okay? I miss you terribly and Leo is bereft.*

But the stalemate continued. I convinced myself that I couldn't respect a serial seducer, while Sylvie must have decided that anyone so square, so snappish, so judgmental, could go to hell.

I watched my new TV and noted how the world was paired: husbands and wives, mothers and daughters, doctors and nurses, lawyers and cops, anchors and meteorologists, wisecracking roommates and quirky friends.

At the same time, companionship and affection were at hand. Ray was chiseling away whenever he got the chance, memorizing my schedule, leaving groceries at my door, massaging my insteps, naming a new fudge "Alice"—constantly reminding me that he had never liked that know-it-all gal across the hall.

If Ray had been inclined, if he hadn't been relishing his elevation to therapist and best friend, he might have said, "Just do it. Go across the hall. Apologize. Or let *her* apologize. You don't know what's going on. She's probably miserable, too." I could have consulted a mental-health professional. I could have called a hotline. I could have paged Leo. If I weren't six months behind on journals, I could have read about smart women prone to stupid choices.

Instead I asked for two consecutive days off and got them. On a Friday afternoon in March, just before the clerk's office at Boston City Hall closed for the weekend, I married Ray.

23
Here Comes the Bride

I WOULDN'T HAVE called it a honeymoon—one night at the first motel we came to after crossing the Cape Cod Canal—but Ray embraced the Upstream Inn as if he'd booked two weeks in Cancún. What kind of guy doesn't take his bride out of town? he asked. What would we tell our kids—that we lived, worked, wed, married, *and* honeymooned in Boston, Mass., like two losers without wheels? So we headed for Falmouth, underestimating the traffic on a Friday afternoon in late winter, traveling light, with a garment bag for Ray, and one canvas tote containing a transparent nightgown that was his engagement gift to me.

He had made a little speech just before the city clerk pronounced us husband and wife, something to the effect of, "Alice and I might be the poster children for 'opposites attract,' but that's why I fell in love with her. If someone put a gun to her head and asked, 'Do you love Ray?' I doubt whether she'd fall all over herself answering in the affirmative. *Yet . . .*" He grinned, squeezed my hand, and repeated *"Yet"* for dramatic emphasis. "I never gave up. I know I have a job ahead of me, and that's spending the rest of my life convincing her that this was a courageous thing she did and an amazing gift to me. So this is just me saying, Thanks, Doc. I know you think it's impossible, but I really love you."

Everyone was looking to me for a reply, for some heartfelt, unscripted wedding vows. I said, "I didn't prepare anything. I've been so buried at work."

Ray grinned. "What did I tell ya? The jury's still out. But that's okay." He faced the clerk again, straightened his shoulders, straightened the knot on his new lavender tie.

The clerk hesitated, then asked if I was entering into this marriage of my own free will.

I said, Yes. Of course.

"Because nothing is binding until I sign the marriage certificate," he continued. "And you're the last wedding of the day. You can take all the time you want. Would you like a few minutes to yourself? Or is there someone you'd like to call?"

"Why?" I asked.

He nodded to his secretary, who steered me to an alcove.

"You don't look very happy," she whispered.

I explained that I was an overly serious person, too serious for my own good. I considered confiding my mother's Asperger's suspicions to underscore the point, but refrained in case the commonwealth required parental permission for brides with disabilities.

"A couple of more things," the secretary confided. "I

noticed that you came without a corsage or a bouquet. Brides usually carry flowers, even if it's just from a bucket in the supermarket. And often friends and family are in attendance."

"He offered to buy flowers," I said. "But I didn't know what I'd do with them in the car on the way to the Cape."

"Her family's out of state," Ray called. "And mine are deceased."

The secretary was frowning at my black suit, hardly a wedding ensemble, but not hospital whites or surgical blues, either. "How long have you known him?" she asked.

"For months. And earlier than that on a professional basis."

"I shouldn't have brought up that stuff about her feeling less crazy about me than I am about her," Ray joined in. "That was my inferiority complex talking. But if that's what's holding us up, then ask her what other possible motive she'd have for marrying me if it wasn't about being passionately in love?" He winked. I knew what the context was: Love on the Murphy bed. Love as a transitive verb. Love as the fruit of pheromones.

"I'm not rich and I'm not handsome," Ray continued. "I *happen* to have a heart as big as Disney World, and luckily I found someone who values loyalty and personality more than good looks and deep pockets."

"Ray and I are extraordinarily compatible," I said, returning to his side, hooking my arm through his, remembering to smile. "Which I believe correlates exceedingly well with marital success." I landed an unscheduled kiss on his lips, which seemed to answer their questions and satisfy all participants.

"Where were we?" asked the city clerk.

RAY USED THE word *honeymoon* in every other sentence he exchanged with the desk clerk, resulting in a plate bearing an apple, a pear, a banana, and an orange, which appeared minutes after we took possession of our knotty-pine suite. We weren't in the main building, but at the far end of the newer, motel-like crescent behind the inn. Despite its boast of fresh fish caught outside its doors, the room's water view was of a scummy pond. The card was addressed the way Ray had registered: Dr. and Mr. Ray Russo. I hadn't thought about nomenclature before that moment, but said, with what I hoped was great delicacy, that my diplomas all said *Thrift;* life might be simpler with name continuity.

He agreed enthusiastically. "Of course," he said. "No person named Alice Russo went to Harvard Medical School, so how can you have framed diplomas hanging on your office walls that don't match the name on the door?"

"I thought you might give me an argument about it," I said.

"Me? The guy who thinks the title 'Dr.' is more important than 'Mrs.'? The guy who met you on the job; who won't let you throw it all away even when you've hit rock bottom? Who promised never to whine about the hours or pull any immature shit like, 'You love your job more than you love me'?"

I said I didn't remember that specific exchange, but

thank you. Such support was very much appreciated.

"Dinner first?" he asked.

He meant as opposed to consummating the marriage. Ordinarily, I would choose bed and sleep, but this was real food, at a table, in a restaurant that had earned two stars in the Mobil guide. I said, "I'm starved."

"I hope it's fancy enough," said Ray.

I said, "I looked at the menu while you were checking out the gift shop, and it seems more than adequate."

Ray ran his hands up and down my sleeves. "I guess I was thinking this occasion calls for a revolving penthouse restaurant with live music and thick steaks and . . . popovers."

"Another time," I said. "Or maybe you can go with your cousins on a night that I'm working."

Ray closed his eyes.

I asked if I'd said something wrong.

"Mary and I . . . God. It makes me angry and sad at the same time. . . . We had a reception at the Knights of Columbus Hall, huge meal, a buffet with chefs carving turkeys and roast beef plus every side dish you could ever think of. And make-your-own sundaes."

I said, "*This* menu is just what I'm in the mood for: fish and chowder and a raw bar."

"If you're happy, I'm happy," he said.

I said I was going to have every course, including dessert. And I'd start with a celebratory drink. Maybe even a margarita, or something festive with cranberry juice.

"Are you going to put on a dress?" he asked.

I said I hadn't brought one, but I'd take off my suit jacket if the dining room wasn't chilly. I reached up my sleeve to pull its cuff into view. See—the blouse underneath? It had a ruffle at each wrist.

"You always look like a million bucks to me," said Ray.

WE WERE INFORMED by the hostess that a rehearsal dinner was taking place at the long table against the wall. Please forgive the excess noise. "No problem!" Ray enthused. I knew what this portended: Ray would introduce himself, shaking hands up and down the table as if he were the special-functions manager. Once seated, I leaned across the bud vase and whispered, "I know you want to jump up and announce the coincidence, but I'd prefer that you didn't."

Ray grinned. "You know me, Doc. Always the salesman. Besides, wouldn't you want to know, if you were toasting this and toasting that, that a few feet away is a couple who should get a little attention, too? Let's say the maître d' tells them on the way out that we're newlyweds. They'd feel bad that they had hogged the spotlight."

"No, they wouldn't."

He patted my hand. "All I need to say is, 'I got hitched today myself, and I hope you have great weather tomorrow and a wonderful life.'"

"Fine," I said. "Go. Chat. Make some new friends."

Ray chucked me under the chin and rose to accomplish his mission. The first man he approached shook his hand tentatively, then pointed to an older man wearing a boutonniere. Ray pumped that puzzled hand. Sentences were exchanged.

He returned to his seat, grinning, not deflated, waving to presumptive ushers he missed on his rounds. After a minute of ostensibly studying the menu, he murmured, "Did they call a waiter over?"

I said, "I wasn't watching."

"Because if I was in their shoes, I'd send two drinks to our table."

"They don't strike me as the kind of people who would do that."

He leaned closer. "Wanna know their story?"

I sighed. "Sure."

"It's the old guy and the dame in plaid on his right. The rest are their kids from previous marriages. Both widowed. Live here year-round. The bride and groom and their dead spouses played mixed doubles."

"Then you must have told them you were a widower yourself."

"I'm laying that one to rest. I'm a husband now. No one's interested in the old sad story."

"Poor Mary," I said.

Ray looked up. "What made you say that?"

"The finality of it. I know you're mad at Mary because she cheated on you, but—"

"But what? I'm supposed to forgive and forget and build a monument in Sullivan Square?"

"I only meant that you don't have to pretend she never existed. You can talk about her as much as you like. You can talk *to* her."

"*Talk to her?* How do I pull that off?"

"I meant you could still visit her grave."

"Fat chance," he said.

I asked where she was buried.

Ray said, "Buried? You mean, which cemetery?"

I said yes, of course which cemetery.

He picked up the wine list and said, "No more talk about wife number one. This is our night. I'm ordering us . . . give me a sec . . . here we go: Sex on the Beach! I don't even care what's in it."

"As long as you don't shout the order across the room," I said.

His finger slid down the menu to an illustrated box. "And lobsters! Do you like lobster? The twin lobsters come with a salad, a potato, and a vegetable."

I said yes, I loved lobster, but "market price" could be astronomical. Let's ask first . . . and did he mean we'd be sharing?

"No way! Ray Russo doesn't order from the right side of the menu on his wedding night. Besides, if they have any business sense, they'll throw in a honeymoon dis- count."

I said I thought that our fruit plate might be the only grand gesture an inn would make in the off-season, so let's not get our hopes up.

"Do I sound like a cheapskate? I hope not. Profes- sional courtesy or not, I'm just so damn happy. I can't believe I pulled this off."

"Pulled what off?"

"This! You and me." A public, louder testimonial was inspired by the appearance of our waiter, a tall young man wearing a brocade vest and the slightly disdainful look of a moonlighting graduate student. Ray continued, "So, there's me, a working stiff, barely graduated from the school of hard knocks. And who do I marry? A woman who graduated first in her class from Harvard Medical School."

"Not first," I murmured.

"Second!"

"Congrats," said the waiter. "Would you like something from the bar?"

"We certainly would," Ray said. Then—in case the waiter had missed the point—"*Especially* since we got married this afternoon at City Hall."

"I think this calls for champagne," said the waiter.

Ray cocked one eyebrow and said with a smile, "On the house, by any chance?"

"Ray!"

"We're also guests of the inn." He shielded one side of his mouth to confide, "Paying the rack rate, I should add."

"I'll see what I can do," said the waiter.

"I hope to be represented in your gift shop soon," said Ray.

I could see the waiter was straining to look interested for the sake of good service and a generous percentage of the bill. "Represented? How so?" he asked.

"Fudge. The best. And that's based on independent testing results. I left a sample with the manager."

The waiter's glance seemed to ask, Arranged marriage? Baby on the way? Someone desperate for a green card? "I'll be sure to put in a good word for your product," he said.

"First-Prize Fudge," said Ray. "That's its actual name."

I gave Ray's shin a poke. "Sex on the Sand," I reminded him, hoping he'd forgo his campaign for complimentary champagne and product placement.

"She means the mixed drink," said Ray. "Make that two."

"Excellent choice," said the waiter, with a bow in my direction.

THE DOUBLE BED sagged just enough to make sleeping a more claustrophobic event than I was used to. Ray was asleep with one cheekbone beached on my shoulder, and, while not exactly snoring, there was a uvular rattling on the exhale. He scratched himself, passed some gas, smiled beatifically. I tried to shrug him off, but that left him at an unnatural angle, neck extended, chin hooked on my shoulder. Didn't heads belong on pillows? Hadn't beds evolved to queen- and king-sized so that body integrity could be maintained during sleep?

In addition to his twitching and eructing, worry kept me awake. Insomnia was new to me, the chronically exhausted intern. I reviewed the sweet parts of the day, which surely outnumbered the embarrassing ones. I considered counting sheep, but opted to review the cranial nerves and the eight layers of the abdominal wall. Still, real life overtook medical minutiae. Panic infected every new subject. Most alarming: I was married. What seemed like convincing arguments yesterday ("Everyone has doubts; every single person who walks down the aisle wonders if he should run like hell in the opposite direction. And you know what? If you change your mind? We can always get divorced") sounded to my nocturnal ears like desperation. What was his hurry? Why *this* weekend and not six months from now?

The ghost of Mary Ciccarelli visited. Why hadn't I asked forensic questions? What was the nature and location of her accident? Had there been an autopsy? Had tissue samples been preserved?

No one, not one living soul except the reservations manager, knew where I was. It would take a private detective to find me, if ever. The pond outside was murky, black, opaque, possibly bottomless. Who would even miss me? Until my parents put two and two together and obtained my dental records, *if* my bloated body floated to the surface, I'd be an unidentified victim, the notorious Cape Cod Jane Doe.

Someone should know my whereabouts. Who could I call? I slipped out of bed. Ray stirred, snuffled, but didn't wake. I took his cell phone into the bathroom and called my home number. "This is Alice Thrift. Just for the record, in case anyone is looking for me, I am at the Upstream Inn, Falmouth, Massachusetts. I married Raymond J. Russo of Brighton, Mass., today, March 15, at Boston City Hall. I'm supposed to return on Saturday, March 16. Most likely you won't need this information."

"Alice?" Ray called. "Whaz wrong?"

I said, "I never told anyone where I was going. I just wanted to leave the information on my answering machine in case of an emergency."

"That's nice," he murmured.

"Go back to sleep," I said.

"You, too, hon," he said. "Come to bed."

I did. I nudged him a few inches toward his own side, and wedged a pillow under his head. He smiled as if these were the ministrations of a doting helpmeet.

"Love you," he murmured.

It was a hard fact to ignore: My husband not only didn't mind me but he adored me. He was so easily gratified, so eager to find tenderness in any custodial act. Wasn't that a compelling enough reason to marry? Wasn't it better to give than to receive?

I felt ashamed that my thoughts had stalled in the sulci of my brain that housed criminal suspicions. Here was a man in pain, a lonely widower, hardworking, undistinguished in almost every way, outwardly unattractive. Yet he was convinced that I brought him joy and relief and, even as a physician on probation, some distinction or pedigree. In Ray Russo's book I was a success—a healer, a curer, an ideal wife.

It could work. It shouldn't matter what outsiders thought, or what inquests I imagined in the dark. I'd call my parents in the morning and elicit their blessing. Eventually they'd send out engraved announcements, and host a subdued celebration.

My colleagues, especially the social-minded nurses and the popular Dr. Stephanie Crawford, would notice the gold band on my left hand. "Alice Thrift?" they'd squeal. *"Married?"*

"Eloped last Friday," I'd say offhandedly, but with a veiled smile. I'd practice in the mirror beforehand.

IT WAS A good thing that Immigration and Naturalization had no reason to examine our union, because, after dropping me off at 11G, Ray announced that he'd be going back to his place.

"To get your things?"

"That. And because of Pete."

"Who's Pete?"

"The dog!"

I said, "You never mentioned a dog."

"Pete's the reason I never could stay over: He acts out when he's left alone for too long, and the neighbors signed a petition. Besides," he said, "if I'm smart about one thing, it's marriage."

Smart about marriage? I asked. How did that correlate with pets?

Ray put an arm around my shoulder and tilted his temple against mine. "In this day and age, any arrangement is normal. Separate apartments, separate cities, separate time zones. This place is such a steal, and my place is not only rent-controlled but doubles as an office. So why go crazy if it means having a whole new set of business cards printed up?"

He walked to my night table and picked up my alarm clock. "Note what time it's set for: five A.M. Once I'm awoken I can't fall back to sleep. Also, I'm used to a little more space. My speakers alone would take up a high percentage of your square feet."

"How many bedrooms does your apartment have?"

"Two. But it's crummy. I haven't kept it up. And Mary was no white tornado, either." I followed him into the kitchen, where he wrote *Grape-Nuts* and *hot sauce* on my magnetized shopping list. He turned around, smiled, and announced, "The next thing on our agenda is telling your parents."

"No hurry," I said.

"Here's what I'm thinking: You say, 'Ray proposed to me and I accepted.' In other words, we're engaged."

"Not 'Ray and I got married'?"

"Unh-uh. Too cut-and-dried. That was just a civil ceremony to make it official, but now we're talking about a real wedding."

I said, "I don't want a real wedding. That's too much fuss; too much pomp and silly outfits."

"Okay. I'm hearing you. What about a party? Because a party says, 'This is our son-in-law. Alice finally tied the knot. Come meet the guy who swept her off her feet.'"

I said, "Maybe, at most, I could go along with a quiet dinner for their closest friends."

Ray opened the cupboard above my sink. "I'm counting four dinner plates. Four salad plates. Three mismatched bowls that look like they came from a yard sale. Two chipped mugs, and one wooden egg cup painted to look like an Indian maiden."

"It's from my childhood," I said. "There used to be a mate."

"My point is, what kind of inventory is this?"

"I have enough as long as I wash them after each use."

"But what about company? What about when we entertain? Are we going to set the table with Chinet and plastic forks?"

I asked if this was the sole motivation for restaging a wedding: the acquisition of housewares.

"Is that so bad? I've seen kitchens get outfitted in one fell swoop, especially if someone throws a shower. Have you heard about registering at a department store? Because when Mary and I got married, we picked things out that we never thought anyone could afford—like a Mixmaster with a dough hook, and a toaster with four slots. And would you believe that her coworkers at Kinko's chipped in and got both pieces for us?"

"What happened to those presents?"

"I gave them away. It was too hard to have them around as reminders."

"Even the appliances?"

"I let Mary's sisters take what they wanted. The rest I gave to Goodwill."

I asked if he stayed in touch with these original in-laws.

"Here's how that came down," he said. "When a daughter dies, even if it's an accident, parents resent the fact that it was their daughter who lost her life, and not their son-in-law. I know that's crazy, but it's human nature. It's not that they want me dead per se; it's just that deep in their subconscience, they're angry Mary was picking up the Chinese food, and not me."

"Is that how it happened? She was picking up take-out?"

"I never told you that?"

I said no. How awful. How senseless.

"People die every day running errands," he said. "She was the one who had the egg-roll craving. I was willing to eat leftovers that night. But I understand why her family severed all ties." He pointed to the telephone: speaking of parents.

I said I'd wait. Sunday was my traditional phone-home day.

Ray smiled. "You know what I think? I think you're dragging your feet. You want to call when I'm not around, because they might go ballistic, and you want to spare my feelings."

I said, "Actually, I do want to talk to them alone."

"You can't say 'I love the guy' in front of me?"

I said, "I could. The more personal the better in Joyce's book."

Ray grinned. "Now I get it. You're going to try to explain the chemistry thing, and you think I'll get embarrassed."

"Something like that," I said.

"Wow. If I told my old lady anything personal, let alone doing it, let alone *enjoying* it, she'd slap me across the face. Wife, fiancée, girlfriend, it wouldn't matter."

I asked when his mother had passed away.

"Where are we? March? A year ago."

"So you lost your mother and your wife at the same time?"

"The winter from hell. First Mary's accident, then my mother's."

"Your mother died in an accident, too?"

"She fell taking out her garbage, broke her hip, and

next thing I knew the hospital's calling me and telling me she has cancer."

"What kind?"

"Whaddyacallit: bone."

"What was the primary?"

"Huh?"

I said, "That's usually a metastatic focus and not a primary. Do you know if it was a pathologic fracture?"

"*Bone cancer* sounded right to me. I didn't know I was supposed to ask about where it started. And don't forget, I was still in shock over Mary."

"Probably breast or lung."

"Too bad I didn't know you then," said Ray. "You could've fed me the questions."

I said it probably wouldn't have changed the outcome. Was she a smoker?

Ray said, "Can we talk about more pleasant topics? Like our upcoming wedding?" He pretended to transform reality into something gauzy with a wave of his hand. "Me relatively handsome in a tux and you in a dynamite white dress, your big happy grin behind a veil which is flowing down from a shiny tiara."

A wedding dress. I felt a pinch in my heart where Sylvie had been. For weeks I'd been trying to forget the death of that friendship, studiously substituting her minuses for her pluses. But now I couldn't conjure what I'd say, on my own, to a bridal saleswoman, or what I'd make of my reflection in a three-way mirror.

"Did I say something wrong?" asked Ray.

I told him the truth: that the phrase *wedding dress* had made me wistful—

"I know, I know. But you're going to get a chance to do it up right."

I said, "Not that. I meant I was thinking of Sylvie; that *wedding dress* was reminding me of past girlfriend diversions. We shopped together once. It was only to Filene's Basement for bras, but it was really fun."

He pointed to the door. "Go. She's right across the hall. Knock on her door and ask her if she wants to have a soul-searching conversation about who hurt whose feelings and how to prevent future misunderstandings. I know how much you enjoy discussing and dissecting your feelings. So here's your chance. What's the worst that'll happen? She'll slam the door in your face?"

"Maybe I could just say, 'I thought you'd like to know that Ray and I were married yesterday.'"

"First," said Ray, "she couldn't care less. And second, we have to get our stories straight: Did we get married yesterday or engaged? We can't have two separate versions floating around."

He picked up the receiver and handed it to me. "It's not gonna get any easier," he said. "Your parents and your friends will still want to know, 'Why in hell would you pick that guy?' My advice is to say, 'Ray wants to marry me,' and see if they say, 'Over my dead body,' or, 'I have to get off and rent the hall.'"

I put the phone back in its charger. "Remind me why we chose a civil ceremony in Government Center if you're so determined to have a church wedding and a big party."

"It's simple," said Ray. "I couldn't wait. I wanted you to be Mrs. Ray Russo ASAP. But when I thought about it, I realized I'd cheated you. I had a big first wedding, but this was all you got—'I do' in a concrete office with a pencil sharpener for a bridesmaid."

I said, "I don't like to lie."

"Is it a lie if we were just sealing the deal, getting ourselves on the books? I don't think so. But you do what you think is right. I gotta get going. The kennel closes at six."

I asked if I could come with him.

"No way! Not until I clean up my apartment. You'd divorce me if you saw the way I lived." He snapped his fingers. "But that gives me a great idea. Why don't I take something of yours back with me so Pete can get used to your scent?"

I said maybe next time. Which would be when?

"I'll come by tomorrow," he said. "And I'll wear my Paco Rabanne."

"I'm working tomorrow, remember? They gave me Friday off in exchange for Sunday."

"Lunch, then?"

I said, "Lunch? You know I can't stop for lunch. I don't even have time to get a wrinkled dollar rejected by a vending machine."

Ray walked to the door, where he'd left his garment bag in a slump. With his hand on the doorknob he said solemnly, "I think you understand why it's a good plan to keep our separate places."

I said no, actually. The rationale was not clear to me at all.

"I want you to miss me. Let's say you can sneak away through the tunnel for a catnap during the day. I don't want to be here, needing a shave, doing paperwork or calling customers. In other words—and I speak from experience—I want to keep love alive."

I said, "You're being awfully modern and liberated."

He grinned. "That's me: Ray Russo, a.k.a. Mr. Thrift." He slipped his wallet out of his back pocket and checked its contents. "You wouldn't have a couple of twenties until I get to the bank on Monday?"

I said there was an ATM in the hospital lobby, through the tunnel, just inside the pneumatic doors.

He checked his watch. "I gotta get Pete," he said.

We were husband and wife now. I found my knapsack, and gave him two twenties, a ten, and the spare key I'd never had use for.

He kissed me in haste. "Call your parents. Then leave a message on my cell."

IT WAS FIVE-THIRTY P.M. and I'd been married for twenty-four and a half hours. As I studied the Mykonos take-out menu, I actually wondered whether Ray was a spy or a G-man. I'd read of dissembling within a marriage, of husbands drawing paychecks from the U.S. Postal Service when the true employer was the CIA. First-Prize Fudge could be a front for some top-secret job that required occasional travel by car around the six New England states.

No, I'd eaten that fudge, and I'd heard fudge anecdotes that only an insider could know. I had no reason to doubt Ray's credibility—except that I'd only known his address, his date of birth, and his middle name since applying for our marriage license.

I selected Greek salad and dolma, but hung up before the restaurant answered. I'd need cash. Was it the ATM that sent me down the elevator, across the tunnel, into the hospital on a Saturday night? Or was it loneliness?

"What's new?" I might ask a fellow house officer across the sneeze shield of the salad bar. "I haven't been around. I had two days off: As a matter of fact, I got married yesterday and have been honeymooning on the Cape."

But when I entered the square beige cafeteria, its lights dimmed as if Saturday night required atmosphere, there were no convivial teams of house officers occupying tables I might join. I saw a few lost souls, and several adults who looked like the depressed grown children of parents on life support. My salad was dressed with chalky ranch, its carrot curls desiccated, my onion soup watery. On my return trip—for coffee and the last piece of coconut cream pie—I came tray-to-tray with Meredith, dressed for midwifery in blue scrubs.

Her greeting—"Alice! Hello!"—was friendly, even warm. "Where are you sitting?" she asked.

I led her to my table, where she lined up her two cartons of skim milk, a banana, and a dish of paprikaed cottage cheese.

"How's work?" I asked. "And how's the fetus?"

"Work is great," she said. "I know I'm supposed to be tired, but I'm all energy. Shaw says it's plain old excitement."

"How is Dr. Shaw?"

"Fine. He asks about you. I think he thinks . . ." She stopped. "I think he thinks that I see you more often than I do."

"And Leo? Is he excited, too?"

"Leo and I . . . are on what we're calling a hiatus," she said.

I waited for her to define that term, and after two deliberate spoonfuls of cottage cheese, she did. "We're being perfectly cordial, but we're not spending time together. It was my decision. First, he hasn't told his family yet. Secondly, I felt as if I couldn't talk about the baby with pure, unalloyed enthusiasm. I shouldn't have to walk on eggshells."

"Don't people often wait to announce the pregnancy?"

"Because they're superstitious. Which is such fallacious reasoning. I mean, what if the worst happened and you miscarried? Would the pregnancy be forever a secret? People don't think like that anymore. If you lost a child, would you hide that fact? Wouldn't you want people to know; your *community* to know?"

My community. "I'd probably keep it to myself," I said.

"Well, that's not me. I've been open and honest about the pregnancy, and I don't think I should have to deny myself the delight I feel every second just because Leo isn't thrilled at the prospect of fatherhood. He's conflicted, and I am so . . . *not* conflicted."

"Were you trying to get pregnant?" I asked.

Meredith said, "Not consciously. Leo, on the other hand, thinks I was using him as a turkey baster."

I understood the reference, but didn't comment. I wondered why Meredith had joined my table, and why she was confiding anything at all unless she thought I'd report back to Leo on her independence and autonomy. "How long has the hiatus been in effect?" I asked.

"Since that dinner," she said. "And I don't mind telling you that your friend Sylvie Schwartz brought out the absolute most cynical side of Leo. I felt as if a lead curtain dropped down between us that night."

I said, "I felt that, too—as if Leo and Sylvie were ganging up on us."

"Us? No. *Me*. I couldn't say anything right. I was the odd man out to the point that I was relieved when I got beeped."

I said, "I've auto-beeped myself to extricate myself from an uncomfortable situation, too."

"Mine was the real thing, and a very long night. Which gave me time to reflect on the whole episode. You know what it reminded me of? High school. And Dr. Schwartz? Did she think I wouldn't notice her sarcasm? I'd never met her before that night, but she was awfully happy to join forces with Leo and make me the butt of their jokes."

I took a bite of pie and a sip of coffee before asking, "Do you know if they've been seeing each other?"

Meredith said, "I thought you'd know the answer to that."

I said yes, she did live across the hall from me. But I'd been keeping to myself. Well, not entirely to myself. Did she remember Ray Russo? From the dinner at Dr. Shaw's?

"Vividly."

I held out my left hand. "We eloped yesterday."

Meredith drew in her breath, then begged on the exhale, *"Why?"*

"For the same reason other people get married. To be together."

She looked this way and that. "So where is he?"

"At home."

"They can't give you one day off after you elope?"

I murmured something about checking up on a Mr. Smith or a Mr. Jones, whose hernia I'd repaired the morning of the wedding. Upon learning the patient had been discharged, I swung by the cafeteria to grab this piece of pie. In celebration.

"Congratulations," said Meredith. "He did seem awfully fond of you." She pinched open the second carton of milk. "But who isn't? You do seem to have that little-girl-lost quality that makes men want to take care of you."

I said, "I most certainly do not."

"I'm just the opposite," said Meredith. "I project self-reliance to the point of overconfidence. Which isn't the worst quality for a single mother to possess." She patted her belly, smoothing the blue cotton so I could see the suggestion of convexity.

I said, "Just because Leo isn't under the same roof as you and the baby doesn't mean he won't be a fully committed father. In this day and age, any arrangement is normal. Separate apartments, separate cities, separate time zones."

"Not where I come from," she said.

"How much time before the baby's due?" I asked.

Meredith looked at her watch. "When I left she was

287

only three centimeters dilated. So I'd say tomorrow. A Saint Patrick's Day baby."

"I meant you."

"Oh. September. Mid."

"A long time to work things out," I said.

Meredith rose. "If I see Leo, should I tell him about your wedding? Or do you want to tell him yourself?"

I said, "I don't think it matters either way."

"Congratulations again," she said, pocketing her banana, gathering the remains of her snack.

"I'll take care of that," I said. "I'm going to be here for a while."

"Thanks. Give my regards to your husband." She smiled. "Maybe one of these days I'll be rushing back upstairs to see you in the birthing chair."

I asked, "What would I be doing in the birthing chair?"

"Pushing. Don't look so shocked. That's the progression I see: marriage, conception, labor, and delivery."

"But I have seven more years of training. Then, if I'm accepted into a plastic surgery—"

Meredith stopped me with a hand on my shoulder. "One piece of advice? You know this as well as I do: You can do a fellowship at forty, but fertility isn't forever."

"I know, but—"

"*Really* have to get back upstairs to Rachel," she said. "I hate to leave my mothers alone, especially the ones without partners."

It was Saturday night and I had no partner, either. "Mind if I tag along?" I asked.

YOU DON'T EVEN have to scrub. You just wash your hands and put on a sterile gown, and there you are, eligible for bedside duty like a pinch-hitting sister-in-law who volunteers for Lamaze. No attendings hover. The patient whimpers, screams, writhes, yet it's no cause for medical alarm.

A nurse named Florida was making an argument for a fetal monitor. Rachel had already threatened to sue: Had she or had she not signed a contract prohibiting fetal monitoring except in the case of dysfunctional labor or meconium-stained fluid?

"What contract?" Florida said good-naturedly. "Show me your contract. What mama doesn't want to hear her baby's heart?"

Meredith swooped down to say, "Hon, I'm back. She's not talking about the fetal scalp electrode."

I asked what else Rachel had delineated in a contract.

"No episiotomy unless the baby's in distress," said Rachel. "No forceps—"

"Don't even own them," said Meredith.

"No Pitocin."

"We don't need Pitocin, hon," said Meredith.

Florida began to say that labor sometimes stopped, so who could say what lay down the road, but Meredith stopped her with a look.

"You new?" Florida asked me.

I said, "I'm in surgery."

"Surgery?" Rachel asked. "What's a surgeon doing here?"

Meredith said, "For the pure sport of it. We're a teaching hospital. You know that. She could be a veterinarian for all that her specialty has to do with you."

I said, "I can get the ice chips."

"Whatever," said Rachel.

I asked how things were. Where were we now?

Meredith said, "Three centimeters when I left. Ninety percent effaced."

"I think there's been some progress," said Florida.

"I didn't think it would be this bad," said Rachel.

Meredith and Florida wrapped a pair of belts around Rachel's abdomen. "How's that?" asked Meredith. "One's for Doppler and the other measures the length of the contractions."

"And here we go," said Florida, readout in hand.

Rachel was flapping her wrists while expelling a string of alliterative syllables that I knew to be the incantations of natural childbirth. Meredith quieted Rachel's hands, and recited the *hee-hee-hoo*s along with her.

When the contraction subsided, I asked what the scientific basis for the breathing exercises was.

"Relaxation and pain management," said Meredith automatically.

"I'm sure someone's done a controlled study," I said.

"Want to walk?" asked Meredith.

"I don't like that," said Florida. "I don't like when they're off the monitor."

"Intermittent monitoring every few laps," Meredith promised. "Every fifteen minutes we'll check back into the room."

"Am I still in the latent stage?" asked Rachel. "Because I'm finding it harder and harder to hold it all together."

"Of course you're holding it together," said Meredith. "And Fir's fine, too."

"What fur?" I asked.

"That's the baby," said Meredith, eyes widened, appealing for my indulgence.

"Is that a boy's name or a girl's?" Florida asked.

"Either," said Rachel.

Florida wrinkled her nose. "Fur? Like a coat?"

"F-i-r," said Rachel. "Like the tree. But all capital letters."

"Not that it isn't pretty," said Florida, "but other children can be mean."

Rachel asked, "Why do people always think it's f-u-r?"

"What do you care what people think?" asked Meredith. She put an arm around the area where a waist normally would be. "Okay! Let's hit the road. Alice?"

"Another," said Rachel, grimacing, clenching Meredith's closest forearm with both hands.

I looked at my watch, because Florida was looking at hers, searching for meaning in its second hand.

"Body relaxed," chanted Meredith. "C'mon. Blow it away. You're at the worst part. It's going to subside. Let your jaw go. Let your shoulders go."

Florida and I waited. Rachel was frozen to one spot, eyes bulging, her face drained of color.

"Breathe," said Meredith.

"Do you need some more to drink?" asked Florida.

Rachel gagged slightly and closed her eyes.

"Does your back hurt?" asked Meredith.

"Don't touch me," moaned Rachel.

"Let's check you when this one's over," said Meredith.

"Don't touch me," she repeated.

"Do it for Dr. Thrift," said Meredith. "She's probably never measured a dilated cervix."

"Who did you say she was?"

"A house officer," said Meredith. "And a friend."

"Maybe next time," I said. "No hurry."

"I'm one giant vortex of unbearable agony, so why should I care who sticks her fingers into me?"

"Have you peed lately?" asked Meredith.

"Not since I got here," said Rachel. "Ironic, huh?"

Meredith said to me, "*Ironic* because she's been peeing every fifteen minutes for the last six months."

"This sucks," said Rachel. "I hate it." And she began to cry, a humpty-dumpty with two belts around her middle, a johnny on the front and a johnny on the back, arms braced against the bed, feet in kelly-green hospital-issue nonskid socks.

"You're doing great," said Meredith. "You're tired. We don't have to check you now."

"I'm feeling sick," Rachel moaned. "I want to throw up."

"No problem," said Meredith. "Just like we talked about."

"I can't throw up in a toilet. I find it disgusting. It makes me sicker."

"Our toilets are immaculate," said Florida.

"We have pretty pink pans," said Meredith. Then, to me: "Would you mind?" pointing her chin toward the bathroom door.

"Wouldn't it be better . . . in there?"

"All she's had is water and a cherry Popsicle," said Florida.

"We don't mind, do we?" said Meredith. "Whatever makes her feel better." She was holding Rachel up by one elbow, so I went around to prop up the other side.

Florida said, "I haven't eaten since I came on duty."

"Go," said Meredith. "I've had my turn, and now I have Alice."

"I'm sick," said Rachel.

"Basin!" ordered Meredith. "Above the sink. Top shelf."

"You won't even miss me," said Florida.

"TELL RACHEL WHAT you did this weekend," Meredith tried as we shuffled along the linoleum, Rachel sagging between us. Meredith stopped every few laps to knead her own lower back.

"Should you be doing this?" I asked.

"I'm fine," she said, "a little sciatica," and immediately turned the conversation to Rachel's well-being, to Rachel's need to breathe in through the nose and out through the mouth when another contraction stopped us cold. "Ask Alice what she did yesterday," Meredith coaxed.

When Rachel only glared, I volunteered, "I got married at City Hall."

Rachel asked, "To whom?"

"My boyfriend."

"They eloped," said Meredith. "Like two crazy kids in Las Vegas."

"Is this supposed to distract me?" asked Rachel. "Because I thought the main thing here was focus. Am I listening to my body, or am I listening to a total stranger's married-cute story?"

"Sorry," said Meredith, but with a wink to me over Rachel's bent head.

I said, "Does your body want to keep walking, or does it want to lie down?"

"I don't know," she said, and began to cry again, loudly, unselfconsciously.

"Want me to get a wheelchair?" I asked.

"We're almost there," said Meredith.

"When does the doctor arrive?" I asked.

"Sorry, kid," said Meredith. "I'm it. No doctor needed, present company excepted."

"I didn't want a doctor," said Rachel. "What would a doctor do? Give me an episiotomy when I wasn't looking, then throw away my placenta?"

"Don't be like that," said Meredith. "We don't discriminate against our brother doctors, right, Alice?"

Who *was* this, I wondered—this formerly less-than-companionable acquaintance who seemed transformed on the job to an angel of imperturbable mercy? I said, trying to copy Meredith's genial tone, "My favorite doctor in the whole hospital is a male obstetrician."

"I'm not an idiot," said Rachel. "Nor am I anti-male. I knew I wanted a midwife and a birthing pool—"

"Which we don't do," Meredith murmured. "Too much housework and timing and disinfecting involved. Plus the pediatricians hate it."

"I saw a video," said Rachel. "It was so beautiful. The warm water made the pain almost bearable."

"Pain?" said Meredith. "Do we call this pain?" Smiling, she steered us back into Rachel's room. "Time to check the baby." And to me, "We're looking for one-twenty/one-thirty/one-forty beats per minute. Something around there."

"I need to pee," said Rachel.

"Leave the door open," said Meredith. "We're right here."

I whispered to Meredith that this experience was different from what I'd seen in medical school.

"How?"

"I don't remember the walking and the talking. Or the talking *back*."

Meredith said things were intensifying. Soon Rachel would be rendered near-speechless, all sound and fury but no debating, so I should hang in there.

"I'm having a bowel movement," we heard from the bathroom. "Is that okay?"

"Uh-oh," said Meredith.

"Something's there!" Rachel yelled.

I followed Meredith, three long strides to the bathroom.

"Are you feeling rectal pressure?" Meredith asked. "Talk to me."

Rachel moaned, then grunted.

"We need to check you," said Meredith. "Don't push.

This could be it. Can you stand?"

"No!"

I stepped forward. "Tell me what to do," I said.

FIR WASN'T EXACTLY born in the toilet, but it was close. Rachel couldn't or wouldn't move herself, all the while insisting that she had to push, that it felt better here, that FIR had chosen this time and place. I saw pain in Meredith's face when she and I tried a double hoist. When Meredith stepped back to put on gloves I said, "Rachel! Your baby is going to fall into fecal matter. I know you don't want to move, but you're much better off in a clean, well-lit place. See the bed? Nice and upright? Not unlike a big comfortable toilet seat, only sanitary. Doesn't that look better?"

"Well lit?" she snapped. "I specifically asked that the lights be dimmed—"

"Do you want it to say *bathroom* on FIR's birth certificate?" Meredith said.

"You're lying," said Rachel. "They fucking don't write—" and the rest of her retort was lost in the worst animal scream yet.

"I have to check you," said Meredith, "but I absolutely *cannot* do it there. You have to listen to me, Rachel—"

"Something's coming," she cried.

"I can't budge her," I said.

"You have to," said Meredith.

I tried what I'd already failed at—lifting, heaving, enlisting—and this time something worked: Rachel was up on her stubborn legs, her slippered feet. Later

296

Meredith confirmed that sometimes we find super-human strength—*her* adjective, *superhuman*—in matters of life and death; or, on this Saturday night, just new life. Finally Rachel was propelling herself with the force of a runaway car in drive toward the safety of the bed and its hygienic field.

Meredith was everywhere—at the door yelling for a warm blanket, for help, for a warmer, for paraphernalia known only to midwives and nurses—yet never seeming to leave Rachel's side. "Knees up," she ordered. "Way up. As far as they can go. C'mon. I'm right here. You're doing great. Now, *push*."

I thought I was standing there helplessly, but I wasn't. For once it was Alice Thrift in the right place at the right time—3:03 A.M. on March 17—when out swooshed a big, messy FIR Patrice Flowers, eyes wide open, into my curiously steady hands.

26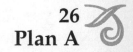
Plan A

I SLEPT FOR two hours, alone, and reported to urology on Sunday. As soon as I crossed the threshold of my first patient's room, a postoperative Mr. Parrish announced that he was in for—*ha ha ha*—a penile reduction. "That stuff about cancer?" he added. "Only a decoy."

I knew it was incumbent on me to smile, to answer in kind, to postpone a discussion of the medical facts, and to assure him that I could handle genital humor.

I faked a notation in order to buy myself a little time. "Please let's not talk about male anatomy," I finally said, shaking my head mournfully. "I'm supposed to be on my honeymoon."

Mr. Parrish laughed, then immediately apologized for what he hoped hadn't been a lapse in good taste. See, a friend of his had sent that card over there—that's a guy's idea of a joke—and he didn't expect that the first doctor he saw after his operation—

"No apology necessary," I said. And what could I do next to put Mr. Parrish at ease but perch myself on the side of his bed to engage him in conversation; to treat—as we were often reminded in medical school—not just the disease but the whole patient. I chose my best conversational gambit, my elopement, abridging it to a short paragraph. Mr. Parrish liked this confidence. He asked thoughtful and paternal questions; I said no, my husband was not in medicine, and yes, he *was* very understanding when it came to my long hours.

"You're an MD?" he asked.

I said yes, and flipped my ID faceup for verification.

"Not a flattering picture," he said. "Which I mean as a compliment."

I said I'd get a new one on July 1. If I lasted that long.

He asked what I'd meant by that. Was I worried about layoffs?

I said only, "It's a pyramid system. More of us start out than finish. For example, only one person can become the chief resident."

"Would you want that job? I mean, being married and all? Is that such a big honor—chief resident?"

When I didn't answer right away, Mr. Parrish jumped in to volunteer that he was a guidance counselor at

Rindge and Latin, in Cambridge.

I said, "It hasn't been easy. I'm trying to figure out where I belong."

Mr. Parrish patted the edge of his mattress. "This is where you belong. Right where you are. Keeping a worried guy company at sunup."

I knew it was a moment to be psychiatric, to ask a meaningful follow-up question, to explore *worried*. But it was easier to divert his thoughts back to my personal life. "Want to hear something strange?" I asked. "I delivered a baby today. By accident. I was invited to watch, and I happened to be in the right place at the right time. I actually caught the baby coming out."

Mr. Parrish smiled. "Now, *that* is what I call a very meaningful event."

"My name's on the record as the doctor who delivered the baby."

"As it should be," he said. "Boy or girl?"

"Girl," I said. "A doozy. Nine pounds, one ounce."

"More fun than this, I bet." He glanced over to where I was performing my nurselike probationary responsibility, recording his urine output. I said, "It's *all* fun. Every task with every patient."

"C'mon. You can't kid a kidder. What about the ones who die on you? And the people who arrive by ambulance bleeding and needing tubes stuck into their windpipes? That can't be any fun. Are you thinking that you have to enjoy every minute or you're not a good doctor? Because when I watch doctor shows—not just *ER* but the docudramas—being unhappy is pretty much the norm."

"Are you giving me a pep talk?" I asked.

He smiled. "What else are you supposed to do to me today?"

I pointed groinward. "Check your site."

He pulled the sheet to the side and yanked up his johnny in friendly, accommodating fashion.

I moved closer and said everything looked good. No redness or weeping. A lovely job.

"You know what the weird part is? I feel okay. It's not like anything hurts, if you don't count a little soreness. It's just that it's already spread."

I dredged up something I had read: that autopsies performed on older men who died in car accidents showed that a large percentage of the victims over the age of seventy had cancerous cells in their prostate. In other words, it was practically a normal state of being.

"But I'm not even sixty," he said. "What's normal for me?"

I thought of Meredith winking over Rachel's head and pronouncing soothing words that weren't 100 percent scientifically supportable. I said, trusting he'd recognize my answer as jocularity, "The good news is, I think you have an excellent chance of dying as an elderly man in a car accident."

"Really? You're not just saying that?"

"Prostate cancer is one of the more treatable ones. And there are new therapies, experimental ones. I can have someone talk to you." I added good news of my own: His urine output was excellent, 120 cc an hour.

"Meaning?"

"Everything's moving. No clots in the urethra. I don't

have to flush your Foley catheter. You're doing great."

"I hope you're right. I hope you're not being Miss Sunshine because someone out there said, 'Be nice to him. He's terminal, but don't give it to him square between the eyes.'"

I said, "No one's ever called me Miss Sunshine. And no; no one sent me in here to sugarcoat anything."

"I'm Al," he said.

"I know. I have your chart."

"It's short for Alphonse."

I said I knew that, too.

"Al and Alice," he said. "Kinda nice. If you don't mind my saying that."

I said, "You can call me anything you want. We're very informal here. All my patients call me Alice."

It was a manifest lie, but so what? On this particular morning I felt like lying.

I TRIED RAY'S cell phone with no success, then called my apartment and reached myself on tape. "Ray," I said. "It's me. I'm at the hospital. I delivered a baby girl last night, sort of by accident. I'll tell you about it tonight. Also, this morning I helped a patient who had a nerve-sparing total prostatectomy. Not help in the medical sense, but just by talking to him. I should be able to get out of here by six . . . okay, never mind. I'll try your cell."

I redialed his number, and, for the first time in the history of our telecommunications, I got the live Ray instead of his voice mail. "It's Alice," I said. "Your wife."

"Can't talk, Doc. I've got Joyce on call waiting. Where are you?"

"Urology," I said. "Joyce who?"

"She's getting your father out of the tub so I can talk to them both at once."

"About what?" I asked, but to no avail. The line clicked and I was overridden.

I STOPPED BY the nursery to sneak a peek at the cleaned-up FIR Flowers.

"Went home," said the nurse, a short, plump young woman named Doreen, wearing a smock patterned with cartoon characters I should have recognized.

"Is that Bernie?" I asked, pointing.

"Bert, Ernie, Cookie Monster," she said, jabbing at faces decorating her broad bosom. "And I'm sure you know Big Bird."

I lied again. I said of course I knew Big Bird. He was an icon; I'd had a Big Bird thermos and a Big Bird chess set.

"Are you Dr. Thrift?" asked this stranger.

It was the old sign on my back: WELL-KNOWN FAILURE/PROBATIONEE. "Why?" I asked.

"I heard about the delivery! Meredith said the baby would've dropped headfirst into the toilet, but you carried the mother to the bed."

"She *did?*"

"I think that's what she said. That she couldn't lift her because of her back, and the baby was crowning—"

I shook my head. "I might have pulled the mother off the toilet seat but I didn't carry her anywhere. She sort of

302

went careening toward the bed."

"Whatever. Meredith said it was a close call. You know what it would have meant if the baby landed in the toilet? And *aspirated?*"

"Bad?"

"She'd be in the NICU, at the very least on a full course of antibiotics, and we'd very likely be dealing with pneumonia."

"Well," I said, "in that case . . . glad I could help." I was going to ask, speaking of near-occupancy in the NICU, if she knew Leo Frawley, but babies were crying and several visitors had gathered at the viewing window, pointing at newborns. I caught on quickly, and wheeled a few Isolettes right up to the window. The homely and the wizened earned the same adoring gazes as the plump and the pretty. I lingered to watch Doreen swaddle two babies tightly, expertly, and change a diaper on the tiniest pelvis one could possess without having earned a berth among the preemies.

"Weren't you on your way home?" Doreen asked. "And didn't Meredith tell me that you're a newlywed?"

"My husband hasn't moved in yet," I told her. "He has obligations back at his apartment."

"Like what?"

I couldn't pronounce the truth—a previously unannounced dog—so I said, "Work. Just like me. Married to our jobs."

"So instead of going home and chilling the champagne, you're floating—delivering a baby here, rearranging the nursery furniture there?" She said it indulgently, adding, "Just don't become one of those insane surgeons who gets in so early and leaves so late that he never sees the light of day."

I asked if she meant *light of day,* literally: i.e., the rotation of the earth on its axis. Or figuratively—*light of day* as a metaphor for self-knowledge?

Doreen said, "I've got babies crying and their daddies watching. Can we discuss this another time?"

"Not important," I said. "Have to run." Pretty sure I knew the answer myself, I silently vowed to leave the hospital by the main entrance and not take the tunnel home.

I WENT DIRECTLY to the answering machine, expecting it would yield my mother, either tearfully shrill or coyly mother-of-the-bride–ish, but there was only my own voice imploring Ray to pick up if he was there.

I jumped when the live Ray called from the direction of the bathroom, "I know, I know. I was supposed to let you handle it. But I had this brainstorm. Come on in. I want to tell you about it."

He was in the tub, his head propped against a vinyl pillow I'd never seen before. "I know what you're thinking: The water's too hot. But I won't stand up too suddenly. Want to join me?"

I said, "What was your brainstorm?"

"The phone call to your parents. It hit me suddenly that *I* had to contact them, not you. Does a woman call home and announce she's engaged? Or does the polite man call the father and ask for his daughter's hand?"

"He doesn't if they're already married."

"I thought about that, and I decided we were going to

follow Plan A, but with a very interesting wrinkle: We don't say 'married'; we say 'engaged.' And I back it up a notch to ask for his blessing."

I said, "And you didn't think that was too important a decision to make unilaterally? And a huge lie?"

"Not to me it isn't. Because let me ask you this: Do you feel married? Do we have one photograph to document it? One present? One piece of wedding cake in the freezer?"

"We're legally married. If I don't feel married it's because you haven't unpacked your suitcase yet."

"*Shhhh.* Hon. No. I'm talking about the way I feel morally and religiously. Lots of people have two cere- monies—"

"So why not say that? Why not say, 'We eloped, but now we'd like to do something more traditional'? Why go through this charade?"

"You're too damn black-and-white," said Ray. "Whereas I live in the gray area. I massage things a little if it helps achieve a goal. In this case, we call ourselves engaged, we register, and in a couple of months we drive down to Princeton for a ceremony and a party. Which isn't just for the presents. It has more to do with making your parents happy and not running off like two bird- brain teenagers with something to hide."

"What did they say?"

"You want the whole thing, from the beginning?"

"Please."

He motioned toward the toilet, so I lowered the lid and sat.

"First I identify myself: 'Ray Russo, Alice's friend.

You remember me from the funeral of your mother. How are you doing?' 'Yes,' she answers, kind of cold. Or maybe I was hearing something else. Like fright; like there had been an accident and I was contacting your emergency numbers. I said, 'This is a social call. Alice is fine. She's at work. But I was wondering if I could speak to your husband?'

"'He's indisposed,' she said. Still no thaw. So I ask, 'Should I call back?' She asks if it's anything I can discuss with her, and I say—very formal, very cool, 'I think you can probably guess why a daughter's boyfriend might ask to speak to the daughter's father.'"

From across the very short distance of my tile floor I listened, but in a state best described as nauseated dread. Ray asking for my hand was Ray lying, and it was painful to see the self-congratulation in his face. I untied my shoes and slowly rolled my knee-highs down, studiously, concentrically.

"Am I boring you?" Ray asked.

"I'm listening," I said.

"So finally your old man picks up the phone, dead serious, and says, like his secretary just told him that some undesirable was on the phone, 'This is Bertram Thrift.'

"'Ray Russo,' I say in return. 'Do you have a minute?'"

I studied my toes, which bore the impression of my knee-highs' cable stitch; I felt for the pulse in my ankle and rested my fingertips there for several reassuring throbs.

"Meanwhile," Ray continued, "I hear suspicion in his

voice. He's being ultracareful. Suddenly it dawns on me: He thinks I'm calling to borrow money!"

"No," I said. "No one would jump to that conclusion."

"Are you kidding? When you live in a house like that, people constantly ask you for money. So, without even trying, I've got him on the ropes: He thinks I'm going to hit him up for a loan, but instead I say, 'I love your daughter very much, sir. I'm calling to ask your permission to propose marriage.'"

I leaned over and put my head between my knees.

"What's the matter?" Ray asked.

I said, my voice muffled, "Just exhaustion. I didn't sleep last night. It's not a vasovagal."

"Bear with me," Ray said. "I'm getting to the best part. Bertie-boy repeats my words, dumbfounded: 'You're calling to ask for Alice's hand in marriage?' I said, 'Hey! I'm an old-fashioned guy. I didn't want to buy a ring or pop the question until I got your permission.'"

Ray stopped to soap the washcloth and attack his armpits.

"And? What did my father say?"

"He yelled, 'Joyce! Pick up the phone!' Your father finally says something like, 'Mr. Russo, I appreciate your calling, but I wouldn't dare encourage you without knowing Alice's mind. This is a free country. Don't take it personally if Alice says no, because she's always put school and medicine before her social life.'

"And you know what I said? I said, 'Not this time. In fact, would you like to make a little wager on whether

Alice accepts my proposal?'

" 'No, I would not,' he says. But I think he knew I was pulling his leg."

I raised my head. "Why wouldn't they have called me? I checked the machine but there wasn't anything."

"They did call, but I picked up. I told them they were going to ruin my surprise. That the scene was set—the candles, the ring, the caviar, the deviled eggs. I asked if they'd limit the conversation to matters outside a potential engagement."

"All of that just rolled off your tongue while your bath was running and while your secret wife was on her way home, wondering when her next date with her husband would be?"

"Secret wife?" he said sharply. "What's that supposed to mean?"

"Me. The lawfully wedded one who now has to live this lie."

Ray smiled. "I picked up a rotisserie chicken at Star Market. You hungry?"

I said no . . . yes . . . what would I say to my parents when I returned their call?

"You say, 'Ray proposed last night and I accepted. I've never been so happy. We're thinking of a June wedding.' "

I stood up, left the bathroom, headed for the kitchen, came back. "Or maybe I'll tell them the truth. Maybe I'll say, 'We eloped on the Ides of March. Everything Ray has uttered in previous conversations is a sham, but it's only because he regrets not having staged a large church wedding with its accompanying rights, privileges, and lavish presents.' "

Ray stood up in the tub, slowly—as medically advised—and wrapped a towel around his waist. "No, you will not," he said.

27

The Opposing Argument

"I COULD'VE CALLED this," he said, reaching for his overcoat. "You're a little pissed off at me, so I'm going to give you some space to think it over."

I asked if he could define "it," because several antecedents were suggesting themselves to me.

"My taking the reins; my setting the scene, i.e., wedding on the horizon versus wedding under our belt." He kissed me fraternally on the cheek and patted the closer buttock. "You'll change your mind because you'll realize it doesn't take great acting ability to get into it: us two marching down the aisle, cutting the cake, dancing the first dance. Which reminds me: our song."

I said, "Song? We have no song."

"We're going to get ourselves one, and the bandleader is going to announce to the wedding guests, 'Ladies and gentlemen. Put your hands together for Mr. and Mrs. Raymond J. Russo as they take the dance floor for the first time as husband and wife!' "

I said, "I haven't said yes to any wedding, and I don't like to call attention to myself on a dance floor."

He had walked to the door as if accepting the expulsion, but now he came back to where I was standing, at the open refrigerator, one hand on the plastic take-out tomb of the chicken. "You know what, Doc? You are one giant wet blanket. The wettest. I make all these plans. I set the ball in motion. I take the reins. And you can't just go along with the smallest white lie because you're so perfect, so in love with the truth. Well, good. You tell your parents anything you want—married, engaged, said yes to Ray, said no—and then you let me know where things stand. Just remember that we're married, and married people are supposed to compromise. Do you think if I went to a dating service I'd pick 'works round the clock' under potential spousal occupation? No. But I know the meaning of the word *compromise*. I am willing to be on call, at your service. Alice is awake on Saturday night between seven and eight P.M.? No problem. I'll be there with my take-out and my ever-ready instrument of pleasure. Did I ever let you down? Did I ever say no once you discovered the bedroom? No, I did *not*. But I guess that's something that polite people don't talk about. Why do you think you agreed to marry me? It wasn't anything you could put a scientific name to. Nothing that'll sound classy in a wedding toast. Because it's plain old animal magnetism."

I closed the refrigerator door and turned toward him. "I don't see what one thing has to do with another. I'm troubled about your lying, and you're saying, 'I provided half of the animal magnetism, so do me this favor and go along with a sham wedding'? Explain to me how one relates to the other."

Ray said, "Don't get me wrong. I enjoyed all of the conjugal stuff. *Especially* after my widowhood and that long layover. No complaints there. Where it gets relevant is that I never said boo to you about our social life. Did we go out to dinner or to parties or go dancing? Did we ever see a movie that wasn't on network television? Or did we just hit the hay because Alice had to be at work at six?"

"Not always," I said. "Still, I don't see your point. And it hurts my feelings to be called a wet blanket by the one person who never seemed to mind that."

"You want a point? It's this: You owe me some fun. Some dressing up and going out. A couple of turns on a dance floor and an open bar."

I said, "Some widowers might consider a big wedding to be in bad taste."

Ray thought this over. "First, don't get me started on Mary. Because I could hold my second wedding on her *grave* and it wouldn't bother me. Second, I think you're talking about guys who are divorced. They're the ones who have to look over their shoulder before planning a big blowout, because nine times out of ten the ex is going to say, 'You've got enough cash for a live band and a week in Aruba, but not enough to make your alimony payments?'"

I had no arguments left in this debate, especially now that he was citing persons who were both imaginary and insolvent. I asked, "Would you like to take half of the chicken with you?"

He looked at his watch. "What if I gave you an hour, hour and a half, and came back at nine? Or whenever. I could be here in five minutes if I just go over to the Shamrock."

"I'll be asleep. Besides, don't you have Pete to consider?"

"Pete," he said. "I thought that whole thing over, and I gave him away. What do I need that responsibility for? With my asshole neighbors leaving threatening notes in my mailbox?"

I was going to inquire as to what kind of a home Pete had gone to, but I didn't. It would have provoked a more elaborate and unconvincing story than I had the stomach for.

I ATE A wing, a thigh, and a drumstick, one eye on the telephone. If I didn't call, Joyce and Bert would have to assume one of two things: that Ray didn't get around to proposing, or that I had turned him down and didn't want to discuss it. Eventually they'd get back to me; as ever, I'd use work as my excuse: too busy, too tired, too professionally downtrodden to take time out for social niceties. If pressed, I would say yes, I accepted his proposal. The love between two people is idiosyncratic, didn't they agree? Ray was good for me. I could see the differences already: I was sleeping less, eating more, purchasing electronics that most people had acquired at an earlier stage in their development. Also, I seemed to be gaining ground in the area of bedside manner, indirectly attributable to Ray's various physical conditions.

I pulled my bed down from the wall. It had been dressed in crisp sheets I'd never seen before, a surprise contribution to my trousseau—white-on-white zigzags that looked like a gala EKG. I lay down, closed my eyes, didn't sleep.

Maybe Ray was not being deceitful in wanting to restage our wedding. Hadn't Princess Grace and Prince Rainier been married in a civil ceremony before the costumed event in a cathedral? Ray had added to his argument that when he made his First-Prize Fudge rounds, a wedding band was an asset. And if sympathetic guy customers upped their orders because they thought Ray Russo had extra mouths to feed, why go out of his way to correct that impression?

I went to the bathroom for a glass of water. "Remind me why I did this," I said aloud in the mirror. I turned off the light, answering in the dark so I didn't have to see my miserable face. Maybe you *are* autistic. You aborted the very friendship that might have improved the baseline Alice. And Leo? What kind of pitiful self-esteem and rash behavior made you donate your bedroom to a cause he wasn't campaigning for?

Good work, Mrs. Russo, and congratulations. You got what you deserved: a husband.

SHE MIGHT HAVE greeted me with a sarcastic "Well. Look who's here." But she didn't. I asked if it was too late or too inconvenient a time to talk.

She opened her door wider to reveal a kitchen table covered with newspapers and something wrinkled and embryonic suspended over a glass with toothpicks. "Have you ever planted an avocado pit?" Sylvie asked.

I said no. I had no horticultural abilities.

"I don't know why I do it," she said. "It's not that I want an avocado tree or even an avocado plant, but when I make guacamole and I see that the seed's sprouted, I feel compelled to buy potting soil."

I asked, "How have you been?"

"Furious," she said.

"At me?"

"That's right, sweetie-pie. One hundred percent at you."

I backed up a step. "Should I leave?"

"No," she said. "I've practiced one side of this conversation in my head a dozen times, so now I'd like to hear the opposing argument."

"Your place or mine?" I asked.

"C'mon in," she said.

She poured two glasses of red wine and asked me to please not spill any on the couch.

We sat down. I was wearing my old bathrobe over an older nightgown, and had walked across the hall barefoot.

"So," said Sylvie, her voice still occupying the new range of iciness, "how have you been?"

"Busy. Trying to improve."

"We're all busy. We all work our asses off, yet some us manage to find the time to walk across the hall and maintain our friendships."

I said, "I just walked across the hall, didn't I? Was it all up to me?"

"Look," she said. "I know you think that I flirted outrageously with Leo and left you flapping in the breeze. That you felt like a third wheel. That you were so mad at me that you couldn't knock on my door and ask, 'What the fuck were you doing tonight?'"

I asked her if she really thought I was capable of blunt

cross-examination, not to mention confrontation.

She closed her eyes for a few seconds, then opened them. "Not really."

I asked meekly, "Is it too late to ask what the fuck you were doing that night?"

Sylvie, while frowning into her own lap, looked across to mine. She reached over and touched the gold band. "Is this what I think it is?"

I said, "It seems so."

She put her wineglass down on her hardly level steamer-trunk coffee table. "No. You couldn't have gotten married. No one gets married while estranged from the very influence who would have counseled her against it."

I said, "I did. On Friday."

"I'm afraid to ask . . ."

"Ray," I said.

Sylvie turned sideways on the couch and tucked both legs under her. "Okay. I'm not hysterical. I'm a rational and scientific person. This requires a detailed account of every word leading up to this shocking news flash."

"We eloped at Boston City Hall."

Sylvie shook her head. "I want to know if you were coerced. Were you a participant or an accessory? Or was it like a surprise outing, where he said, 'Follow me. I can't tell you where we're headed, but dress up and bring your birth certificate'?"

I said, "No, I was a full participant. You have to be. I got a blood test and I signed the papers, and when the city clerk asked me if I was reluctant, I said no."

"But Alice . . . marriage! That's, like, a giant leap.

You're supposed to do that when you've exhausted the field and when you can see yourself having sex with only one person for the rest of your natural life. And— no small matter—that you love that person desperately."

"Desperately?" I asked. "In what sense?"

"Desperate-good," she said. "Not desperate-pathetic."

I said, "Well, I did feel a kind of desperation. I mean . . . it's complicated. It had something to do with his filling the void after we stopped speaking—"

"*We?* You and I? Because I flirted with Leo? Jesus!" She closed her eyes again. "That's not the point anymore, is it? The issue on the table is you marrying Ray for reasons I'm trying to fathom. So, please continue. I won't interrupt unless provoked."

"I know you don't like Ray that much, but if you—"

"He's an operator! I sensed that the first time I laid eyes on him."

I said, "Once you get to know him, he's very sweet. And very devoted."

"Really? How come he always cleared out around midnight and never stayed over?"

I said, "That has nothing to do with devotion. He has a dog—*had* a dog—who couldn't be left alone. Besides, I have to get up at five-thirty, so it isn't fair to him to have to live by my timetable."

"*'Isn't* fair'? Present tense? Is he still slinking out after he performs his marital duties?"

I said, "That's a harsh thing to say about a person's husband." I gestured around her studio. "Could you live here with another person?"

Sylvie said quietly, "I honestly think I could. If it was the right person, I'd want to."

"We need two bedrooms," I said. "He has a home office. And his apartment is rent-controlled."

"What about love? Is that a factor here?"

I said, "I do love him."

"I've loved a lot of guys, but I haven't married one yet."

"You're different than I am. I'd be a failure at having affairs. I can't even talk to an attending, let alone follow him into a fluoro suite for an assignation. That's a big difference: Five minutes after you met Leo you were able to carry on a successful flirtation. Which I don't mean as criticism."

"Which we'll get to, believe me. But first you." She leaned in, nearly eyeball to eyeball. "To recap: Being of sound mind and body, you went through with this marriage. What aren't you telling me?"

"Nothing. It just happened."

Sylvie said, "But I haven't heard the *why* yet. Something else had to be driving this plunge. Maybe I should look into this; maybe he took out several million dollars in insurance policies on his new bride, naming himself the beneficiary."

"Wouldn't that require a physical?" I asked.

Sylvie said, "Do you even know yourself what the inducement was? Not to mention the rush?"

I said, "Ray thinks that the main stimulus was animal magnetism."

"But it's not as if you were saving yourself until marriage, correct? That was several decades ago, when people used to run off and elope because they were dying to do it, and marriage was the only ticket."

I said, "Correct. I wasn't saving myself."

"Am I overlooking something obvious here? Like, you're pregnant?"

I said no, I wasn't pregnant. How could someone in a surgical residency, with seven years—

"Shush," said Sylvie. "I know. You're preaching to the choir here."

I said, "I wanted to get better. I was searching for a cure."

She touched my forearm. "Cure?" she whispered. "Is something wrong that you haven't told me? And does Ray know?"

"Ray *does* know. Ray picked up on it the first time we met."

"How bad?" she asked, her voice hoarse. "Give it to me straight."

I said, "It'll sound self-pitying. And I know you'll feel that it's your duty to—"

"Say it," said Sylvie. "What did Ray diagnose that your colleagues missed?"

I didn't want to confess, but Sylvie was pressing. And Sylvie was back.

"How lonely I am," I said.

28
The Wife-Bride

IF I COULD understand why I found myself on June 29 walking down the aisle on my father's rigid arm, behind my sister, who was looking put-upon in sea-foam silk chiffon, toward Ray Russo, in white tie and tails—train tickets to Niagara Falls in his breast pocket—then perhaps I could describe, to an onlooker's satisfaction, the psychological contours of Alice Thrift's mind.

Bear with me.

The morning after my détente with Sylvie, Joyce and Bert drove up from Princeton without advance notice, and followed signs for the Department of Surgery. It had been a good day. At morning rounds, Mr. Parrish had glanced around the semicircle of residents' faces, smiled when he spotted mine, and announced, "Hey! There's my favorite doctor. Good morning!" Heads turned dubiously in the direction of his salutation—downward, to the bottom rung of the residency program—then back to Mr. Parrish with looks that said, Is the patient delusional?

I said brightly, "Good morning! How are you feeling?"

"Like we talked about. A little discouraged about the prognosis, but otherwise hanging in there."

"You'd better hang in there," I said.

"Dr. Thrift?" said the attending with a puzzled smile. "Could you give us an update on Mr. Parrish's post-op course?"

Stepping up to the bed with my best posture, head erect, I gave it all I had. I discussed his urine output, his test results, his meds, and, without blinking, showed all in attendance his neat, dry wound.

"Is it okay if she sticks around for a couple of minutes?" Mr. Parrish asked.

"We're doing rounds," snapped a senior resident who'd never given me a break or thrown me a bone.

"I'll tell you what," I said. "I'll finish rounds, then I'll come right back. Unless you think it can't wait."

"It can wait," said Mr. Parrish. "And I certainly don't want to get you into trouble."

The same senior resident snickered.

I said to Mr. Parrish, "Don't mind him. He's amused by the notion of me ever encountering trouble."

"Not that the rest of you aren't doing a great job," Mr. Parrish said.

"He works with teenagers," I explained. "He believes in positive reinforcement."

"My wife's coming in at noon," Mr. Parrish added. "Think you could drop by then and meet her?"

"Me?" asked the attending.

"I was pretty much thinking of just a social chat with Dr. Alice. Our younger daughter talks about going to medical school, and I thought . . ."

"Has your wife talked to the oncologist?" asked the surgeon, his sterling-silver pen tapping the clipboard.

Some of us sucked in our breaths audibly. Mr. Parrish's face changed. He was back to his lymph nodes, his diagnosis, his fear.

I said, "I'd love to meet Mrs. Parrish. And you never mentioned any daughters, let alone one who's thinking about medical school. You'd better give me her phone number so I can talk her out of it."

He tried to smile.

Through the thin blanket, I squeezed an ankle.

320

"Back in a jiff," I said.

THE TRIP FROM Princeton to Boston takes approximately six hours, which meant that my parents must have left Einstein Drive at one A.M. after digesting Ray's phone call, then not hearing from his intended. The department secretary paged me. "Your parents are here," said Yolanda. "And I'm supposed to tell you that it's not an emergency. They're fine."

I said I was still on rounds. Could she please send them to the cafeteria, and could they take seats by the door so I could find them? She repeated my directions. I heard my mother ask, "How long do rounds take?"

Yolanda said, "Interns don't take coffee breaks. Am I correct in assuming this is an unscheduled visit?"

My father said, "We're her parents. We didn't think it necessary to make an appointment to see our daughter."

The secretary asked me, "Is it safe to say that you'll get there as soon as you can, but you can't name an exact time?"

"Pretty much," I said.

I tried to concentrate, to answer the questions about electrolytes and medications and differential diagnoses that were the walking pop quizzes of my daily grind. I found myself murmuring to a junior resident, someone who'd never to my knowledge taken part in the sport of humiliating Dr. Thrift, "My parents are waiting for me in the cafeteria. I think they're here to talk to me out of marrying the man I married."

The resident said, "I'm not good at stuff like that."

We could exchange only one sentence at a time, cryptically, between patients' rooms, and sometimes less if the chief resident was nearby. During my next opportunity I asked, "Can third parties get marriages annulled?"

"My wife's a lawyer," said the resident. "I'll ask her tonight."

I said, "By tonight, I'll probably be on the psych floor."

"I get it," he said. "As an inpatient. It was a joke."

"Correct," I said.

I returned to Mr. Parrish's room as soon as I could. "I know that you weren't trying to play favorites or put a gold star on my forehead during rounds," I told him, "but I want you to know how much it meant to me."

He pushed the button that made the head of his bed rise. "Alice? Are you crying?"

I said, "I didn't tell you I was on probation. I have two weeks left before they decide whether I stay or I go. And even though I'm improving, I doubt whether anyone has noticed."

Mr. Parrish smiled hopefully. "Are you saying that because I was happy to see you this morning, I might have raised your stock a couple of points?"

I said, "This isn't very professional of me to be discussing any of this. Especially with you worried about your own health."

"Bullshit," said Mr. Parrish. "What else can I do to help?"

I plucked a tissue from the generic gray hospital box. "Not a thing," I said. "Just get well and completely cured and dance at your daughters' graduations and weddings."

"I wouldn't mind dancing at *your* wedding," he said. "As long as we're being unprofessional."

"Too late," I said. "Remember? I eloped on Friday."

"Eloped," he repeated. "Now, there's a word you don't hear very often."

I confided that my parents were downstairs, and that in a few minutes I'd have to sit down with them and—

"They were up for the wedding, and now they're taking off?"

I nodded weakly. How much could I burden Mr. Parrish with? Too much already, I feared. The whole patient I was treating in this room was turning out to be me.

I NEGLECTED TO slip off my wedding ring, so the principal reason for the parental mission—"Don't do anything rash"—evaporated as I lifted a Styrofoam cup of coffee to my lips.

"What's that thing on your left hand?" my mother gasped.

A better liar might have had an answer ready or, thinking ahead, a naked finger. I said, "Oh, that. My wedding ring."

"Do you mean an engagement ring?" she asked.

My father reached over to inspect the offending item. "Where's the diamond?" he asked.

I pointed out that, in the course of a day, I peeled several dozen pairs of exam gloves off my hands, and that a diamond would make my life that much more difficult.

My mother asked, her face hopeful, "So you went out immediately and bought the wedding bands, and you're wearing them in advance as some sort of promissory gesture?"

I could have agreed vigorously, but I remained silent.

"So he popped the question?" my father prompted.

"Why didn't you call us?" asked my mother.

I took the ring off my finger. "This isn't a gesture. It's a bona fide wedding band."

My ever-polite father did something that astonished me. He plucked the ring from my fingers and bounced it on the linoleum. "The hell it is," he said. "You didn't marry that drifter! You'd never do that to us."

My mother continued to smile, but it hauled a worried question behind it: That's it? We're too late to derail a future wedding?

"Are you saying that you ran off and got married after your boyfriend spoke to us last night?" my father demanded.

I said no. We went to City Hall on Friday.

"Dating the man is one thing . . ." my mother said.

I asked, "Let me understand: Is it the not telling you or the basic marrying that's got you so angry?"

"Pick up the ring, Bert," my mother said. She turned back to me and said, "Do you think we're so superficial that our grievance is not being able to spend twenty or thirty or fifty thousand dollars that is earmarked for your wedding? On seeing our only nongay daughter in a beautiful dress and train and veil, walking down the aisle? Or do you think it's an unprovoked marriage to a total stranger?"

"The latter?"

"Who is he anyway?" my father demanded. "And I'm praying you know the answer to that. Because, frankly, I worry that you'd take up with the first guy who lavished attention on you—"

"Or not even *lavished!*" my mother cut in. "Because I'm not sure you know the difference between lavish attention and . . . and . . . perfunctory dating."

"And what's this nonsense about him calling me up and asking for your hand *ex post facto*. Am I in a time warp?"

I picked the ring up myself and put it back on my finger. I handed them my keys. "I cannot spend one more minute away from the floor. If you need to discuss this further, you can go to my apartment. Mom knows where it is. Take a nap or go out and have a drink. I'll try to leave here by six."

"Six tonight?" asked my father.

"We're too upset to nap," said my mother.

"I could nap," said my father. "We left in the middle of the damned night."

"Eleven-G," I said. "You'll have to lower the Murphy bed."

"Will he be there?" asked my mother.

I said, "I honestly don't know."

I PAGED SYLVIE. I said, "If you get home before I do, could you knock on my door? My parents came up this morning, and the earliest I can get out of here is six."

"And you want me to do what?"

"I don't know. Charm them? Entertain them? Show them what a nice, healthy friendship I can have with a normal person?"

"Did they come up to kidnap you or do an intervention?"

"Something along those lines."

"How much do they know?"

"They saw the wedding band. They're appalled."

"I'll do my best as hostess," said Sylvie, "but I can't promise any support for lover boy. I mean, if they ask what I think of him, I'm not going to give a testimonial."

"You could say, 'I don't know him at all,' or, 'Let's wait for Alice.'"

"Or, 'I hear noises coming from the apartment which indicate a rather rambunctious conjugality.'"

"Go ahead," I said. "My mother wouldn't blink."

"Now I'm curious," said Sylvie.

I FOUND MYSELF alone in an elevator with Dr. Charles Greenleaf Hastings. "How's your back?" I asked.

He snarled, "I'm not intimidated by your veiled references to that misbegotten and regrettable night."

"How's your back?" I repeated.

He jabbed the elevator button marked 6 repeatedly with his thumb.

"Yoga's good," I said. "But of course nothing beats bed rest."

"Aren't we clever," he said.

The door opened at 4 to admit a transport worker and his elderly, wispy-haired wheelchair patient holding a sleeve of X rays. Hastings fled prematurely, pushing past the new passengers without apology.

"Don't mind him," I said once the doors had closed. "He's famously rude."

"Surgeon, right?" asked the transport worker.

"He had to escape because I intimidate him," I explained.

"Cool," said the transport worker.

"*She's* chatty," said the patient.

"I'm really not," I said.

A NOTE SAID, "We're across the hall. Needed more chairs. S."

I knocked and entered. My parents were on her couch. Sylvie was perched on its arm, a pan of fudge on her lap. All three were listening to the defense, dressed in a blue blazer and a button-down shirt, apparently presenting his opening argument. Never before had I heard Ray Russo more sincere, more earnest, more unguarded in his salesmanship. When he saw me in the doorway, he looked up. He didn't rush over to embrace or kiss me for courtroom effect. Instead, he offered an apologetic smile that said, Do you believe what I walked into? Tough audience. I'm going for it. I'm pulling out all the stops.

"Don't get up," I said.

The presentation stopped just the same while everyone greeted me. Ray brought a chair from the kitchen. Sylvie pretended to take my coat, a ruse to get my ear. "Ray didn't know that *they* knew the wedding had happened, so he was pitching 'Why I Want to Marry Alice' and digging himself deeper."

"How was your day, hon?" Ray called.

"Sit down," said my father. "Mr. Russo was about to explain this whole mess."

"Anyone want another drink before we resume?"

asked Sylvie.

"Water," I said.

"Alice has heard all of this," Ray began, "so I'll be brief. But here goes: My mother was a kid when she had me. She and my father eloped because her parents wanted her to give the baby—me—up for adoption. But they were madly in love. No one thought they were going to make it because both sets of parents cut them off without a cent. My dad got a job pumping gas at an Esso station, and my mom worked the lunch counter at Kresge's five-and-dime until she got too big too hide her stomach. In those days, people didn't like pregnant women out in public like they do now. So she went back to their one-room apartment, even smaller than this—"

My father asked, "Is any of this relevant?"

"Absolutely," said Ray. "It addresses the very relevant question of me and my relationship to celebrations. Basically, I had kids for parents, kids who were on the outs with their families. No baby shower for my mother, no party after my christening, no birthday parties unless you count a cupcake with a candle in it and a Hoodsie. It took years and a couple of more kids before my grandparents came around, and mainly it was to help out because my parents had split by then. But still, how do you make up for a whole lifetime of not observing special occasions?"

"I don't see how this relates to Alice," said my mother.

"Or the various pretenses you put forth in your phone call," said my father.

I said, "I was a party to this. You're all acting as if I

were an innocent bystander."

"You *were* an innocent bystander," said Ray. "You were at work when I called them—without your knowledge or permission."

Sylvie frowned at me and put her finger to her lips.

"Thank you," said Ray. "Okay. As some of you might have heard, I was married before. Only Alice knows that that marriage wasn't all that it was cracked up to be. My first wife cheated on me with a coworker for the entire duration of our marriage. Needless to say, it was very painful and very . . . what's the word . . . ?"

"Emasculating?" said Sylvie.

"No. More like *ironic,*" said Ray. "Because if I'd known about all the fooling around before Mary died instead of after, I wouldn't have suffered in the same way when she passed. I threw away an entire year of my life being the grieving widower." He held up his hand to avert the question nearly visible on my father's lips. "I know," said Ray. "You think Alice was the first warm body that came along when my period of mourning ended, but it wasn't like that. Friends were throwing phone numbers at me; throwing actual *girls* at me— inviting me over for dinner or out for a drink, and I'd get there: Surprise! Another blind date, another coworker or cousin of some buddy's wife. But nothing was happening here"—he rapped the left side of his chest. "*Nada.* Until I went to the hospital one day—not because I was sick; I'm as healthy as a horse—and discovered that a whole other species of woman existed, someone who doesn't come on to a man, or flirt, or even know how to. A total professional." He smiled sheepishly. "I gotta admit: I found that something of a novelty. From that moment on, all I could think about was, How do I get this incredible woman to give me the time of day?"

My mother's head swiveled reflexively and diagnostically in my direction, then back to Ray.

"This incredible woman who was a doctor with a very bright, financially secure future," amended my father.

"I hope," said Ray, "that that isn't a roundabout way of accusing me of being a golddigger."

"I'd say not roundabout at all," murmured Sylvie.

"My question is this," said my father. "If everything was aboveboard and not a plot to march Alice down the aisle beneath our radar screen, why did you elope, then pretend you didn't?"

"Am I the only one who thinks the answer is obvious?" asked Ray. He strode to my chair and stroked my hand. "I know it looks like we were being impulsive, but it was purely time management. Your daughter, as you know, works like a maniac. When she was able to beg two consecutive days off—which, if you translate that into doctor-time, it's like two *weeks*—we went to City Hall. And then, when the dust settled, and because of my emotional history, we regretted not having a proper wedding, and I in particular regretted not going through the proper channels. I guess I don't see why everyone wants to put this under the microscope. We ran off, thinking it would be romantic, and—despite my previously expressed lack of respect for my former wife— I did have to consider whether or not a big blow-out was in poor taste for a widower. And then, when all was said and done, it turned out to be pretty damn depressing to get married at City Hall without one single relative in attendance, not a flower, not a note of music, not even a handshake when it was over, or a honeymoon. That's when I said to myself, 'This sucks. What was I thinking? Is this any way to get married?' Oh, and I forgot to mention: I was especially concerned, since it was Alice's first time, that she should get the works."

My father said, "We have related concerns." He waited a few long seconds. "Which I might put under the general heading of suitability."

When no one spoke, I surveyed every face. Ray looked undeflated. My father wore an expression of strained diplomacy, while my mother's was utter confusion—Will I be planning a wedding or not? Sylvie, looking the most uncomfortable, stood up. "As much as I don't want to appear inhospitable," she said, "I think this is a family discussion that should take place in private."

My father said, "She's right. Let's go back to Alice's room."

"Am I invited?" Ray asked.

"I think that's the whole idea," I said.

My mother said, "Lovely to meet you, Sylvia. I know I'll see you again."

"Take the fudge," said Sylvie. "I'm trying to cut back on caffeine, not to mention fat grams."

"What're you talking about?" said Ray. "You look great. If ever there was someone who didn't need to go on a diet . . ."

"Gee, thanks, Ray," said Sylvie. "And Alice? You'll call me when your company leaves?"

Ray asked, "Is this the kind of Q and A we could have at a restaurant? Alice is probably starved."

My mother said, "Is there a decent place close by where people can carry on a conversation?"

"This is Boston," said Ray. "You name it, we have it: quiet, loud, big, small, gourmet, Chinese, Italian, seafood, sushi—"

"Are we driving back tonight?" asked my mother.

My father said, "Could we please just move across the hall and tackle these subjects one at a time?"

We did. I had to lower the bed to accommodate all of us. Without a stranger as a moderating influence, my father barked increasingly rude questions at Ray. About his income. About his job history and security. School? Brushes with the law? Life insurance? Debts? Liquidity?

I winced with each question, eliciting my own reprimand from my father. "I'm only asking what I assume you already know; what any prudent woman would ask before jumping into marriage with a relative stranger who seems to have a lot of time on his hands."

I said, "Actually, Dad, since I wasn't arranging a marriage or calculating the size of my dowry, or granting him a mortgage, or sitting on a co-op board, there wasn't any need to ask for his last ten income-tax returns."

"She fell in love, Bert," my mother said.

"And vice versa," said Ray. "Head over friggin' heels."

"And he proposed," my mother continued. "And, because it was his second marriage, he didn't think it was appropriate to have a big wedding, so they eloped, and then he regretted cheating Alice out of something more formal and meaningful. I just can't see anything sinister in wanting to get it right."

"No one said anything about *sinister*," said my father. He turned to me. "Alice? Do you understand why we would find this whole thing unnerving?"

I nodded.

"Because Alice is a chip off the old block!" said Ray. "*Unnerving* is her middle name. But I understand that. I know she finds the prospect of shopping for a wedding dress unnerving. And getting her hair done and choosing stainless. And auditioning bands, not to mention hitting the dance floor in front of hundreds of people—"

"And all those thank-you notes," trilled my mother.

I looked at her. She'd married off her impaired, unpopular daughter. Her husband's objections had been voiced and noted. Alice wasn't asking for an annulment. The mother of the wife-bride could now move forward and fashion a fabulous wedding without worrying that—short of divorce—the groom would change his mind.

I looked at my husband, who looked back at me. "Alice?" he said. "Sweetie?"

Have I mentioned that this is a cautionary tale? One gets swept up in these things. One's doubts get pushed into a section of the brain that doesn't trigger speech, and where other people's zest for wedlock jams the pathways that send warnings to a bride.

"Anyone?" said my father.

"I really love her," said Ray.

"End of June?" asked my mother.

GOOD NEWS: DR. Kennick passed me in the hall, one day before his verdict was due, and announced rather blandly, "Oh, Thrift? You've been taken off probation."

"And put where?" I asked.

"Back in the lineup."

"Thank you," I said.

"Heard you were holding your own."

I said, "I think so, too."

He took a few more steps, then turned around again. "Did someone tell me you got hitched?"

"*I* told you. I asked for two consecutive days off last month so I could go to Cape Cod."

"Did I grant them?"

I said yes, thanks again.

Clearly it was only etiquette that impelled him to ask, "Who's the lucky guy?"

"No one you know," I said. "Raymond Russo."

"Physician?"

"Businessman."

"That's good: occupational hybrid vigor—each of you bringing complementary talents to the marriage."

I said, "Well . . . I'd better get back to my patients. Thanks for the vote of confidence."

"Hang in there, Thrift," he said. "I've seen worse."

I called after him, "And where are they now?"

Vaguely, he brushed the air with his right hand, this direction and that, with a final gesture toward the world outside. Translation: anesthesiology, pathology, mother-hood, law school.

RAY EMBRACED THE wedding chores traditionally per-formed by the bride. He registered for gifts in depart-ment stores up and down the eastern seaboard and for appliances in high-end catalogs. He leafed through bridal magazines for inspiration on formal wear and flowers, and enlisted his cousin, a full-time beautician and part-time calligrapher, to address the invitations. I came home one night to find seven wedding dresses in my size arranged rather artistically across my bed, with a note that said, *Pick your favorite, I'll return the ones you don't want. Almost got trampled in the One Day Only Bridal Rush. Some look dirty it's just from being tried on so we'll send it to the cleaners. P.S. I'm not superstitious are you? I won't remember the dress by the time 6/29 rolls around.*

I knocked on Sylvie's door, wearing a big gauzy one with a hoop skirt, and holding its back closed because I couldn't finesse the buttons tracing my vertebral column. She opened the door and emitted a yelp—some-thing between pleasure and pain, not easily character-ized.

"Do you like it?" I asked.

I could see she was hesitating, so I assured her, "You don't have to be diplomatic. There's six more."

"This I gotta see," she said, closing her door and fol-lowing me. Inside my apartment, after she buttoned me, she went straight for the array of gowns. "Hideous," she said, of the first one she held against her body. And then, of the next three: "Can't do acetate . . . too Southern belle . . . too *Starship Enterprise*."

I said, "Don't blame me. Ray picked them out."

"With you along?"

"No. By himself. Because he thought it was the only way I'd get one. Apparently there are strict seasons, and you can't just get a June wedding dress anytime you please."

"Although," said Sylvie, examining the tags, "I daresay Filene's Basement isn't as sensitive to those issues as, say, Priscilla of Boston."

"I'm supposed to choose one, and he'll return the rest."

"Does the groom usually pay for the dress?"

I said no; I'd reimburse him.

"Let your mother reimburse him! You don't have to spend your hard-earned salary on a dress you didn't want in the first place. Besides, she's getting a bargain: three hundred and ninety-nine bucks for something that must've cost five times that much in its original state."

"Could you unbutton me?" I asked.

"You're going to need a lot more than a dress," Sylvie said, working the silk knots out of their slippery loops. "There's the foundation garments, the stockings, the shoes, the veil. Ray can't do everything."

"Does one have to wear a veil?"

Sylvie turned me around by the shoulders so she could deliver a meaningful stare. "You don't have to do anything. You can wear a feather headdress or an orchid behind one ear. Or not walk down the aisle at all if a little voice inside your head is telling you to run like hell."

I said, "We're already married, so don't get dramatic. This is for my parents."

She went back to the dress candidates with a sigh. "The worst," she said, tossing a much appliquéd and pearl-encrusted model to the floor. She reached for the last one. "Not bad except for the stains."

I said, "I'm not supposed to consider its state of cleanliness."

"I see: a twofer," said Sylvie. "Something old *and* something new." She glanced at its price and its original tag. "Bergdorf's. Very nice. And no froufrou. Let's see this one on you."

I obliged. It had a zipper for easy access, a no-nonsense approach to straplessness—straight across, high on the sternum—and a slit from knee to ankle for ease of ambulation. Sylvie motioned with an index finger: pirouette, please.

"Too anything?" I asked.

She stepped back. "We've got a winner, as far as I'm concerned."

"It's kind of pink."

"Blush," she pronounced, dragging the *ssshhh* out until I laughed.

I looked down at myself. It fit. It wasn't necessarily me, but it wasn't a dress for a bridal Barbie, either—no layers, no lace, no embellishment at all.

Sylvie said, "I bet some New York deb ordered this at Bergdorf's and then for whatever tragic reason had to cancel the wedding, so it went to their sale rack, but then someone stepped on the hem, and it had to go to Filene's Basement. My guess is it was originally thousands and thousands of dollars."

I said, "Ray has good taste."

Sylvie looked up. "No one ever disputed that."

In a flash she had pulled off her T-shirt and stomped out of her scrub pants, leaving on a hot-pink lace bra and transparent purple underpants. "Button me up," she ordered, her voice muffled inside the bodice of the most ornamental and twinkling model. "This might be as close as I ever get."

I said, "Do you really believe that?"

"I'm not the marrying type," she said. "Which I say with no self-pity whatsoever."

"You never know. Look at me."

Sylvie shook her head. "Don't confuse my faux popularity with wife potential. I attract men through sheer hard work, which is required because I'm not conventionally attractive. Men are very susceptible. That's where I reel them in: Love me and leave me, permission granted."

I sat down on the edge of the bed, and Sylvie joined me, both of us in bridal finery. I said, "Whoever told you that you weren't attractive? Not those boys on the high school football team. Not your fellow physicians."

"Some men might find me attractive in a kind of freaky bad-girl way, but trust me—I'm not what you want to bring home to Mother."

I said, "If I had a son, I'd be thrilled if he brought you home."

Sylvie patted my hand. "I know you would."

"I'd like to be a little freaky in a bad-girl way myself. I just don't think I have the basic building blocks."

"I'll be fine. I've got my life all figured out. I'll stay unencumbered, date-raping my fellow house officers as needed. And then, when I'm forty, I'll adopt a baby girl from China. Or, Plan B: artificial insemination from some smart, good-looking, athletic yet musically gifted volunteer."

I smiled. "Or *not* artificial."

"Too complicated. And too messy. Look at Leo and his love-child problem. He wants to do the right thing, but he doesn't love Meredith."

I would not have exhumed this topic, but this was Sylvie, fearless confronter of all things awkward. I said, "Okay. Is this the point where you confess that you slept with Leo?"

Sylvie said, "*N-O*. We did not go down that road. Yes, we danced; we might even have danced close. And yes, I thought about it. But in the end I was saved from sin because Saint Leo said, 'I think you're a very nice woman, Sylvie, *blah blah blah,* but I'd hate myself in the morning.'"

"And what did you say?"

"I didn't want to look morally clueless, so I nodded sadly and said, 'You're so right. I'd hate myself, too.' And that's the irony. That's why I was so hurt when you assumed the worst: I could have fucked him to kingdom come and you wouldn't have been any less mad at me."

I said, "I was stupid. I'm sorry. I overreacted."

"It's okay. It's not as if you weren't technically correct. I mean, if it had been up to me . . ."

She tilted sideways until our shoulders knocked. "So when are we reaffirming the sacred vows?"

"June twenty-ninth."

"Am I invited to this shindig?"

I said, "Of course. You're first on my guest list. Invitations are going out . . . sometime or other."

"Is Leo on your list?"

I said, "Should he be?"

"It would give me someone to drive down with, and to sit with at the reception. Besides, he was your roommate for six months. He's exceedingly fond of you."

I said, "He's not exceedingly fond of Ray."

"That's the human condition, sweetie-pie: people you love marrying people you hate."

"Did he tell you that he hated Ray?"

"No. Certainly not. It was a figure of speech. Besides, I promised myself that I was going to mind my own business."

"Do you see Leo?"

"Sure. We wave across the cafeteria and occasionally sit down for a cup of coffee. But he's very careful to mention how complicated his life is at the moment, meaning, 'Not interested in you, Dr. Schwartz.'"

"But his life really *is* complicated. Only a very shallow guy is going to jump into bed while he's figuring out if he wants to be with the mother of his child."

"First of all, they're all shallow. Second, in many ways it's preferable. I dated a guy who was a messenger for a law firm—absolutely no ambition whatsoever except to look great in spandex. He never complained, except occasionally about the weather, and about office buildings with no numbers."

I said, "I think I'm like that: simple. I get up when the

alarm rings. I go to work. I have a cheese sandwich and chocolate milk for lunch. I read and memorize and take notes. I do what I'm ordered to do: Run this to the lab. Get the results. Hold this. Stitch this. Inject this. Intubate that. If someone wants to date me, I accept. And if they want to marry me, I get a blood test."

"Alice. Unh-uh. Please don't talk like that. Because if you start sounding ambivalent, I might have to exercise that speak-up-or-forever-hold-your-piece option from a back pew."

"You can't. We're already married. Wedding number two is just for show. It doesn't change anything."

"But . . ."

"But what?"

"Nothing. Nothing substantive. My own prejudices and *mishegaas*." She shook her head firmly, eyes closed.

"You can't turn back the clock," I said. "Not that I want to."

I could see her searching for something benign, for an answer free of wedding animus.

"Are you worried that we'll need a two-bedroom, and I'll move away?" I suggested.

Sylvie patted my stooped and strapless shoulder. "Yes," she said. "You're right. That's it. Geography. *C'est tout.*"

RAY GRANTED MY mother sole discretion over reception decisions. Not only was it her house, her caterer, her florist, her daughter, and her signature on the checks, but it was time for Ray to go forth and sell his wares. On May 1 he headed north with routes highlighted in yellow and carnival locations circled in red. I asked why he didn't expand his customer base to gourmet and souvenir shops, those places on the Mohawk Trail and Martha's Vineyard that sell maple candy and saltwater taffy. And what about all those ski resorts?

"I try," he said. "Believe me. If it has a sign out front and a jar of beef jerky by the register, I pull over."

He informed me that most of northern New England was not covered by his cellular provider, but he'd call me whenever he entered a service area. He spent the night on April 30, enjoyed marital relations, and was dressed and ready to go when my alarm sounded on May 1. "I know it'll seem like a long time," he announced, sample cases in hand, "but this is good. When you spot me standing at the altar, I'll be a sight for sore eyes."

I said, "Are you saying this is a two-month road trip?"

He said, "You can't be surprised when we're talking about a huge territory, with islands and ferries and thirty-mile-an-hour speed limits." He took out his map and laid it across my lap. "I don't think you understand how big New England is. If you figure the distance between here and Presque Isle, to take one example, and figure a dozen stops every hundred miles, not only is it going to take two months, but I'll be cutting it short to get back in time."

I said I had no idea.

"This is what I save my energy for. This is *Around the World in Eighty Days*, only without the trust fund. This is me sleeping in budget motels or pulled over on some creepy backwoods road because I'm nodding off at the wheel."

I said, "Ray, under no circumstances should you sleep by the side of the road."

"I sleep in my car," he said. "There's only been a couple of times that anything bad happened."

"Were you attacked?"

"Robbed. But now I try to pull over into campgrounds."

"Is it a question of money?"

He shrugged.

"You didn't want to ask me?"

He said, "I have my pride. I scrimp wherever I can. When you work for yourself, you're the guy you turn your expenses in to. It's a hell of a way to make a living."

I pointed toward the kitchen. "Please bring me my wallet."

Ray said, "I can't have it both ways: 'Marry me, Alice. Be my wife. Whoops, sorry, that didn't count. Let's do it over. Let's be engaged.' Only a loser would take money from his fiancée."

I said, "I'm your wife. I have money in the bank. If I want to give you some, you should accept it."

"How much?"

I looked in my wallet. "I have six twenties. Is that enough?"

He asked if a couple more twenties were possible.

I said, "If you didn't mind running down to the ATM."

"Password?" he asked.

"Edema," I said, and spelled it.

He tapped his temple. "Can I tell you what's really going on up here? I want your parents' approval. I think

343

it's time to back off and let them put their signature on this wedding. I'm putting my nose to the grindstone to demonstrate that I can take care of you as good as any guy you might have picked up at the country club or the library."

I said, "I've never been to a country club in my life. Besides, no one has to take care of me."

"You're not saying you don't want me to go on this trip, are you? Because you knew when you married me that I'm not a guy who sells fudge over the phone."

"It just seems a little sudden. And a little long."

He smiled. "You know what you're saying? That you're going to miss me." He smoothed the map across my knees. "Look: Here's Boston. And here's me, driving along these highways all by myself—no colleagues to shoot the shit with and eat lunch with, no neighbors across the hall."

"You could bring some audio books," I said.

"That's not my point. My point is, who's going to miss their partner more? You or me?"

"You?"

"No question. How can you even compare the two? Me living out of a car, the smell of cocoa fat turning my stomach by about day three. Do you think I'd be doing this unless I absolutely had to?"

I said no, of course not. Sorry. Here's my bank card. Bring it right back.

"When I first met you I thought, This is a girl who will always understand that work comes first." He kissed my forehead and murmured, "I'm doing this for us. You believe that, don't you?"

I said I did. And the disturbing part? I meant it.

A WEEK LATER, I received an invitation to my own wedding—Mr. and Mrs. Bertram Thrift requesting the pleasure of my company at the marriage of myself to Mr. Raymond Joseph Russo, seven weeks hence.

How had I landed on my own guest list? Was it meant to be a sample? A souvenir? A sign that I'd be on the outside looking in? It turned out to be the act of the calligrapher/cousin and her low IQ, but still it was unsettling. I sent the preaddressed RSVP card back promptly to the hosts, and checked off, after considering the options, "Chicken."

30
A Free Woman

SORRY, NO; NOTHING dramatic happened at the actual ceremony.

Everyone said I looked my best. The dry cleaner had worked magic, returning my dress spotless, sized, stuffed with tissue paper. My shoes matched the cream-pink of my dress, and I surprised everyone by wearing my mother's pearls and a nearly red blossom behind one ear. As for my bouquet, I couldn't say; I left that up to other people.

My mother had decorated the church with weeping figs and other cumbersome potted plants, requiring a nursery as well as a florist. The groom's side of the aisle was sparsely populated: a few unnamed relatives, the female guests of cousins George and Jerome—best man and solo usher, respectively. There was a woman said to do Ray's books; another woman said to be the switchboard operator at the parent confectionery company. If there were others in attendance, I've forgotten.

I found the ceremony overly ambitious for what it was, a reenactment. We recycled the gold bands that we had used the first time. In modern Unitarian terms I promised to love, respect, treasure, listen to, learn from, share with, and celebrate Ray, who then promised to do the same. Upon being pronounced husband and wife, Ray kissed me in a fashion I found too fervent for the occasion. "It's been ages," he told the Reverend Walter Webb.

One would think that the recessional would be a blur, tears of joy compromising my vision. But not so. I noticed every face, every peculiarity of expression: my aunts Janet and Patricia looking at Ray in appraising fashion; neighbors from Einstein Drive looking anxious to get home before guests blocked their driveways; Leo in a dark suit and Sylvie in a black dress, visibly worrying from the last pew.

Following the congregation's environmental guidelines, the guests showered us with birdseed in lieu of rice. Some flung their allotment, I noticed, with more force than others.

IT WAS GRAY and humid with temperatures more than 100 degrees Fahrenheit, with the tent adding to the oppression. Thunder could be heard to the north and west. Ray's dance-floor dreams had to be downsized when the reception moved indoors. Waiters were enlisted to remove the Bokhara and its pad from the first-floor study, uncovering the hardwood floor and enough dust to make my mother call for the vacuum.

The food, everyone said, was fabulous—raw fish suspended in spicy emulsified liquids housed in martini glasses, to name one particular smash hit. The ice sculpture was meant to be a representation of my hospital—I recognized the cylindrical parking ramp on its face—but it quickly melted into formlessness. The bartender was hailed as a martini genius, with much of the banter concerning which subcategory and hue of the house drink guests had selected. "Open bar!" Ray announced more than once, directing traffic toward the gins, the vodkas, the dry vermouths.

Whether it was the advice of parents worried about our earning potential, or merely custom, the majority of our guests slipped checks to Ray, who managed to look both surprised and deeply humbled at the appearance of each white envelope.

"Want me to put those in my purse?" I asked.

"Eventually," he said.

It wasn't like other weddings. Maybe it was the setting, or the "Fêtes by Frederick" van in the driveway, or my mother's stricken look, but it reminded me of the receptions I'd attended after each grandparent's funeral. I asked Ray why his family was so underrepresented. Hadn't we each invited seventy-five?

"Saturday's a workday," he said. "Plus some felt a little intimidated by you."

"Without ever meeting me?"

"On paper, I mean: MIT, Harvard Med. The fact that

the reception was in Princeton, New Jersey. On Einstein Drive. Some of them have never been outside Suffolk County."

He took a sip from his green martini. "Besides, who needs more people scrambling to get in line when they blow the lunch whistle?" He grinned. "Not me."

"And I suppose that's fewer thank-you notes to write," I said.

"Are you kidding? You send a present whether you show up or not."

There was a loud squeal of feedback—my mother with a microphone in one hand and a brackish martini in the other. "Please, everyone. Gather around. I promise I won't filibuster, and I promise that there will be music and more of Frederick's brilliant food." She patted her French twist and took a deep breath. "In today's world, a mother never knows if she'll ever be standing up before friends and relatives, toasting a daughter's marriage. But here I am, raising my glass to Alice and Ray." She smiled bravely. "When I first saw these two together, I didn't think *soul mates*. In fact—and I can't believe I'm going to confess this—I thought he was her driver. But it didn't take too long before I understood the dynamic. Ray is fun-loving, pragmatic, street-smart. Alice, on the other hand, is the consummate professional. Work and science trump people every time. Or so I thought. As the person who has known Alice longer than anyone else, who felt her heartbeat under my breast for nine months, who nursed her, raised her, drove her to her various enrichment programs and competitions, I think no one is better qualified than I to say that my baby has found, against all odds and across a great figurative distance, a man who sees beneath the surface . . . a man who has discovered that Alice's heart speaks volumes even when it's inarticulate or mute. Yes, she's the scientist. But he's the one who put her under the microscope to discover what was pumping and clotting and surging through those undiscovered veins. And although Ray is something of an unknown—by which I mean a relatively new acquaintance—a parent only has to see the way he looks at Alice to feel that this wedding is a cause for celebration and gratitude and, well, *relief* might be too strong a word, so I'll just say *peace*. Please join me in raising your glass in a toast to the bride and groom . . . to Alice and Ray . . . to a whole—*w-h-o-l-e*—that is greater than the sum of its parts."

Everyone raised their glasses, including Ray, who mouthed a quivering "Thank you."

I felt an arm around my waist—Sylvie's. When the *hear hear*s subsided and the tray-bearing waiters resumed their rotations, she whispered into my ear, "Can Leo and I talk to you in private? Maybe upstairs?"

Ray, at the same time, was pulling me toward the few square yards of hardwood that had been designated as the dance floor.

"Let me get this over with," I told Sylvie.

Though my mother had won the music battle, engaging a violin, a flute, and a harpsichord, Ray squeezed in a deejay to administer the mandatory first dance, the father/daughter dance, a mother/father dance, and sundry novelty dances that evolved into lines.

Guests applauded as the Righteous Brothers CD

brought forth "Unchained Melody" and the bride and groom. It was incumbent on us to smile and exude marital happiness. Absent that, to chat. I asked, "How was the swing through the Monadnock region?"

"Didn't I talk to you after that?"

I said, "The last call was from Concord."

"Which is when I finally got phone service. It's the capital. People who live in that state must have ridiculous roaming charges."

"Luckily," I said, "I was able to follow your progress on-line through the debit withdrawals. At least I knew you were staying in motels and eating three meals a day."

Ray led us into a pivot and a mild dip. "You mad?"

"I left messages. I thought we'd have a chance to discuss these things before today."

"I'm a little superstitious," he said. "Mary and I had dinner together every single night for a week before our wedding. Need I say more? By the way, I love the flower in your hair. I'm going to take a nibble."

"It's poisonous," I said.

He landed a kiss proximal to the flower anyway. "Where's your old man? He's supposed to cut in."

"Did you get my message about work?"

Ray said, "Remind me."

"I'm no longer on probation."

"That's my girl," he said.

Nothing was premeditated, but as soon as I introduced the topic, I grasped its probative value.

"Go on," he said, his voice confident. "I'm holding my breath."

I said simply, "I'm out. On my ass. A free woman." I snapped the fingers he was holding against his chest. "Just like that: 'Thrift? Sorry. It's not working. You'll have to clean out your locker by midnight tonight.'"

Slowly, expertly, he said, "Sweetheart. You must feel terrible. Are you okay? Why didn't you tell me?"

"I tried. You were out of range."

"But you still have a job, right? It's like you didn't get promoted. Like you're staying back a grade?"

"No. It's like getting kicked out."

"But just from being a surgical intern, right?"

"From anywhere. I'm washed up."

"I know you're joking," he said. "I know you're still a doctor. That doesn't go away."

"I'm afraid it does in my case," I said.

His dancing slowed to a near standstill. "You're saying that with all the hospitals in Boston, you can't come up with something? You can't call up your old teachers at Harvard Medical School and ask them to make a few phone calls on your behalf?"

I shrugged. "If I wanted to I could."

"You're gonna want to, believe me," said Ray.

I sighed. "The word's already out: Tear up the application of anyone named Alice Thrift."

Ray said, "You could apply as Alice Russo." His voice brightened. "Or you could move to another city where they don't usually get Harvard Medical School graduates."

"That would have to be pretty far away."

"You do what you have to do," he said.

Until then, I'd been assuming that a scrupulous non-liar such as myself would reveal by song's end that she'd been kidding. Instead I said, "I know this comes as a shock; I know how much you were looking forward to being supported in a style to which you were hoping to become accustomed."

"What about the apartment? Do you have to give that up if you're laid off? And what about health insurance? What if one of us gets sick?"

"I'll keep my black bag," I said. "I can treat any number of diseases at home."

"How're you gonna pay for those vacations in South America fixing the faces of the poor if you're not pulling down a big salary the rest of the year? How are you going to make *those* dreams come true?"

I said, "I can't. But here's the bright side: I'll be around. I'll be a real wife, which will make you an actual husband."

Ray said nothing. He motioned to my father, who was surveying us from the bar.

"Don't say anything to him about my job," I whispered. "It might spoil the wedding for him."

My father, obediently, tapped Ray's shoulder. The preselected music changed to "Isn't She Lovely?" Paternal relatives applauded.

Ray didn't linger. "Take good care of her," he said.

"Where's he going?" asked my father.

I said, "Probably to look for Mom. That's the protocol: The groom dances with the mother of the bride if his own mother is dead."

"Your mother's needed elsewhere," said my father.

I smiled and nodded because we had an audience.

"No one else is joining in," I noted.

"It's not a dancing crowd," he said.

I LOCATED SYLVIE and Leo on the stairs, one pink and one blue martini in their respective hands. Sylvie insisted the pink drink was just the accessory I was missing, if not a remedy for what appeared to be my bridal fidgetiness.

"She's never wrong," I said.

"So," said Leo. "What's new? I haven't heard much from you lately."

"Likewise," I said.

"She got married," said Sylvie. "She got into a groove at work. She pulled her job out of the fire. She got married all over again."

Leo bent down from the step above Sylvie to clink glasses with me. "Congratulations on most of those," he said.

"What's new with you?" I asked.

"Me? Hardly anything. I'm still in the NICU. I'm still living in the same place. Still fathering children promiscuously all over Greater Boston."

"Are you drunk?" I asked.

"On three and a half martinis? Absolutely not."

I said, "I never accused you of being promiscuous."

Sylvie said, "Let's be nice. No one wants to look back on this day with any more regrets than are absolutely necessary."

I said, "I delivered a baby with Meredith. Did she tell you?"

"She mentioned it."

"She was amazing. So calm. Very empathic. Fun,

even. I was really impressed."

"Exactly the circumstances of my meeting her," Leo said. "Which is to say at her absolute best."

"So then what?" Sylvie asked. "You witnessed her winning bedside manner, and you thought, 'How do I get me some of that?'"

Leo said, "And while you try to solve the mystery of me and Meredith, I'll try to figure out how the friendship between you and Alice ever got off the ground."

"We discuss this ourselves," I said.

Leo said, "Why is it that Alice doesn't have to make sarcastic comments about the mother of my child? In fact, she takes time out on her wedding day to say, in effect, that she understands what I might have seen in Meredith for one brief shining moment."

"An opposing view," said Sylvie, "which I say with undying affection, is that Alice is altogether too nice." She patted the carpet next to her. "Sit down, cookie. We have to speak to you."

THEY HADN'T BEEN looking for trouble. They hadn't come to spy or to eavesdrop. But Ray, they said, before the ceremony, talking outside the church among his pals—the best man, the usher, and their dates—seemed agitated. Very.

"Not nervous," Leo clarified. "Angry."

"They're his cousins," I said. "It could have been some unrelated family feud."

"Did you see the cousins' dates?" Sylvie asked me. "Shiny turquoise dress on one? Barbed-wire tattoo on the other?" Her fingers circled one of her own biceps.

"Just in passing," I said. "On my way back up the aisle."

She touched my shoulder from the step above. "Let's go outside," she said.

We walked down the slate path to the backyard, under the empty tent, to what would have been the head table. "You must know more than you're telling me," I said.

Leo shrugged. He fished out his olive spear and drained his glass.

"I heard the name Mary," said Sylvie.

I said again, "These were his cousins. Of course the name Mary would come up at Ray's second wedding. I'm sure they were ushers at the first."

"I couldn't help myself," said Sylvie. "I strolled over, pretending to be gregarious, dragging Leo. I stuck out my hand to the one they'd been calling Mary, and said, 'We don't know a soul here. I'm Sylvie and this is Leo.' She shook my hand, limply, stupidly. No name offered. 'And you are?' I asked. One of the cousins said, 'This is Donna. She's with me.' Which of course made it incumbent on *me* to remark on the not-insubstantial diamond on the fourth finger of her left hand. I said, 'Beautiful ring, Donna. Are you two engaged?' Immediately, her left hand disappeared behind her. Ray mumbled something about a former dead fiancé."

"Do you see where we're going with this?" Leo asked.

"Not entirely."

"Premature widowhood running rampant?" said Sylvie. "A woman named Mary who inspires a string of lies from your low-residency if not entirely absent groom?"

"And then when we checked her out again, inside the church," said Leo, "the ring was gone. She must have slipped it inside her purse."

I said, "I don't understand what this adds up to. Do you think this is Mary, the dead wife?"

"Or undead," said Leo.

"Or wife-to-be," said Sylvie.

I shook my head. "There must be more you're not telling me. You wouldn't throw this grenade into the middle of my wedding if you had only circumstantial evidence."

Leo shrugged.

"What else?" I said.

They both winced. After a moment Sylvie said in a small, flat voice, "I carded her."

"You what?"

"Carded her. Very unobtrusively. A truly conscientious bartender isn't supposed to serve minors, even if it's a private party."

I said, "You're not a bartender, and she's not a minor."

"I've tended bar! I viewed it as a citizen's carding. She ordered a green apple martini—same as Ray, I noticed—and suddenly I found myself saying to the bartender, 'I'm sorry, but I'm doing a fellowship in hepatology, and I get very upset when I see an underage drinker being served.'" She paused.

"Did he ask to see her ID?"

"He had no choice."

"And she complied?"

"It was either that or make a scene. Besides, she had

356

no clue that her name would mean anything to anyone at a wedding in Princeton, New Jersey. *Plus* she got to enjoy a little victory and mutter 'Fuck you' when she turned out to be thirty."

"Did you see the license yourself?"

"Of course! The bartender showed me."

"Professional courtesy," said Leo.

"And the name of this thirty-year-old?"

Sylvie checked with Leo first.

"Not Donna," he said.

After a long pause I said, "I guess he told the truth about a couple of things."

"Still," said Leo. "There could be a plausible explanation."

"Name one," said Sylvie.

"A person of science wouldn't be allowed to say that the ghost of Mary Ciccarelli had come back to see her husband remarry, would he?" Leo asked.

Sylvie shook her head.

"I don't know what this means," I said.

Leo said, "It means *you'll* be the widow when I get through with him."

I said, "Even if she crashed the wedding, I can't believe she'd come back to my parents' house."

Sylvie stood up and started to pace. "Big fucking hilarious joke. As if Alice would never catch on; as if Alice would never realize that she was getting married under the nose of his girlfriend or fiancée or whatever the hell she is."

"Alice *didn't* catch on," I said.

"Alice doesn't expect people to lie," said Leo.

"Please go get him," I said.

"He'll never tell the truth," said Sylvie.

"Go get him," I said.

THE DEFEATED TWO-MAN search party, Leo and my father, were gone a long time.

"Honey—" my father was saying, all the way from the back door, along the slate path, to where I was sitting. "Honey, it's okay—"

"No sign of him," said Leo.

"What about his cousins?"

"Gone."

"Did anyone see them go?"

"We didn't ask," said my father. "We didn't want to raise any suspicions—"

"In case they went out for cigarettes and might breeze back any minute," Leo tried.

"And I didn't want your mother getting hysterical," said my father.

"What would be the point of his taking off?" asked Sylvie. "If he's come this far; if this is some trick, some swindle, to marry Alice, wouldn't he have made his move after the ceremony?"

"The checks," said my father. "Those don't materialize until the reception."

Sylvie said, "No one goes to all this trouble for a couple of wedding checks."

Everyone looked at me. "He wasn't planning to run away. He thought I was going to be a rich doctor—"

"Who wasn't going to be around enough to cramp his style," Sylvie added.

I pulled the limp flower from behind my ear and tossed it over my shoulder. "He's gone," I said. "I told him I had no job and no prospects . . . and I might have implied that we were homeless."

Sylvie bit her lip. When that didn't work, when her twitch of a grin couldn't be suppressed, she clapped her hand over her mouth.

"I wouldn't jump to conclusions," said Leo. "Maybe he got a little heat stroke and had to lie down."

"Could someone give me a phone?" I asked.

Sylvie fished hers out of her purse and handed it to me. I dialed, and Ray, being Ray, answered.

"It's your wife," I said.

"Hey! Where are you?"

"At my wedding."

"I looked all over for you."

"And when you couldn't find me, you thought you'd head home?"

"My cousins wanted to see the sights. They'd heard of Princeton, the college. They all saw *A Beautiful Mind*."

"Are your friends enjoying a good laugh? And have you found an ATM yet?"

"We can stop payment on those checks!" my father yelled.

"We're just getting some fresh air," said Ray. "Jerome's allergic to shellfish. He didn't have any, but he ate a canapé that must've been next to a shrimp. I didn't want to bother you or your doctor friend."

"Put Mary on," I said.

"Mary? There's no Mary here."

"Put Mary Ciccarelli on the phone," I yelled.

"Put Ciccarelli on the goddamn phone," my father said, even louder.

I heard whispers, then a businesslike "This is Mary."

My voice shook. I had no script, no oxygen. I finally blurted out, "Are you aware of the fact that everyone thinks you're dead?"

"Not *everyone,*" said Mary.

"Just me? Is that what you're saying? The bride? Who would now like to ascertain your relationship to the groom?"

She repeated the question, her hand muffling the receiver.

Ray was back. "Alice, I told you. She's George's friend." He chuckled, the least convincing sound that ever bounced off a satellite. "I can't even say *girlfriend* because Georgie would get pissed at me. This is, like, their second date."

"Are you a pathological liar?" I asked.

"Why do you always ask me that?"

"Are we married?"

"Totally."

"Legally?"

"Of course, legally. You were there for both of them!"

Sylvie said, "Ask him if he was married before."

"Ask him if he's a bigamist," said my father.

"Maybe he was going to have her murdered," said Sylvie. "That's not unheard of."

"Alice?" Ray was saying. "You still there, hon? Would it help if I talked to your father?"

I said, "What did you want?"

"To get this straightened out. As soon as we drop the girls off at the bus station, we're coming straight back to the reception."

"No. I meant, what did you want from me? From the beginning?"

"Our connection's breaking up," said Ray. "Can this wait until we're face-to-face?"

"Don't come back here," I said.

"I'll get a restraining order," my father yelled.

"Leo's threatening mayhem," I added. "He went to a tough high school in Brighton where the kids beat each other up."

"What parish?" Ray asked affably.

"Dinner!" my mother sang, first from a window, then, her face worried, from the back porch.

"Alice? Doc—" I heard from the phone as I passed it back to Sylvie.

"Good-bye, asshole," she growled.

"Bert?" my mother called. "What's wrong?"

"You go in, Dad," I said. "The food will get cold."

"It's supposed to be cold."

"Tell Mom what's going on. Tell everyone. You'll make a lot of people happy."

"It's a sauna out here," said Sylvie. "You come in, too. We'll find a table in some remote corner."

"We'll dance," said Leo.

I watched my mother's face change as hostess mortification set in; as the buffet line took shape behind her.

The musicians came outside on break, carrying plates heaped with food. Thunder rumbled, but the rain held off. Someone produced a cigarette, and I smoked it.

THE NEW YORK TIMES wasn't going to stop the presses for something as trivial as a runaway groom. As a result, I received presents and congratulations for months, returning every one that Ray hadn't cashed. My thank-you note was something of a form letter: *As much as I would have gotten great use out of your lovely (soup tureen/wine carafe/pressure cooker/croquet set), I am returning it because my marriage to Ray didn't work out. It's hard to explain, but my parents would be happy to elaborate. Thank you for your thoughtfulness. I hope you saved the receipt. Sincerely, Alice.*

Ray, it turned out, had broken no laws of the commonwealth. Lying was punishable by nothing, especially when its victim was an allegedly adult woman who married freely and volunteered her bank card with express instructions to make a withdrawal. I consulted a lawyer, who listened to my tale of woe and advised, gently, that I take my bad judgment and romantic blind spots to the other kind of counselor.

There was some early hope that Ray had been previously married and never divorced, rendering the ceremony at City Hall illegitimate. My father hired a private detective without my consent, which led only to the discovery that in all of Ray's forty-five years, he'd been nothing worse than a serial fiancé. The truths we learned were these: We were legally married. He lived with Mary Ciccarelli the entire time he was wooing and wedding me. The diamond ring on Mary's finger was his, bought on layaway, eventually pawned. There was no dog. He did sell fudge, but in the manner of a Girl Scout selling cookies—once a year and door to door.

We didn't see each other until the hearing. On the witness stand, he insisted that it was a real marriage based on love. That he loved me and I loved him. That our marital relations were frequent and awesome. That he'd been lied to, and promised a nose job. That he was devastated. Which was why he, the injured party—currently on disability due to documented mental anguish—was compelled to ask Dr. Thrift for alimony.

The judge ruled, swiftly and edgily, for the plaintiff—me.

I WENT BACK to work immediately, on July 1, a rung above the new batch of petrified interns. Two out of seven were women. The first opportunity I had to pull them aside I said, "If anything goes wrong, which it will, come talk to me. When Dr. Kennick says, by way of a compliment, 'I've seen worse,' know that he's referring to me, and that I lived to tell about it. Here's my phone number. Call anytime."

Dr. Kennick, in his vagueness, decided that he liked me. It's not that I improved so dramatically, but more that he credited me with being the intern who asked for a week's vacation, then changed her mind, sacrificing her honeymoon for the good of her team.

I no longer want to be a plastic surgeon. That particular pursuit belonged to the world on the other side of the embarrassing fissure, the Ray Russo Pass, that I have only recently vaulted. And as various advisers have noted, repairing the lives of the shunned in places far removed from the hospital might have had more to do with altering myself than with saving the world. Dr. Shaw suggested I think about OB-GYN, and I was tempted. We discussed it over several lunches, but in the end I decided to stay where I was rather than start over in something requiring a Shaw-like level of compassion around the clock. I was better suited, it turned out, to do what surgeons do—cut to the problem, excise it, and get out.

On this side of the crevasse is what Sylvie calls "Alice Thrift, A.D."—after divorce. The new me enjoys residential peace and elbow room on the upper floor of a two-family house in Brookline Village. There are three bedrooms; we let Leo have the large one, with the alcove for a crib, for that distant day when John Paul, born in September, is weaned. Aunties Sylvie and Alice can't wait for him to spend the night.

Paternity is demanding, and Meredith is never very far away. Her daily phone calls recount the baby's milestones, his sleep, his various intakes and outputs—much more than anyone but a NICU nurse-dad would want to know. On alternate nights, for the sake of uninterrupted meals, we let the answering machine pick up.

Sylvie is chief resident in medicine this year—an honor she kept to herself the whole time my career was on the rocks. The three of us joke about going into private practice one day—*joke* because an internist, a general surgeon, and a NICU nurse would not make any sound professional sense. Leo dubbed this silliness the Convenient Clinic—one flight down, open nine to five, naps as needed because we'd live above the store, a rotating chairmanship, no male attendings, and never a cross word.

OVER THE PAST few months, we three have jointly purchased a dining room table and a hooked rug, fully recognizing that the day might come when one of us will have to buy back his or her share. When I say this aloud, Sylvie barely looks up from her bowl of cereal or her potting soil. "It ain't going to be you, cutie," she always says.

"Who's this Leo?" my therapist asks weekly. "Tell me more."

I throw out a few neutral biographical facts, the kind that one could learn from his CV—age, job title, last school attended. But nothing more. Confidentiality notwithstanding, certain things are sacred.

Sylvie pushes, too, and has abandoned all subtlety. She'll order two curries or two burritos, buy a bottle of wine, set two glasses and two plates, beep herself out the door, and insist that she couldn't possibly return before midnight. At my divorce party she made a toast, a very convincing mother-of-the-bride impression. "To Alice," she began, patting an imaginary French twist, "the social misfit and bookworm I love with all my heart."

"Hear hear," said Leo.

I know Sylvie; I know she had more to say, more laughs to induce with stored-up Ray jokes and Joyce Thrift bloopers.

But her face grew solemn. She raised her glass higher. "What a good place to stop," she said.

ACKNOWLEDGMENTS

I thank the gods of publishing for my kind and gifted editor, Lee Boudreaux, and my agent/champion, Ginger Barber.

As ever, I owe at the very least my soul to Stacy Schiff and Mameve Medwed, eager and artful first readers and the best audience a gal could have.

I am grateful for the attentions and talents of Brian McLendon, Sally Marvin, Robbin Schiff, and Amy Edelman of Random House; Marty Asher, Russell Perreault, and Jen Marshall of Vintage; Laurie Horowitz of CAA, and Elyse Green of the William Morris Agency.

I thank Christopher Potter of Fourth Estate for his faith in my books and for their British home.

Alice particularly thanks: Dr. Robert Austin, verisimilitude coach, proofreader, and unwitting supplier of phrases I pounced on; Dr. Steve Lee, onetime surgical resident, who had tales and traumas to recall wryly; Eileen Giardina, labor and delivery nurse, who helped me bring FIR into the world; and Tim Farrington for his way with words.

ABOUT THE AUTHOR

ELINOR LIPMAN is the author of *The Dearly Departed*, *The Ladies' Man*, *The Inn at Lake Devine*, *Isabel's Bed*, *The Way Men Act*, *Then She Found Me*, and *Into Love and Out Again*. Her work has appeared in *The New York Times*, *The Boston Globe*, the *Chicago Tribune*, *Gourmet*, *Salon*, *Self*, *More*, and *Yankee Magazine*. She has taught writing at Simmons, Hampshire, and Smith colleges, and won the 2001 New England Book Award for fiction. She lives in Massachusetts.

Center Point Publishing
600 Brooks Road ● PO Box 1
Thorndike ME 04986-0001 USA

(207) 568-3717

US & Canada:
1 800 929-9108